The Ungovernable series:

Zero Day Threat
Jailbreak
Time Bomb
Insider Threat
Firewall
Trojan Horse
Security Incident
Threat Agent
Attack Path

THREAT AGENT

R.M. OLSON

ISBN-13: 978-1-990142-06-2

To my wonderful beta readers, without whom this series would never have actually worked:
Shauntel, who very kindly cut all my terrible work to pieces;
Darci, who showed me when things weren't working, and more importantly, why they weren't;
Frances, Amber, and Becca, who put up with aaallll my ridiculous plot questions;
Leslie, Mellissa, Katherine, Kristin, and Mel, who made me believe my books were actually half-way decent;
and Kevin, who pointed out the worst of my technological inconsistencies.
Thank you! <3

THREAT AGENT:

An individual or group that has the potential to exploit a system's vulnerabilities, and/or damage or harm the system or the organization through other means.

1

Masha, day 1, early

The Prasvishoni night was cold, the bitter wind whipping snow around Masha's face. She hunched down into the collar of her thin jacket, squinting through the blowing snow at the darkened streets ahead.

She knew exactly where she was going. She'd been planning this trip since she was seven years old.

Ahead of her rose a dark block of apartment buildings, barely visible through the blizzard. They were almost indistinguishable from the other apartment blocks along the street, but if you looked closely enough, you could see the minute differences. Extra security measures, for instance, and prefab walls built thickly to withstand explosions.

This was a place for people who had money, and enemies. People powerful enough to cause the government trouble, should things go sideways.

Masha stepped into the entrance, partially sheltered from the biting wind, and paused a moment, shaking the snow from her scarf and coat.

She'd expected her hands to be trembling. But they were perfectly steady.

She touched the building's com, tapping through to the correct apartment.

"Hello?" The woman's voice was groggy with sleep. "Who is it?"

"This is Alonya Kozelva," said Masha calmly. "You requested I come."

"Ah. Yes. Alonya." The woman's voice now was slightly more awake. "Come in."

The door clicked as the lock unfastened, and Masha stepped inside.

From inside, the difference between this and the regular apartment buildings was much more pronounced. Instead of dingy, mildew-y prefab walls, these walls were smooth and painted. The carpets on the floor were thick and lush. And perhaps most surprising of all, it was clean.

The hololift gleamed in the corner of the lobby, shiny and modern. Masha stepped into it and murmured, "Floor five."

The apartment she was looking for was at the far end of the fifth-floor corridor. Masha hesitated at the door for half a second, then pulled her scarf over her face and tapped firmly.

The door swung open.

It took all of Masha's willpower to conceal her quick intake of breath.

She hardly recognized the woman in front of her.

She'd aged since the last time Masha had seen her. She was perhaps in her sixties, but she looked eighty, her skin wrinkled, her sunken eyes wary and suspicious.

She pulled the door open wider. "Well?" she demanded impatiently. "Don't just stand there, come inside." Her eyes darted around the hallway, as if searching for something—or someone.

Masha smiled behind her scarf, and stepped through the door.

The inside of the apartment was obviously fine, subtle touches of wealth accenting the small space, but Masha ignored them. "Ex-minister Slavenka," she said quietly. "It's good to see you, finally."

The woman glared at her suspiciously. "You're Alonya?" Her voice was brusque.

Masha inclined her head.

Slavenka glanced around again quickly, unease evident in her face and posture. "Very good." She paused. "I assume I don't have to explain to you what's been happening?"

Masha shook her head. "No. I'm aware of the situation." She studied the woman as she spoke.

She'd obviously lived a prosperous life, at least by the standards of the Svodrani System—her face had the soft roundness of someone not accustomed to missing meals, and her body didn't bear the marks of hardship carried by most of the people in Prasvishoni. But the nervous set to her posture, the unconscious movements of her hand, the faint, almost imperceptible trembling in her fingers, spoke of someone who'd lived with fear for a very, very long time.

Masha couldn't hold back her slight smile. But her scarf around her face was enough to conceal it.

"And you understand our arrangement, I assume," the woman continued. "You will go in as undersecretary to the Under-minister of Internal Affairs. You will raise my suggestions in government meetings, as I direct. You will keep me appraised of anything unusual. And you will arrange for my protection at all costs."

Masha's voice was quiet. "Slavenka. You always were a careful one. I've known you for a long time, after all. But then, you never really knew me at all, did you?"

The unease in the woman's expression was crystallizing into fear.

"Of course I don't know you. I was told by someone I know and trust that you could do what I needed. But I don't know you, and I have no wish to."

"I'm certain that's true," Masha murmured. "But we don't always get what we wish for. And we can't always trust who we think we can."

Now the fear in Slavenka's face was sharp and obvious. "Who are you?" she demanded. "Why haven't you taken off your coat? Let me see your face."

"Be careful what you ask for," said Masha quietly. Slowly, she loosened her scarf, letting it fall away.

If the woman's expression had been panicked before, now it was a blank terror. "Masha," she whispered. "Masha Volkova. How did you—"

Masha smiled gently. "Come now, Slavenka. We've worked across from each other for years. Such a greeting for an old colleague."

Slavenka's face turned up into a twisted parody of a smile, sick with dread. "Masha. You're right, we've worked together for years. I —don't know what they told you, but you must believe me that—" She was backing away slowly, towards the kitchen. Her hand fumbled for something tucked inside her sleeve.

Masha was still smiling, that same faint, pleasant smile, even though her heart pounded in her ears. "Don't bother," she said. "Did you really think I would come here without a blocker set on my com? None of your calls for help can get out. None of your bodyguards will hear you scream."

"What do you want?" The woman's voice was practically shaking. "What do you want from me, Masha?"

"I think you know," said Masha. "I think you know exactly what I want, and why."

"Whatever happened was a long time ago. It was years ago, years and years. We all make mistakes. Unfortunate things happen, things outside our control. You've worked in this government for how long? You know what we have to do to survive."

The woman stepped back again, as Masha took another step towards her. She felt, oddly, perfectly calm—that cool detachment she'd perfected over the years settling across her like an impenetrable shield.

"You're right," she said, in that same mild voice. "I know exactly what it takes to survive." She took another step. "And I know what it takes to get ahead."

Slavenka's hands were shaking, the whites showing around her eyes. "I told you," she tried again, her voice a terrified whimper. "Look at me. I'm an old woman. I'm not the person I was. Whatever happened, however many years ago—"

"No," said Masha, her voice gentle and merciless. "You're not the woman you were. The woman you were was a small, unimportant undersecretary. The woman you were didn't live in an apartment like this one. She hadn't spent years enjoying the fruits of her labours."

"Masha—"

Masha was still smiling, that strange calm still bleeding through her, even through the rapid pounding of her heart. "You were young, and ambitious. And you wanted more than just to survive. You made that clear when you contacted Alexia Patrova, after she'd murdered her way into the position of mafia krestnaya, told her she could do what she needed to, and you'd take care of the police. And after the mafia enforcers went through the city, making examples of everyone who wouldn't pay Alexia's protection fees—you were suitably rewarded for it." She paused. "That was the day my parents died. I watched them. They weren't the only ones, of course, but when you're seven years old, you don't think of that. You only think of the looks on their faces as they choke on their own blood."

"Masha, I swear—"

"Of course. None of this was what you intended." Masha smiled slightly. "I saw the kill orders you put out on me and my crew, once you knew who I was. But getting rid of your past is harder than it looks, isn't it? You never know when someone might come back from the dead, looking for revenge."

Slavenka wasn't speaking anymore, her eyes darting back and forth in frantic panic.

"Do you know the name of the boyevik Alexia sent to kill my parents?" asked Masha, conversationally. "He was a young man at the time. But he rose in the ranks, just like you did. His name was Grigory Korzhakov."

She saw the realization wash across the woman's face, the grey tinge to her skin growing more pronounced. "What do you want?" Her voice was harsh. "What do you want with me?"

Masha didn't answer, just slipped her hand casually into the pocket of her pilot's coat and took another step, the smile never fading from her face.

Her foot crossed the threshold between the entryway and the kitchen.

Slavenka's expression changed suddenly, fear turning to one of savage triumph. Masha tried to step back, but it was too late—the force-field current jolted through her body, freezing her muscles, pinning her in place.

"You thought you could threaten me, Masha." Slavenka's voice was vicious, the brutality that Masha had known lurked just under the surface in full display now. "But you miscalculated, for once in your life. Ever since I found out who you actually were, I've been prepared for this. I had no idea that your parents would die when I spoke to Alexia. I didn't concern myself with details. But it seems ironic, doesn't it—your parents' death got me my position, and your death will secure it." She paused. "Believe me Masha. There are important people who will be very grateful to see you dead." She twisted something on her com, and the invisible restraints around Masha tightened.

Masha closed her eyes, drawing in a shallow breath. Her heart pounded so that it felt like it would break through her ribcage, and a bitter nausea rose in her throat at the flood of memories from the past seventeen years—working across from Slavenka, smiling and laughing with her, making pleasant conversation in the hallway. All the time hiding her disgust, her gut-clenching hatred, her visceral revulsion at the woman's presence.

The woman who, it appeared, would kill her.

Slavenka turned to the small kitchen table behind her. "Don't worry," she said, her voice hard with malice. "I'll make your death quick. I heard your parents took some time to die, so you're lucky, really." When she turned back, there was a heat gun in her hand, small and deadly. "I've set this force-field into my com signal," she said. "Until I release it, you can't move more than a finger."

She lifted her pistol in a shaking hand, her eyes cold.

Masha closed her eyes, just for a moment, straining against the force that held her.

She could still see the look on her father's face as he died.

There was the shuddering hiss of a heat-blast.

For a long moment afterwards, there was silence.

Slowly, Slavenka toppled forward, face still frozen in an expression of vicious hatred, a small, blackened hole burnt through the centre of her chest.

The force that bound Masha released as Slavenka's fingers relaxed from the device.

Masha smiled grimly, and glanced down at the small, round hole her hidden heat pistol had burned through the pocket of her pilot's coat.

Moving a finger was all she'd needed, in the end. Slavenka hadn't been the only one who'd spent years preparing for this meeting.

Masha stepped over the body without glancing down at it. Her heart still pounded strangely, but her legs were perfectly steady.

She looked quickly around the apartment. Slavenka would have kept her government codes here somewhere, and there were various other items that could come in handy.

She searched quickly and efficiently, and was finished within fifteen standard minutes.

At the doorway to the kitchen, she paused a moment, a strange reluctance slowing her movements. Then, at last, she knelt beside the burned body.

Slavenka lay face-up. She looked old and frail now, no trace of viciousness or violence left in her slack features. There was that small, almost imperceptible stiffness to her expression, the hint of death closing in. No pain—the death had been too quick for that.

For half a moment, Masha saw her parents' faces, the tears running down her father's cheeks, her mother's eyes wide with horror.

This death had been peaceful in comparison.

It was a shame. But it couldn't be helped. She had work to do.

Masha patted the woman down calmly. It took her only a moment to find the small ID tucked inside the front of her jacket. After all, she'd been planning to give it to Masha—or Alonya—to begin with.

Masha tucked it carefully into her own pocket. It wouldn't even need to be forged—her contact had made sure that all the biometrics matched.

She stood, glancing around quickly to make sure she hadn't missed anything, and stepped carefully over the body to the door.

They'd find Slavenka in the morning. With the government in its current state, the assassination of an ex-minister couldn't possibly come as a shock.

Masha closed the door behind her and walked briskly back to the hololift. When she reached the lobby, she paused for a moment before stepping back out onto the street.

Decades of planning had brought her to this point. And this, here, was the final stage.

She took a deep breath, touching the ID in her pocket. Then she pulled her scarf up around her face again and stepped out into the icy Prasvishoni night, turning towards the sprawling block of government buildings.

No point in going back to her freezing apartment. Undersecretaries typically got an early start.

She had every intention of being a stellar undersecretary.

2

Jez, day 1

Jez woke in warm, drowsy comfort, and nestled her head into the warmth.

Then, like every damn day for the last however many weeks, she jerked awake, cursing under her breath. Because the warmth was Lev's shoulder, and they weren't supposed to—

And then she remembered, and the rush of relief that washed over her was as thick and dizzying as the panic she'd felt a moment before.

She was here, with Lev. On the *Ungovernable*. And somehow, some ridiculous way, they'd figured it out. She didn't have to run away, or leave, or pretend she didn't care. And she'd never realized how this —waking up next to him, curled in his arms—had been the only thing in the entire system she'd actually wanted.

She blinked hard against the unexpected tears, and when she could see again, she glanced over at Lev.

He was lying next to her, one arm tucked around her, his face peaceful in sleep.

She watched him for a few moments, and she honestly hadn't known that you could love someone so much that just looking at them could make your chest tighten, and almost choke off your breath.

She leaned over and, very gently, kissed him on the cheek.

He stirred slightly, his arm tightening around her instinctively, but didn't wake.

She smiled to herself and kissed him again, this time on the corner of the jaw.

He gave a sleepy moan and stirred again.

This time, she kissed him in the hollow behind his ear, and he moaned again, eyes still closed.

By the time she'd kissed her way down his neck to his chest, his eyes had blinked open, and there was an expression there that made her heart pound a little faster than it had been.

"Jez," he mumbled sleepily, pulling her closer.

She bit softly at the corner of his neck.

He drew in a quick breath. "Jez—" His voice was much less steady now.

She grinned wickedly, grazing her teeth along his collarbone, and he groaned.

He rolled over slightly, pulling her closer, his body warm against hers. He was definitely awake now, and the look in his eyes was making her heart skip in a strange and undeniably pleasant way.

She winked at him, running a hand across his bare chest, and traced her fingers languidly down his stomach. He gave an incoherent growl, tightened his uninjured arm around her waist, and rolled her on top of him, pulling her into a long kiss. She closed her eyes and leaned into him, and something about the taste of him on her tongue, the press of his body against hers, the way his hand ran down her back, sending delightful shivers up her spine—

Well, now that she thought about it, maybe waking up next to him wasn't the *only* thing in the system that she wanted.

It was … sometime later before they made their way onto the main deck of the *Ungovernable*.

The others were gathered around the conference table, going through a pile of what looked like every damn thing on the damn ship, stowing items into packs as Tae frowned down at a list on his holoscreen.

Lev sat down on one of the chairs, pulling Jez onto his lap, and she acquiesced readily.

Ysbel shot them a flat look, but there was faint amusement under it. "We were all wondering if the two of you would show up at some point."

Jez smirked. "Hey now, maybe we were a bit busy."

Ysbel's look grew, if possible, even flatter. "Believe me, we all gathered that." She paused a moment. "You could work on being a little quieter, while you're at it. And I think after last night, everyone on the ship would happily pitch in for a cot that doesn't squeak."

Jez's grin widened. "What, jealous?"

Ysbel rolled her eyes. "No. I am not jealous. But I would like to be able to actually sleep at night."

Jez winked at her. "Hey, I'm willing to bet there are a couple cots on this ship that don't squeak." She turned to Lev. "Me and genius boy could try them out. I mean, hell, it'd be a sacrifice, but the things I'm willing to do for this crew—"

From the look on Lev's face, he fully supported this suggestion, and would happily get started then and there.

Ysbel gave an exasperated sigh, and Tae glared at them.

"I'm not sure if either of you remember, but we're actually in the middle of a full-on revolution at the moment," he said. "So if you could spare some of your attention—"

Jez rolled her eyes and settled herself a little further onto the Lev's lap. "Fine, tech-head, if you're going to put it that way—"

He gave her a look of unmitigated exasperation, then turned to Lev. "Lev. How are you feeling?"

Lev looked over at him in blank incomprehension, and Jez would have snickered at the dreamy look on his face, if it hadn't basically mirrored her own. "I'm sorry, Tae, what was that?"

Tae put his head in his hands. "Lev," he said in a flat voice. "I'm not sure if you remember this, but you were shot. With a heat gun. Less than twelve hours ago. Does that ring any bells?"

Lev stared at him for a moment, glanced down at his shoulder, then sighed deeply and ran a hand over his face. He looked back at Tae with a slightly rueful expression. "I'm—sorry. I'm a little distracted at the moment, I'm afraid."

"I'd gathered that," said Tae through his teeth. He took a deep breath, shook his head, and said, "Look. I get it. If I had my way, you and Jez could have a private room on the ship, and nobody would bother you for the next month. But—" he sighed. His face was lined with worry and strain, the bruises from yesterday standing out in sharp relief against his dark skin. Blood from where his head had hit the wall during the explosion still matted his hair, and looking at him, Jez felt the euphoria of the morning fading.

Lev sobered as well. "Sorry, Tae," he said quietly.

Tae shook his head, a slightly wry expression on his face. "Look, I get it. It's just—"

Lev nodded. "It's just there are people out there who are going to die if we don't figure this out," he finished.

Tae sighed.

"Alright then," said Lev. "I suppose we'd better figure it out." He looked around. "Were you discussing anything while you waited for us?"

Tae gave another tight shake of his head. "No, just packing up everything we might need—mostly my tech and Ysbel's weapons and explosive components. Once we're back behind the barricades, it might be hard to get out again. I don't know if we can really plan much until we have a better idea of what's happening in the city." He paused. "I think we're about ready to go, if you are."

Jez glanced around the ship one last time as the rest of the crew assembled outside in the cramped smugglers' bay, and took a deep breath. She closed her eyes for a moment, running her hand along the *Ungovernable's* smooth paneling, breathing in the faint fragrance of crystallized sap and old wood mingled with the mechanical smell of a long-haul ship.

The smell that meant home. The smell that meant no matter what happened, she was on her ship, and things would be alright.

Then she stepped out the door and walked slowly down the loading ramp.

Lev waited for her at the bottom of the ramp. He had a small smile on his face, but his expression was overlaid with concern. "Are you going to be alright?" he whispered as she came up to him.

Jez glanced back at her beautiful ship for just a moment, and swallowed hard. "Yeah," she said softly. "Yeah, figure I will."

Lev took her hand and squeezed it, his face turning serious. "Jez," he said. "We'll get you back to your ship, I promise. One of these days, we'll get you back here, and you won't have to leave it again, not unless you want to."

"Yeah," she said quietly. "One day. But—right now we've got crap to take care of. And hell, maybe being away from her hurts like a damn heat-blast in the gut, but—but I guess I found something even more important than flying. Guess I didn't think that was going to happen."

Lev was watching her in that way he had, his eyes soft, something in his expression that always made her chest tighten, just a little. "Yes," he said, his eyes catching hers. "I suppose the same thing happened to me." There was affection in his tone.

She grinned, and swallowed again. "Well then, guess we better get a move on and save the damn system. Because I'll be honest, doesn't look like you and me are going to get any more alone time until that happens."

Lev chuckled slightly and pulled her in for a quick kiss. "That's more than enough motivation for me. So. Saving the system it is."

The small smugglers' bay where they'd stored the *Ungovernable* was just on the edge of the docking district, a kilometre or so north of the university. Jez looked out the hangar bay door cautiously, then beckoned the others forward, and they followed her warily into the streets.

Even with the sun peering reluctantly over the horizon, the air was bitter cold. The snow from the blizzard of the night before coated the streets and alleys, plastered up against the prefab brick walls of the dingy warehouse buildings around them.

Ysbel pressed Misko closer against her shoulder, her expression grim. "I don't like this," she said in a terse voice.

Jez glanced around.

The streets, at this hour of the day and in this part of the city, should be filled with people, going about their own business, and trying not to intrude on the business of anyone else who might, for example, shoot them dead.

Today, the streets were completely empty.

Which meant things were dangerous enough that even the damn smugglers and long-haul crews were staying indoors.

Jez grinned, resting her hand on the heat pistol shoved into her belt. "Well, Ysbel, I know you've been wanting to see how the mods you put on this work in real life. It's looking like we'll have a demonstration."

Ysbel pulled out her own pistol, not even bothering to respond.

They made their cautious way down the deserted streets. Jez's heart hammered in her chest, and she moved so that her body would shield Lev from any stray heat-blast that might come their way. She could tell that he'd noticed, and that he wanted to protest, but had realized it would do absolutely no good.

She grinned to herself.

It wouldn't have done. She was damn well not going to watch him get shot again.

They'd made it almost three-quarters of the way through the empty streets around the docks when the first shot rang out.

Jez shoved Lev down, and from the corner of her eye saw Ysbel half turn, shielding Misko's body with her own. Another shot fizzed past them, and this time Jez saw where it came from. She raised her pistol and returned the favour.

The air of the street glowed momentarily white hot, and there was a muffled scream from behind an alley wall.

"Ysbel!" said Jez over her shoulder. "I ever tell you how hot—"

"Piss off," Ysbel grumbled, but Jez could tell she was smiling.

And then the entire street lit up, heat-blasts lighting the air around them, the hiss and crackle of them sharp in the silence of the street.

"Guess that's our cue," Jez muttered. Ivan put his arm around the still slightly unsteady Tae, Jez pushed Lev ahead of her, and they ran for their lives.

The shots followed them down the street. Jez wasn't counting, but she figured there were at least five shooters, maybe more.

She swore as one of the heat-blasts hit so close it almost scorched a hole in her damn jacket.

"Jez! Are you—"

"I'm fine, genius," she said through gritted teeth. "Keep moving."

Behind her, Tanya slowed for a moment, turning so that her body sheltered Olya from the blasts. She fired three times in quick succession, and there were three strangled shouts of pain.

"Who's shooting at us?" asked Lev, his voice tight.

Jez rolled her eyes. "Figure we can talk about that when we all get out of here alive. Come on!"

He stumbled, and she swore, catching him by his good arm and pulling him after her.

Behind them, Tae and Ivan were pounding down the streets. There was sharp pain on Tae's face, worry in Ivan's.

Lev was breathing heavily, his feet stumbling on the rough cobblestones. "Jez, turn here," he panted. "There's a back street that will get us there faster."

In the distance, Jez heard the whine of police sirens. She swore loudly, and Tanya shot her a disapproving glance over her shoulder.

"Hey, Tanya," she drawled breathlessly. "Figure if the kids are going to learn to swear, now is a pretty damn good time."

Another blast lit the air beside her, and Lev cursed, his voice tight with pain.

Jez swore again, her heart jumping into her throat. "Genius?"

"I'm fine." Lev's voice was strained. "Just run."

They pounded down the street, around the corner, down another street. Lev was still on his feet, but his face was ashen, and she could hear his laboured breathing. Tae, half-supported by Ivan, was muttering into his com.

"Up ahead, next left," murmured Lev.

They rounded the corner, and there ahead of them were the barricades.

Three figures stood on the barricade walls, faces grim, heat pistols in their hands. She recognized all three of them, and her heart skipped in relief.

The hiss and sputter of their covering heat-blasts almost drowned out the rapidly approaching sirens.

"Tae! Get in here!" shouted Dmitri as soon as they were close enough. He scrambled down the barricades and grabbed Tae's other arm, half-dragging him inside. Vera was there too, and she caught Lev around the waist, supporting his other side, and the three of them stumbled behind the shelter of the barricades. Peti, above them, was still firing at their pursuers—at least, Jez assumed so, from the whine of heat-blasts outside. Ysbel, Tanya, and the two children appeared a moment later, breathing heavily, faces pale with strain.

"Is everyone alright?" Demetri snapped.

Jez glanced around quickly.

Tae had collapsed against the wall, breathing heavily. Ivan was beside him, face worried and hand on Tae's arm. Lev sagged against her, breath coming in short, painful gasps. Tanya had dropped Olya with Ysbel and joined Peti on the barricades, her heat pistol firing with deadly accuracy.

Jez propped Lev against Vera and yanked out her own heat pistol. "They going to come in here? Because if they are, we better be ready for them. I'll take the opening there, Ysbel, you—"

Vera shook her head wearily. "No. They won't try to come past the barricades. At least, not yet. They've had chances, but I don't think they're up for the kind of firepower that would take. They're just shooting at anyone they find in the streets."

Sure enough, when she listened, Jez could hear the sounds of the sirens fading in the distance.

She drew in a long breath, sagging back against the wall beside Lev. "So," she said at last. "Guess I know where to come for a good time these days."

Vera chuckled, but her expression was grim. "The streets are a mess. We heard the shooting all night. I—" Her voice choked, and Jez felt a sudden twist of sympathy.

These idiot students were just kids. They'd had no damn idea what they were getting into.

Then she remembered Lev's choked gasp, and she turned in sudden panic. He was leaned up against the wall, face pale, but when he caught her eyes, he managed a smile.

"I'm fine, Jez," he said in a strained voice. "Although I've come to the reluctant conclusion that running from the police is not an activity that's conducive to restful recovery from a heat-blast injury."

She glared at him skeptically, and he gave her a small smile. "Honestly, I'm fine." He tried to straighten, and grimaced slightly. "Inasmuch as 'fine' can be applied to having been shot less than twenty-four hours previously."

"You're starting to sound like me," she said with a reluctant grin. His smile in return was fond, and her heart stuttered, like it always did, and there was something in her chest, something tight and warm and almost sickeningly grateful.

She could have kissed him right there—maybe done a little more than just kiss him—but—

She glanced at the weary, drawn faces of the students and street kids surrounding them.

This probably wasn't exactly the time for that, much as she wished it was.

Finally, Tanya and Peti climbed down from the barricades and joined the rest of them, their faces grim.

"So," said Ysbel quietly. "What do you think, Lev?"

He sighed, and glanced down at his shoulder ruefully. "I'm sorry, I'm—afraid I wasn't quite as coherent as I normally am for most of our discussions last night."

Jez fought back a quick shudder at the memory—Lev crumpling to the ground, face bloodless, a heat-blast seared through his shoulder. The sick pain in his expression, the way his face had gone slack when he fainted—

Lev must have noticed the tension in her, because he pulled her closer, giving her a small smile before turning back to the others. "At any rate, if I understand the situation correctly, the entire city has broken out in rebellion, the police have been instructed to use any means necessary to stop it, the government has gone to hell, the gangs are running rampant in the streets, someone is working behind the scenes with the police to stir up trouble, the gangs and the police have joined forces, and as far as we can assume, Masha is now actively working against us. Have I more or less remembered everything correctly?"

Tae sighed again. "I—think you've captured it fairly well."

Lev turned to Vera and Dmitri. "I assume you've gone through the supplies you have left? How long will we be able to hold out here?"

Vera glanced at Dmitri and shrugged. "A week or so? There was some food storage in the school cafeteria that we've been using, but it's not going to last forever."

For a few moments, there was silence. Jez glanced around at the grim expressions on the others' faces, and despite the warmth of Lev's arm around her, she had to repress a small shudder.

This wasn't like anything they'd done before. This wasn't just some job they were pulling now—this was life or death, for more people than she really liked to think about.

3

Masha, day 1

"So. You're Alonya." The man across from her scowled, his face pinched in an expression of permanent distaste.

The lines on his face and the shakiness in his hands were more pronounced than she would have expected—if her information was correct, he was in his mid-fifties. Alcohol had probably played a part, if she had to guess. Certainly not an uncommon vice among the government under-ministers.

Masha gave a small, polite smile. "Yes," she said. "Slavenka recommended me to your office."

"Oh, she did," said the man in front of her sourly. "But if you think this is going to be a cushy job, just because you have friends who have pull—"

"I have no qualms about working hard," said Masha, her voice still pleasant. "I do understand that in a place like this, one must work if one wishes to achieve anything."

The man scowled at her, clearly not placated.

Under-minister Adrik was a washed-up bureaucrat, and it showed. He clearly had no idea how to play the games that were required to get ahead in government. Games Masha had known from the moment she arrived in the office as a fresh-faced university graduate.

Honestly, he seemed to have survived this long by simply being too unimportant to bother with.

He glared at her for a few moments longer, then leaned back in his seat. "We all must work if we want to achieve, you say," he said at last. The sneer in his voice was a familiar one—someone happy to take out his frustration on anyone with less power than himself.

"I was under the impression that's what I was hired for," said Masha, her voice still polite.

"Well. You'd best get to work then," said the man, his tone acerbic. He glanced around the office, then waved his hand vaguely. "Tidy up my information chips and my paperwork, for a start. If you're working for me, you take what I give you."

"I wouldn't dream of protesting," said Masha.

He kept his eyes on her suspiciously as she looked around the office.

It was cluttered from what looked like years of neglect. Remnants of food cartons, old dishes, even something that looked like an old shirt, were lodged in corners and under shelves.

She smiled wryly to herself.

She'd done worse jobs, certainly.

For a while, he watched her as she worked, his face still twisted with dislike. Eventually, though, he seemed to conclude she could be left to her own devices, and turned back to his desk.

She picked up a dirty shirt in the tips of her fingers to get to a pile of yellowing paper documents, and was jolted by an unexpected memory—Ysbel and Tanya, their faces wry, manner businesslike, working beside her to clear out a filthy, rodent-infested apartment, quietly, so as not to wake the sleeping children.

She pinched her lips closed.

She'd made her choice, and she wouldn't change it even if she could.

She worked quickly, her progress bringing her around the desk closer to Adrik. He didn't seem to notice, still scowling down at his holoscreen, and she tapped her com discretely.

The mods Tae had set up were still working, as she'd expected they'd be.

When she was behind his chair, she stumbled, bumping into him heavily.

He swore. "Watch yourself," he growled.

"I'm terribly sorry," said Masha, her tone a mix of apologetic and embarrassed. "Do forgive me."

"You'll be more careful, or I'll send you packing, Slavenka or no."

"Of course. I'm so very sorry. I'm not usually that clumsy." She ducked her head in embarrassment, glancing surreptitiously at her com.

She hid a smile.

The full copy of Adrik's com would make for interesting reading tonight in her apartment.

Again, a memory flashed in her mind—Tae, face drawn with exhaustion, hair falling into his eyes as he scowled down at his com, putting the finishing touches on the mod she'd just finished using.

It had been—extraordinary, honestly, to work with people like her crew.

She shook her head.

Without them, doing what she had in mind would take more effort on her part than she'd grown used to. That was all.

She'd been working in silence for almost an hour when Adrik glanced up at her again.

"Alonya," he said shortly, pulling a chip from his desk. "I need this message to go to the undersecretary to minister Elena."

She raised an eyebrow. Adrik was old-school, yes, but surely he understood that sending an undersecretary to do an aide's work was public humiliation.

Perhaps he was too stupid to realize the insult. Or perhaps he simply wanted to demonstrate who was in charge.

She took the chip he held out. "Of course, Under-minister," she murmured, biting back a small smile.

Either way, he was playing perfectly into her hands.

"Bring me lunch on your way back, since you'll already be out. Cheburek, please. And be back within the hour, unless you'd like your position to go to someone else," he called after her.

She didn't acknowledge either the words or the arrogance in his tone, just let the door swing shut behind her.

She paused a moment outside the door and glanced quickly up and down the hallway, one hand resting on the heat gun concealed in her pocket.

The entire building hummed with unease. The only people in the hallways at the moment were the ubiquitous aides, who should be running the errand she was running right now.

She gave a wry smile. Perhaps Adrik's intentions had been stronger than just humiliating her. With the government in the state it was, sending her out now could have been him angling to get her killed.

The long, wide government hallways had always been the ideal place for political machinations—a way to catch someone's shoulder, pull them aside into a private conversation that could appear casual, in a way a conversation in an office could not. Had the hallways been built narrower, she'd often thought when she worked here, the government might have completely ceased to function.

Now, the hallways were dead. The few unfortunate souls who had been forced to walk them were tense with fear, hands shoved in pockets where, Masha had no doubt, heat pistols had been carefully tucked that morning.

When she reached the drab door that marked the undersecretary's office, she tapped lightly, calling out, "A message from Under-minister Adrik."

A moment later, a woman's voice called, "Come in."

The door lock clicked, and Masha pushed the door open and stepped inside.

A woman, perhaps late forties, sat behind a small, uncomfortable desk. She gave Masha tight smile as she entered. "I'm sure I don't need to tell you to lock the door behind you."

Masha nodded, pressing the lock. When it clicked, the woman visibly relaxed.

"You're here from Adrik?" Her tone was curious.

Masha nodded. "I'm his new undersecretary." She kept her expression completely blank.

The woman frowned, looking at her more closely. "He sent his undersecretary to bring me a message?"

Masha gave her a wry smile. "Yes."

The woman was looking her over in a calculated fashion. "Who recommended you to the post?" She pulled up her holoscreen and glanced through it quickly, then smiled. "Ah. Slavenka. Adrik is living on the edge again, is he? I didn't think he be quite so brave as to insult her this openly."

Masha raised an eyebrow. "You're—not fond of him, I take it?"

"I think that speaks for itself. Considering he thought sending you on an errand to someone as insignificant as me would be a stinging insult to Slavenka." The woman's tone was dry.

"I'm sorry," said Masha.

The woman shook her head. "Believe me, I've been aware for some time about he views those of us who he outranks." The bitterness in her voice was stronger than Masha had expected.

She hid a smile and held out the chip. "I suppose you want this?"

The woman stood, coming around her desk to take it. "Yes, I suppose I should look at it, after all that."

Masha paused a moment. "I—do apologize, but—do you know where I might purchase cheburek?"

"Why do you need—" the woman broke off abruptly, her expression turning dark. "He didn't ask you to—" she stopped, lips pressed tightly together. "There's a vendor on the corner of Pravital and Reka street," she said at last. "He should have cheburek. Believe me, you don't want to be on the streets any longer than you have to be."

"As bad out there as it is in here?" asked Masha wryly.

The woman shook her head, her expression grim. "Worse."

Masha nodded. "Thank you. I—appreciate the warning."

She slipped quietly from the room, but she felt the woman's eyes following her.

Good. Let the rumours spread.

When she got back to Adrik's office, a bag of hot street food in her hands, she saw his eyes flick towards her. But he pretended to be enthralled by whatever was pulled up on his holoscreen for several standard minutes while she waited patiently. Finally, he glanced up, his scowl deepening when he caught her eye. "So you're back, finally," he snapped.

"I have been, for quite some time," she said, in her most pleasant voice. "But it appeared you were working far too hard to notice."

There was nothing he could say to that without admitting his attempted insult, and he was clearly furious about it.

He snatched the bag from her hands, and she let go of it without comment.

"And you made a mess of my office this morning," he snapped. "There was an information chip I needed, it was sitting right here —" he gestured to a spot on the desk.

"I do apologize," Masha murmured. "As you asked me to organize the office, I put it with the chips in this pile—" she turned, bending over a shelf, and let the chip she'd palmed earlier slide into her hand.

"Here it is," she said, turning back with a small, apologetic smile.

He scowled at her for a moment and snatched the chip from her hand. "Be more careful next time."

"Of course," she murmured.

The mods on her com were just as good as she'd expected them to be. He likely wouldn't notice the changes at all—the numbers she'd tweaked, the names she'd slipped in.

But someone would. And someone would make the requisite assumptions.

Killing Slavenka had been personal. This was merely business— the first step on a carefully charted path.

Still, after meeting Adrik—she wouldn't feel the slightest bit of guilt when she brought him down completely.

4

Ysbel, day 1

Ysbel glanced around quickly as they took their seats around the makeshift table in the small shelter the students had set up earlier. Someone had brought in a heatsink from one of the university dorm rooms, and it clanked and groaned to itself in the corner, pumping out just enough heat to keep them from actually freezing.

The faces of the students around the small table were grim.

Her students.

They'd been so young, a few months ago.

Her own children had never had a chance to be that young. She'd kept them from the middle of the battle the day before, but now there was nowhere for them to go.

Olya was pale-faced and terrified, and Misko's head was buried in her shoulder. But they weren't crying. Because even at eight and six years old, they knew crying could get them killed.

"Alright," Lev began.

Tae's com crackled. "Tae! It's the police! They're back, I—I don't know—"

Tae swore and scrambled to his feet. "It's Ludie, she's standing watch—"

The others jumped up as well. Jez already had her pistol in her hand, and Ysbel grabbed for the padded bag of explosives she kept around her neck.

"Caz. Can you watch the children?" she asked in a tight voice, detaching a quietly whimpering Misko from around her neck.

Caz nodded grimly.

Tanya had already sent Olya over to him with a gentle push.

With a final glance at her children, Ysbel ducked out of the tent, and she and Tanya sprinted after the others.

By the time they'd joined them on top of the barricade, she could see the police at the far end of the street. There were only a handful, and it didn't look like they had heavy-duty weapons, but there was a grim desperation in their faces, and the way they held their guns.

Ivan hit the voice amp on his com and called, "What do you want?"

Tae leapt forward, cursing, and shoved Ivan down, and the air above their heads crackled with heat.

Ysbel dropped to her stomach as lasers and heat-blasts lit the air around their heads.

"Whatever it is they want, I think it's safe to assume talking is not it," said Lev wryly. He'd climbed up after the others despite his injured shoulder. Because of course he had, because Jez was here, and he wouldn't leave her to go alone if he could help it.

Jez was crouched beside him, grinning. "Talking with those bastards is overrated anyway," she drawled. She poked her head up for just long enough to squeeze off a quick shot, then dived down again as the air around where her head had been sizzled with heat.

Beside Ysbel, Tanya was calmly taking aim. She raised her head carefully and fired three rapid shots.

The shots were followed by three shouts of pain.

Ysbel frowned as the small huddle of officers moved closer to the barricade under the covering fire.

Why were they here? There was no way they could honestly believe a dozen officers could take on everyone inside the barricade.

But the way the officer in the back was standing, the object he held half-concealed in his hand—

She sucked in a quick breath. "They've got an explosive."

Tanya nodded, face tight. "Jez. Cover me," she said tersely. "I'm going to try to take them out."

Jez grinned. "Do you one better."

There was just time for a look of dismay to register on Lev's face, and then Jez had leapt to her feet on top of the barricade.

"Hey, you bastards! Got kicked out of basic training because you didn't know how to shoot?"

She dived to the ground as a blistering barrage of heat exploded around her, then jumped up again and sprinted for the other end of the barricade.

Tanya was already standing, moving towards the entrance to the barricade like a shadow, pistol raised. Ysbel followed her, crouched low.

From the other end of the barricade Jez cursed, and then Tanya's shots cracked out in sharp succession, and the police officers went down one by one without so much as a groan.

The officer closest to the barricade fell, an explosive rolling from his limp hand. Ysbel jumped to the street, snatched it up, and threw it overhand back towards the officers.

The police line broke, the officers scrambling for their bikes, and a moment later, they were gone.

A moment after that, the street where they'd been exploded in a blinding blast of noise and rubble.

Ysbel's shoulders dropped in relief, her heart still pounding wildly.

She glanced up, and Tanya gave her a small smile. She pocketed her pistol and reached down to help Ysbel up.

On top of the barricade, Lev slapped his com. "Jez!" he snapped, his voice frantic. "Are you—"

"Relax, genius," Jez panted. She was limping towards them. "I'm fine. Just tripped on one of the damn chair legs on the damn barricade and sprained my ankle."

"Jez," said Lev, in that calm voice that he reserved for emergencies and utter panic. "When you say you sprained your ankle—"

"I mean, I sprained my ankle." Jez dropped down beside them, wincing at the movement.

Lev closed his eyes, clearly gathering his composure. "Jez. I'd—feel better if Tanya took a look at it. If you don't mind."

Jez gave him an odd look, then shrugged. "Yeah, guess that would be fine."

Tanya stepped over to her, shaking her head. "You know, when I said cover me, that's not exactly what—"

Jez grinned. "Yeah? Well, from what I could see, it worked pretty damn good."

"Except for the part where you nearly died," Ysbel grumbled, coming over.

"Hey, that assumes those bastards were fast enough to catch me. Which they weren't." She sounded smug.

"You're lucky," said Tanya at last, looking up. "It's just a sprain."

Jez was still grinning. "You say lucky. I say damn good."

"Damn good at almost getting yourself killed, perhaps," Tanya muttered.

"Tanya. Jez is a very good judge of what she can and can't do," said Lev quietly, and Ysbel and Jez both turned to stare at him.

Emotions flickered over Jez's face—surprise, uncertainty, relief, and then an expression that probably meant that she was currently wondering if there were any beds available, squeaky or not.

Tanya caught Ysbel's eye, smiling ruefully.

Tae sighed. "I'll talk to Felix, see if his kids can take watch. They were killers for the Blood Riots, and they're all pretty decent shots."

Ysbel shook her head.

Every so often, she was reminded again what they were working with—mostly kids who'd never held a gun before a few weeks ago.

A few moments later, a ragtag band of street kids clambered up beside them, led by a skinny kid who looked to be about fifteen or sixteen, with a wary expression and a hostile set to his posture. The kids carried weapons that were ancient, but deadly looking, and much too big for them.

Tae spoke to the skinny boy quietly for a moment, and the boy nodded, face set.

Lev helping a limping, swearing Jez down the back of the barricade, and the rest of them followed him. When they were back in the tiny shelter, and Misko was huddled back on Ysbel's lap, Lev looked around quickly.

"I guess that answers our question as to whether they're still worried about barricades," he said.

"I don't think it was ever a question," said Ivan. "The barricades are a symbol for the rest of the city. They're going to be a target, as soon as the police have the time and attention to spare."

"And we're not prepared to go up against that kind of firepower," said Lev quietly. "From what Vera told us, we don't have the supplies to hold out under a siege, either."

Ysbel glanced over at her wife.

Ivan was right. The only reason Tae and his friends had lasted behind the barricades for as long as they had was Jez running interference in the government. And now that was gone.

"I suppose, then, our best bet is to make sure that they don't get the time or the attention to focus on us," said Lev at last. "We need a clear picture of what's happening outside, and what's happened to everyone who came out to help us yesterday. Then we can maybe make a plan."

"I'll go," said Tae at last.

Lev frowned. "Tae. You were hurt yesterday. Someone else can—"

Tae scowled at Lev. "Listen. The streets are a mess. I'm not sending anyone else out into something like that. Besides, I still have the police scanner set up on my com."

Ivan put a hand on Tae's shoulder and gave it a small squeeze. "I'll go too," he said. "You'll need someone to come with, in case you run into trouble."

Tae opened his mouth to protest, and closed it again, and Ysbel smiled slightly despite herself.

"Alright," said Lev at last. "Be careful. I'll be on the com. Report in whatever you see. If you run into problems, call in." He gestured out the tent door at the scanty, makeshift shelters, the homemade barricade, the grim-faced students and street kids, some of them limping, many of them bandaged. Few of them armed. "We might not have much, but we'll figure something out. And I wouldn't put it beyond Jez to liberate a police bike if she had to." His tone was a mixture of amusement, affection, and resignation.

Jez looked over at Tae and winked.

Ysbel sighed, and pulled the padded bag of explosive from under her shirt. "Here," she said, reaching inside it. "If you're going out, I'd just as soon you do it with enough explosive power to take out a few city blocks."

Tae took the explosives gingerly, looking like he'd rather face down the police unarmed and single-handed. "Well, at least if they catch us, you and every other person in the damn city will know about it," he muttered.

Ysbel cracked a smile. "That's true. But try not to get captured. I don't like to waste explosives."

His smile was a little more genuine this time. Then he sighed and pushed himself to his feet. "Come on, Ivan. I'm guessing Lev wants this information sooner rather than later."

Ysbel looked around at the small, ragged group of them—injured, exhausted, crouched in their makeshift shelter behind their makeshift barricades that had been blown to ash only the day before.

Ivan had been right—the reason people had dared to take to the streets now, after years of corruption and abuse, was because they saw these barricades—this small, ridiculous group of students and street kids—as a beacon of hope.

But she could see the unease in Vera's face, the pale fear in Dimitri's. Their families were out there. And they knew how costly keeping the police distracted could be.

She pulled Misko closer, and he squirmed in protest. She managed a small smile, even through the hot, familiar anger welling in her chest.

Before she'd met Masha, when she'd thought her family was dead—she'd learned how to use that anger. She'd learned how to embrace it.

If that's what it took to bring Masha down, and keep these children safe—because they were all children, the students and the street kids just as much as her own two—then she could do that again.

5

Tae, day 1

The streets outside the barricades were unsettlingly quiet, and the bodies of the handful of police officers Tanya had shot earlier lay where they'd fallen—it spoke to how busy the police were that no one had come back for them.

At least in this weather, they were unlikely to rot, so they wouldn't be dealing with the stench on top of everything else.

Ivan looked grim, his lean face tight with strain. "We couldn't have done anything else, not without letting the police take out the barricades," he said quietly. "But—" he shook his head. "They're not going to forget this. They're going to be looking for blood." He gave a quick, strained grin. "On the bright side, they were looking for blood already. So maybe this doesn't actually raise the stakes that much."

The unnatural silence of the streets lasted for maybe three blocks past the edge of the barricades. And then they began to hear the noises Tae had been expecting—distant sirens, voice amps, people shouting and yelling.

He exchanged glances with Ivan, and they turned down a narrow street leading towards the sound.

When they reached the end of the small alley next to the nearest red cluster of police on Tae's scanner, he slowed. Ivan came up beside him, and they peered out, Ivan's hand resting on Tae's shoulder.

"What are they doing?" Ivan whispered.

Tae shook his head.

Ahead of them, grim-faced officers in riot gear had set a narrow parameter around a block of apartment buildings in the projects. They'd blocked the surrounding streets with barriers, and they were standing in front of them, weapons drawn.

As Tae watched, someone hurled a projectile from an upper window, shouting, "Down with the fascist police!"

The projectile bounced harmlessly off the cement, metres away from the nearest officer, but the officer raised her weapon. "Stand down," she shouted into her voice amp. "Stand down, or I shoot." Without waiting for a response, she raised her rifle to her shoulder.

Tae just had time to realize it was a laser gun, rather than a heat gun, and would easily reach the distance, then the window shattered, a long line burned into the sill around it.

There was a strangled scream from inside, and Ivan's hand on his shoulder tightened.

He ducked back into the shelter of the alley and tapped his com. "Lev," he whispered. "The police have an apartment block cordoned off here in the projects. I'll send you through the coordinates."

"Alright," said Lev after a moment. "Caz and Peti and I will start mapping it out. Do you know what they're doing?"

"No. I'll let you know if we figure it out."

He tapped off his com and glanced at Ivan.

Ivan had turned back to the apartment, and something about the sharp cut of his profile, the long, clean lines of his body, the dark curl of his hair against the brown of his skin, shot an unexpected ache through Tae's chest.

He closed his eyes and swore under his breath.

"There's nothing we can do here," said Ivan at last, turning away, his voice quiet.

"I know," Tae whispered back, a hard knot of guilt and worry tightening in his stomach.

The next place his scanner showed a large police presence was the same—another apartment block cordoned off, a tight police patrol, officers in riot gear.

And another, a few city blocks later.

And another.

He frowned as he tapped yet another set of coordinates through to Lev. "I—think I see what they're doing," he said into the com. "They're separating people off. They were overpowered yesterday when everyone joined us, and I think they're trying to prevent that happening again. These blocks must be where people were causing trouble. They want them to believe they're alone, and there's no help coming."

"That makes sense." Lev's voice was grim. "It might keep the police distracted for a bit, trying to segregate everyone off like that, but if they manage it, they'll have the city back under control within a couple days."

"It's not taking as many officers as you might think," said Tae, words sharp with worry. "They're patrolling, but they're also setting up force fields. They'll be able to keep those up and defend them with just a couple officers."

There was a moment of silence from the other end of the com. At last Lev sighed. "Just keep sending through the coordinates. Let's get this mapped, and we'll figure things out from there."

Tae glanced around the almost-deserted streets. The sun was already past its reluctant zenith, the dim, clammy glow of it turning the streets a pale orange as it drooped towards the horizon. "We're almost finished, I think," he said. "Just a few more places, and we'll head in."

He tapped off his com. Ivan gave him a small smile, and they started off again, pulling their scarves up around their mouths against the growing late-afternoon chill, walking close enough that their shoulders brushed.

And then, ahead of them, came the sharp blip of a siren, turned on and off quickly, and the hiss and fizz of heat guns.

He glanced at Ivan, and saw the tension he felt reflected in Ivan's face.

They started towards the sound at a half-run.

The noise of heat guns grew louder as they got closer. Then they came around a corner, and Tae stopped abruptly.

Ivan swore through his teeth.

In front of them stretched a large, sprawling encampment town, the makeshift homes and shelters of those unable to get housing vouchers, because of their family name, or poverty, or some offence, real or imagined, against a government official sometime in the past, but with just enough money or pull to avoid joining the street kids.

Grim-looking police officers in full riot gear surrounded the shantytown, just like they had the apartment blocks, patrolling a tight parameter. They'd shut down the entire area, force field barricades blocking off any entrance or exit, their weapons drawn and ready as they patrolled.

And from inside, Tae could hear shots, screams, children crying for their parents.

He felt sick.

Damn it to hell. He hadn't wanted this. He hadn't meant for this to become a bloody revolution. He'd just been trying to keep his damn friends safe.

Ivan glanced over, as if reading his thoughts, and put a hand on Tae's arm. And like always, despite everything, Tae could feel his muscles relaxing at the pressure of Ivan's hand.

"Something like this would have happened anyways, Tae," he said. "Between Grigory and Olyessa fighting for power and the government cracking down, the people I talked to in here seemed to believe that if something didn't change, they'd end up getting killed regardless."

His voice was gentle, but there was sharp strain on his face, and pain in his eyes.

Tae gave a short nod, his teeth clenched. "Fine. But this, right here, is happening because of us. And we're damn well not going to let them deal with it alone."

They crept cautiously around the edges of the shantytown. As Tae had suspected, the police had effectively closed down every exit and entrance. Still, from the sounds from inside the cordoned-off area, some people were fighting back anyway.

Two police officers stepped out from one of the entrances, dragging a struggling man between them. They shoved him to the ground, and as he pushed himself to hands and knees, one of the officers stepped forward, swinging his shock-stick.

It hit the man across the back of his head, and he crumpled.

A girl, not older than twelve, ducked between the police guarding the entrance and ran to him. She was sobbing, and she grabbed the unconscious man under the arms and tried to haul him back inside.

"Get back," one of the officers snapped.

"Let me take him," she whispered. "He's my papa. Let me——"

The other officer grabbed the girl by the shoulder and shoved his shock-stick into the side of her neck. Her body went stiff as the current jolted through her, and when he pulled the stick back, she collapsed beside her father.

Tae swore, his hand tight on his heat gun.

Ivan's face was pale.

Damn it to hell, these were the people who'd risked their lives to save him and the street kids and the students the day before.

They were Ivan's damn friends.

"Ivan, listen," he whispered, pulling a small metal sphere out of the padded bag Ysbel had handed them. "You think the police would be less excited about fighting people inside the shantytown if they're worried about what might be happening outside?"

Ivan raised his eyebrows. "They might."

They crept down the small alleys, keeping to the shadows. Their caution was hardly necessary—the police were fully focused on it was happening inside the shantytown.

At least, for the next three minutes or so.

Half a block down from the police cordon, Tae glanced around quickly. The explosive he'd chosen wasn't a big one, but it should get the police's attention. He nestled in the doorway of an abandoned building that looked like it had been used to trade street drugs, before the streets had erupted into chaos.

"Ready?" he whispered.

Ivan nodded.

He set the timer on the controller, and they took to their heels.

They'd made it maybe six blocks by the time the timer finished counting down. There was a muffled roar, a spray of debris visible even from six blocks away, and shouts of alarm over police voice amps.

Tae and Ivan exchanged grim smiles, and Ivan leaned in and kissed Tae quickly, the warmth of his kiss much too brief.

And again, something about the pull of Ivan's shirt as he straightened and turned, the way it tugged against the wiry muscles of his chest and arms, slid through Tae like a knife, so he had to close his eyes for a moment.

There would be time for that eventually. If he could keep them all alive that long.

The last sickly glow of the setting sun through the forcefield was slowly fading as they headed back towards the barricades. Ivan reached over, taking Tae's hand in his as they walked, but he was still unnaturally quiet, and Tae watched him from the corner of his eye. His lips were pinched tightly, his face paler than normal.

He'd hardly smiled since the day before, when they'd both almost been killed at the barricades. The memory of the look on his face, when Tae had told him to go back without him, leave Tae to be killed, still made Tae feel slightly sick.

He hadn't had a choice. That had been the only option.

But Ivan's face still bore traces of the horror of those desperate moments.

They were only a few streets away from the barricades, and Tae could already feel his shoulders relaxing, when they rounded a corner, and he ran full-on into a police officer.

"What the—" the officer started, grabbing Tae around the arm and yanking him up. "You're one of those damn revolutionaries!"

Tae reached for the heat-pistol in his pocket, but before his hand closed on it, a shock-stick slammed into the side of his head, and the world went momentarily unfocused.

The shock-stick hit him again, this time in the ribcage, and he tasted iron as the current jolted through his body.

He felt, rather than heard, the heat-blast, the blow-by heat crisping the edges of his jacket, and then the hand holding him loosened, the shock-stick clattering to the ground, and he collapsed onto the cement.

"Tae! Tae, are you alright? Tae, talk to me——"

He blinked, and the blur bending over him resolved into Ivan's face, bloodless and drawn with worry.

"I'm alright," he muttered through the throbbing in his head. "I'm fine. Just help me up."

Ivan pulled him to his feet and into a tight embrace, kissing him desperately. Tae leaned into him, but it took him a moment to find his balance.

"Come on, lean on me," said Ivan quietly. "We've got to go. I think he put a call out."

Tae nodded unsteadily, and they set off as quickly as his stumbling feet could carry him. His head throbbed, and his muscles were still shaky enough from the electric current that he was leaning most of his weight on Ivan, but they reached the barricade and slipped inside before the police bikes, sirens wailing, came around the corner, pulling up when they saw the defenders with their heat guns.

"Tae! Are you alright? What happened?" Caz was there, and Peti.

He squeezed his eyes shut for a moment and straightened. "I'm fine," he mumbled. "I wasn't being careful, and I ran into an officer. Ivan took care of him."

"Are you sure?" Caz's voice was tight with worry.

Tae managed a small smile. "Caz. I'm fine. It was nothing."

He glanced back.

Ivan was standing at the edge of the barricade, eyes closed. He was supporting himself against the wall, pain etching his face, and Tae's breath caught in sudden panic.

"Ivan! Ivan, are you alright? Were you hurt?"

Ivan opened his eyes and tried to smile. "I'm fine. I wasn't hurt. I'm—just sorry I didn't get to you faster."

Tae frowned. "It's alright. I'm alright. Thanks to you, I mean."

Again, Ivan tried to smile, but it didn't reach his eyes. "Probably better get to the medic tent anyways, get looked at," he said.

Tae nodded, and Peti took his arm, steadying him as he started toward the tent.

But he couldn't help a backward glance at Ivan as he went. And he couldn't help the mixture of helplessness and anger constricting his chest at the look on Ivan's face.

Ivan was here because of him. Ivan was hurting because of him.

And there was nothing he could damn well do about it.

6

Masha, day 2

"Where did you put the damn info chips, Alonya?" Adrik snapped.

"They're in your bag," said Masha calmly, watching as he fumbled about on his desk.

He glared at her. "And I'll need the statistics I asked for, the street disturbances under prior Secretary Generals."

"I prepared them, as you requested," said Masha. "They're on the chip in the outside pocket of your bag."

"And what were the conclusions?" he grumbled.

"I prepared a graph. If you open it, you'll see that there have been seventeen instances of street disturbances in the past century. I've broken them down by number of people involved, level of violence incurred, how close together they were in years to account for any copycat impact, and any concessions made by the government. The numbers support, broadly, the proposition you intend to present."

Adrik dropped back into his chair, passing a hand across his face. He looked, for a moment, older than his years, weary and almost pathetic.

Masha felt no sympathy. This had been coming for a long time.

When he spoke again, his voice was as weary as his expression. "Alright, Alonya. I didn't want to bring you to this meeting. I think it's no secret I don't like you, and I don't trust you. And I'm certain you've heard by now that your patron, Slavenka, is dead. Murdered. I could throw you out in the streets tomorrow, and no one would care. But—" he gestured helplessly. "I'm getting too old for this. And you, useless as you are, can at least remember the facts and figures you looked at yesterday."

Masha nodded her head in a gesture that could have been agreement, or could have been submission. "The meeting's in fifteen minutes' time," she said, her voice calm and carefully modulated. "I'll prepare everything I need to."

He glared at her in sudden irritation. "Don't bother trying to fool me, Alonya," he snapped. "You came in this morning prepared for the meeting. You knew what I'd ask."

Masha inclined her head again, without actually answering.

Five minutes later, they were walking down the corridors towards the general conference room. The hallway this time was slightly more crowded—since enough important ministers were attending, police had been redeployed from the street protests to keep the most egregious assassination attempts from occurring in full view.

The expressions on the other ministers' faces were cautious, and their aides walked with weapons clutched in their hands. They didn't even bother to hide them at this point. Everyone knew what was happening.

Masha caught more than one minister glancing in surprise or faint disapproval at her and Adrik, he walking deliberately ahead of her, she carrying his bag.

She kept her expression neutral, her eyes straight ahead.

The atmosphere was no less tense inside the conference room.

Ministers sat or stood, talking in curt, hushed tones, and security guards rimmed the walls, riot shields down, grim expressions on their faces. If she hadn't realized how bad things were, this scene alone would have told her everything she needed to know.

At the opposite end of the table from her, she caught sight of a familiar face. Zhenya looked up as she entered, and for just an instant she caught a flicker of surprise in their expression. They hadn't expected to see her as an undersecretary, no doubt—after all, she'd gotten them in as a full minister.

She gave them a bland, pleasant smile that conjured no recognition, and let her eyes wander around the rest of the room.

She and Adrik weren't the last to arrive, but they were close—only two ministers walked in after them. At last, a woman who must be Branka stood, tapping her knuckles sharply on the table.

"Ministers," she said, voice cutting through the hushed murmur of conversation. Her tone was sharp, but the noise didn't die immediately. She rapped the table again. "Ministers, please. Take your seats. My hope is that we can deal with this in an expeditious manner."

Reluctantly, the ministers quieted. The other undersecretaries sat next to their assigned ministers, but Adrik gave an imperious wave of his hand, gesturing Masha to stand behind him.

Masha noticed how Branka's eyes flicked over her quickly, a small frown creasing her face, but the woman didn't comment.

When everyone had taken a seat, there was a moment of silence. At last, Branka spoke. "For those of you who may be unaware, after our most recent reorganizations in government positions, I am the Minister of Government Affairs. The Secretary General has asked that I take charge of the response to the governmental crisis caused by Grigory and Olyessa's demise, and I intend to do so."

Masha raised her eyebrows.

The woman was something of an unknown quantity. In Masha's time here, she'd worked behind the scenes, but now, it appeared, she was making her play. By invoking the Secretary General, Branka was making her position clear—she was confident enough in her ability to deal with the situation that she was willing to tie herself to the outcome publicly.

Ambitious, then.

That could prove useful. Or dangerous.

"I have asked that you each prepare a report to present at today's meeting. I assume you've done so." She glanced around the room. "To begin, I will ask that Under-minister Dmitrov please provide his report on the situation in the streets."

The under-minister over the Commissioner of Police in Prasvishoni stood and gave his brief report.

Masha watched him, forcing her face to remain expressionless.

It never would have gotten this out-of-hand if her damn crew had actually listened.

But—as much as there was a part of her that rebelled at the thought, this could provide her with an even stronger position than she'd planned for. As long as she had the means and the will to take advantage of it.

When Dmitrov sat down, another minister rose to give her report, this time on the activity of the street gangs.

At last Branka turned to Adrik. "Minister Goran informed me he's delegated this particular internal security matter to you. Please present your report, followed by recommendations."

"Hand me the information chip," Adrik snapped over his shoulder, not bothering to address Masha by name. She didn't comment on his rudeness, just pulled the chip from the bag by her feet and handed it to him. He snatched it from her fingers without looking at her, and slipped into his com, pulling up his holoscreen.

"If you examine this graph, which I've prepared from a hundred years' worth of street disturbances, you'll see that the most important overarching factor in how quickly the government was able to reassert control over the protests was the amount of government force used," he said in a monotonous voice.

"Then can you explain the inconstancy in the graph there?" asked one of the ministers across the table, raising her head.

Adrik looked to the chart for a moment, and Masha could picture his scowl. "My undersecretary will explain that," he said at last. "Alonya?"

Masha gave a small smile, ignoring Adrik's warning glare, and stepped forward. "Of course." She turned to the minister who'd asked the question. "As you will note, if you look at the side of the graph, the apparent discrepancy comes here, during a transition of power. One can surmise that the ability of the Ministry of the Interior to do their job was affected by the internal disturbances at the time. This is borne out by data, as we can see on the next chart." She swiped the screen. "The assets deployed in that instance were a fraction of what they could have been. Which proves, I think, the general point—that if an uprising is not put down at the start with sufficient force, the cost and the ultimate loss of life associated with dealing with it goes up exponentially."

"And wouldn't you agree, Undersecretary, that this is also a time of particular instability in the government, considering the situation with the mafia?" the woman asked. "I assume we must also take that into account."

Masha nodded with a slight smile. "Of course. However, as you'll see, I've laid out the variables that appear to have played a significant role in the disaster you reference. You'll note the majority of these do not apply to our current situation—the lack of resources, for instance. Through our contacts with Olyessa, prior to her unfortunate demise, we were able to procure a large number of physical assets which, if I understand correctly, are en route to Prasvishoni as we speak." She glanced at Branka, who gave a short nod of confirmation.

"And of course, despite the current divisions within the government, the police and the army are still under the control of their respective ministers. In addition, with the unrest in the boyeviki and the street gangs, the streets are in turmoil, certainly. But they are not united under one cause as they were in the incident you referenced." She looked around the table with a pleasant smile. "Therefore, you'll see that even the apparent anomaly in fact supports our proposed use of force."

"That's enough, undersecretary," Adrik growled. He was glaring at her with a look of pure hatred. He hadn't missed her apparent slip of the tongue, when she'd referred to who had prepared the information.

She nodded and stepped meekly back, and he stood, eyebrows lowered, expression venomous. "As my undersecretary explained, the amount of force I propose to use against the street disturbances is both historically sound, and logistically practical." He glanced around the room.

"I understand you have additional information you would like to share in private," said Branka at last.

He nodded brusquely. "I've been putting it together for the last two weeks, ever since we were first informed of the rumours regarding Grigory. If it turned out to be true, street disturbances were inevitable. I thought it best to be prepared."

"Very good," said Branka, with a brusque nod. "In that case, let's move on to a report by Minister Sorana."

The meeting lasted just over two standard hours. Masha was secretly impressed—she'd expected it to drag on much longer. She stood silently behind Adrik's chair, shifting her weight slightly to relieve her aching feet, but didn't let her expression change. The look on Zhenya's face, though, when they glanced in her direction, was changing gradually from one of surprise to one of calculation, and she hid a smile.

When the meeting was over, Branka turned to Adrik. "Would you join me in Minister Goran's office, then?" she asked. "I'd like to see this information you've prepared."

Adrik nodded and rose. "Alonya," he said over his shoulder, "go back to my office. Finish up the research I assigned you yesterday, please."

"Of course," Masha murmured.

When she reached Adrik's office once more, she dropped into the chair behind his desk with a small sigh of relief. It had been a while since she'd been expected to stand through a meeting, and her feet ached.

She closed her eyes for a moment, and let a small smile play across her face.

Things were progressing nicely.

Then she sat up with a sigh and pulled up her holoscreen. Probably best to familiarizing herself with the situation in the streets while she waited.

It took less time than she'd imagined—only fifteen standard minutes or so before the knock came at the door.

"Hello?" she called.

"Undersecretary Alonya?"

It was a voice she recognized very well, although its owner wouldn't recognize her. She'd been very careful, for seventeen years, to ensure that the only people who would remember her were people she wished to remember her.

"Yes? What do you need?" She kept her voice pleasant and bland.

"It's Minister Goran. I'm here with Branka. Would you be so kind as to let us in?"

She stood and tapped the lock. The door swung wide, and the two ministers stepped inside.

Goran was tall and broad-shouldered, his face carved deep with lines of age and weather. He'd served in the military himself for several years before being assigned minister of Internal Defence and Security.

"Please, sit down," said Masha politely, closing the door behind them. "Under-minister Adrik isn't with you?"

Minister Goran looked around, frowning. "Where's your desk?" he asked.

"I'm—afraid the under-minister neglected to request one," she murmured. "A regrettable oversight, I'm sure."

Goran took the chair behind Adrik's desk and leaned forward, steepling his hands in front of him and fixing her with his piercing gaze. "I apologize for the intrusion, Undersecretary, but when did you begin work here?"

"Yesterday," said Masha, voice still carefully neutral.

Goran shot a meaningful glance at Branka, who nodded, her face grim.

"I assume you assisted in preparing the presentation for the ministers' meeting," he continued. "But the information Adrik showed us today in our private meeting—was that something you had a hand in?"

Masha shook her head, letting faint confusion flicker across her face. "No. He—informed me that my services would not be required for that."

Goran watched her for a few moments longer.

Her heart was pounding.

Minister Goran was notoriously suspicious, and notoriously close-mouthed. Masha had taken that into consideration, of course, but as her crew had so aptly demonstrated over the past few months, there was no way of taking providing against every variable.

At last, though, he gave a sharp nod. "I hear there was no love lost between the two of you."

Masha dropped her eyes. "I—don't know that I'd—" she began.

Goran shook his head brusquely. "His behaviour was in full view today in the meeting. And I've heard the same story from others who he'd have no reason to attempt to impress."

Masha let the confusion on her face sharpen.

Goran sighed. "I suppose there's no point hiding the tokens. Under-minister Adrik has been arrested. Thankfully, I have my own sources of information other than the compromised report he attempted to present to me today, and thankfully, I trust them. A disaster was averted, and at a time like this, that's more luck than we should expect. But." He spread his hands on the desk. "This puts me in a difficult position. With the current upheaval in the government, I don't have time to find a ready replacement." He paused. "Your presentation today—I assume you researched and prepared it?"

Masha nodded.

He had no idea, of course, exactly how much research and preparation had gone into, not only the report, but the tainted chip the unfortunate Adrik had presented in his private meeting.

Still, it had proved worth the effort.

"And I assume that before Slavenka recommended you for this position, she assured herself that you were familiar enough with the necessary information to serve under the Under-Minister of Internal Defence, correct?"

"Of course," Masha murmured.

He slapped his hands on the table. "Very well then. For the time being, Undersecretary Alonya, you will take on the Under-minister's responsibilities. Finding a replacement for Adrik may take days, or weeks, depending on how quickly we bring this situation in the government to heel, and until then, you will report to me directly." He leaned forward, his eyes boring into her. "I will expect you to perform your duties competently, until you are replaced. This includes putting an end to the situation in the streets, by whatever means necessary."

Masha ducked her head. "I'm honoured by your trust."

He gave her a grim smile. "Perhaps you'd best see what the job entails before you thank me. As I'm certain you know, an undersecretary is not a position that will allow you to deflect blame, should things go badly with the situation outside."

"I am very aware of that," she said quietly.

He pushed himself up from his seat and gave her a brief nod. "Very well." He glanced around the room. "I suppose you may as well make use of this office. I'll expect daily briefings, and I'll expect them to be as well-researched as your presentation today. I will not be understanding of mistakes."

"Of course," she murmured again.

"I'll see you in my office tomorrow morning. I've granted you access to the confidential information pertaining to your temporary position. I expect you'll be able to locate what you need."

"I'm certain I will," she said.

When the two ministers had left, Masha sank into her chair, heart still pounding strangely.

Her first play had gone exactly as she'd planned. But there was an unexpectedly bitter undertone to the victory.

And as much as she hated to admit it, she knew very well why.

Her crew, right now, were crouched behind barricades, hunting desperately for a way save the lives of a group of ragged revolutionaries.

Revolutionaries she'd have to crush, ruthlessly, to win what she needed for her final victory.

She took a deep breath and allowed herself a small, wry smile.

For seventeen years she'd worked in this corrupt, parasitic government, watching as ministers gave orders that would kill street children, took bribes and looked the other way as gangs warred over streets and innocent people died, funnelled money from starving precincts into their own pockets. For seventeen years it had sickened her, and she'd pasted on a pleasant smile and pretended she didn't notice. For seventeen years, she'd swallowed down her fury, her disgust, her horror.

And now, finally, she was holding tokens in the game she'd spent those seventeen years preparing for.

One play down, two to go.

Whatever her crew believed to the contrary, this was a goal worth sacrificing everything for.

7

Jez, day 2

Jez sauntered into the small shelter, tossing the explosive Ysbel had given her and catching it neatly.

Lev glanced up at her entrance, a quick sequence of emotions flashing across his face—that soft look he always got when he saw her, followed by a sudden alarm as he realized what she was holding.

She winked at him.

Tae must have noticed a moment later, because he yelped, swore, and started to scramble to his feet from the other side of the small fire they'd started for warmth. "Jez, are you bloody well trying to kill us?"

She grinned. "Don't figure I need to at this point. Got enough people trying to do the job for me. But anyways—" she turned to Lev, still grinning. "Just talked to Ysbel. She figured this little beauty would cause a hell of a distraction, but then she was going on and on about some crap about it blowing all the rest of us into the damn stratosphere, so I said, why not throw it on a skybike, drop it at some warehouse somewhere far enough away it won't kill us all when we make some fireworks with it, and she said that would be a great idea, except with the streets the way they are you'd have to be a damn lunatic to get through them. And hell, figure there's at least one of us here who fits that description, so—" she shrugged. "Anyways, guess I'm stealing a skybike."

Lev closed his eyes, the strain sharp on his face, and for a moment something twisted in her chest.

He'd looked like that far too often over the last few days.

"Hey. Genius." She dropped the explosive into her pocket and took him by the arms, pulling him around towards her.

He closed his eyes and sagged against her for a moment, and again, she was hit by the terrifying, breathtaking realization—that Lev hurting hurt her. That she needed him to be alright. That she would do anything for him to be alright.

She slipped her arms around him. "Hey. I'll be fine."

He opened his eyes and tried to smile at her. "I—I know you will. This is your expertise, Jez, and I trust you. I—I just—"

"I know," she said quietly. She leaned in and kissed him softly, which—OK, which actually, now that she thought about it, kissing Lev was basically always a good idea, and he seemed to think so too.

"Be careful," he said at last, voice only a little unsteady.

She winked at him, and gave him one final kiss before she turned and left.

She slipped through the barricade, glanced quickly around, and started off down the street, keeping close to the edge of the buildings. She pulled her heat pistol from her pocket, holding it loosely in one hand, although honestly, against police in full riot gear, it wouldn't really do much even with Ysbel's mods.

She found her first skybike, with a police officer on top of it, about four blocks out. The officer wasn't actually paying much attention to her, seeming entirely set on whatever the hell he was supposed to be doing.

She grinned to herself, grabbed a piece of loose prefab from the street, and lobbed it at him.

When it bounced off his helmet, he decided pretty damn quickly that she was worth his attention. He spun his bike, and she jumped back as a heat-blast scorched the wall behind where she'd been standing. She weighed her heat-gun in her hand.

Yes, he had riot gear with a heat shield. But—

She stepped smartly out of the way of the bike and swung up behind the officer as he shot past. Before he could even open his mouth to protest, she spun her pistol in her hand, shoved his chin forward, and brought the butt of her pistol down on the base of his skull.

He slumped.

She hit the restraints, and he tumbled into the streets.

She tapped her com, grinning. "Hey genius, got my bike."

Lev, day 2

Lev stared into the fire. He was dimly aware of the dull pain in his jaw, and it took a moment to realize it was because he was clenching his teeth hard enough to hurt.

He closed his eyes for a moment and forced himself to relax.

Jez would be fine. Everyone would be fine. This would work.

It had to.

He jumped at Jez's voice through his earpiece. She was clearly grinning, and clearly exceedingly pleased with herself.

"I—won't even ask how you got the bike," he said, smiling despite himself.

Honestly, he didn't think his nerves would take knowing.

"Guess you'd better send the coordinates." The jauntiness in her tone betrayed nothing of the fact that she was carrying an explosive device of unknown capabilities, manufactured by Ysbel, while riding a stolen police skybike through a city that had devolved into total anarchy.

"Sending through to your com." He tapped his com, pulling up the map with the marker on it indicating a vacant warehouse he and Ysbel had decided was far enough away from the barricades, and from any other inhabited building, that it likely wouldn't kill anyone.

"On it," said Jez.

He could hear, faintly, shouts and yells through his earpiece, the whine of sirens, the distorted voices of police officers shouting through voice amps.

He closed his eyes and took a deep breath, then another.

Anything he could say or do now would only distract her, and that was the last thing in the system she needed.

"Just—try to keep the police from going to investigate what you threw, so we don't kill any of them in the explosion," he said at last.

"Figure that won't be a problem, considering how close they're staying on my damn tail. Must like my company. And I sure as hell don't plan on sticking around after I drop the thing."

Vera, who'd wandered into the tent, listened to the proceedings with raised eyebrows, her eyes going from Lev's com to his face.

"You—you and she—" she said after a moment.

Tae glanced over at Vera with an expression of grim resignation. "Yes. Believe me. He and she. I've walked in on enough to guarantee that 'he and she,'" he muttered.

"You—I mean, forgive me for saying this, but you actually sound —relatively sane. How have you not had a heart attack yet?"

"Sane is relative," Tae mumbled.

Lev managed a small chuckle, even though he wasn't sure if his heart would actually start beating again until Jez was back here, in the tent, and in his arms. "I—believe there's still time for that," he murmured.

"On my way in," drawled Jez over the com, and again he jumped. "Got some friends with me. Figure Ysbel and Tanya want to prepare a little a welcoming party?" In the background, he could hear sirens, and the faint sounds of shouting.

"We already have one ready," Ysbel grumbled. "We've worked with you before, you crazy lunatic. Come in over the east end of the barricade, a few metres to the north of the entrance. We'll have the wires pulled back for you."

"See Ysbel, and this is why you're so damn hot," said Jez. "Be there on my bike in thirty standard seconds." She paused a moment. "Or in fifteen standard seconds, but off my bike and in pieces."

Lev closed his eyes and gritted his teeth and counted down. From outside the shelter, the sound of sirens grew louder, and then he heard Jez's whoop of delight through the com, and a muffled, sputtering string of explosions.

He left his eyes closed for a few moments, breathing in and out until he was pretty sure his hands had stopped shaking. Then he stepped out of the shelter and caught Jez as she swaggered over, pulling her into a tight embrace.

"See, genius?" she whispered. "Nothing to worry about. Anyways, couldn't die before you followed through on all those things you were whispering in my ear that you wanted to do to me this morning."

He swallowed hard, and she pulled back, grinning, and gave him a wink that made him temporarily forget how to speak.

Tae had come up beside them, resolutely averting his eyes.

Lev sighed and turned to the others, without taking his arm from Jez. "Alright," he said. "Vera and Dmitri, you weren't here for the discussion last night. Peti and I went through the information Tae and Ivan brought back. This is what we mapped out." He tapped his com, bringing up the holoscreen, and expanded it so they could all see. "It appears they're trying to cut us off from each other, as Tae surmised. And once they've put up force fields around each of these areas, it will free up the officers to come finish us off. So—" He turned back to the map. "I think our best bet—perhaps our only bet at this point—is to make sure they can't do what they planned. The more area we force the police to control, the more of them we occupy in just maintaining the status quo, and the more of a chance we have."

Dmitri frowned. "So—you're suggesting we break these other places out of the police cordons?"

Lev nodded.

Vera bit her lip for a moment. "And if we do that—you realize these are residential areas. If the police block off this whole section of the city, the people there won't have a choice. They'll be dragged into this whether they want to or not, and they could die for it."

Lev took a deep breath. "I know," he said quietly. "We'll be pulling this entire sector into a revolution. But—if we don't, everyone who had anything to do with this, even tangentially, will be killed. The street kids, the students who stood up for them, every person who flooded the streets two days ago, risked heat guns and shock sticks to keep the people behind this barricade from being shot or tortured or beaten to death. And not just them. Do you think the government won't track down their family and friends? Do you think the gangs will forget the names of people who took a stand against them?"

There was a hard knot in his chest as he spoke. Because, of course, everything he'd said was the truth. But then, so was everything Vera had said.

For a few moments, there was silence.

At last, Ivan looked up from where he was standing beside Tae, his arm around him. "We talk about pushing people into a revolution," he said, his voice quiet and grim. "We talk as if there was a chance for someone to sit this out. But the police are in the middle of a crackdown. There's going to be war in the streets of Prasvishoni. Everyone in this sector will be dragged into it, one way or another. The only question now is, will it be a war between revolutionaries and the government? Or will it simply be a slaughter?"

Vera looked at him for a long moment, then nodded slowly. "Maybe before I met Tae, I wouldn't have believed that," she said. "But after these last few weeks?" She gave a small shrug. "You're right. We were innocents. We had no idea. But—I think we do, now."

Ivan smiled, although the haunted look was still there in his face. "For a bunch of innocents, you did a surprisingly good job of starting a revolution."

She chuckled, then sobered, turning back to Lev. "Maybe you're right. Maybe this is the only way to keep people alive."

Lev sighed.

It would have been nice to be wrong, this once. But they'd been over this last night—they didn't have another viable option.

"Tae is going to jam the police lines, and the explosive Jez planted will be a distraction," he said. "Tae already hacked us through to the people who are inside the cordons. On our signal, they'll attempt to break out. And hopefully, between all of that—"

There was fear in Vera's face, strain and uncertainty mixed, but she just nodded again.

Lev bit the inside of his cheek, watching her. She'd faced execution only a couple days ago. She'd been under siege as long as

Tae had—longer, even, if you counted the time the police had them cut off in the university. And she didn't even have a reason to fight, except that she didn't think what was happening was right.

The same reason Ivan had to fight, and Dimitri, and the other students and street kids—everyone else behind this barricade.

And yet, they were still here.

And they were all counting on him to find a way out of this.

Ysbel ducked into the tent half a standard hour later.

"Are you ready?" he asked her.

She smiled grimly and pulled a controller from her pocket. "Believe me. I'm ready."

"Tae?"

Tae nodded.

Lev took a deep breath and tapped the com line Tae had set up between the buildings.

"On my mark," he said quietly. "Two. One. Now."

Tae hit the command on his com, activating the blocker he'd planted into the police lines, at the same time as Ysbel tapped the controller to the explosive.

For a moment, nothing happened. Then a low *boom* rumbled through the streets, the cement under their feet trembling with it.

"Well," said Vera finally. "If that doesn't do it, I don't know what would."

Tae tapped his com on, and they listened as police officers shouted and swore, their voices fuzzing and indistinct over the newly jammed lines.

Tae smiled. "That should make it a bit more complicated for them to put together a response," he said. His voice was quiet, but there was a bitterness in it that Lev hadn't heard there for a long time.

"Can you tap us into the government lines?" Lev asked. "I'd like to hear the response, if possible."

Tae nodded, tapping something into his com. A moment later, they heard a sputtering outrage of voices. "If they're discussing what happened, it'll be over this line," he said.

Within ten minutes, judging from the panicked calls through the government lines, the police had been overwhelmed. Within twenty, the besieged would-be revolutionaries had broken through the police cordons. And within half an hour, it was clear the police wouldn't be able to take their positions back.

They looked at each other, relief on their faces. Dmitri was grinning widely, and Vera gave a low, delighted laugh, slapping Tae on the shoulder. "We did it!"

Tae was smiling as well.

And then, through the com, Lev caught a name he recognized, and he held up his hand for silence, frowning.

"—saying it's the same crew. They got visuals on them when this all started. Lev Antov, Jez Solokov, Ysbel Kovac, Tae Bezdomnikov, Masha Volkova. And there's rumours that Ysbel's wife is with them. None of that's good news."

"We'll instruct the police to set their biometrics into the system. If half of what I've heard about them is true, getting rid of them is going to be our first priority if we want to get this under control."

Lev glanced around at the others.

Jez was grinning. That wasn't, however, particularly reassuring.

"Well," said Ysbel at last. "We may have just declared war on the government. But it looks like they've returned the favour."

8

Masha, day 3

When the knock came at her door, Masha was expecting it. She sighed and shut down holoscreen, standing to unlock the door.

An aide stood there, practically quivering with nerves, and somehow, the fear in her face gave Masha a slight pang.

The girl was young—hardly older than Tae—and she'd likely never seen chaos on this scale before.

Masha forced her face into a pleasant smile. "Yes?"

"Undersecretary Alonya?" The girl's voice trembled ever so slightly.

"Yes?" Masha said again, patiently.

The aide swallowed. "Minister Goran would like to speak with you."

Masha give a brisk nod, and stood, picking up her bag from the floor.

She'd had it ready since she'd heard what her crew had done. Because she had no doubt it had originated with them.

She hadn't been surprised, exactly. The government likely had no idea what they were up against, with her crew behind those barricades. Putting this rebellion down would be bloody work indeed.

The thought still had the power to make her slightly sick.

If they'd damn well listened to her—

No. Tae would never have agreed that the lives of his friends were expendable. No matter what, he'd always have done what he did, tried to find a way to save everyone, and no matter what, the others would always have gone with him.

They hadn't lived as long as she had.

They couldn't save them all. No one could.

She straightened, and turned back to the young aide. "I'm ready. Shall we go?"

The girl nodded, her body tense.

Masha frowned, studying her more closely. There were tear-streaks down her face, and terror in her eyes.

Masha had spent seventeen years training this out of herself. At the end of the day, if she wanted to save the many, she had to ignore the one. And she'd learned, finally, after years of practice, to ignore a young aide with tear-streaks on her face.

And yet somehow, she found herself asking, "Are you alright?"

The girl looked up at her, startled, and pasted a smile on her face, but it didn't reach her eyes. "I'm fine, thank you," she said.

Masha raised an eyebrow.

The aide turned away quickly. "There—one of the aides was killed in the hallway this morning," she said, her voice slightly choked.

"And you'd never seen someone killed before," said Masha.

The girl nodded, not looking at her.

"I'm sorry," said Masha quietly. "The first time is the worst, if it helps."

The girl looked up again, surprised. At last, she said in a low voice, "I—didn't think it would be like this." The words sounded as if they were being dragged out of her. "I—in university, they talked about the government, how coming to work here helped keep the system running, kept people safe. That they paid you enough to send back to your family. I—I didn't think it would be like this." Her voice shook.

Masha hesitated a moment, then reached out and put a hand on the girl's shoulder. The girl flinched, as if expecting a blow.

"I'm going to tell you something I learned young," Masha said, her voice coming out harder than she intended. "They lie to you. That's how they stay in power. They make you think it's for the good. And sometimes, someone lying dead in the hallway is the only way you figure out the lie."

The girl was staring at Masha, and Masha cursed under her breath.

She damn well knew better than this. But there was something about the intensity and the vulnerability in the girl's face that reminded her uncomfortably of a certain long-haired, scowling street-boy, and she found she couldn't help herself.

"Thank you," the girl said quietly. "I'll remember that." She paused a moment, then looked up at Masha again, her face strangely vulnerable. "But if—if they lie to us, if everything they told me was a lie—then why are you still here?"

"Because sometimes, it's the only way to change things."

The young aide studied Masha for a long, long time. At last, she nodded. "Thank you," she said again, quietly, and Masha was surprised by the warmth that sparked in her chest at the words.

She pushed it away resolutely, rearranging her face into its normal bland smile. "At any rate, I have a heat gun. I expect nothing untoward will happen on the way to Minister Goran's office."

The aide nodded, swallowing hard, and they walked down the hallway towards the minister's office.

Goran was waiting when they entered, his face dark with anger. He nodded curtly to the aide, who gave a deferential nod and ducked out the door, closing it behind her.

"Alonya," he snapped, once they were alone. "I assume you've familiarized yourself with the situation on the ground."

Masha nodded. "I assumed you'd want a report first thing this morning, so I prepared all the information I was able to gather."

He gave her a brusque nod, gesturing to a chair. "I understand you were only given access to much of the information as of yesterday afternoon. But the situation has progressed to the point that I cannot afford patience. I need someone who's up to speed and well briefed, and fully prepared. If you can't—"

"I am fully briefed, and prepared to present you with my recommendations," said Masha.

He paused, frowning. "Your recommendations?"

"Of course," she said. "I've gone through the previous briefings, studied the actions we've taken thus far, and calculated their relative effectiveness, taking into consideration the size of the police force, the weapons available, and the number and distribution of the protesters. I believe I've been able to identify some useful patterns. If I may?"

He was still frowning at her, but he gave a brusque nod.

She tapped her com, pulling up the holoscreen. "You see here, I've marked out the location of the explosion that served as a distraction, and the places where insurgents and protesters were able to break the police line. It would appear the insurgents' primary strategy, at this point, is simply to keep their fellow protesters out of the grip of the police.

"This is understandable—they've essentially declared war on the government, and they'll be rightly concerned about the consequences. However, I don't believe that at present they pose an existential threat to us. They've taken no overtly aggressive actions, and it appears they're still attempting to regroup and form a strategy."

She swiped to a new screen. "As you may recall from yesterday, I've been studying the precedents for such an insurgency. I believe that if we don't antagonize the rest of the city further, the revolutionary fervour will die down. The people were stirred up by some unfortunately leaked audio and visuals from the police crackdown on the university students. When the police turned their attention to the citizens who'd come out in protest, the citizens who were rioting in anger began rioting in fear. And fear is a powerful motivator. But now—" she shrugged. "They're no longer in immediate danger. They've barricaded themselves inside their sector, demonstrating that their motivation is more fear-based than aggression-based. Therefore, I suggest for the moment our best move is to pull the police back. Hold the line, keep their sector cut off from the rest of the city—but nothing more. Don't add fuel to the fire. If we can keep the insurgency contained, and cool the flames of those who are only partially committed, our job becomes much simpler."

Goran scowled at her. "You're advocating for us to treat these revolutionaries with kid gloves. Shall we offer them supplies as well, and blankets against the cold? These are people who attacked our police force, killed officers."

Masha gave him a small smile. "Perhaps I did not explain myself sufficiently. I'm advocating to pull the police back, yes, to let things cool down. And to wait, until the weapons we purchased from Olyessa arrive. From the briefings you give me access to, they should arrive in a matter of days. And then—" she broke off, spreading her hands. "We destroy the barricades, and the people behind them, so thoroughly that it's clear to everyone that a revolution is hopeless."

He was watching her consideringly now, but his face was still creased in a scowl. "You're aware, of course, who's behind this. A woman by the name of Masha Volkova, and a crew of criminals she assembled. She has created more chaos in this system than perhaps any other person currently living." He shook his head, pinching his lips together. "This is the crew that took down Grigory Korzhakov, and Olyessa Janovik, if the rumours are true. You think if we don't push them, they'll sit peacefully behind their barricades and wait for us?"

Masha gave a small smile, ignoring the sudden twist in her chest. "No. I do not believe that. But where are they likely to be? Not on the outskirts, with the half-committed government officials, worried for their children, or the people in the projects. If they're here, they're behind the barricades. And so, we focus our efforts, cut off their communications, keep the officers there day and night. But we don't start trouble. Until the weapons come in. And then—" she let her sentence trail off delicately.

Of course the police would start trouble. Leave them there, outside the barricades, with a bunch of students and street kids who'd been defying them, cut off any outside monitoring—of course they'd start trouble.

But she wouldn't have been the one who suggested it.

And besides, her crew would be able to handle it.

She was almost certain.

Goran nodded slowly. "Perhaps you're right. And once the weapons are here and we can take out the group behind the barricades completely, these protests will fall apart."

Masha nodded, keeping her smile calm and bland.

She wouldn't let herself think too hard of how her crew had looked last time she'd seen them—Lev shot through the shoulder, barely able to stay on his feet, Tae, circles under his eyes like bruises, dried blood matting his hair, Jez, still staggering from the aftereffects of the poison that had almost killed her—for a moment, she felt again the sick jolt of panic, stepping into the drab government apartment to see Jez lying on the floor, shaking and half-conscious, her eyes wide with fear. The helpless pleading in Lev's expression when he looked up at her, Jez cradled in his arms, the way Masha's hand shook as she plunged the needle into Jez's vein, with enough antidote to either cure her, or kill her.

Jez would be shaky for a while.

Masha still needed her crew—but they were smart. They'd survived worse.

"And I assume you're getting updates on the weapons, and how they'll be distributed?" she asked.

"That's my concern, not yours," he snapped. But she caught the way his eyes darted to a chip storage on the shelf in the corner of the room.

She nodded. "Very good." She paused a moment. "Do you need anything else from me?"

Goran shook his head. "I'll take your suggestions into consideration."

"Thank you. I'll send the underlying data, as well my research, through to your com once I'm back in my office."

He nodded, and dismissed her with a wave of his hand.

When she opened the door, the aide was waiting, leaning against the opposite wall. She'd clearly been instructed to escort Masha back, and Masha wasn't surprised. Everything in Alonya's record would suggest she was nothing more than yet another calm, boring, completely uninteresting civil servant in a list full of boring, uninteresting civil servants, but Goran hadn't survived to get where he was without exorbitant amounts of suspicion.

The girl straightened quickly. "Undersecretary? The minister asked if I'd wait to bring you back to your office."

"Thank you—" Masha paused a moment. "I'm sorry. I don't believe I asked your name."

The girl looked up, startled, and Masha smiled despite herself.

"Um. I'm—my name's Radka."

Masha nodded gravely. "Thank you, Radka."

They were silent on the walk back to Masha's office. But Masha couldn't help but notice, after she unlocked the door and stepped inside, the look Radka shot her before she turned away—a sort of camaraderie, mixed with gratitude.

The door clicked shut, and Masha closed her eyes for a moment.

It didn't matter. The kid was just an aide, and if she was smart, she'd realize that pinning her loyalty to an undersecretary wasn't good for job prospects in the government.

And the girl looked smart, despite her obvious innocence.

She took a deep breath and crossed over to her desk. She dropped into her seat and tapped her com. The number would have been in Adrik's confidential information, if she'd needed it, but she had it memorized from years past.

She'd known she'd have a limited amount of time to prepare for the second stage of her plan. She'd have to work quickly, if she wanted to keep Goran from getting suspicious

The com buzzed a moment, and then a male voice answered.

"General Osip," he said, his voice rough. "Who is this?"

"My name is Alonya," said Masha pleasantly. "I'm sure you've heard of the unfortunate incident involving Under-minister Adrik. As I was asked to fill his position temporarily, I thought perhaps a discussion between the two of us could be productive."

By the time Masha's com read 1800 Standard, she could hear the murmur from the corridors of her colleagues heading for home.

She sighed and stood, stretching out the stiffness in her back, and picked up her work bag.

At the door, she hesitated for a moment, touching the small heat pistol in her pocket instinctively. Funny, after all these years and all this time, to still be afraid. She'd have thought she would have gotten over that years ago, but, she supposed, something like fear never really went away.

She joined the crowd, merging in among the hurrying bodies, making sure that she was seen and noticed. As she neared the door leading outside, she slipped into a small side corridor that she'd used more than once in her time in the government. It led nowhere, really, but it looked like it might, and so no one took notice of someone turning down it.

And at the far end was a small storage closet, long abandoned. Once, it must have been used for cleaning supplies or some such thing, but now it lay empty and dusty.

She tapped her com against the lock, and it clicked open. She smiled to herself when she pulled the narrow door open—the box she'd set here years ago as a makeshift stool was still there, covered now with a thin layer of dust.

She pulled the door closed and settled down to wait, leaning back against the cool prefab wall. As the noise and footsteps from outside faded, she pulled up her com screen, scrolling through to the information she'd been studying earlier.

She had far too much to do to let any time go to waste.

When at last she looked up from the numbers and figures on the holoscreen, it was 2100 standard, and halls were long since silent.

She sighed quietly to herself and stood, wincing slightly at the cracking in her back and hips.

She wasn't the twenty-something she been when she first arrived in government—like the girl Radka. Although she doubted she'd ever been as innocent as that girl.

She pushed the door open a crack and glanced outside.

The emptiness of the narrow sliver of the main hallway she could see told her that most, if not all, of the ministers had gone home for the night, or else settled into their offices for a long evening of work. Quietly, Masha pulled the door shut and retrieved the cleaning-staff uniform from the bottom of her bag. She pulled the garment over her head, tucked her hair into her scarf, slipped an ID chip override into her com, and let her shoulders droop into a despondent, exhausted slouch.

Then she stepped out the door.

She didn't have a cleaning cart, but it was less about your disguise, and more about the atmosphere you carried with you. And so she trudged down the hall with the bored, tired step of someone who'd walked the same halls every night for far too many years to count, and who'd likely walk those halls until the day they died.

Where the hallway split off, she glanced down at her com as if checking her night's detail, sighed, and started towards Goran's office, her stomach tight with a mixture of nerves and anticipation.

When she reached the door, she tapped her com against the lock. It clicked open, and she let out a breath of relief.

She forced her hands steady as she stepped through the door, pulling it closed behind her. As if this was just one more task on an endless list.

Once inside, she hit the scanner on her com, doing a quick check for bugs. They were there, of course, but the blocker Tae had installed on her com from their previous job would be enough to keep them from picking up anything more than a blurred shape. Even so, she wandered slowly about the office, dusting and tidying in a desultory fashion, until she reached the shelf that Goran's eyes had flicked to momentarily when she'd asked about the weapons.

She ran her fingers across the smooth surface until she felt the chip storage. Tae's lock-pick, set into her com, vibrated, and there was a soft *click*. She slid the top back and reached gently inside.

There. A small information chip. The only one in the shallow space. With a quick breath of relief, she palmed it.

As she slid the storage closed, she heard a small noise from behind her.

The lock on the door, clicking open.

She froze instinctively, her free hand reaching for her heat pistol.

But whoever it was, it was too late to hide.

She took a deep breath, heart pounding, and forced herself to turn casually.

Goran stood in the doorway, with two aides who were clearly serving as bodyguards.

For a moment, the three of them stared at Masha. Then Goran jerked his head, and the aides stepped quickly forward.

For a split second, Masha's fingers almost closed around the small pistol in her pocket—but if she did that, even if she survived the shootout, it would derail her plan. And she didn't have time for that.

So instead she stood still, eyes wide with fear, as the aides grabbed her and yanked her arms behind her back, shoving her to her knees on the floor.

"Who the hell are you, and what are you doing here?" hissed Goran.

Masha blew out a quick breath of relief. He hadn't recognized her.

But then, people seldom did—she'd spent her entire life learning to be forgettable. And so now, with a change of clothes, a change of posture, the scarf around her hair and neck partially obscuring her face, she was entirely unrecognizable as the self-assured undersecretary she'd been earlier that day.

"I asked, what are you doing here?" Goran snapped.

"I—I was cleaning your office. That's what was on my schedule for tonight." She allowed her voice to come out high and shaky.

He glared at her. "Show me your schedule."

"I—" she began again, voice wavering.

"You what?" he snapped.

She swallowed hard, and gestured with her chin at the woman holding her arms behind her back.

"Let go of her hand," said Goran, his voice resigned. "But keep your weapons on her. My office isn't scheduled to be cleaned until tomorrow morning."

The woman let go of her arm, and, hand trembling, Masha held out her wrist with the com. He touched his own com to hers and read through her ID, frowning. He paged through to the schedule, then glared back up at her. "Who prepares the assignments?"

She shook her head, swallowing hard, as if too frightened to speak.

Goran turned away in disgust. "Get her out of my office. And make sure nothing's been touched."

The aides wrenched her to her feet, and she whimpered pitifully.

The chip, clutched in her hand, was cutting into the flesh of her palm.

If they noticed it before she was outside—

One of the aides stepped out from behind her, checking the office quickly with a scanner. As he moved closer to the chip storage, Masha found her breath coming faster.

Most scanners wouldn't be sensitive enough to pick up something as small as an information chip inside a storage compartment. But some would.

Slowly, the scanner moved along the wall, and then along the shelf, and then, inexorably, towards the com storage.

She could, if it came to it, probably still kill them.

The scanner passed the shelf. Masha let out a breath, almost dizzy at the spike of relief.

"Nothing seems to be missing," said the aide.

"Then get out of here," said Goran, gesturing dismissively at Masha. "Tomorrow I'll look into who sets the cleaning schedules. I don't like that they've changed, not with things the way they are right now." He glanced around, then reached down and picked up his office bag, left beside the door.

Masha had to bite inside of her cheek hard to keep from almost hysterical laughter.

All that because he'd forgotten his bag.

The aides hauled her out of the office, and Goran followed, closing and locking the door behind him.

"Follow her out," he said curtly to one of the aides. The man nodded, gesturing Masha ahead of him down the hallway. It wasn't until they were outside in the snow, and the door to the government buildings had clicked shut behind them, that he holstered his weapon.

"Get out of here. Go home. I have your ID number, and you'd

best hope that we don't find anything missing tomorrow."

She gave a small, frightened nod, then shuffled off down the street.

When she was out of sight, she slipped into a shallow doorway, watching for any signs she was still being followed.

She waited for a few long minutes, the snow whipping around her face and biting at her exposed skin. Winters in Prasvishoni were not for the faint of heart.

Tae had slept out in nights like this, on the streets.

She tried to ignore the painful twinge at the thought.

Her cheeks had long since grown numb, and her fingers and toes ached from the cold, before she eased out of the doorway and back into the street.

Her tiny apartment was still cold when she stepped inside, but at least the heatsink had managed to cut the chill. Still, she didn't take off her coat when she came in—it wasn't warm enough for that, not yet.

It likely wouldn't be.

She sat down on one of the hard chairs and slipped the stolen chip into her com, pulling up the holoscreen. She'd have to find a way to replace it before Goran noticed it missing, but in the meantime, best to find out everything she could.

She pulled the screen up and began swiping through the various pages of information. And then she stopped, frowning.

Someone was making requests for weapons. Someone was designating which weapons should go where, and giving instructions to the police. And it wasn't Goran.

She frowned deeper, scanning the lines of text.

They were encrypted with the highest security. But there was no hint of the identity of the person making the requests.

A small tickle of unease began in the back of her brain.

Masha knew every person in the chain of command. Every name, every face. She'd studied the lists until they were burned in her memory.

And none of them were giving these orders.

She shivered.

Whoever this was, they were powerful. Extremely powerful. And —she frowned down at the list of orders and requisitions, a small chill in her stomach.

Everything she was doing here was to save lives. Her crew might not understand that, but the sacrifices she was making were necessary, and as minimal as possible.

Whoever this was wasn't concerned about lives lost, not if their orders were any indication.

Whoever this was intended a massacre.

Slowly, Masha tapped off her holoscreen and stared blankly at the wall in front of her.

She'd always known that once she got here, she'd have to work quickly. More so since her crew had parted ways with her.

But it seemed her timeline maybe even shorter than she anticipated—at least, if she wanted anyone in the streets to survive this.

9

Tae, day 4

"Ready? Lift," said Tae, pulling up on the edge of the heavy dresser.

Ivan, on the other side, lifted as well, and they staggered forward.

"You sure you two should be doing that?" Jez called from the top of the barricade as she saw them approaching. "I mean, I appreciate the help and all, but I'm pretty damn sure that both of you just about got killed not too long ago."

"Says the person who just got over being poisoned," grumbled Tae.

She grinned at him. "Yeah. Like two weeks ago. Basically the longest I've gone without someone trying to kill me for—" she shrugged. "Hell, can't even remember how long."

"I think there were plenty of police officers trying to kill you a couple days ago. If I remember correctly," he grunted, stumbling on a broken cobblestone and almost dropping the damn dresser.

Jez laughed and jumped off the barricades, coming up beside him to help guide the heavy, awkward piece of furniture into a gap in the barricade. "That doesn't count. They were just trying to kill me because I was stealing crap and blowing crap up. It wasn't personal."

Tae dropped his end of the dresser into place.

Ivan laid his carefully down as well, then stepped back, looking over the makeshift barricade with a practised eye. "It looks better. We'll want to put something heavy there—" he gestured, "but structurally, this isn't bad. The main thing is, we want it to be easy for us to get up from our side, but hard for anyone to climb up from the outside." He glanced around, frowning. "Actually, in cold like this, we could take some water, soak down the front of the barricades. It should freeze solid, make it a little more difficult for someone to get up."

Vera glanced over from where she was helping guide an overturned university desk into a gap in the wall. "That's a good idea," she said, the weariness in her tone not quite masking her enthusiasm. "I'll get some of the students on it."

"And we know bloody well it'll actually freeze, considering I'm basically turning into a block of ice right now," said Jez cheerily. "And so is tech-head, by the looks of it."

He scowled at her, then started after Ivan, who was already headed back towards the university.

Ivan turned as Tae caught up, attempting a smile, but his eyes still held the haunted look that had been there for far too long.

Tae touched Ivan's hand. "Are you—is everything—"

Ivan hesitated a moment, then he put his arm around Tae, pulling him close, the gesture almost desperate. Tae slipped his arm around Ivan's waist, and he could feel the tension in Ivan's body as he leaned into him.

They walked together towards the university, but when they reached the entrance, Ivan paused. His face was weary, lines of exhaustion and strain cut across it, his dark eyes tight and distant.

"Ivan," Tae said quietly. "Just—go lie down for a bit. Get some rest. You haven't stopped for even a minute."

Ivan faced straight ahead, mouth set, like he was afraid to let even a hint of emotion show. "You almost died a few days ago, yet here you are," he said at last. His tone had a forced lightness to it, and Tae scowled.

"Ivan. Please. I—listen, you—" Tae trailed off. He wasn't sure how to say what he wanted to say. How looking at Ivan, seeing the hurt in his face and not being able to do anything about it, choked him.

Ivan turned and took Tae's arms gently.

Tae was acutely aware of how close they were standing, of the pressure of Ivan's hands on his arms.

They'd kissed. They were boyfriends. And perhaps Tae didn't have much experience with love, but the thought of being away from Ivan, for any reason, was a physical, dizzying pain.

But somehow, standing so close their bodies were almost touching, Ivan's hands on Tae's arms, Ivan had never seemed quite so far away.

Ivan rubbed his hands absently up and down from Tae's elbows to his shoulders, but he didn't meet Tae's eyes, and his jaw still held that tension Tae remembered so well from the pleasure planet, in the days after Ivan had almost been killed.

"Tae," he said at last. "Listen. I'm—I'm alright. I'm fine. This is something that has to be done, and I know how to do it because I've done it before."

"You're not fine," said Tae. His breath was coming a little too quickly, a mix of guilt and anger twisting inside him. "Maybe I'm just a dumb street kid, but I'm smart enough to see that."

Ivan's hands tightened around his arms, and he looked Tae in the face for the first time that morning. "Don't say that," he said sharply.

"You're not a dumb street kid, Tae. You're—" His voice choked just a little. "I just—I can't talk about it right now. I can't. I'm—I'm sorry." He let his hands drop and turned away abruptly, but not in time to keep Tae from seeing him blinking back tears.

There was a set to his shoulders, as if one sentence, one word could crack him wide open.

For a moment, Tae wanted to. He wanted to grab Ivan, spin him around, hold on to him and not let go and make him talk until it all spilled out across the cobblestones and they could somehow make sense of it together.

But Ivan was already half-way towards the dorms. "I'll grab some chairs from the common room," he said over his shoulder.

Tae heard the words he wasn't saying—he'd take something he could do alone, for now. For this trip.

He watched Ivan's retreating figure, slender and elegant. The contained grace of his movements sent a familiar ache of longing through Tae's whole damn body, and left him feeling, somehow, like he'd been hit in the stomach.

Damn this. Damn this to hell, damn this whole thing to hell. Why hadn't Ivan stayed behind on the casino ship, where he could have taken the next transport back to Prasvishoni, or wherever else he'd wanted to go? Or even stayed on the damn pleasure planet, with Galina and Radic and the others?

He closed his eyes, fighting back the tightness in his chest.

Ivan was right about one thing, at least—they were all exhausted, but none of them could afford to rest yet.

He was helping one of the kids from Felix's gang carry out another student desk when Matija called over the com.

"Tae!" Their voice was tight with strain. "Police officers. Coming in fast."

Tae slapped his com. "How far?" he asked tersely.

"I don't know. But Ysfir called it in, and her post is only a ten-minute walk from here."

Tae cursed, dropping the desk and sprinting for the makeshift command tent. He tapped his com to the crew's closed loop as he ran. "Lev! Ysbel! Police are on their way!"

"How many? How far?" Lev's voice was tense.

"Just under a kilometre, I think. I don't know how many."

He reached the command tent and ducked through the door, panting. Lev was already on his feet, and Ysbel had her pistol out, one arm around Tanya's waist.

"Are the children somewhere safe?" Tae snapped.

Tanya nodded. "They're with one of the students. He's back in the dorms, and we barricaded the door. If the police get through the barricades, he'll take them out the back and get them away."

It made a gruesome sort of sense—if the police got through, they'd be too busy in the ensuing bloodbath to worry about two children.

Tae took a deep breath and turned to Lev. "Are we ready for this?"

Lev's face was serious. "As ready as we can be. The street kids?"

Tae give a tight nod.

"Good." Lev smiled. "At the very least, I hope we're still able to give them a bit of a surprise."

Vera tapped her com through to the general line. "Everyone in position. Bring your weapons. If you don't have weapons, stay the hell back. This might get ugly."

Tae could see the concern in her face. But he couldn't reassure her, because she was right.

Dimitri waited outside the door. His face looked just as exhausted as Vera's, skin paler than usual, the dark circles under his eyes matching the ones under hers. "I've got everyone in position," he said. "The street kids are up on the barricades, the ones that can help fight, and the others are waiting for Tae." He glanced at Tae, and sudden concern tightened his eyes. Tae wondered, for a faint, ridiculous moment, exactly how awful he must look for Dimitri to look that worried.

"Are you—sure you're alright?" Dmitri asked in a low voice.

Tae gave a small, grim smile. "I don't think not being alright is an option."

Dimitri watched him for a moment, his face still cut with concern, then turned away. "I'm going up in the barricades."

"We'll come with you," said Lev. He grimaced as he stood, and Tae was almost tempted to tell him to stay back, because he'd damn well been shot with a heat gun five days earlier.

But he didn't bother. Lev wouldn't stay behind if Jez was up there, and besides—

He gave a short shake of his head.

Besides, five days to heal from a heat-blast injury was starting to look like a luxury at this point.

They clambered up the barricades and gathered on the top.

Vera had been as good as her word—the entire front of the barricade was soaking wet, the water already freezing in the chill morning air.

The police sirens in the distance were approaching rapidly, and Tae's stomach tightened.

There were a lot of them. He couldn't tell how many, but a lot.

And then they came around the corner at the end of the street, and he sucked in a quick breath.

There must have been a hundred officers, all in riot gear, helmets pulled low over their faces, sirens on their skybikes howling like wounded animals.

He glanced up involuntarily, but of course Ivan had already dealt with it—between the rows of thin, glistening wire they'd strung up in the alleys and over the entire square in the previous days and weeks, visible only when the light struck it a certain way, and the blocker field Tae had set up around the barricades, it would be suicide for the police to try to get on top of them.

The police bikes came to a halt fifty metres or so from the barricade, forming a small, tight cluster. They dismounted, pulling out weapons, and moved into a formation Tae knew all too well— officers in the front lifting their riot shields to form a phalanx, officers in the back with their shock sticks at the ready and heat guns pointed through the cracks between the shields.

They were waiting for something. And he had a pretty damn good guess what it was.

It came into view a few moments later—a massive gun, pulled behind a small, in-atmosphere cruiser. The sight of it sent a jolt of thoughtless panic through him, choking off his breath.

He could still see bodies on the ground when he closed his eyes, the brilliant, impossible red of the blood against the greyish-white snow. Vanya, body broken and lifeless. Students he knew, street kids he knew, their bodies sprawled on the ground like discarded dolls.

"Tae?"

Lev's voice was sharp with concern, and Tae took a deep breath, trying to force his brain to stop, trying to pull himself back to the present.

A hand rested on his shoulder, and he jerked his head up. Ivan stood there, his expression tight with sympathy and concern, and somehow, Tae could breathe again.

Ivan gave him a small smile, but from the look on his face, he was seeing the same things Tae was.

The officers worked quickly, unloading the gun from the cruiser. There were out of range of any of the defender's weapons at the moment, and the bikes formed an additional protective shield.

He knew when the gun was ready, but the sharp, high-pitched whine that still haunted his nightmares. The officers started towards the barricade at a quick jog, the gun pulled along behind them with a massive antigrav.

"They'll try to get in close," said Lev quietly. "They'll want to kill as many of us as they can in the first few shots, keep anyone from getting out in the confusion."

Ivan turned to Vera. "You got everyone without weapons back from the wall?"

She nodded, and then they all dropped down as the officers came into range, and heat-blasts sizzled and crackled through the air around them.

Tanya had set a sniper gun into the top of the barricade, and was firing at a steady pace. On the other end of the barricade, Felix shouted to his kids, shoving them into position. They were releasing a blistering amount of heat from their pistols, but the officers' guns were longer range, and they weren't close enough for the street-weapons to do any good.

The officers slowed as they crossed into range of the defenders' weapons, staggering from the sheer volume of the heat-blasts aimed in their direction. One of them stumbled, hit squarely in the chest by Tanya's sniper fire, but even with Ysbel's mods it wasn't enough— police riot gear was designed with heavy firepower in mind, and although their heat shields glowed a bright orange, they held.

The officers pushed forward, as if against a heavy wind, but they were still coming. Tae looked up for a moment from his own weapon, glancing at Lev. Lev's forehead was creased in concentration, and he was firing methodically, and for a moment, Tae almost laughed.

Who would have thought the calculating, analytical, slightly disheveled scholar he'd met months ago would one day be standing on top of a barricade, shooting at an oncoming group of police officers?

One of the shots from Tanya's sniper gun knocked an officer's face shield up, and a second shot dropped the man, but the others hardly paused. They were close now, maybe twenty metres away.

At the back of the phalanx, a handful of police officers had crouched down to unload the gun from the antigrav.

"Get down," Tae hissed through his com. "Heads behind the barricades."

Not that it would matter. If he'd miscalculated, there was nothing in the system that would save them now. He glanced around quickly, checking that the street kids were down—

Someone grabbed his jacket sleeve and yanked. He fell, caught off balance, and a pair of arms caught him. "Tae. You need to follow your own advice sometimes," whispered Ivan's familiar voice, warm and faintly amused. "Some of us would prefer you didn't get shot either."

Tae tried to smile, but his stomach was clenched too tightly.

The officers stepped back from the gun.

He couldn't breathe.

If the mods he'd spent the last four damn days setting up didn't work—

There was a long moment of silence.

Another.

And then cursing from the police officers, and he sucked in a breath, almost dizzy with relief.

Ivan grinned at him, and Ysbel gave a short chuckle.

"Remind me never to get on your bad side, Tae," she said. "I don't know if I could make weapons faster than you could disable them."

"It only worked because they were stupid enough to use the same model of gun as last time," Tae muttered.

"Like I said," said Ysbel, still sounding amused.

Outside the walls, a small knot of officers were frantically working on the gun, but the rest were firing on the ragged group of defenders.

"Tae," hissed Caz over the com. "You coming?"

"I'm on my way. Hang tight." He slithered backwards off the barricade and strode quickly to where Caz and Peti and a handful of other street kids waited.

"You ready?" Caz asked tersely.

Tae nodded, pulling out his heat pistol. "Come on."

He ducked through the narrow gap in the east barricade and started down the small alley that opened onto one of the larger streets.

He glanced quickly behind him at the ragged handful of street kids and gritted his teeth.

Yes, they'd been behind the barricades, and yes, they'd all had to fight to survive. But these were the kids he was supposed to protect, damn it. The kids he was damn well supposed to keep safe.

And here he was, dragging them into danger yet again.

They reached the mouth of the alley, and Tae peered out before beckoning the rest of them forward. It looked like Lev and the others had succeeded in keeping the police busy—the street here was empty.

They crept down the street and paused at the mouth of another narrow alley.

The police had stopped—what, fifty metres away? This should be far enough.

He hoped.

Caz came up beside him, and Tae glanced over, struck once more by how young the boy was.

And besides Tae, he was the oldest of the street kids.

They ducked into the darkness of the alley, the shadows from the abandoned apartment buildings and empty warehouses around them cooling the already-chill air. The crunch of snow under their feet was unbearably loud in the silence.

The alley bent, and he could see the shaft of light from the other end, the orange-yellow of late afternoon.

"I'll go first," he whispered. "I'll call you on the coms if it's safe." He slipped out of the alley, not waiting for Caz's protests.

An officer had been left behind to guard the bikes, but he was several metres away, watching the barricades.

Tae bit down hard on his teeth.

Whatever was happening there, there was nothing he could do about it right now. He'd have to trust that Lev and Ysbel and the others had it under control.

He crept towards the officer, pulling the thin tube Ysbel had given him from his pocket. She'd been working on it, but it wasn't a long-range weapon—he'd have to be within a meter of the man, probably.

Tae's foot slipped on a loose stone, and the officer turned, his eyes going wide.

Tae swore and leapt forward. The man grabbed for his com, his mouth opening to shout an alarm. Tae pointed Ysbel's device and hit the button, and the man slumped, unconscious, to the ground. Tae closed his eyes, silently gasping out a prayer of gratitude that it had worked, and that in the scuffle he hadn't accidentally turned the thing on himself instead.

Damn it to hell, Ysbel could keep the weapons she was developing until she had the bugs worked out next time.

He looked around quickly, but none of the officers at the barricades seemed to have noticed anything amiss.

He tapped his com. "Caz. It's safe. You can come out."

The rest of the street kids had joined him within a few moments.

He'd set a hot-wire into their coms, but the police had put physical locks on the bikes as well. There were looks of grim satisfaction on the kids' faces as they set to work with their makeshift tools, yanking apart the lock-bars, or smashing them with a well-placed blow of a mallet or stone.

Tae glanced nervously over his shoulder. The amount of noise they were making—

Still, the amount of noise they were making was nothing compared with the shouts and screams and firing weapons around the barricades.

The officers, it appeared, had given up trying to fix the gun, and were now trying to swarm the barricade and overwhelm the defenders by sheer force. The ice Ivan had suggested, though, was making it difficult work, and the defenders were throwing down bricks, prefab blocks—even bits of furniture—on the heads of their attackers.

An officer fired, and there was a shout of agony from the top of the wall.

Tae turned grimly back to the bikes.

Nothing he could do to help them right now.

Jez had asked them to bring back as many bikes as they could, and already a couple of the kids seemed to have their bikes ready to go.

Tae turned, surveying the bikes. He grabbed a likely looking one, and set to work prying off the lock-bar.

And then, from behind him, came the wail of an alarm.

He spun.

One of the younger kids must have triggered something, and stood there frozen, a horrified look on his face.

Tae cursed. "We've got to get out, now!"

Half a dozen officers had turned from the barricade, and now they were sprinting towards them, guns drawn. They'd be in range in moments.

Tae grabbed the frozen kid, pulling him out of the way, and touched his com to the bike, typing something rapidly. The alarm shut off as abruptly as it had begun, and Tae lifted the kid bodily onto the bike, firing it up.

"Go!" he hissed.

Caz was behind him, grabbing the kids who hadn't finished with their hot-wires and shoving them onto bikes behind kids who had.

The police officers were close enough now that their shots were heating the air around them to an uncomfortable temperature. A few more steps, and they'd be in range.

"Caz, get the rest of the kids out of here," he snapped, ducking behind the bike and yanking out his pistol. "I'll try to keep them busy for a minute."

Damn it, they had heat shields that even Ysbel's mods wouldn't get through.

He grabbed a twisted chunk of metal, detritus from one of the mangled bike locks, and threw it as hard as he could. He hit the helmet of the officer in front, and she staggered back, her helmet coming loose and tumbling to the ground.

For just a moment, he saw her face. She wasn't much older than Lev, really, and she was surprised, and maybe a little afraid—

He squeezed the trigger.

The blast hit her full in the face. She teetered, and fell.

Two of her companions dropped down beside her, but he knew damn well there was nothing they could do.

He felt sick to his stomach.

"Tae! Get on!"

He turned to see Caz behind him, mounted on the last of the hot-wired bikes.

"Caz! Go! I'll—"

Caz's body jerked, his eyes going wide with pain. Tae choked out a curse and grabbed for him, catching him as he fell.

"Caz!" His voice was frantic, shaking. "Caz—"

Another blast hit so close he could smell burning, and when he glanced down, the edge of his coat was charred.

He swore helplessly, then swung up behind Caz's slumped body and hit the throttle. The bike shot forward, Caz swaying limply against him at the acceleration.

Tae thought maybe his heart would actually stop.

Caz stirred. "Tae—" His voice was tight with pain.

Behind them, the whine of skybikes hummed like angry insects. Tae slapped his com. "Lev. We're coming in with the bikes, but they're after us."

"We've disabled the skybike traps where I showed you," said Lev tersely. "Just come through."

"I told you, they're bloody after us! They'll be able to get in as easily as we will!"

"I'll worry about that. You get in here."

Tae swore and slapped off his com.

The street kids ahead of him might have had no idea what they were doing, but they'd managed to point their bikes' noses towards the barricades. But the police were gaining on them rapidly.

Tae slowed his bike, turning over his shoulder to squeeze off a shot at the first officer who rounded the corner.

He'd seen how the antigravs on the bikes were constructed, and he was pretty sure if he could hit one—

His shot hit home. The bike sputtered, coughed, then tumbled out of the air, sending the officer rolling across the filthy alley floor.

"Where are you?" came Lev's tense voice over the com.

"We'll be there in about twenty seconds," said Tae through his teeth.

He yanked the bike around the last corner, in time to see the first of the street kids pull her bike over the barricade. The others followed close behind, and Tae hit the throttle on his own bike, shooting over the barricade seconds before the police officers rounded the corner.

He yanked the bike to a stop and jumped off, catching Caz as the boy slumped. He didn't even look to see what was happening behind him—in the back of his mind he heard an explosion, but he didn't have the attention to spare. Panic squeezed his chest, and Caz was limp in his arms, and Peti was off her bike and running towards them, her face desperate.

"Caz?" Her voice choked on the words.

And then Ivan was there, lifting Caz from Tae's arms as tenderly as if Caz were an infant. "Come on, let's get him to the medic tent."

Tae couldn't do anything but follow, his throat so tight he couldn't speak even if he'd wanted to.

Ivan laid Caz down in one of the cots, bending over him, and Tae blinked against the sudden dizziness. "Is he——" he started, but he couldn't finish the sentence.

Ivan straightened. "He's fine." He paused a moment, his voice rueful. "Relatively speaking. He's still alive, and it's not fatal. I think he's just passed out from the pain." He turned to a student who'd followed him inside. "Get me a blast kit and a medical knife, please."

The student nodded and ducked behind a partition into the back of the tent.

Tae closed his eyes and kept them closed, afraid of moving, because he was so dizzy at this point he wasn't sure he wouldn't just fall over. Then Ivan crossed over to him and pulled him into a tight embrace.

"Tae," he whispered, his voice thick with emotion. He broke off, pulling Tae tighter against him.

For a moment Tae stood there, soaking in strength from Ivan like water into a sponge, the press of Ivan's body against Tae's, the strength of his arms, the smell and feel of him, slowly clearing away the dizziness.

At last, though, Tae straightened and turned to where Caz lay.

The boy's face was bloodless, but he was breathing. The shot had hit him low down on the thigh, and the sight of burnt fabric clinging to seared flesh almost made vomit rise in Tae's throat.

The student returned with a heat-blast kit, and Ivan crossed back over to the cot. He knelt beside Caz and started cutting the charred fabric away from the wound, hands gentle.

Peti entered the tent a moment later. "The other kids are safe," she said tersely. "I checked. And none of the police got through the barricade."

Tae sucked in a quick breath.

Damn it to hell.

He'd just about lost it when Caz had been shot, and Peti, Caz's own sister, had been the one to hold it together, make sure everyone was in and there were no emergencies to be dealt with, before she even came in to see him.

"Ivan says he'll be fine," he said, through the knot of guilt in his throat.

Peti nodded and went silently over to stand beside Ivan as he worked.

Ivan's hands were gentle and sure, and for just a moment Tae couldn't drag his eyes away from the scene.

He shook his head. If there was still fighting at the barricades, there was a chance they'd need him.

"I'll be back," he mumbled.

Ivan cast a worried look at him, but only nodded, and Tae stumbled out of the tent door.

The memory of the way Caz's body had slumped against him still sent nausea churning in his stomach, but he made his way to where Lev and the others were gathered on the barricade.

Lev turned quickly at his approach, concern in his face. "Are you alright? Did anything—"

"Caz got shot," said Tae wearily. "Ivan says he'll be alright."

Lev frowned, the concern in his face growing sharper. "Tae—"

"What happening out here?" Tae asked shortly.

Lev gestured over the edge of the barricades. "They're gone. I don't think they anticipated we'd be so well-prepared for them. And the fact that you were able to get out of the barricades and around behind them—it frightened them as much as we'd hoped. Maybe they'll be less willing to focus all their force on one attack in the future."

Tae nodded, too exhausted to even feel relieved. "Was—was anyone—"

Lev's face tightened, the crease between his eyebrows deepening. "No one was killed," he said finally. "But—"

"What happened?" Tae snapped.

Lev shook his head. "Tae. It's alright. Minor injuries, mostly. Some heat-blast wounds, none of them fatal, two concussions. And one of Matija's kids was knocked off the barricades and broke an arm on the way down."

Tae drew in a deep, steadying breath, trying to force the shaky adrenaline from his muscles.

It could've been worse. It could've been much, much worse. They'd been absurdly lucky, honestly.

"Are you sure you're alright?" said Lev quietly. "You look like you're about to fall over. Here, sit." He pressed a hand on Tae's shoulder, pushing him down on the edge of the barricade, his face full of concern.

Tae shook his head and tried to smile. "I'm fine. It's nothing. It's —"

Lev watched him, his gaze uncomfortably perceptive. "I hate this too," he said at last. "If there was anything else that we could do—"

"Hey, you two sourpusses." Jez scrambled over the top of the barricade, wearing a jaunty grin and sporting a black eye.

Lev's posture stiffened. "Jez?"

She rolled her eyes. "I'm fine, genius. Anyway, gave those bastards hell on that bike tech-head brought back. Bet they won't feel like coming around here again for a while." She paused a moment. "Did you know," she said chattily, "that Ysbel's mag explosives will just kind of follow along behind a bike for a couple seconds before they latch on, if you get them close enough?"

"How many officers did you—" began Lev, his voice a studied calm.

She laughed. "Ysbel set them as percussive blasts, so I didn't kill a single damn one of them. Just knocked the bastards off their bikes." Her grin faded slightly. "I'll be honest though, figure if anyone deserved to be killed—"

Lev shook his head. "Enough of them died today. We don't need to give them any more reason to come after us."

Jez nodded, but her lips were pinched tightly, and Tae wondered suddenly if the 'minor injuries' Lev had referred to were worse than he'd made them sound.

Lev sighed quietly. "If Masha's the one behind this—and I think we have to assume that she is—I'm increasingly coming to believe that our only hope is that there are still reasonable members of government who outrank her, who are sympathetic to our position. We'll need to be as careful as possible not to do something that would prevent that."

Tae's mind flashed back, for a moment, to the face of the police officer he'd killed.

She hadn't been very old. How many assignments had she been sent on, before he shot her?

Caz, slumped against him on the bike, lying senseless on the cot in the medic tent, Peti kneeling beside him, her face drawn and horrified.

The haunted look on Ivan's face that wouldn't go away, the pain in his eyes.

Damn bloody Masha to hell.

He knew what had happened to her, how she'd watched her parents' murder. Perhaps he shouldn't blame her for doing whatever she needed to get back at the people who'd killed them.

But—

"Tech-head?" Jez's voice seemed to come from a long way off. "You OK?"

Tae gave her a small, humourless smile. "I'm fine." He stood quickly, turning away before she could ask him any more.

10

Masha, day 5

Goran sat watching her, face grim. Masha could read nothing from his expression.

"Alonya, sit," he said, gesturing to a chair in front of his desk. "I assume you haven't heard what's happened in the streets?"

She took the proffered seat, trying to hide the way her heart pounded. "No, I had not." She kept her tone carefully modulated. "I understand they've cut off all the newscoms and put all the briefings under the highest classification."

"They have," he said shortly.

There was a moment's pause.

"And?" she prodded delicately. "Did something happen? Ringleaders captured or killed, perhaps?"

She hadn't meant to ask the question, but it had been burning under her tongue since she'd learned that there'd been an attack on the barricades.

He scowled. "Unfortunately, no."

The rush of relief was so strong it almost made her dizzy, and she was absurdly grateful that she was already sitting down.

"That is truly unfortunate," she murmured after a moment.

"It is," Goran said, his voice grim. "More unfortunate, however, is what happened to the police force we sent. Three officers dead, and seven others badly injured. And in return, they injured a few students and shot a street-kid." He snorted in disgust. "That wasn't all—the rebels disabled the gun, and stole a dozen skybikes. As you know, our resources are not unlimited. And if they could steal a dozen skybikes right from under the officers' noses, they could have come from behind and turned the attack into a slaughter, if they'd wanted to. They were sending a message, and I think all the officers know it. The police are demoralized and frightened, and the rebels in the other parts of the city—rebels that you, Alonya, requested that we leave alone—are ecstatic." He glowered. "I trusted you to come up with a workable plan, and it's resulted in a disaster."

Masha smiled up at him blandly, trying to keep her breathing steady.

They'd shot a street kid.

She didn't have time to think about that right now.

"If you recall, I advocated waiting until we had sufficient resources to take decisive action. It was the police commissioner, if I understand correctly, who gave the order to take on the insurgents behind the barricades immediately. Considering there were only three officers lost, rather than a mass slaughter, this was likely the best possible outcome." She paused, leaning forward. "But you're right. We can't afford another misstep. As I see it, you have a choice —listen to a hot-headed police commissioner, whose actions have resulted in three police deaths and a disastrous blow to force morale, or follow my suggestions. If something like this happens again, it may not be possible to contain the fallout."

Goran watched her for a long time, his gaze challenging, but she met his eyes.

At last, he gave a short nod. "Very well, Undersecretary." She heard the intended bite in his use of the title. "You've proven prescient. We'll follow your lead. But I warn you—if this goes badly, you will suffer the consequences of it."

"I fully understand."

He sat back in his chair. "Alright. So, Undersecretary, since you're the expert in the field—what's our next move?"

She pretended to consider.

She'd had her response prepared for some time now—she'd guessed her crew would make short work of a simple police assault on the barricade, even with the ion cannon. But it would be imprudent to let a man like Goran know that.

"I still believe it's in our best interest to focus on containment," she said at last, slowly. "Put a curfew in place on the street, tighten down the restrictions in the areas we have contained. Make it more difficult for others to join the group behind the barricades. And—" she paused for a moment. "We can allow them to use the gangs as enforcement." The words tasted bitter on her tongue. "If there needs to be unrest put down—and I emphasize, only if there is unrest that threatens to break out of the containment areas—then use the gangs. They have considerable practice in keeping order."

She knew very well what 'keeping order' meant to the gangs. And she knew very well that the police force—angry, frightened, upset at the challenge to its power—would be looking for the slightest excuse to set their attack beasts loose on the people opposing them.

People would die, and it would be on her head.

How many deaths could be justified, to save the system?

She wasn't certain. But she knew damn well that she'd long since passed the point where she had the leisure to worry about the calculation.

Goran was frowning at her. "What makes you think the police are working with the gangs?" he asked, a cautious note in his tone.

She raised an eyebrow. "Was Adrik not supposed to have mentioned it? I assumed he wouldn't have said anything if—"

Goran scowled, swearing under his breath. "Adrik shouldn't have known. Thank the Lady he's locked up somewhere he can't cause any more harm." He took a deep breath and looked up at her. "I'll consider your suggestion."

"I would appreciate that." She paused. This was the most delicate part. "If you would like me to continue to advise you on policy, it would be extremely helpful if I am given full access to the information pertinent to the policies on which you would like my advice. Knowing the police have brought the gang members and boyeviki on board to assist allows much more flexibility in a response. And if you were to provide me with information on everyone who is in position to give orders to the police, or direct the weapons distribution ..." She let her words trail off delicately.

"Of course," said Goran, standing.

Masha fought back a small frown. She hadn't expected him to acquiesce so easily.

He turned and pulled a chip off a shelf on the other side of the room from the one she'd taken last night, and replaced in the early hours of the morning. "I believe this should answer your questions," he said, turning back and handing it to her.

Masha nodded, letting her face show nothing. "I shall be sure to study it. Thank you."

"Of course." He turned back to his desk. "Now that you have the necessary information, I will expect a full report sent to my com by tomorrow morning. I'll call you into the office if I have questions."

"I'll get to work on it immediately," she murmured.

Guran had pulled his holoscreen in front of him and was frowning down at it, clearly indicating that, as far as he was concerned, the conference was over.

But she could see the slight tension in his posture. She'd trained herself to recognize the small signs of strain on people who were expert at hiding it.

Goran was expert. But he couldn't hide everything.

She took a deep breath.

This may prove to be a miscalculation. But things were moving too quickly, and there were too many things she didn't understand, too many players she wasn't aware of. And once their tokens landed on the table, it might be too late to counter them.

"I—did have one further question," she said diffidently, pushing back her chair and bending down to pick up her bag.

"Yes?" Goran snapped, glancing up from his screen.

"Adrik mentioned something else to me, while he was … discussing my role. He mentioned that his position was constricted because it was being co-opted by an individual named Myrni."

The effect of the name was almost enough to startle Masha. Goran's head jerked up in surprise, his expression icy cold, and for a moment she thought he'd go for a heat pistol.

She forced her hands to remain loose, her posture calm.

He shoved back his chair and stalked around his desk to stand over her. He was tall, and broad, and he stood close enough to force her to look up at him.

She let her posture signal subservience, although it wasn't a role she was accustomed to.

"Where did you hear that name?" he hissed. "Tell me."

"I'm sorry if I've misspoken," she said apologetically. "Had I known it was information I was not meant to have access to—"

"Where?" His voice snapped out, sharp as a blade.

She raised her eyebrows and met his furious gaze. "As I said. Adrik told me exactly what I told you. And," she added, allowing a hint of wryness to creep into her voice, "from much the same position as the one you are currently speaking to me from."

He glared at her, and she forced her breathing to slow.

He might shoot her, right now, but he might not.

And she couldn't risk her position.

He let out a long breath, stepping back slightly. "I apologize," he grunted, but his expression was sharp and suspicious. "It's a vicious rumour that's been circulating, is all—a mysterious person pulling strings behind this insurrection. It's nonsense, of course, but it stirs people up, and scares my under-ministers. So I would appreciate it if you wouldn't mention it again."

"Of course not," she said. "I do apologize." She picked up her bag and turned to the door. "I'll send my report first thing tomorrow."

Goran nodded, evidently engrossed once again in whatever was on his holoscreen.

But the tension in his posture was even more pronounced than it had been before.

He'd been lying to her.

And whatever he was lying about terrified him.

When she stepped out into the hallway, Radka jerked to attention, and Masha bit back a small sigh.

"Undersecretary?" the girl began, but Masha gave a quick shake of her head, forming her face into an expression forbidding enough that the girl shut up.

They walked back to Masha's office in silence, and Masha was grateful for it.

Her mind was spinning, thoughts tumbling over each other.

At the door, she paused to hit the key on her com.

Radka cleared her throat. "Undersecretary?" she began, her voice uncertain. "Is—did the meeting not go well?"

"It went well enough," said Masha brusquely. "Now, if you'll excuse me—"

"It's only that, like I said, I have some friends who are aides to some of Goran's superiors. I could talk to them, and maybe they could—"

Masha closed her eyes, trying to fight back the sudden ice forming in her chest. "No," she snapped, more harshly than she'd intended. "I'll give you one piece of advice, Radka. Don't trust anyone here. Don't risk yourself for someone in government. Not me, not anyone. Loyalty like that will get you killed. Do you understand?"

The girl stared at her for a moment, then gave a small, frightened nod.

"Good," said Masha shortly. She shoved the door open, stepped inside, and closed it sharply behind her.

Once inside, she dropped into her seat, letting her bag fall to the floor beside her, and lowered her face into her hands. The icy panic she'd thought she'd brought under control that morning washed over her in waves.

They'd almost been killed. Jez, Lev, Tae, Ysbel, Tanya, the children. Ivan. That student who'd once saved all their lives, Dmitri, and his friend Vera. They'd almost been killed, and she would have been the one who'd given the orders.

A street kid had been shot, Goran had said.

Not Tae. They would have taken pains to identify Tae. But—

For a moment, an image flashed in her mind—Tae, his face gaunt and horrified, posture slack with shock, as they stood with hands bound by armed guards in a small room in the Strani House, and Olyessa mentioned, off-hand, that his friends had been killed.

Olyessa had been wrong, and the mafia hadn't ultimately killed them.

But perhaps Masha, finally, had.

She squeezed her eyes shut and pushed back the wave of nausea, forcing herself to breathe.

It shouldn't be this hard.

It was just a street kid, someone she'd met perhaps twice.

Tae's friend.

She took a deep breath and straightened, pulling up her holoscreen. She'd need to have the report together for Goran by tomorrow morning, and she had plenty of work to do.

But ... somehow she couldn't seem to focus on her work.

At last, reluctantly, she tapped her com.

"Undersecretary Alonya." Zhenya's expression over the holoscreen was a mixture of smugness, curiosity, and what looked like genuine pleasure. "I'm delighted you're contacting me."

"Minister Gavril," she said, keeping her voice carefully neutral.

"What can I do for you?" they asked.

"I recently returned from speaking with Minister Goran about our strategy in response to the insurrection in the streets. He has given me rather a free rein in coming up with strategies to contain it. But it occurs to me that if I had more precise information on what had happened yesterday at the barricade—"

Zhenya nodded again, the calculation sharpening in their eyes. "Of course," they said. "And what exactly would you like to know?"

She took a deep breath. "It would be helpful if I had full details of everything that took place. Including a list of dead and injured on both sides. I had been led to believe you had connections which could provide you with insights in the matter."

"Ah," said Zhenya, their voice ever so slightly amused. "I see. On both sides, you say." They paused. "And what would you be willing to provide me in return for this information? A small favour in exchange for a small favour?"

"You certainly would not find me ungrateful in the matter of small favours. Even an undersecretary can be a useful friend," she said lightly. "Or a dangerous enemy."

"Of course," said Zhenya, their voice smooth. "I'll track down the information you requested. For, of course, both sides of the interaction." There was a tone in their voice that told her they knew exactly what she was asking.

Masha tapped off her com and sat for a few moments, staring blankly at her desk.

She had enough work to do.

But the look on Tae's face kept playing itself over in her mind, interspersed with the sound of Radka's quiet, vulnerable voice.

Was what she was doing worth it? Betraying people who'd trusted her, using their lives as currency?

But—Radka, and a hundred thousand other people like her, lived in a system where they were used up and thrown away, their own lives fodder for any ambitious government official looking for a step up, no matter how many bodies had to line the path to get there. And with Grigory and Olyessa gone, there would be wholesale slaughter if Masha didn't step in. If she didn't do whatever it took to change things.

If she didn't, possibly, sacrifice her crew.

How many lives was her pathetic sentiment worth?

She knew the answer. But somehow, it didn't warm the ice that had formed in her stomach.

11

Ysbel, day 6

"Mama?"

Ysbel glanced down at her daughter. Even in the dim light of the makeshift shelter-come-meeting room, she could catch the hint of worry in Olya's face. It had been there for far too long, but had grown sharper in the last few days.

Something in Ysbel's chest hurt to see it.

She tried to smile. "Yes, my love?"

"When is mamochka coming back?"

Ysbel heard the unspoken question—would Tanya come back?

It was the same question she had every time someone she cared about left from behind the barricades.

She gave Olya another small smile. "It will be a little while yet, my love."

Lev looked up from where he was sitting on the other side of the small shelter. He'd been frowning in concentration, his holoscreen pulled up in front of him, but he smiled at Olya. "Olya. I need some help over here interpreting data. Would you come give me a hand?"

Olya stood with a long-suffering sigh, but there was a sparkle of pride in her eyes as she crossed over to Lev. "I guess I can, for now," she said in a self-important voice, and Ysbel smiled to herself.

Even with everything going on, she was unutterably grateful that, between Lev, Jez, and the others, her children were still able to smile.

Although—she shook her head wryly. Tanya hadn't been overly amused by Jez's method of keeping the children entertained, which mostly consisted of teaching them how to gamble, how to swear, how to swear while gambling, and how to cheat at tokens.

Honestly, though, given enough time with Jez, they'd pick up those skills by osmosis, if nothing else.

Jez sauntered into the tent a moment later, an irrepressible grin spread across her face. "Hey, you plaguers," she said cheerily. "Gonna do anything other than sit in the damn shelter all day?" She shivered. "Can't blame you, though. Damn cold out there."

Lev had looked up at her entrance, and was watching her with that faint smile he got every time he saw Jez, equal parts love, concern, and raw, untempered lust.

Jez winked at him, and his expression went visibly hazy.

Olya glanced between the two of them, gave another long-suffering sigh, and hopped down from her seat beside Lev.

"Olya?" Lev glanced down at her, shaking himself out of his revery.

She rolled her eyes. "Just go kiss Aunty. I'll help you with your work when you're finished."

Ysbel bit back a chuckle at the look on Lev's face.

"Why do you think I was going to—" he began carefully.

Olya rolled her eyes again. "Because you and Aunty kiss every time you see each other anymore. Especially when you don't think anyone's there."

This time, Ysbel couldn't hold in her snort of amusement.

"How … do you know what Aunty and I do when no one's

there?"

"I said, when you think no one's there." Olya's tone was slightly smug.

Lev's expression now said he was frantically going over everything he and Jez had done over the past few days when he'd thought they were alone.

Jez snickered, dropped down next to him, grabbed his face in both her hands, and kissed him thoroughly enough that within about three seconds, Ysbel was very certain that there was now only one thing on Lev's mind, and it had nothing to do with whether or not they were being observed.

After a few moments, Ysbel cleared her throat.

She cleared it again, more loudly.

She was about to resort to more drastic measures when Tae stepped into the tent, his face creased with concern, turned towards Lev, and gave an involuntary yelp.

Reluctantly, Jez released Lev, and even more reluctantly, Lev drew back, blinking, and apparently trying to reorient himself to a world in which Jez's lips were not pressed to his.

He cleared his throat, shook his head, and said, his voice only slightly unsteady, "Tae. What is it?"

Tae was looking fixedly at the back of the tent, his expression one of grim resignation.

"Tech-head. Relax," said Jez. She was still grinning, but there was a slightly dreamy look to her face. "Even genius here can't talk and snog at the same time. So you're safe to look."

Tae sighed and turned back around, shooting a glare in Jez's direction. "For the Lady's sake, Jez," he said through his teeth. "I would just like, for once in my damn life, to be able to walk in here without stumbling over someone making out with someone else."

Jez winked at him. "What, jealous? I could call Ivan in here, bet he'd be happy to—"

"Jez!"

She snickered, and Ysbel bit back a grin.

"Lev," said Tae, still through gritted teeth, ignoring Jez. "I thought we were going to be planning in here."

Lev sighed. "We are. We're just waiting for everyone to show up."

"And we figured, while we were waiting—" Jez broke in, with a broad wink.

Tae glared at her, and Ysbel smiled despite herself.

"Ysi. Are you there?"

Ysbel slapped her com. "Tanya? What's wrong?" Something about the slight hesitation in her wife's voice tightened her chest with dread.

Which was ridiculous. Tanya was fine. Of course she was fine, this was what she was good at.

"Ysi, I'm sorry." Her voice was a strained whisper. "I need help."

For a moment, Ysbel stared at her com blankly. Then she scrambled to her feet, sudden terror flooding through her.

Tanya couldn't be hurt. It was impossible.

She ignored the alarmed looks from the others. "Where are you? I'm coming."

"Solovey Street."

"If you're going out from behind the barricades, probably better take someone who knows how to fly." Jez was on her feet too, her grin sharp and dangerous, and Ysbel's heart stuttered with desperate gratitude.

"Skybikes," she snapped. Jez nodded, and a moment later, they were sprinting across the open square.

"Ysbel. What do you need?" Tae's voice through the com was

worried.

Jez grinned and tapped her com. "Figure I can be a damn good distraction while Ysbel gets Tanya out of trouble, but we'll need a way in and out of the barricades for our bikes."

"I'll get someone over there," said Tae.

Jez turned to her. "Did Tanya send coordinates?"

"No. She just said Solovey street," said Ysbel shortly. "But she can't be too far—she wasn't planning on going beyond the police blockade."

Jez winked. "See you there." She swung onto the nearest bike and leaned forward, shooting over the barricades where a student and a street kid were hurriedly pulling down a section of the wire netting.

Ysbel followed close behind.

They didn't speak as they rode, and soon Jez was out of sight. Ysbel gripped the handles of the bike tightly enough that the patterned surface gouged her palms, her teeth clenched so hard they hurt.

"Lady, please," she whispered, the words catching in her throat.

Tanya had to be alright.

"I found her," came Jez's voice through her earpiece a few moments later. "I'll send you the coordinates. I'm getting the damn police off her tail, but you should probably get her out of here." There was worry under Jez's jaunty tone.

Ysbel glanced at the coordinates on her screen, then leaned forward on her bike.

She hardly noticed the streets flying past under her, every drop of her concentration focused on flying.

Tanya had to be alright. She had to be. Ysbel couldn't lose her wife again …

After what seemed like an eternity, she rounded the last corner and yanked her bike to a halt.

Tanya leaned against the side of a building, her face deathly white. Blood stained the front of her shirt and soaked down her trousers, but she smiled when she saw Ysbel.

"Ysi." Her voice was weak. "Don't worry, I'm alright."

Ysbel's heart was skipping strangely as she jumped from the bike and strode over to her wife.

"Tanya," she whispered.

Tanya tried to stand, and swayed on her feet. Ysbel caught her, her body shaking with tension. Tanya's skin was cool under her hands, and she choked out a curse. "We've got to get back. Let me carry you. Please."

Tanya's eyelids drooped for a moment, but she forced them open with an effort. She nodded and reached up, brushing Ysbel's cheek with a hand. "I'm glad you came."

"I'll always come for you." Ysbel's voice caught, and she blinked back tears.

Tanya sucked in a quick breath as Ysbel lifted her, then let it out through her teeth. Ysbel closed her eyes for a moment, cradling her wife like a child. Tanya's slender body was limp in her arms, heavier than she remembered, and suddenly, achingly fragile.

Tanya. Wistful, beautiful Tanya, who'd always been so much stronger than she looked.

This couldn't be happening.

"Can you hold on while we ride?" Ysbel's voice trembled, and she couldn't stop it.

Tanya smiled weakly. "Ysi. I only lost some blood. I'm not about to die. I'll be alright."

Ysbel set Tanya carefully onto the bike and mounted up behind her, pulling her wife against her chest. She could feel Tanya's heartbeat, rapid and weak, feel the warm, wet stain of blood soaking through her shirt and trousers where Tanya was pressed against her.

She swallowed back the sickness in her throat, hit the throttle, and started for the barricade, holding the bike as steady as she could.

The ride back was endless, the twists and turns of the street that she'd hardly noticed on the trip here stretching out into infinity.

"Ivan," she said in a low voice, tapping her com against her thigh. There must have been something in her tone, because when Ivan answered, his voice was sharp with concern.

"What is it?"

"Tanya's hurt. She's lost a lot of blood."

There was a short pause. "When you get in, bring her straight to the medic tent," he said grimly.

"Hey Ysbel, you and Tanya out of the way? Because I've got about six police on my tail, and it looks like they're planning on shooting me out of the sky." There was a pause. "Or at least, trying." There was no mistaking the jaunty tone in Jez's voice.

"I've got her. Get back behind the barricades, you lunatic pilot, before I have to come get you, too."

"On it, Cap'n," Jez drawled. In the background, Ysbel heard the hiss of a heat gun, then Jez's delighted whoop.

She clenched her teeth.

She reached the barricade a moment later and maneuvered through the opening in the netting. She pulled the bike to a stop outside the medic tent, and before she'd finish sliding off, Ivan was there with a couple frightened university students he'd conscripted to help.

She ignored them, lifting Tanya and carrying her into the tent herself. Her wife was still breathing, but her eyes were closed, the blood standing out in sharp relief against the pallor of her skin.

She laid Tanya on the cot, kissing her forehead before straightening. Tanya's eyes fluttered for a moment, and Ysbel bit back another choked sob, running a hand gently along her wife's face.

Then she stepped back to give Ivan room.

Her arms ached to hold Tanya, and the wet of Tanya's blood chilled her skin in the cool air. She closed her eyes for a moment, trying to stop her muscles shaking.

She wasn't sure how long she stood there as Ivan and two of the students surrounded Tanya, cutting away her torn tunic and mopping up blood.

She didn't want to watch. But she couldn't turn her head away.

Blood had never bothered her. But this—the sight of this much blood, knowing it was Tanya's—made her dizzy in a way she'd never experienced.

"Ysi?"

She started at Tanya's voice, and crossed quickly over to the cot. One of the students stepped back to let her through, and she dropped down beside her wife. "My love," she whispered. "My heart, what happened?"

Her voice was shaking so badly she could hardly speak.

Tanya reached up and brushed a tear from Ysbel's cheek, her fingers shaking with weakness, and Ysbel caught her hand and pressed it to her lips, squeezing her eyes shut against the tears.

"I'm alright, Ysi," said Tanya, her voice barely a whisper. "Honestly, I'm fine. I lost some blood, that's all."

Ivan glanced up from the other side of the cot, where he was bent over, carefully sealing a bandage over the wound. His face was drawn, written over with strain and exhaustion, but he was wearing a faint smile. "She's right, Ysbel. You got her here in time. She'll be weak for a while, but it won't kill her."

Ysbel closed her eyes and dropped her forehead against the edge of the cot. "Tanya," she said at last, voice choking.

She'd never worried about Tanya going out from behind the barricades, any more than Tanya worried about her working on explosives. Because who was going to be able to hurt Tanya?

The shock of it numbed her, the thought that she could have lost Tanya—lost this woman who was her whole heart, her whole life—draining the strength from her muscles.

"Ysi, I'm alright. I promise." Tanya tried to smile, even as her eyelids drooped with weariness.

"Tanya, I love you," she whispered.

"I love you too, my Ysi," said Tanya, her voice weak. She gave Ysbel that wistful smile she loved so much, and Ysbel felt the tears welling in her eyes again.

Suddenly, Tanya drew in a short, sharp breath, her face tightening with something like pain. "Ysi. I'm sorry. I tried to stop it, but—"

"Stop what? Are you hurt somewhere else? What happened?" Her heart was pounding fast enough to make her dizzy.

"No," said Tanya softly. "But—" she paused a moment. "We'd better call the others in here. Everyone is going to need to see this."

"I'll get them," said Ivan, and he stood and slipped out of the tent.

Jez sauntered in a few moments later. The sleeve of her jacket was scorched, but she appeared unharmed, and Ysbel was almost surprised at the strength of the relief that washed over her at the sight of the lanky pilot.

"Hey Tanya, still alive?" she asked, peering down at the woman on the cot.

"Yes, Jez," said Tanya quietly. "Thank you."

Jez grinned. "Well, figured if you died, I'd just start teaching Olya some more smuggler terms, and you'd probably have come back from the dead to stop me." She paused a moment. "Although," she continued, tilting her head as if considering, "looks like you'll be out of commission for a while anyways, so you won't exactly know—"

"Believe me, Jez." Tanya's voice took on a tinge of ice, weak as it was. "I'll know exactly what you teach my daughter. And if you'd like to remain alive—"

Jez snickered and winked at Tanya. "Hey now, Olya's almost nine. Should have seen the things I was getting up to by the time I was almost—"

"If you plan on getting any older than you are today, Jez—" began Tanya, her voice growing even colder.

Jez gave a snort of laughter, turned, and strolled out of the medic tent, calling over her shoulder, "I'll see what's taking those other plaguers."

Ysbel glared after the pilot for a few moments with a mixture of amusement and irritation.

Until she'd met Jez, she'd never realized that you could be willing to die to keep someone safe, and at the same time want to actually strangle them.

Tanya gave a long sigh. "She does that on purpose, doesn't she?"

"I suspect she does," said Ysbel dryly. "It's hard for me to imagine someone being that irritating on accident."

By the time the others were gathered in the medic tent, Ysbel had managed to dry her eyes, although she couldn't bring herself to let go of her wife's hand.

"The children?" Tanya asked quickly as Lev stepped inside.

He gave her a weary smile, taking a seat in the corner. "Hello Tanya. The children are fine. I sent them to play with Caz and Peti for a bit." He hesitated a moment. "I—didn't tell them what happened, only that Ysbel had brought you back, and that I was going in for a meeting with you. I thought you'd want to explain it yourself, so I told Olya you'd talk to her when we were finished."

Tanya nodded, her face softening slightly. "Thank you."

Jez, who'd been wandering around the small space, dropped down beside Lev, and he put an arm around her, pulling her onto his lap.

Ysbel exchanged glances with Tanya.

It would be a more productive meeting if Lev could form a coherent sentence.

At last, though, when they were all seated, Lev gave a reluctant sigh and loosened his arms from around Jez. "Alright, Tanya. What happened?"

Tanya took a deep breath, her expression sobering. "I'm sorry," she said, voice quiet. "I … wasn't able to—" She closed her eyes for a moment, and Ysbel squeezed her hand gently, her throat tight with worry.

Tanya pulled up her holoscreen, her hands shaking slightly. "I'll—send it to your com, Lev."

Something about her voice made Ysbel suddenly certain she would not want to see whatever Tanya had brought back for them.

Lev pulled up his com screen and expanded it, then started the recording playing.

It was a video, the quality poor, the image shaky. Ysbel frowned at it, trying to make sense of the blurred picture.

Then she sucked in a quick breath.

It was an apartment complex.

And it was burning.

For half a second, the sight of those flames, the screams of adults and children from within, hit her like a physical blow, and she closed her eyes, trying to remember how to breathe.

Tanya's face pressed to the window of the cottage, the screams of their children as Ysbel was dragged away—

The first time she'd thought she'd lost her wife, her family.

She forced herself to look back at the screen.

"Who did this?" asked Lev softly, a tone in his voice that Ysbel had only heard there a few times.

"The gangs," Tanya answered softly. "It was the Blood Riots, I think. The people inside the complex had been throwing rocks at the police. I arrived just as a rock hit an officer. He went down, and they pulled him back, and then the captain made a call over the coms. The Blood Riots showed up a little while later. I—" her voice broke, just a little. "I was going to go help, but … someone had been tracking me. It was—one of my old classmates."

Ysbel sucked in a quick breath.

"An Internal Security agent?" asked Lev, worry sharp in his tone.

Tanya nodded. "It took me longer than I'd hoped to get away from him, and he gave me this before I did." She gestured at the bandage that stretched from her hip to her ribcage. "By that time—" She shook her head. "There was nothing I could do. I—" She paused a moment, as if collecting herself. "I—tried, but I could barely walk."

The video cut off abruptly, and Tanya gave a humourless smile. "And that's when the police saw me."

"Did the police try to stop this?" asked Vera in a hollow voice.

"No," said Tanya. Her voice was barely audible, and she was clearly struggling to stay conscious. "They talked with the Blood Riots before it happened. Then they stepped back and let them through."

No one spoke for a few moments. Ysbel's heart was pounding far too rapidly, and the sick, shaky rage rising in her throat threatened to choke her.

There'd been children in that building.

And someone had tried to kill Tanya.

"Is—is there anything—maybe we can—" Tae's voice was thick with horror.

Lev shook his head, face grim. "Did you see the timestamp on the video? Even if there'd been something we could have done, it's far too late now."

For a few moments, no one spoke. There was a grim look on Lev's face, and his jaw was set. Ivan had an arm around Tae, but she couldn't tell if it was to comfort him, or to keep him from jumping on a skybike and taking off towards the apartment complex, regardless of what Lev had said.

"Tae, I'm going to play the video again," said Lev quietly. "You had scanners set into Tanya's com, right?"

Tae nodded mutely.

"Good," said Lev. "I'd like to see where the orders came from."

Ysbel forced herself to look away as the video began playing. Tae, however, was crouched beside Lev, his own holoscreen pulled up, and was tapping something into it rapidly.

At last, he looked up at Lev with a grim, humourless smile. "Got it," he said, expanding his screen.

Lev frowned down at it for a moment. When he looked up again, his face was even grimmer than before.

"I have the IDs associated with the orders of the officers there," he said in a low voice.

"Well?" snapped Ysbel. Her nerves were too taut for her to wait until Lev had finished thinking through his response.

"There was—someone in the ministry who authorized the gangs

to work with the police to keep order. I believe the exact words were —" he glanced down at his com. "'The police are to stand back, not attack the barricades at present. If there are disturbances that need to be taken care of, they're authorized to call on the Rims or the Blood Riots for assistance.'"

"And who was this person in the ministry?" asked Tanya softly.

Lev gave her a grim smile. "Difficult to say. It was an undersecretary this originated with. Something of an unknown quantity. Which is understandable, since she only began working there six days ago."

Jez's face had gone bloodless, and Tae made a sort of choking noise. Ivan's face was dark with anger, but the hand he placed on Tae's shoulder was gentle.

"She gave the order that authorized the police to use the gangs as enforcement?" asked Tanya at last.

Lev nodded again.

Jez reached out and took his hand, and Ysbel wasn't sure if it was to reassure him, or her.

Maybe both.

She couldn't speak. The choking horror of what she'd seen caught her tongue.

Lev was clutching Jez's hand so hard his knuckles were white, but with his free hand, he pulled up the holoscreen again. "That's … not all, though," he said finally.

"What else did Masha do?" Tae's voice was hard and bitter, and half-choked with tears.

"It's … not Masha this time," said Lev. He was frowning down at his holoscreen. "Masha, or at least, this person we can safely assume was Masha, authorized them to work with the gangs. But it wasn't Masha who gave the orders for what happened. Because there was an order. It looks like there was a request sent out, right before the gangs went in, and there was a response that came from the government."

"Who sent it, then?" asked Tanya.

"I—don't know. Their ID is completely concealed. I can't even see their rank. But—" Lev looked up at them, his face grave. "But their code name is Myrni."

There was a long silence.

"That's the person Masha wanted information on, right?" said Tae at last. "I guess we can assume they found each other."

"Maybe," said Lev slowly. "Or maybe there's a player here Masha doesn't control." He closed down his holoscreen with a quick gesture. "Tanya. You said you ran into an old classmate?"

Tanya nodded.

"Correct me if I'm wrong," he said, "but there aren't many people who'd have the authority to command Internal Security agents."

"Very few," said Tanya quietly. "I could name each of them when I was in training."

"Whatever Masha's done, I'm certain even she hasn't gotten to that level in six days." He glanced around at the rest of them. "There's someone here I don't know. And, if my guess is correct, Masha doesn't know either. And whoever it is has more power than I'd really like to think about." He shook his head in frustration. "I wish I knew what they were doing. I'd expect the police to have come after us by now with all their weapons. I don't know why they haven't."

"I've been thinking about that," said Dmitri quietly. "Like you said, the police have pulled back. It could be caution, or it could be a trap. But—it's possible that the moderates in the government are finally speaking up. There are factions in the government, but there are still people like my mother, who aren't in anyone's pocket. And there are plenty of government bureaucrats whose kids are behind the barricades right now—or if not their kids, kids like theirs. My mother's an under-minister, and my father's secretary to a powerful minister. There will be a heavy internal push for calmer heads to prevail."

Lev frowned. "We can't afford to wait much longer. We don't have much left in the way of supplies—a few more days, maybe, but we've already had to put people on short rations." He looked up at Dmitri. "The police have had you cut off for weeks. Why would they negotiate now?"

"Last time, the police were doing everything in secret," said Dmitri grimly. "They cut off communication to the university. Until Tae hacked us through to the general line, no one knew what was going on. But a week ago, everyone saw. Everyone in the damn city saw what they were doing, and they came out on the streets in protest. It's not going to stay a secret any longer."

"Vera? What are your thoughts?" asked Lev at last.

Vera nodded, slowly. "There's no guarantee. But like Dmitri said —this isn't a secret anymore. I can't imagine the parents of all these students won't be calling for a peaceful solution to this. And if we can open negotiations, there'll be plenty of internal pressure to end this in the least painful way possible. Even if it means clemency for the insurgents and protection for the street kids."

Lev bit the inside of his cheek, and Ysbel could see the uncertainty in his expression.

She couldn't help but sympathize.

Perhaps it would be just that easy, and she was so jaded from her years of prison, and then running with this crew, where it seemed that everything that could go wrong did, that she was no longer able to recognize a simple solution when it presented itself.

At last, Lev nodded. "It may be the best strategy we have," he said. "Make enough trouble to let them know we can be an inconvenience, but keep from killing anyone we don't have to. Show them we're holding back. Give the pacifists a day or two to make their positions known, then try to open negotiations. We certainly aren't going to out-fight the government forces, not with what we have here. Our supplies won't last much longer, and I don't know how we'll get more. So that may be the only survivable option." He shook his head wearily, and Jez put a hand on his knee in an unconscious, sympathetic gesture that almost surprised Ysbel.

It was odd, sometimes, to think how much they'd all changed since that first afternoon so many months ago, when they'd sat glaring at each other in Masha's small, eclectic office.

Ysbel stayed by Tanya's bed as the others left the small tent. When they were alone, she sat down beside her wife and pulled her into a gentle embrace, even though the muscles in her arms were shaking, and she wanted to crush Tanya into a hug, hold her where no one would be able to hurt her again. The cold, sick panic, that had been there since she'd heard Tanya's strained voice over the com that morning, still twisted through her stomach.

She glanced over at her wife's pale, drawn face, the neat bandage under her blood-soaked shirt.

They'd been lucky this time.

But who knew how long their luck would hold?

12

Masha, day 6

"You're entirely mistaken." Branka's voice was cold, her eyes narrowed as she glared up at Masha from behind her desk.

Masha ducked her head contritely. "I am sorry. My com's time stamp has been acting up—the message I saw must have been the one you sent yesterday, asking for my report. I thought it was from this morning. I do apologize for interrupting you."

"I'll ask a technician to see that the timestamps on your com are updated so it won't be a problem in the future," said Branka, her voice softening slightly.

Masha nodded. "Thank you, Minister."

As she turned to leave, she glanced quickly back at the small stack of information chips piled haphazardly on the corner of Branka's desk.

The chip she'd surreptitiously deposited there as she stepped inside was tucked in near the top. Branka would have to go through the entire pile soon, judging by the "urgent" markings on the chips. And Masha had far too much confidence in her own skill at forgery to worry that the extra chip would be noticed.

She'd studied Branka's files thoroughly. And despite the woman's lack of visible status, Masha was quite sure that, if the information on the chip had the desired effect, Branka would be fully capable of doing what Masha needed her to do.

She pulled the door closed, and it locked with a quiet click.

As she made her way down the corridor towards the building's exit, someone stepped into her path. She moved aside automatically before she noticed who it was.

"Alonya," said Zhenya smoothly, falling into step with her. "What a pleasure to run into you."

She gave them a bland smile, even though her heart had begun to pound quickly. "I assume you have news for me?"

Zhenya's smile broadened. "Of course." They reached into their pocket and pulled out a small chip. "I believe this contains all the information you requested. Do be aware that I've timed it to erase itself in four hours' time. As you might imagine, a source such as the one I have is valuable, and I'd prefer not to compromise them."

She took the chip from them, her fingers somehow steady. "You always did play your tokens from a closed hand."

They studied her with faint amusement. "Perhaps it would ease your mind if I told you the details. Your information is correct—a street kid was shot. I believe his name was—" Zhenya tapped their fingers on their chin in thought. "Caz."

Masha managed to keep her face impassive, her expression one of polite interest, despite the icy dread in the pit of her stomach.

Zhenya waited a moment, as if expecting a question. Then they smiled. "You're not going to ask, are you? He's still alive. He was injured, but a mutual acquaintance of ours apparently dragged him back across the barricades to safety."

Again, she managed not to let her relief show in her expression.

"You may wonder why I was willing to do this without any

reassurance besides your word that I'd be paid back," they continued, still smiling. "But we have mutual friends, and you showed me on the pleasure planet that you would go to great lengths to protect a friend."

Masha glanced at Zhenya sharply. "It would be a tragedy if something happened to them," she said quietly. "For them, certainly. But not only for them."

Zhenya shook his head. "I'm not making threats, Masha. I'm far too intelligent to try to blackmail you. I only ask that you uphold your end of our bargain."

"Have I ever not?"

"No. You've always done exactly what you promised. But I've watched your career, Masha. The day you decide to break your promise is the day I'll be killed. Which is why I thought it prudent to remind you of my insurance policy. I do have my sources, after all."

She gave them a small, polite nod, and stepped past them.

There was an icy cold in her chest that had nothing to do with the bitter Prasvishoni winter outside.

She pulled her collar of her jacket up as she stepped through the door into the blowing snow. It was dark—this time of year in Prasvishoni it was always dark before you left your office, and she knew her way through the streets of Prasvishoni at night almost as well as she knew them during the daytime.

She tucked her scarf over her face, squinting against the bitter wind, lowered her head, and started towards the small apartment she called home.

Her mind kept replaying Zhenya's words.

Caz, the tall, skinny boy with the haunted eyes who'd spent an evening in a hangar bay with them, and who'd looked at her with such desperate gratitude when she'd found the kids an apartment.

The look on Tae's face, when he'd thought Caz and the others had been killed.

Zhenya knew her weak spot, and they wouldn't forget it.

She walked faster, as if somehow she could walk fast enough to stop seeing the look on Tae's face, picturing the skinny, dark-haired street boy he'd die to protect lying limp and senseless on the icy Prasvishoni streets. The calculating look in Zhenya's face when they'd made their unspoken threat.

She couldn't afford this. She'd never been able to afford this, and she'd thought she'd put it behind her.

When she reached her tiny, dingy apartment, she dropped down on the couch, pulling the holoscreen up in front of her.

There was a dull, exhausted ache starting behind her eyes, but she didn't have time to waste.

She looked quickly through the chip Zhenya had given her.

As she read, she couldn't stop a slight smile, despite the knot in her stomach.

It was clear Zhenya believed they still had her. They hadn't figured out her ultimate plan. They didn't realize how well she'd learned, over her lifetime, to sacrifice what needed to be sacrificed.

Yes, she'd wanted, desperately—more desperately than she like to admit—to know what had happened to Caz. But there was information on this chip that Zhenya would never have let slip, if they'd had any idea of its importance to her. As far as they were concerned, they were simply giving her the small indulgence of making sure her favourite crew of misfits and outcasts was still alive.

She studied the chip carefully, jotting down the important details on a writing pad, until the four hours were up and the information on her holoscreen flickered and disappeared as the chip was wiped.

But she had everything she needed.

She sighed heavily as she stood and stretched the stiffness from her muscles, then she shivered, pulling her jacket tighter around her.

She wasn't unaccustomed to sleeping in layers for warmth—when she'd been young and just starting out in government, she'd lived in an apartment not unlike this one, where there was a very real chance you'd freeze to death overnight if you didn't.

Still … she was getting soft. The thought of her warm, comfortable cabin on the *Ungovernable* sent something like homesickness washing over her.

She shook her head to brush away the thought and the accompanying memories, crossed the icy floor to the bedroom, and shut off the lights.

But whether it was the conversation with Zhenya, or the cold, or the thought of Tae's face when his friend had been shot—despite her exhaustion, it took her much longer than she'd expected to fall asleep.

She woke with a start hours later. She was gasping for breath, and it took her a moment to recognize the familiar, bleak walls of the apartment and remember where she was.

She closed her eyes, trying to calm her racing heart.

The scene from her dream was still sharp in her memory, cut in crisp detail across her eyelids.

A rough table leg under her hand. The scent of her father's laundry soap as the tablecloth brushed across her face.

The view, through the gap where the tablecloth was pulled carelessly to one side, of the kitchen of the apartment where she'd grown up.

The bodies, lying on the floor—the gruesome tableau of blood and broken flesh that had once been her mother and father. The sound of their screams, ringing in her ears.

She'd woken to that sound for months afterwards. But she'd never told anyone. As far as her aunt knew, her parents had died in a house fire. Then, as now, she'd started awake, gritting her teeth closed against the screams, and stayed like that until her heart rate finally slowed.

She hadn't woken to that dream in a very long time. But now that she had, the memories were back, cutting through her mind as sharp as a knife.

There was a tiny sound, just on the edge of her hearing.

She frowned.

It hadn't been only the dream that had wakened her, then. It had been something else ...

The noise came again—a small, slight scraping, the sound a hand might make brushing across a door frame.

She lay very, very still.

It had come from outside her bedroom door.

Silently, she slid from her bed, pulling the heat pistol from under her pillow as she did so. Her fingers brushed the tiny chip beside it, but she didn't disturb it.

There was the tiny, almost inaudible click of a lock scrambler against the door. Then the door inched open.

The clinical part of her mind was coolly analyzing her reaction— her pounding heart, the sour tang of fear in her mouth.

She had moments.

There was her bed, and behind the bed a small dresser, and beside that, a storage shelf. And if she remembered correctly, a small space between the dresser and the wall, where the shelf had been pulled out just a little.

Moving as silently as the person outside the door, Masha slid into the narrow space.

The door pushed slightly wider, and the figure slipped inside, silhouette dark against the dark of the room.

Masha stood very still, her hand resting on her heat pistol.

The figure crept into her bedroom, steps so silent that they were all but inaudible, and moved to stand over her bed. She could tell the moment they noticed she wasn't there—the faint tensing of their posture, like a desert-dog searching for a scent.

They turned slowly, scanning the room, the outline of the pistol in their hand visible in the dim half-light from the streetlamp outside the window.

Carefully, Masha loosened her hand from the butt of her gun.

Whoever this was, they were a professional. Which meant they'd be wearing a heat shield.

Moving so slowly her muscles ached, she crouched until she could reach the top of her boot. Gently, she worked the hilt of a long, thin gutting knife free from its concealed sheath.

The figure turned, facing in her direction. All it would take was a quick heat-scan, and they'd know exactly where she was.

She tensed, bracing herself.

She'd get one chance.

A loud crash sounded from outside her apartment, and Masha almost jumped. The figure started in surprise, glancing around quickly.

The crash was followed by muffled, slurred cursing, and the sound of someone getting unsteadily to their feet.

"Damn door—won't—won't open like it should—" the slurred voice trailed off into unintelligible curses, and the speaker pounded loudly on the door of Masha's apartment.

From across the hall, a man's voice called out, "Shut up, you dirty drunk!"

Someone rattled the door to Masha's apartment again, then

swore. "Not—not my damn door," he grumbled, as if it were a personal insult.

The figure in Masha's room made a quick, disgusted gesture, then slipped out the door. A moment later, Masha heard the soft click of a window closing in the outer room.

She slumped against the wall, heart pounding. At last, she tapped her com and pulled up Tae's scanner.

No heat signatures in the apartment. She was alone.

Cautiously, she opened the door to her bedroom. By the light of her com, she could make out faint markings on the windowsill where the latch had been forced.

It was an old apartment. Understandable that the window had been easy to get through.

But no one in the government should have known where she was staying.

She pulled out her heat pistol, and melted the latch shut. It wouldn't protect against a determined intruder, but then, she doubted the assassin would be back tonight.

Still—she glanced around, then balanced an empty tin mug on the edge of the sill, just out of sight. If someone tried to force the lock, the tin mug landing on the hard floor should make enough noise to wake her.

She shivered.

This was always a risk in her chosen path. She'd known that since she started down it as a young girl. Still, her hands trembled, just a little, as she opened the door to her bedroom.

She bent over her vacant cot, feeling under the pillow, and retrieved the small chip she'd planted earlier. She slid it into her com and pulled up the holoscreen, smiling slightly as the data populated.

She'd hoped the assassin would bend over the cot before realizing she wasn't there. It had only been a moment or two, but enough for the scanner implanted in the chip to do its work.

She glanced through the lines of data quickly. She'd been correct in assuming they were a professional, judging from the specs on their weapons tech.

Then she frowned.

Biometrics matching hers had been set into the assassin's weapon. That was no surprise—it was the most logical explanation for how they'd tracked her so easily. But—

But there was a name linked to the biometrics.

Masha Volkova.

She stared at the name for a long moment, something cold clutching her chest.

It wasn't Zhenya—not now, when they believed they had her exactly where they wanted her. And no one else should have any idea who she was.

If they knew who she was, why not disclose it? Why this assassination attempt?

She shivered again.

She didn't know who this was, or what they were after. But her timeline had suddenly contracted. She couldn't be killed before she finished her plan. She'd worked too hard, sacrificed too much.

But she knew, deep down, that that meant nothing at all.

13

Jez, day 7, early

Jez grinned, bouncing a little on her toes. It was dark, the only light the scattered campfires behind the barricades and the dim orange glow of the faded streetlamps.

The bitter morning air bit her skin and stung her teeth, but her lips still tingled from Lev's kiss a few moments before. His dark eyes had been full of concern, and she could read the exhaustion and strain in them, but there'd been that gentle look in his face that always made her heart skip a beat, the fondness in his expression as he watched her. And something a hell of a lot better than fondness in his kiss, when he'd pulled her against him.

The memory sent a pleasant shiver through her whole body.

Hell, she was about ready to take out the damn Prasvishoni government herself, just for the chance to get Lev alone in a room again.

A skinny kid who couldn't have been more than fifteen or sixteen stepped up beside her, glaring at her sullenly. "Guess you're working with me, then," he muttered in her general direction. "Better learn how to keep up."

Jez is grin widened. "Here's the thing," she drawled. "I'm leading this crap-show, because genius there asked me to, and I trust him. So you'll do what I say, long as we're out there. Once we get back, you don't have to listen to a damn thing I say for the rest of your life. But you can't agree to that, you don't come."

The kid—Felix, she was pretty sure his name was—stared at her for a moment, then his face darkened with anger. "Who the hell do you think you are?" he hissed. "Think you're tough, do you? Hell, I could take you with one hand behind my back. I'm not damn well following orders of some skinny, worthless—"

"Scrawny, mouthy, disrespectful—" Jez grinned. "See? I can do it too. But you're damn well going to take orders from a skinny, worthless, scrawny, mouthy, disrespectful pilot, or like I said—" she shrugged.

Felix took a step towards her, hands clenched into fists. "I'm here because of Tae," he said softly. "I don't know who the hell you think you are, but you don't get to tell me what to do."

She studied him. Kid was mad—fair enough, she'd probably be pretty pissed off herself in his situation. But hell, he'd learn to live with it. Because she'd seen enough of this bastard to know he'd either screw up the plan, or get himself killed, and she wasn't about to let one of tech-head's friends die if she could help it.

The boy reached for his weapon. Or at least, where his weapon had been.

He cursed.

From the corner of her eye she could see Tae, his posture tense, Ivan's hand on his arm the only thing holding him back from coming to her aid. Lev, though, was just watching, a small smile of amusement on his face.

She took a deep, happy breath.

Funny how something as simple as someone trusting you could

handle a situation could make your whole body feel warm, even middle of a damn Prasvishoni winter.

Even better if the someone trusting you happened to be someone you had the hots for, and who had the hots for you right back, and—now she was thinking about it—

She sighed, and turned her attention back to the matter at hand.

The kid was still cursing, patting his pockets down in disbelief. He turned, presumably to grab a gun from was one of his companions, but she stepped in close and whispered, "Looking for this?"

He glanced down at the heat pistol in her hand—a street weapon that had probably belonged to the Blood Riots, if she was any judge—and started violently. He grabbed for it, swearing, but she pulled it out of reach.

From the look on his face, he was about to try to kill her with his bare hands.

She winked. "Trick I picked up in one of the zestavas was when I was doing smuggler runs. Guess even scrawny worthless pilots can learn a thing or two."

"Damn mud-eating pickpocket," he hissed. "You think that'll impress me?"

Jez shrugged. "Don't really care, honestly." She tossed the pistol towards him. He gave another surprise cursed, snatching it out of the air.

A moment later, it was pointed at her face.

"That was damn stupid of you," he said quietly. "Damn bloody stupid. I like Tae. But I don't like him enough to keep from shooting you in the damn face."

Jez's grin widened, her heart pounding, adrenaline pumping through her muscles. "Sure," she drawled. "You could shoot me, if you wanted. At least, you could try. But here's the thing—you're not the first damn bastard tried to kill me. Grigory Korzhakov tried it, not too long ago. And Olyessa Yanovik. Hell, and the government, and Lev's old professor, which, I'll be honest, creepy old bastard, that one. And Vitali Dobrev. And Lena. Well, Lena tried it a few times."

The anger in Felix's face was gradually being replaced by wariness.

"So," she said. "You want to try your luck? Sure. But if you do—" she grinned wolfishly. "You'd better be damn sure you get it right. Because you sure as hell won't get a second chance."

Felix glared at her, but his expression wasn't as certain as it had been a moment earlier.

She raised an eyebrow. "Look. You can come with and follow the rules, or you can stay here. Don't really care which. But you try to use that pistol on me, and I promise you one thing—you'll live just long enough to damn well wish you hadn't."

For a few moments, they stared at each other.

Felix was still scowling, his pistol still pointed at her face. But she could see the tells—the uncertainty in the set of his posture, the way his eyes couldn't quite hold hers.

He wasn't sure of her. Maybe he wasn't afraid yet, but he was starting to wonder if he should be.

He dropped his arm and turned away in disgust.

"Your friend's a damn lunatic," he muttered in Tae's direction.

"Yep," said Jez cheerily. "But anyone who wants to come along with the damn lunatic best get their butts onto their skybikes."

She turned to where the bikes were leaned up against the corner of an alley. Felix grudgingly followed suit, gesturing to four ragged, skinny kids that apparently made up his gang to do the same.

Before she swung onto her bike, Lev stepped forward, putting his hands on her arms. The look in his eyes made her heart skip a little.

"I sent you the coordinates to the places you'll need to hit," he said quietly. "Tanya's working with Tae on getting into the government databases to see if there's anything I missed. If you need anything—information, specs, anything—call me. Please."

She gave him a wink. "Any excuse to talk to a hot scholar-boy."

He chuckled reluctantly, then sobered. "Be careful, OK?"

"Yeah," she said. "Yeah, I will."

Hell, he was standing so close, and the way he was looking at her —she leaned forward and kissed him, the kind of kiss that sent butterflies dancing through her stomach and made Lev slide his hands down her back, tightening his arms around her. When she finally drew back, her whole body felt light, and her legs were a little less steady they had been.

Lev looked like someone had hit him over the head.

"Come back soon," he whispered, and something in his voice made her want, very badly, to come back very, very soon indeed.

She kissed him again, lightly, and swung up, gripping the icy handles of the bike.

She closed her eyes for a moment.

It had been way too damn long since she'd last been in the sky.

She glanced over her shoulder. Felix glowered at her from his own bike, his expression a mixture of irritation, exasperation, and simmering hate.

"Hope you fly as well as you talk," she said. Then she hit the throttle and leaned almost parallel with the cement, and the bike shot forward in a glorious burst of acceleration that left her insides far behind and brought a grin to her face so wide that she could hardly stand it.

She skimmed over the top of the barricade where the students had made a gap in the network of strung wires, slipped down a few alleyways, and then popped up into the flight-lane above the buildings, slowing enough that the damn smart-mouth street kid could catch up. When he was about in shouting range, she started off again, forcing herself into a more reasonable pace, even though it just about killed her.

Through the haze and distortion of the city force field, she could see the faint, washed-out stars, obscured by the city's creeping mist and the uneven glow from the brightly lit government buildings. No one was out on the streets, not at this hour, and especially not since the entire dam city was in an uprising.

She didn't blame them. Be as much as your life was worth, probably.

Even through her heated gloves, her fingers tingled with the cold, and her face was raw with it.

As they neared the police building, she dipped back into the alleys again, slowing even more. Much as her entire body ached for the tear of the wind against her face, the walls of the alleys brushing the sleeves of her jacket, pancaking one of Tae's friends against an alley wall probably wouldn't be the best use of everyone's time.

At last, she idled to a stop. Felix and the others stopped their bikes as well and slid off.

She couldn't tell in the desultory light from the streetlamps, but she could've sworn that Felix's face was grimmer than it had been before he'd gotten on the bike. He didn't say anything, though, and she grinned to herself.

Jez glanced around. "Alright, four of us on watch, two of us to plant the explosives. Don't want anyone on their own, not with this many damn police around."

Felix gave a brusque nod, then gestured with a jerk of his chin to the other kids. They didn't seem to need more than that, breaking off and sliding silently into the narrow streets on either side of the alley.

Jez eyed Felix dubiously. "Guess it's you and me then."

His eyebrows lowered. "You got a problem with that?"

She grinned. "Not particularly. But I thought you might."

"Worked with the damn Blood Riots," he muttered. "Figure I know how to work with people I hate."

"Good," said Jez cheerily. She reached inside her shirt for the padded bag of explosives Ysbel had given to her. Well, given might be a bit of an exaggeration. She'd handed them over with a look of deep foreboding, muttering that if Jez came back as something that had been scraped off the alley walls, it wasn't her fault—she'd damn well explained to Tae how she felt about Jez going anywhere with explosives. And when Jez asked, with a grin, if Ysbel was actually worried about her, Ysbel grumbled something about being more worried about the entire damn city of Prasvishoni with Jez and a bag of explosives set loose on it.

Jez pulled out two small spheres, guessing the ones she wanted by feel, and handed one to Felix. He gave a short nod of acknowledgement, and they crept down the alley towards the brightly lit police building, its bare white walls rising higher than her head.

"Bloody cowards," Felix muttered. "Brave enough to send their damn drones after street kids, but they hide behind their damn walls when there's a chance the street kids'll fight back."

Jez raised an eyebrow at him. "Considering how you and your killers fight, don't actually blame them."

He glared at her, as if trying to parse her words, then his scowl deepened, and he turned back to the gate.

Jez studied the wall thoughtfully. Lev had showed her the layout of the police station. She knew where she wanted the damn thing to land—right in the back corner of the building, where it would blow the supplies but probably not kill anyone—and she was pretty sure she could get it there.

Or she'd blow herself up, but hell, what was life without a few risks?

She took a step back, gauging the distance, and tossed the explosive in a low arc. It glittered in the dim light as it skimmed over the wall, just low enough to pass under the lattice of laser sensors—or at least, she assumed so, considering they hadn't all been blown to hell.

"Are you plaguing insane?" Felix choked. "You could have killed us!"

She grinned at him.

He rolled his eyes to the sky in exasperation and started cautiously up the wall, scrabbling for handholds, but being impressively quiet, all things considered. He reached the top, pulled out the explosive, and tipped it over the edge of the wall, then scrambled back down.

He glared at her, then turned back to the alley. "You coming?" he hissed in a disgusted tone.

She bit back a smirk and followed.

He tapped his com, whispering something into as they reached the bikes, and moments later the other four reappeared beside them, as silently as the thick morning fog.

"Any trouble?" Felix asked.

"Nothing," said a tall girl, who looked to be maybe fourteen.

He nodded, and jerked his head towards the bikes. The kids scrambled on, and Jez swung up on her own bike. She leaned over to Felix. "For a kid who doesn't like listening to orders, you sure as hell know how to give them."

The glare on his face hardened, and for a moment, she thought he might go for her. She grinned, and he turned away sullenly.

She hit the throttle on her bike and leaned forward, and they shot off down the alleyway.

By the time they'd planted their explosives in the second police station and started off again, the faintest hint of grey smudged the edges of the horizon through the maze of tall buildings.

"Gonna have to hurry this up," said Jez quietly into her com.

When they reached their final target, the light on the horizon had grown brighter, casting the streets in shades of grey-black shadows.

She stopped the bike a couple streets away and slid off, rubbing her numb hands to warm them.

Behind her, Felix was speaking quietly to the other kids.

"Come on," she whispered over her shoulder. "In a bit of a hurry here."

Felix glared at her, then sauntered over slowly. "See, some of us aren't afraid of the police," he said, his voice a slight sneer. "Some of us know how to use a damn weapon. How to actually fight, not just use cheap tricks they learned in a filthy off-world zestava."

Jez grinned, her heart pounding in a tight anticipation. "Lots of talk from the kid who lost his gun to a cheap trick from an off-world zestava."

Felix's face darkened.

From the corners of her eyes, she could see the other kids moving slowly around behind her. She turned so her back was against the wall, and gave Felix a dangerous grin.

"Alright, you dirty bastard," she said in a low voice. "You want to try this? Hell, there are five of you, and only one of me. And you're all damn killers, kill people for fun, right? So sure, go ahead. We can have it out right here, right in the middle of the damn street." She paused a moment. "Or, we can bloody well act like adults, and do what we came here to do. Your choice, you scum-eater."

For a moment, none of the kids moved.

Jez was wearing a grin that showed all her teeth. She could feel the comfortable weight of the heat pistol in the pocket of her jacket, and she knew damn well that every single one of those kids had enough dirty weapons on them to turn this place into a battlefield.

But at last Felix turned away, jerking his head at the kids. They faded back as well, off to the side alleys, presumably to keep watch.

Or to try to ambush her. But hell, she'd never liked boring jobs.

"Fine," Felix said through gritted teeth. "You're right, there's more important things to do than try to take out some skinny, useless pilot."

"Says the funny-looking street kid who can't figure out where the throttle is on his damn skybike." She winked at him, and tossed him an explosive. Then they crept forward.

This time, as they approached, she could hear voices from inside the walls, raised in anger or alarm, she couldn't tell which.

She exchanged glances with Felix, and they edged silently closer to the walls.

"… doing outside our walls? How could they have gotten so close?" There was a moment's pause. "Where did you see them?"

She didn't wait for the response, her stomach already tight with anticipation. "Listen," she began in a low whisper, turning to him. "Looks like we'll have to—"

Then she caught sight of his face, and bit back a curse.

He was wearing a small smile, his eyes narrowed and his expression savage.

"What the hell did you do?" she hissed.

He shrugged. "Can't help it if the police saw one of my kids.

Guess that means we're going to have to take care of it."

Jez narrowed her own eyes and stood quickly. She tossed her explosive over the fence, then snatched Felix's neatly out of his palm, tossing it before he had time to react. He spun, face dark with fury. "You don't—" he began in a low growl.

"You're not damn well doing this, not on my damn watch," said Jez through gritted teeth. "You want to bring the whole damn force down on us? Lev said buildings only, no people."

Felix smirked at her. "Oh, and you do everything that soft scholar bastard tells you? I saw you—one kiss, he's got you off your damn head. Just following orders like a good little soldier." He leaned closer. "If I kissed you, you'd do everything I say too?"

She gave him a tight grin. "Sorry, kid, you're not nearly hot enough. Got standards, you know." She turned, starting towards the alley where the other street kids had disappeared. "And you'd better damn well hope, for your own bloody health, that when I find your kids, I don't find a dead police officer with them."

She was halfway jogging down the street, and she could hear Felix's footsteps, soft on the pavement behind her.

Could be the bastard had pulled his own weapon and was lining up a shot, but hell, at this point, she almost hoped he'd try.

She rounded the corner and came to an abrupt halt.

Two of Felix's kids were facing an officer. The officer's gun was drawn. And behind the woman, Jez could see the two other kids creeping closer, weapons ready.

Damn it to hell. Blowing up police stations was one thing. Shooting down an officer in cold blood, six on one—that was gonna bring a pile of crap down on them that they weren't damn well ready for. Just to satisfy the pique of some bastard smart-ass street kid.

"Hey!" she shouted.

Five heads whipped around.

"What—" the police officer began, but Jez was already moving. Before the woman could finish her sentence, Jez had reached her, grabbed her by the arm, swung her around, and planted a knee in her stomach. The officer collapsed, choking, and Jez yanked off the woman's helmet, slamming the butt of her pistol into the woman's temple.

The officer groaned and went limp.

Jez stood, breathing heavily.

"Who the hell do you think you are?" Felix hissed. He turned to the other four kids. "Alright, she's down. Kill her. Leave the body outside, let the plaguers know we were here."

"You're damn well gonna have to go through me first," said Jez through her teeth.

Damn these street kid bastards to hell, the last thing in the plaguing system she wanted to be doing right now was protecting a police officer.

She grabbed the woman under the arms, turning her back on Felix deliberately, and hauled her towards the station entrance.

"Solokov." Felix's voice was soft with menace. "That officer was threatening my kids. You heard Tae—we can kill an officer if they were gonna kill us first."

She yanked the limp body into the pool of light from the front entrance of the station. Then she turned back to Felix, keeping her body between him and the officer.

"Listen, kid—you're a lot of damn things, but you're not stupid. And right now, you're damn well going back to the barricades, and you're not coming out with me again. I'll take bloody Mila before I take you."

"Sure," Felix said, his mouth pulled back in a sneer. "You let me kill that officer behind you, and I'll happily go back to the damn barricades. I don't work with softies, damn bleeding hearts trying to protect the poor, innocent police. You know how many of my kids I've watched killed?" His voice was still sneering, but she could hear the choke of emotion under his words. "Watched three of my kids gunned down by the police. You want to know why I agreed to be a killer for the gangs? It was the only way I could stay alive. Kill the other street kids, or watch my own kids die." He took a step towards her. "Three kids, Solokov. Three damn kids shot by these bastards. And now one's lying on the ground in front of me, and you want me to bloody walk away?"

Jez reached into her pocket, hand on the hilt of her heat gun. "Look," she said quietly. "I don't like these bastards any more than you do. But we're not ready for what would happen if we kill an officer outside the barricades. Blow up a police station or two? Sure. They see that, they know we could have hurt them and didn't. They figure, they leave us alone, maybe they stay alive. They're scared, they give us time, they give those idiots in the government time to decide not to kill us all. But we come out hunting them? Then, the only way they stay safe is to take us out. So yeah—I don't blame you for hating this bastard. Far as I'm concerned, we could send her into space without a space suit and the system would be better off for it. But I have friends behind that barricade, and I'm not about to watch them die because you couldn't keep your temper. So you want to kill her, you'll damn well have to kill me first."

A slow, ugly smile was spreading across Felix's face. He reached into his own pocket. "You say that like I haven't been wanting to kill you since I damn well met you."

"Jez! Are you there?" Tanya must have been calling on the group's general channel, because all the street kids started at the sound.

Jez glared at Felix, then tapped her com against her leg. "What is it?"

Tanya's voice was tense. "I'm in one of the databases. The police have brought in a new gun, and it looks like they're getting it ready to use. It's at a weapons depot not too far from where you are. They'll be moving it soon, but if you can get there and take it out—"

Jez winked at Felix. "Just finishing up some business. Figure we're just about done."

"Good. If you're going to do this, it's now or not at all."

"Oh, we'll be there," murmured Jez. She tapped off her com and turned back to Felix and the other street kids. "Your choice," she said. "Leave this bastard here, head back to the bikes, and take out the gun—or, try to take me. Maybe you walk out of this alley, maybe you don't, but either way, that gun breaks down the barricades next time the police stop by."

Felix's face was dark with fury. The other four street kids watched him, faces tense, waiting for a command.

At last he snorted in frustration and jerked his chin towards the skybikes, and the kids started after him down the alley, casting dark looks at Jez as they went.

When Jez was sure they were far enough away, she stepped away from the police officer, who'd begun to stir. She sighed heavily, turned, and kicked the door hard. There were voices from inside, and approaching footsteps, and she turned and sprinted down the alley after the street kids.

The door creaked as she rounded the corner, and someone gave an exclamation of surprise, then she'd reached the bikes.

She swung up and shot Felix a challenging grin. The way his eyes narrowed told her that he'd keep up or die trying, and honestly, at this point, she didn't really care which. She leaned over her bike and shot off.

She slowed as they got closer to the weapons depot. It was in the heart of the warehouse district, which meant wide, empty streets with basically no shelter.

She dropped down between the buildings, twisting through alleys until she was a couple blocks away, then pulled to a stop.

The street kids arrived a few minutes later.

She grinned at Felix as he shot into view. "Thought you were planning on keeping up."

He didn't deign to answer, just jumped off his bike, looking like he wanted to go for his pistol and was barely restraining himself.

"Tanya, we're here," said Jez into her com. "Send me the specs."

A moment later, her com beeped softly, and she glanced down at it.

The layout was simple—there was a small loading entrance in the back, and from there, a few narrow service corridors that should take them through to the weapons bay.

"Be careful," said Tanya tersely. "It will be busy if they're getting weapon ready to move."

"Yep," Jez drawled, tapping off her com.

She glanced over at Felix.

He scowled. "Same as before. My kids keep watch, you and me take out the gun."

Jez nodded, and they started silently towards the back entrance. She pulled out one of Tae's lock scramblers and clipped it onto the door, and a moment later, the door swung gently open at her touch.

She stepped cautiously inside, resting her hand on the butt of her heat gun.

The long hallway was empty, at least for the moment.

She breathed a quick sigh of relief and beckoned the others, and Felix's small gang followed her inside.

At the first intersection between corridors, she paused, pulling up the diagram Tanya had sent. "We'll go this way," she whispered, pointing at the screen. "If your kids stay back here and here, they should be able to keep an eye out."

Felix gave a terse nod, and the other four melted silently away in the direction she'd indicated. Then she and Felix crept towards the weapons bay.

When they reached it, Jez opened it a crack and peered through.

"Hey Felix," she whispered over her shoulder. "How quiet you think you can be?"

"What are you talking about?" he grumbled.

She grinned. "Couple soldiers in the weapons bay. Don't think we have time to wait around for them to leave. Can't kill them, which we already had a chat about. So—" she raised an eyebrow.

"I can be as quiet as I need to be, you plaguing smuggler," he growled.

"Good," she said cheerily.

The officers were on the far side of the room, examining one of the large troop transport vehicles. Plenty close enough to shoot Jez and Felix down without even having to aim, but hell, she'd been in tighter situations.

Silently, she slipped through the door. After a moment's hesitation, Felix slipped in after her, leaving it cracked open—if they were getting out of here, they wouldn't have time to be fumbling around with a lock-scrambler.

She looked around quickly.

The massive street-cannon was sitting in the open, halfway across the room, maybe twenty metres from where they stood. No real cover between them and it, but then, probably didn't matter—if the officers turned, they'd see the door cracked and sound the alarm. Or just shoot her and Felix dead.

She started forward, tested her footing carefully at every step—places like this, easy to step in an oil slick and slip, and, at least in this situation, easier still to get your damn head melted in.

When they were only a couple metres away, she slipped three explosives from her pocket, one for each muzzle on the gun.

Across the room, one of the officers glanced up casually.

Damn it to hell.

As the expression on the officer's face flickered through from puzzlement, to confusion, to shock, to alarm, she grabbed Felix's arm, slipping the explosives into his hand. "Get those in the guns," she muttered. "I'll keep them looking at me."

Before he had time to protest, Jez yanked the heat pistol out of her pocket and started towards the officers at a dead sprint. They scrambled for their own weapons, and she fired off a shot that melted a hole in the siding of the troop transport next to their heads.

"What the hell do you think—"

Jez fired again, hitting the front of the transport this time. The shielded metal glowed a dull orange momentarily, and Jez gave a small sigh of satisfaction.

Damn, she loved working with Ysbel's weapons.

The officers had their guns out now, and she dove to the ground as a heat-blast sizzled over her head, then rolled upright and ducked behind another transport.

"There's someone in the weapons room," one of the officers shouted into his com. "Looks like she's trying to take out the troop transports."

Jez grinned to herself, placed the muzzle of her heat pistol against the engine compartment, and pulled the trigger. Black smoke rose from inside the machine, carrying the thick, astringent scent of burning metal. She stepped back, coughing, and the two officers rounded the corner of the transport where she was hiding, their pistols raised.

Jez winked at them, and slipped around the side of the transport as they pulled their triggers. Heat seared the air where she'd been standing, and they charged after her.

She slipped around the corner again, just ahead of them. They paused, and after a quick, muttered conference, split up, sprinting around the transport in opposite directions.

Jez grinned and dove out from behind the transport as heat lit the air above her head, running in a half-crouch towards another transport. She tapped her com as she ran. "Felix. Got the explosives in?"

"Yes." His voice was strained. "What the hell—"

"Get out. Leave the door open—I'll be coming through in a jiff."

She reached the transport and yanked open the door, slid into the cockpit, and hit the controls. The control chip had been left in, thank the Lady, and the machine powered up with a low hum. She let out a long, blissful breath. Something about feeling controls under her fingers, even controls of a clunky old beast like this one—

One of the officers reached for the handle. Jez slammed the throttle forward, and the transport jerked, lurched, and barrelled across the open floor.

She could hear shouts from the main hangar door, and a moment later, a dozen officers appeared in the opening. Her grin widened, and she shoved the throttle even harder, pointing the transport at the opening.

Officers dived out of the way as she hurtled towards them, but at the last moment she yanked back on the controls, pulling the transport into an ungraceful swerve towards the transport the officers had been inspecting earlier. She pushed the throttle all the way forward, then pointed her pistol and fired at the controls.

They melted.

She grabbed the door handle, yanked it open, and dived out, landing in a roll. She'd half expected to be dodging heat-blasts before she got her feet under her, but the officers' eyes were glued to the impending collision. She leapt to her feet and sprinted towards the back door of the weapons bay.

One of the officers glanced up, then shouted, pointing in Jez's direction.

The two transports collided with a bone-numbing crunch.

For half a second, the eyes of every officer in the room jerked involuntarily towards the disaster.

Jez dived through the partially opened door and slammed it shut behind her. She leaned against it, panting.

Felix was waiting for her, still scowling. "Come on," he said. "They'll be after us any second."

They took off down the empty hallway. Felix hit his com as they ran. "Kasimir! Nadia! Meet us at the back door—we've got to leave in a hurry."

They reached the back door, and a moment later, two of the kids skidded to a stop beside them.

"Where's Kasimir?" Felix snapped, voice tight with concern.

They heard a boy's voice through the com. "Felix! They caught us, I'm sorry, I'm—"

His voice cut off.

Felix and Jez glanced at each other, faces grim. Then Felix turned to Nadia and the street boy that stood beside her. "Get out, wait for me by the bikes. If I'm not back in ten standard minutes, go without me."

"If we're not back," said Jez with a sharp grin at Felix. "Not letting you get into trouble by yourself."

He glared at her, then seemed to realize arguing would be a waste of breath.

They turned and sprinted down the hallway where the other two street kids had disappeared.

They heard voices long before they could see anything, and they slowed. Ahead of them, the corridor turned, and according to Tanya's specs, led into a mess hall.

That must be where the kids were. If they hadn't been shot already.

She glanced at Felix and saw on his face that he'd come to the same conclusion. He took a deep breath, clearly prepared to burst in, even though he must know as well as she did it would be suicide.

She grabbed his arm.

He turned to glare at her. "I'm not leaving my kids to—"

She rolled her eyes. "Not asking you to. But figure there's a better way in than getting ourselves made into barbecue." She cut a meaningful glance at the ceiling.

Felix frowned, and she rolled her eyes, pulling out her heat gun.

The ceiling panels melted with one shot, and she took a few steps back, and, with a running jump, caught the edge of the latticework, pulling herself up. Then she flattened herself onto her stomach and put a hand down to Felix. He was still glaring at her, but he caught her hand, and she pulled him up after her.

He scrambled through the melted hole, pulling himself up beside her. She jerked her head down through the open space towards the mess hall, and he nodded grimly.

It wasn't tall enough to stand, so they made their way through the dusty, cobwebby space on hands and knees until they reached what Jez was pretty sure was right over the mess hall. She leaned down, pressing her ear against the ceiling panels.

The murmur of voices below resolved into words.

"I'll ask you one last time: what are you doing here?" a woman's voice snapped. "Who are you working with? Why are you trying to take out the transports?"

There was no answer, and a moment later, there was the sound of a sharp slap.

From beside her, Felix sucked in a quick breath and put a hand on the ceiling panel, as if to yank it back.

She grabbed his arm. "Wait. We go in now, there's a good chance they get shot in the confusion."

He hesitated, then finally, reluctantly, he nodded.

She rummaged around in her pouch, and then grinned. "This should help," she whispered, pulling one of Ysbel's gas bombs out of the bag. She stripped off her coat, shoving it in Felix's hands. "Don't have a good rope, so you'll have to tie this together with your coat."

"What—" he began.

She held up the gas bomb. "When I drop this, everyone down there will be out in about five seconds flat. Including your friends. Shouldn't affect us up here, because the gas is pretty heavy, tends to stay low. I'll jump down there, grab the kids, and you haul them up with this, then drop it down for me again. Don't think I'll have the breath to be able to jump and haul myself up again after that."

Felix glared. "Why don't I go down and get the kids?"

She raised an eyebrow, deliberately looking him up and down. "I might be a skinny pilot, but I figure I've got about ten centimetres and fifteen kilos on you. We'll get one chance to get those kids out, and we sure as hell won't have time for more than one trip through that smoke. So I go."

He was still glaring at her, his eyes narrowed. Finally, he muttered, "Fine."

She nudged the roof panel aside just enough to peer through.

Six or seven officers down there, plus the two street kids. The kids' hands and feet were bound with mag cuffs, and from the bruises some of the officers wore, they hadn't gone down without a fight. The boy was sporting a black eye, and blood dripped off the girl's lip and chin, staining the front of her tunic.

And OK, maybe the little bastards had tried to jump her not too long ago, but—hell, they were kids. The girl couldn't be much more than twelve.

Jez was smiling grimly as she tipped the smoke bomb through the narrow opening.

The officers turned as it hit the floor, surprise registering on their faces, and then a thick fug of smoke exploded from the tiny sphere.

Within seconds, the first of the officers was down. In less than a minute, everyone in the room had slumped to the ground.

Felix's face was drawn, expression strained. "If you hurt them—" he began in a choked voice.

She rolled her eyes. "Told you. I know what I'm doing. Be ready to haul them up."

She took a deep breath, pulled the ceiling panel all the way back, and jumped to the ground.

The thick, heavy gas wound its way into her nose and tickled her lips as she landed, and she had to fight back the urge to cough.

She glanced around quickly, halfway disoriented, then started for the two cuffed figures. When she reached them, she threw one of them over her shoulders and grabbed the other under the arms.

Damn it to hell, she was running out of air, and who knew two skinny kids could possibly be this awkward to carry?

She heaved the other kid onto her other shoulder and staggered to her feet. Her head was pounding, and her lungs burned as she stumbled towards where she was pretty sure the open ceiling panel was, although in the haze, it was hard to tell.

"Over here," Felix called, and she stumbled toward the sound. Something brushed her face, and it took her a moment to realize it was their makeshift rope. She shrugged one of the kids off her shoulder, tying their limp body under the arms with a quick knot, and jerked at the rope. A moment later, the kid was pulled up through the ceiling panel.

Her lungs ached, and black spots were starting around the edge of her vision. In about thirty seconds, she was going to breathe in whether she wanted to or not.

The coat came down again, and with fumbling fingers, she tied the other kid into the makeshift harness. It took her three tries to get the knot tight, then she gave a tug, and again, the kid was pulled up.

The floor swayed under her feet, and she reached out to catch herself before she realized she wasn't standing near anything she could catch herself on.

He should have already dropped the rope again.

Unless—

Her stomach sank.

Damn. Damn it to hell.

She was a damn innocent. All this time and she was still a damn innocent. Felix had wanted to kill her since that morning, and she'd just damn well handed him the opportunity on a credit chip.

She was going to die here. She was going to bloody die, and she wouldn't even be able to say goodbye to Lev.

Stupid reason to be upset, but in the end, that was the thing that hurt the most.

"For the Lady's damn sake, grab on!"

She looked up with a start. The jacket sleeve dangled in front of her face, and she grabbed for it desperately. Her lungs hiccupped and spasmed, trying to draw in a breath. Someone yanked up on the makeshift rope, but her fingers didn't seem to want to hold on, and she could feel her grip slipping—

A hand grabbed her wrist and yanked her up, and she gasped in a breath, and found she was breathing clean air.

She collapsed on her stomach on the ceiling tile, gasping and choking, still dangling halfway out of the ceiling panel.

As the black dissipated from her vision, she saw Felix crouched beside her. He was peering at her with what looked like actual concern on his face.

"You OK?" His voice was rough. "Sorry it took me so long. Couldn't get the knot untied—had to cut it loose with my damn gutting knife. You alright?"

"I'm … fine," she gasped. Her muscles were shaky, and her chest still ached, but she managed to pull herself up into the space above the ceiling.

To her shock, Felix grabbed her arm and helped her.

She glanced down at the two unconscious street kids. "Only one way to get them out of here," she muttered, crouching down and slipping one of the kid's bound wrists over her head, so he was slung around her back like a heavy, unwieldy knapsack. She hoisted him up as Felix took the other kid, and they started off at a half-crouch back the way they'd come.

Behind them there was a shout, abruptly cut off. Presumably an officer had discovered the scene, and been promptly knocked cold by the gas. But it wouldn't last—once the door was open, the gas would clear quickly.

When they'd gone far enough, Jez pulled out her heat gun, melted another ceiling tile, and she and Felix jumped down and jogged for the exit, the unconscious street kids bouncing awkwardly on their backs. They slammed the door behind them, and from inside, an officer shouted the alarm, and then they were running down the icy Prasvishoni streets.

When they reached their bikes, Jez cursed. "Felix, you take the kids back to the barricades."

He scowled. "No way in hell. What are you doing?"

"Not gonna leave these bikes for the damn police," she muttered, yanking out her gutting knife and slicing a strip from her tunic. "And I fly these things a hell of a lot better than you do."

Felix rolled his eyes. "Nadia! You got binding twine?"

The street girl pulled something from her pocket, tossing it at Felix. He snatched it out of the air and handed it to Jez. "Use this. I sure as hell don't want to see you naked. Tie one bike to yours and one to mine."

The shouts from the officers grew suddenly louder. They must have opened the back door, which meant they had maybe a minute at this point.

She sighed. "Fine." She wrapped the bikes together neatly, then slid onto hers. "But you damn well better cut it loose if you can't keep up. Easier to get a new street bike than a new damn street kid, probably."

"Worry about your own self," Felix muttered, but to her shock, she saw the hint of a smile on his face.

Jez hit her com as they shot forward. "Got the explosives planted. Tell Ysbel if she wants to make some noise, now would be a good time."

"You're safe?" Lev's voice was strained.

"Yep," she drawled.

Safe was relative, anyways.

A moment later, a *boom* shook the streets of Prasvishoni. Matching balls of fire rose from the weapons depot behind them, and where the police stations must be—or had been.

She glanced over at Felix, and they grinned at each other, despite the icy wind cutting through their thin tunics. "Hey," she said through the private line. "You didn't you too bad back there, you scum-sucker."

"Yeah? You didn't do too bad either, for a skinny ugly plaguer."

She was grinning as they shot back towards the barricades. Her arms ached with cold, and her bike shook with the added strain of the loose bike tied on beside it, and the speed they were flying was probably dangerous—but honestly, she couldn't have cared less.

14

Masha, day 7

When Masha approached her office the next morning, two police officers stood outside the door, waiting for her. They held their weapons in a businesslike way, their stances ready.

Masha hid a smile.

"Alonya?" one of them asked as she stopped by the door.

"I'm she," she said. "What's the meaning of this?"

"We're here on orders from Minister Branka," said the first officer. "There was an unfortunate occurrence in the building last night, and the minister wanted to assure your safety. She requires your presence at a meeting this morning."

Masha raised an eyebrow. "And did Minister Branka see fit to explain what happened?"

The officer scowled. "If the minister wishes to explain, I'm certain she'll do so," she snapped.

Masha gave a small shrug. "Very well. I assume I'm to follow you, then. Please lead the way."

When Masha stepped into the meeting room, she could feel the eyes on her.

At least two dozen ministers were gathered around the table, many of them surprisingly important. For a brief moment, she felt a spark of fear.

Either things had played out as she'd intended, or she'd been found out, and she wasn't certain which.

Then she noticed the preoccupied looks on the faces turned towards her, and her shoulders relaxed.

"Undersecretary," said Branka, gesturing to a seat. "Please. We've been waiting for you."

Masha kept her expression one of polite curiosity, and sat.

Branka glanced around the room with a slightly wry expression. "No one officially knows the news I'm about to tell you. However, I'm certain many of you have heard unofficially." She paused a moment. "For those of you who have not, Minister Goran is dead."

A buzz of whispers started around the table.

Masha watched Branka out of the corner of her eye.

The woman was very good. She'd managed to give the news with an air of complete detachment, and now she stood looking around the room, expression placid, but mildly concerned.

When the murmurs had faded, a man in the back said gruffly, "How?"

"Assassination," said Branca curtly.

There was a look of hunted fear in the faces around the table now. Goran had been a high-up minister. If he could be killed, none of them were safe.

None of the people in this room knew, of course, what had been on the information chip Masha had planted in Branka's office the day before. If they had, they would have been much less surprised.

No one around the table would have seen the internal security files Masha had seen, either. And likely none of them knew exactly what Branka was capable of, as Masha did.

The assassination of Minister Goran, for one thing.

"With the current crisis, it's vital that we deal with any potential fallout up front," Branka continued. She turned to the man at the end of the table. "Minister Pasha. You are in charge of internal government security."

The man looked nervous. "I am, but the details—"

Branka cut him off with a curt gesture. "I'm aware the details are delegated to your staff. I'm not blaming you for what happened. However, I request that you take personal charge going forward. The rest of the ministers and staff in this building need to have enough confidence in their personal safety to remain at their desks during this crisis."

The man nodded, clearly unhappy with the situation.

"Speaking of the current crisis," said another woman, "Goran was in charge of the response to the insurgency. It seems to me the most urgent task now is to find someone to replace him."

"I fully agree," said Branka. "That's why I've asked Undersecretary Alonya to be present." She turned to Masha, studying her with her piercing gaze. "Undersecretary," she said. "As I'm sure you are aware, this is a highly unusual request. However, we are dealing with highly unusual circumstances. I understand that you are fully briefed as to the situation in the streets?"

Masha nodded.

"Very good." Branka turned back to the others at the table. "I suggest, then, that we ask the undersecretary to step into the vacant position on a temporary basis, until we are able to procure a suitable replacement for Goran."

There were some grumbled protests and looks of discontent, but the fact that no one raised an audible objection told Masha exactly how desperate the ministers were.

She hid a smile.

Branka scanned the room, then give a brusque nod. "Very well. Since there appears to be no objection—"

"Minister Branka," said Masha smoothly, half-rising from her seat.

Branka turned in surprise, frowning. "Undersecretary?"

Masha gave her a pleasant smile. "You asked that I step into Goran's position and take over his responsibilities. I'm willing to do so, but there are conditions that would have to be met."

Branka's frown deepened, and there was a definite hint of frost to her expression. "May I ask what such conditions might be, Undersecretary? I was under the impression that you would be thrilled to receive this honour. Considering how willing you were to step forward when Minister Adrik was removed from his position." Her last words contained a bite to them.

"I am very aware of the honour you're bestowing on me," said Masha, voice still in low and pleasant. "I am also aware that my immediate predecessor was violently killed less than twenty-four hours previous. When Goran asked me to take over the defence of the streets and putting down the insurgency, responsibility for the ultimate decision rested with him. Now—" Masha gave a small shrug. "If I accept your offer, should something unfortunate occur, I'll be the next in line for the assassin's heat-blast."

"You are not my only option." Branka's tone was icy. "There are plenty of under-ministers who would leap at this chance."

"Perhaps," said Masha. "But how many of them know the situation like I do? Who else knows the details of the sabotage the insurgents carried out this morning? Who else was aware we're currently running off of generator power in this building? Or which key pieces of infrastructure they'd have to take out for us to lose power completely? This is a situation that does not afford time to bring a new person up to speed."

Branka's eyes narrowed to slits. "What are you requesting, Undersecretary?"

Masha smiled. "I need full autonomy. I need the authority to use every tool at my disposal, without being tied up in bureaucratic struggles. To that end, I must be named as a full minister, and it must be announced, by someone with your influence, that I have full power within the scope of my ministry. That's the only way I will be able to deal with this situation."

"You're asking for something ridiculous," snapped Branka.

"Am I?" asked Masha. "How do you propose I deal with this crisis, where the situation on the ground can change in the blink of an eye, if I have to go through four different ministers, each of whom will want some favour or payback in return for their stamp of approval? The streets will devolve into chaos. I understand your unwillingness to raise an undersecretary to a full minister. But what I'm asking is eminently reasonable."

She glanced quickly around the table. The looks on the minister's faces were furious, but still, none of them voiced a protest.

She and she alone knew the information Goran had been working with, the names and identities of his informants, what he'd been planning and why. And everyone at this table knew it. Goran had been somewhat of a legend, even in government, for playing his tokens from a tightly clenched fist. And everyone at this table realized by now that if they did not agree to Masha's demands, whoever else they chose was unlikely to ever get those details.

"If I were to agree," said Branka at last, reluctantly, "I assume you would accept a full performance review at the end of this crisis. I may be able to get you appointed acting minister. But even I can't pull enough strings to get you authorized as a full minister with no external review or committee meetings. And," she added, "as you have so helpfully pointed out, time is of the essence."

Masha hesitated a moment.

Let Branka think this was a concession. Give the woman a win.

At last, she nodded slowly. "Acting minister, then," she said. "With a review after the crisis is over. But I will expect everything else that I requested, and I will expect you to ensure it moves quickly. If I am to take on this position, I expect to be starting to strategize a response within an hour, and by that time, I need every minister, under-minister, or any other official with whom I might be working, to have an update on my status, and instructions to obey me as if I were Goran, from this moment forward."

Branka was still glaring at her, but she gave a short, sharp nod. "Your proposal is acceptable, Undersecretary."

"Acting Minister, now, correct?" said Masha quietly.

The anger lines around Branka's mouth sharpened, but she nodded. "I apologize. You are correct. Acting Minister Alonya."

"Thank you, Minister Branka." Masha stood briskly, pushing back the chair. "If that's all, I would like to get started. It will take me some time to go through the information my predecessor left." She turned to Branka. "Would you be so kind as to arrange for his files and information chips to be sent to my office?"

"Of course," said Branka, her voice still cold. "I appreciate your devotion to duty." She paused. "I received some additional information regarding the situation on the streets. It involves the gangs, who, I believe, you authorized to assist the police. However, as you pointed out, you have plenty of work to do, so I'll send it through to your com."

A tendril of unease wound around Masha's chest at the tone in the woman's voice, but she nodded politely. "Minister Branka,

Ministers. Thank you for your confidence. I hope not to disappoint you."

And she turned, opened the door, and stepped out of the room.

Acting Minister. Her next play, gone off without a hitch.

She had business to take care of. And after that—one more move remaining.

Radka was waiting for her, her expression a mixture of tension and boredom. When she saw Masha exit, she straightened comically quickly. "Hello Undersecretary," she said. "I'm to take you back to your office when the meeting's done." She glanced uncertainly at the closed door. "Is—the meeting done?"

Masha gave a terse shake of her head. "For me, yes. I've been given an assignment, and I'm afraid it will keep me busy for the foreseeable future."

Something had happened with the gangs. And from the expression on Branka's face, it had been something very, very bad.

She couldn't tell if the nausea in her stomach was from imagining what had happened, or for her own role in whatever it was.

It didn't matter. After the attempted assassination the previous night, she no longer had the time to wonder about right and wrong.

Maybe she never had.

"Undersecretary?"

She looked up, startled, to see Radka watching her with concern.

"Are you alright?"

"I'm fine."

"Did something happen in the meeting?" The girl's voice was quiet.

Masha scowled at her. "That is not something that I wish to discuss."

"If—if there's anything I can—"

"No." Masha cut her off sharply. "I told you before. I am not your friend. No one in these buildings is your friend. If you don't learn that lesson, you won't survive. Now please, take me to my office with no more conversation. Do you talk with every minister you escort to their offices?"

She made her tone as harsh as possible.

The girl gave a meek nod, but the look on her face wasn't hurt, or even anger.

It was sympathy.

Masha cursed internally.

She had more important things to worry about than an aide who likely wouldn't last out the month.

An aide with a brother who worked here as well, who she worried about. A mother at home, sick, and the father working as an undersecretary to the Transport Minister.

Masha gave a brusque shake of her head.

She didn't have time for that. She'd never had time for that.

When she reached her office, she unlocked the door and stepped through without sparing Radka a glance. She locked it behind her, then sat slowly at her desk and pulled up her com screen.

The file Branka had sent was flashing on her com.

She tapped it open.

The moment she saw, on the video footage, the police captain murmuring instructions to the leader of the Blood Riots, she knew what would follow.

She forced herself to watch anyways.

When it was over, she closed down the holoscreen.

She felt sick, the guilt and fury burning inside her strong enough to make her dizzy.

This was her fault.

She took a long breath and dropped her face into her hands, closing her eyes for a moment against the images seared across her eyelids—a burning apartment building, people screaming, desperate faces pressed to windows.

But only for a moment. There was work to do.

She raised her head, took another deep breath, and tapped her com.

"Alonya," answered a man's voice immediately.

"You have the shipment of weapons," said Masha, the words more statement than a question.

"Of course," he said. "I've been holding them in a secure location, as we discussed. No one in any official capacity knows they exist, other than you and me. As you instructed."

"Your help has been invaluable," said Masha, with a small, grim smile. "I'm now in position, so you may officially release news of their arrival."

"I'll do so."

"Thank you." She tapped her com through to another line.

"Undersecretary Alonya?" a woman's voice answered.

"Acting Minister Alonya," Masha corrected.

"Ah. Congratulations on your promotion, Acting Minister." There was faint amusement in the woman's tone.

"Thank you," said Masha with an answering smile. "I just finished speaking to an official in charge of weapons distribution. Your soldiers will be receiving new weaponry within the hour, I expect. Likely faster. He is a very efficient man. General Osip, I believe, has already cleared your orders."

"Very good." The woman paused. "And I assume—"

"Yes," said Masha calmly. "We will proceed as discussed."

There'd been a time that she'd wondered, years ago, if her voice would break as she gave the order. If she'd have a twinge of hesitation, a momentary second thought.

But she'd seen the video. Her voice was perfectly steady.

"Of course, Acting Minister," said the woman. "I'll stream the results through to your com as they come in."

"Please stream it along the general government lines as well," said Masha. "I suspect there will be a number of ministers who'd be interested in the results."

"Of course," said the woman, and again there was that hint of amusement. "You are likely correct."

Masha tapped off her com, and for a few moments, sat staring at nothing.

Her stomach was tight.

Nerves?

No. Not nerves, although it felt like nerves—the tightness in her muscles, the adrenaline tingling in her fingertips.

Anticipation.

She smiled slightly and leaned back. After a moment, she pulled up the holoscreen and slid it around in front of her, turning it to the government channel.

This, she'd been waiting her whole life to watch.

"Acting Minister! Acting Minister Alonya!"

There was a loud pounding on the door.

Masha looked up from the screen with a start.

Her stomach was still tight, her muscles still shaky with adrenaline, but for once, she couldn't hide the grim smile on her face.

This—this hadn't made her sick at all. Much as she'd once thought it might.

"What is it?" she called.

"Minister Branka would like to see you immediately. In her office."

"Of course," called Masha pleasantly. "Give me a moment to gather my things."

Radka was waiting when she opened the door. Her expression was a mix of confusion and fear, and Masha caught herself thinking that this girl would not do well in government until she learned to become less transparent.

And feeling an entirely unexpected pang of regret at the thought.

"What's—what's happened?" Radka whispered, her voice trembling slightly. "I—I don't know what's going on, but everyone's terrified. Was someone else assassinated?"

Masha hadn't intended to respond, but the girl's eyes were so frightened—

"In—a manner of speaking," she found herself saying. "But nothing that should affect you."

She tried to ignore the relief in the girl's face, and kept her expression carefully blank.

When they reached Branka's office, Radka tapped timidly on the door. "Minister Branka. I've brought the Acting Minister, as you requested."

There was a moment's pause. Then Branka said, "The door is unlocked. Please ask her to come in."

There was an unfamiliar tone to the woman's voice.

Radka pushed the door open, and Masha stepped inside without glancing in her direction.

Branka sat slumped behind her desk. The brown of her skin had gone an unhealthy colour, and she seemed to have aged fifteen years since that morning.

"Alonya. Please have a seat," she said, her voice heavy.

Masha sat, her face still a pleasant blank.

For a long moment, Branka was silent. At last, she raised her head and looked at Masha.

Masha saw, with the twinge of satisfaction, the fear behind her eyes.

"I assume you are aware of what happened in the streets, about twenty minutes past." It was a statement, not a question.

Masha nodded. "Of course. I was the one who gave the order."

Branka stared at her for a long moment. At last she shook her head in a stunned disbelief. "How many gang members and boyeviki, do you think, were in the city, Alonya?"

Masha smiled politely. "I can give you an exact number. Seven thousand five hundred and thirty-two, as of this morning." She paused. "Now, none."

Again, Branka paused a moment before she responded. "They were working with us," she said at last. "They agreed to help the police, put their differences aside to help us bring down this insurgency."

Masha leaned slightly forward, resting her forearms on Branka's desk. "And what do you think would have happened once we'd finished with the insurgency?" She wasn't sure that she'd managed to fully conceal the hiss of hatred in her voice. "They would have taken over our police force. They would have infiltrated the government again. We would have been exactly where we were months ago, when Grigory turned on us the first time—completely reliant on them, their power, their weapons. We would have brought down one insurgency, only to welcome in another. At least under Grigory and Olyessa, there was a structure. This rabble had no leadership. It would have been chaos, anarchy, until someone managed to murder their way to the top. And we would have been dragged into it."

"Seven thousand five hundred and thirty-two," said Branka again, her voice hollow. "In ten minutes. Seven thousand five hundred and thirty-two people dead. How could you?"

Masha caught Branka's gaze and held it. "Minister Branka," she said, her words sharp and crisp. "You gave me full authority to do as I saw fit to stop this insurrection. This is what I saw fit to do."

Branka seemed to rally slightly at the sharpness in her tone, her eyebrows drawing into a frown. "And how, exactly, did you believe that killing our biggest allies would assist in putting down the insurrection?"

Masha took a deep breath.

Giving the order to kill the gangs—she'd been perfectly calm then. Odd, how this was the part that made her voice want to shake.

"Everyone in the street will have seen what happened," she said quietly. "Everyone in the street will have seen the special op forces gun down every member of the Rims, the Blood Riots, the boyeviki, in a matter of minutes. They've seen what we can do. They're scared now, terrified. And—" she hesitated, for the slightest of moments. "And now I believe the pieces are in place to take down the insurrection."

"What's your next move?" Branka's voice held an undercurrent of fear.

Masha smiled, despite the sick tightness in her stomach. "We take out the barricades. Completely. In the same way we took out the gangs. We use the special ops first—I doubt the insurgents will survive that, but if they do, we'll move on to next options. We bring the ringleaders back for questioning, and kill the rest. Once the head is cut off the sand snake, the body may thrash for a while. But it will be over. And we'll be free from not only the insurgents, but also from the murderers who wished to take the mafia's place."

"I expect," said Branka slowly, "the Secretary General will look very favourably on whoever was instrumental in putting down this insurgency."

Masha raised her eyebrows. "I hope you're not insinuating I would take such drastic measures for personal gain."

Again, that spark of fear in Branka's expression.

She'd underestimated Masha, and she knew it. And she didn't know by how much, and it terrified her.

"Of course not," she said at last, hatred and fear battling in her tone. "I wouldn't dream of making such an insinuation."

Masha stood, still smiling slightly. "Is that all you need from me at the moment?"

Branka nodded, her face still haunted. "I—believe it is."

"Good," said Masha. "I have several matters to attend to." She nodded farewell to Branka and stepped out the door. Radka was waiting for her, as always, but Masha ignored her completely, leaving the girl to trail along behind her.

She couldn't stop and think, not for one moment. She couldn't afford the luxury of regret. She'd do what needed to be done, and deal with the rest when it was over.

When she was back inside her office, she leaned up against the door, legs suddenly weak. For a moment, she wasn't sure if she could handle the short walk from the door to the chair behind her desk.

But she could always do what was necessary, when it came to it.

She took a deep breath and crossed over to her desk.

For a moment, after she sank into her seat, she studied the information chips spread out on her desk.

She'd won her play that morning, yes. And she'd taken out the gangs. But there was one more thing she needed before she could make her final move. One more thing that would be by far the most difficult task yet.

As powerful as Branka, or Grigory, or Olyessa, or Vitali had been, none of them had been a match for her crew.

The crew she was now going up against.

She hesitated a moment, then pulled up her holoscreen and brought up video Branka had sent to her, earlier.

She forced herself to watch again, the entire thing. Even stripped of the shock, the images had the power to turn her stomach.

She'd been the one to authorize the police to work with the gangs to contain the insurgents. She'd known something like this would be a possibility, and she'd decided the risk was worth the benefit. This was the result.

But …

She paused, frowning, then flipped back through the still frames of the video.

What had happened there … she was willing to swear that what happened there had been under orders. She'd seen the way the police captain reacted to the message on her com before calling for the gangs, seen the way she'd spoken with the gang leaders before they'd come in.

Someone was giving orders. And she'd looked through Goran's files—it hadn't been him. He and she were the only two people who should have been authorized to give those orders.

She looked closer at the image. For just a moment, the officer who'd been recording had jiggled the vid screen, and there was a fraction of a second where he'd caught an image of the captain's com screen, reflected in her heat visor.

Masha expanded the screen until the foggy image resolved itself into something legible.

Then she sucked in a quick breath, dropping back into her chair.

She recognized, suddenly, the telltale signature in the corner of the com message.

She'd seen it twice before.

Once three days ago, just a fragment of it, caught in her scanner as it scanned the files of an assassin leaning over her bed.

She hadn't recognized it at the time, because it had been only a fragment.

But now, seeing the whole thing, she realized where she'd seen it first.

Months ago. In the basement of a university, on a program that would kill her and her crew and enslave the entire system.

Evka.

She felt as if all the oxygen had been sucked from her lungs.

She'd known, of course, that Evka was still alive. But she'd thought they had more time, that she'd finish her plan long before the woman would be ready to make her move.

But time was a luxury that she'd never had. And now it wasn't just a race to save Prasvishoni before it crashed and burned.

If Evka won, she'd destroy the system.

15

Lev dropped to his stomach as a smoke bomb sailed towards them, hitting the barricades and bouncing off back into the street.

He lifted his head cautiously and fired at the officer who'd thrown it, but the police had learned by now exactly how far away to stand, and by the time the blast reached her, it was hardly warm enough to melt the ice from her uniform.

Another smoke bomb flew through the air, this one landing on the barricade near him, and he jumped backwards as the smoke hissed out of it. A student and a street kid sprinted over, throwing a bucket over the top of the smoking cylinder, then pouring the contents of a water bottle through a hole in the bottom of the bucket.

Lev coughed and rubbed his eyes at the sharp sting of the residual smoke. From across the barricade, Jez shouted something about plaguing scum suckers.

And then there were startled exclamations from around him, and he blinked hard against the smoke, clearing his eyes in time to see the officers scrambling for their bikes.

They mounted up, and a moment later, were gone.

He stared at the students on the barricades around them, but they looked as confused as he was.

"Lev? What did you do?" Tae's voice came through the closed loop.

Lev tapped his com, frowning. "I didn't do anything. I assumed you had."

There was a moment of silence. When Tae spoke again, he sounded as uneasy as Lev felt. "The street kids standing watch outside the barricades said they're gone completely. They just—left."

"Hey genius," said Jez, coming up to him. "What did tech head —"

"It—wasn't him," said Lev quietly.

Jez cocked her head at him, then grinned, but he could see the worry behind her expression. "Maybe it's just been too long since any of us took a shower."

Ysbel joined them, and for a few minutes they stood watching the suddenly quiet streets.

And then, in the distance, there was a thick hissing and fizzing, like water boiling on a heatplate.

He glanced over at Jez and Ysbel.

Jez looked as confused as he was, but Ysbel's face had gone very pale.

"Somebody's shooting," she said, her voice tight.

"Lev, Jez, Ysbel—you need to see this." There was something about the tone in Tae's voice that tightened Lev's stomach.

When the three of them reached the shelter they were using as a conference room, Tae had his holoscreen pulled up and expanded. It took Lev a moment, as he stepped inside, for his brain to register what he was seeing.

And then it did, and he had to turn quickly away.

Beside him, Jez gave a choked curse, sounding a little like she wanted to vomit.

"What—" Lev began, and then had to swallow hard.

"It's the gangs," said Tae quietly. "The gangs, and the boyeviki. Blood Riots, Rims, all of them."

Lev forced himself to turn back to the screen.

It was over now.

It must have been over in a matter of minutes.

All that was left were the bodies, strewn across the street.

"Who did this?" His voice was strangely calm.

Tae had reached out unconsciously, supporting himself on one of the shelter walls. He looked almost as sick as Lev felt.

"I can't tell," he said, his voice hollow. "They had uniforms I didn't recognize. I thought you might." He tapped the screen and dragged the image backwards a few seconds, then froze it.

Lev leaned in, frowning, trying to ignore everything in the image except the uniforms of the people with the weapons.

Then he sucked in a quick breath and looked up. "It's the army special op forces. And from the look of it, the weapons Branka requested when Jez was still in the government have arrived." He shook his head. "No wonder that was over so quickly. They wouldn't have stood a chance, not taken by surprise like that."

"But why? Why would they take out the gangs?" Tae still sounded sick. "They were working with the government. Why—"

Lev could see on his face the moment Tae realized what Lev had already guessed.

"It's Masha," Tae said quietly.

Lev nodded. "It has to be."

"So," said Ysbel. "She's done what she's always wanted to do, finally."

"One of the things, yes," he said quietly. "She'll come after us next."

"Why?" Jez's face was sick, her voice almost a whisper.

"I don't know," said Ysbel grimly. "But look at what she's done. If all she'd wanted was to take out the gangs, she wouldn't have needed those weapons. These are what you'd use to take out a city block. Or a barricade."

"Lev?" Jez whispered.

He'd promised himself he wouldn't lie to her. And he couldn't break that promise, not even for this.

He met her eyes, and gave a small nod.

Jez turned back to the screen, and there was something about the look on her face that made a sharp, hot anger rise in Lev's chest.

Damn Masha. Damn her for hurting Jez, damn her for making him stand here and tell the woman he loved more than anything in the system something that would cut her open like a damn gutting knife.

"Jez." He slipped his arm around her waist. "I'm—sorry. But—Ysbel's right. What just happened, with the gangs—that wasn't just revenge. That was strategy. After a display like that, who will dare make trouble when she finally takes this barricade down? That was always what they had to avoid, the whole city rising up. That would have been more than they could control. Now she can do it without a whisper of resistance."

Jez stared at him for a moment, and there was a vulnerable look to her face, and for a moment, he wasn't sure if she was going to cry, or swear.

But she did neither, just gave a brief nod. "Yeah," she said softly. "Yeah, guess that makes sense."

For a moment, none of them spoke.

Lev was still swallowing back sickness in his throat.

He had no love for the gangs. He'd seen what they could do—what they had done.

But so many people. So many dead.

"Well," he said at last, forcing a smile. "I suppose now that we know her endgame, we can focus on a counterstrategy." He sighed. "We were hoping that more reasonable heads in government would prevail, and we could end this with a negotiation. But this is Masha's game now. And she won't stop until she gets what she's after, whatever that is."

"So if we can't negotiate, what's our other option? Die?" Ysbel's voice carried a grim humour.

Lev shook his head. "No. We stop her."

"How?" asked Tae, incredulously.

He shook his head. "We take down the government ourselves."

There were a few moments of silence.

Then Jez gave a shaky grin. "One thing about you, genius—you don't think small."

"Masha won't stop trying to kill us," he said quietly. "If she has the power to do what she did, she certainly has the power to block any attempt at negotiations. I don't know what her game is, and I don't know what she's after, but keeping us alive doesn't seem to be part of it. We're almost out of food and supplies as it is. Even if we could convince her not to kill us, what we're fighting—the police killing street kids, killing protesters, crackdowns in the poor parts of town—it won't stop." He shook his head. "I would have preferred a peaceful solution. But—I don't think that's an option anymore."

16

Jez, day 8, early

"What the hell's taking them?" The girl's words came out as a white puff in the dark of the frosty morning.

Jez grinned at the kid—Nadia, she was pretty sure her name was. One of Felix's. "Not nervous, are you?"

The girl scowled. Jez gave her a wink, and she turned away, muttering something sour.

"You know," said Ysbel to the girl over her shoulder as she passed behind them, "You can tell Jez to piss off if you want. That's usually how I deal with it."

"She says that," said Jez in an exaggerated whisper. "But really, she thinks I'm hot. Flirts with me all the time."

"Piss off," Ysbel growled. Jez snickered.

Every muscle in her damn body was pulled as tight as a suspension-wire on a ship, and prickles of anticipation danced up and down her spine.

Masha was planning to damn well kill them. Not by accident, not because some part of the plan had gone wrong.

This was the plan.

She could still see the look on Masha's face in the tiny hotel room that had been their prison on the casino ship however many weeks ago, the haggard weariness in her face, the greyish tinge to her skin, the pain behind her calm expression. *"I'm not good at trusting people. So don't screw this one up for me, OK?"* Jez had said. And Masha looked at her, and for an instant, Jez saw behind the bland mask she wore. For an instant, she'd seen a real person behind Masha's calm exterior. Someone desperate, hurting, unsure. Afraid.

She'd seen her own damn self.

Because hell, probably the rest of the crew should have given up on her a long damn time ago too, and they hadn't. And—well, she couldn't bear to give up on Masha, either.

And she'd been damn well taken in. She'd thought she'd learned her lesson, but she hadn't. All it had taken were some damn idiots to care about her when they really probably shouldn't have, and suddenly she was the same gullible innocent she'd been as a kid.

The thought was like a splinter of steel working its way into her chest.

She closed her eyes for a moment and took a deep breath, because she didn't have time to deal with this right now.

"They're on their way." Tae's voice through the com was low and strained.

Despite everything, she could feel the adrenalin-grin spreading its way across her face as she opened her eyes.

She crawled on her stomach to the edge of the barricades and peered over.

The streets in front of them were still dark. She couldn't see much of anything through the cold morning mist, except for the dim glow of streetlamps. Probably wouldn't have been able to hear anything either, except they'd spent the whole damn night getting ready, and at this point every single one of her nerves was strung so tight that she'd probably have been able to hear a swamp-rat skittering across the cement three blocks away.

And she sure as hell could hear the unmistakable sound of the special op forces approaching.

They were much quieter than a group of probably a hundred soldiers with heavy weaponry and guns should be. But there was the small scuff of boots against cement, a whispered command, the soft sound of breathing. The ineffable sense of too many people in too small of a space.

And then she saw them.

They appeared from the mist like damn ghosts, their tactical gear the same greyish-white as the fog. Their faces were obscured by heat visors, their gloved hands clasped around long, deadly looking laser guns and heat rifles. They didn't speak, simply moved into position. The first row of soldiers dropped to one knee, levelling their high-powered laser rifles, and allowing the row behind them to raise rifles into place as well.

And in the centre, between them …

Jez sucked in a quick breath as the weapon rolled into place.

It was an ion cannon, but obviously designed for street fighting. It looked, honestly, more like a ship's cannon than anything else. Even in space, if she saw something like that pointed in her direction, it would have scared the living hell out of her.

This could take down a barricade without even trying.

Nadia's breath hissed in through her teeth.

No wonder they'd been able to wipe out the gangs in minutes. Everything about these soldiers said they were here for one purpose —killing as many people as possible with as little fuss as possible.

She swallowed down the bitter taste of fear.

Waiting was hell. All she wanted was to do something—anything, really. But there wasn't a single thing she could do right now that would make a damn difference.

For one endless moment, there was no movement at all, the scene frozen like a still-screen.

"On my count." The terse command cut through the mist like a knife. "Three."

The gunners pulled the weapon up with practiced ease. Jez's heart was pounding so fast she was almost dizzy.

"Two."

They locked it into place.

Damn this to hell. Damn all of this to hell, there was something about standing in front of an ion cannon when it was loaded and aimed at you—

"One."

There was a moment for an intake of breath.

"Fire."

The gunners hit the lever, and the soldiers bent over their rifles.

Nothing.

The soldiers stopped, confusion evident in their movements, and Jez blew out her breath, her entire body going shaky with relief.

"Think you took them by surprise, tech-head," she whispered into her com.

"It worked?" Tae sounded almost desperate.

Jez glanced out into the streets. The soldiers had yanked up their weapons, turning them over, fiddling with the controls. The gunners were bent over around the massive gun, postures tense.

"Well, considering the fact I'd be a damn red mist right now if it hadn't—" she drawled.

There was a bitten-off curse that sounded like Lev's, and she felt a momentary twinge of guilt. When she'd come out here, Lev had already looked like he was about ready to pass out from the strain. The fact that none of them had slept a wink the entire damn night hadn't helped.

She winked at Nadia. "See, kid, that's why you want to be on the side of the damn tech-head who knows how to work with EMPs."

The soldiers were clearly professionals. It took them only a moment, apparently, to realize what Tae had done with his EMP pulse and readjust. They dropped their useless weapons at a sharp command from their captain, and in their place, pulled out long, deadly looking curved knives and blunt clubs with metal-reinforced ends.

But honestly, this was the kind of thing Jez was good at.

Well, being beaten to crap was also a thing she was good at, but hell, you'd never win a fight if you were afraid to get beaten up now and then.

"Get ready," she whispered into her com. "I think we made them mad."

Jez could see the fierce anticipation under the tension in Nadia's face.

"Guess you're not so mad about us being killers now, eh?" the girl whispered.

"Nope. Figure there's a time and a place for everything," Jez whispered back, grinning.

The captain barked another sharp order, and the soldier started forward at a quick jog. The ones in front carried grappling hooks, manual ones that attached to their wrists, since the electronic ones were now useless.

Jez grabbed a chunk of prefab from the pile beside her. Her whole body ached for action, and she couldn't stop her grin.

And then the first wave of soldiers skidded and stumbled, some of them losing their footing entirely, others flailing wildly, trying to keep their balance.

Jez gave a quick snort of laughter.

The thin slick of water they'd poured across the cobblestones the night before had frozen hard and smooth, and it was next to invisible in the mist. The soldiers who were still on their feet were trying desperately to stay there, and the ones who'd fallen were trying desperately not to be trampled.

And, of course, when Ivan and the others had poured the water, they'd measured the distance precisely.

Jez lined up, and hurled the chunk of prefab as hard as she could.

It hit a soldier who'd been struggling to his feet and sent him down again, knocking another soldier over as he grabbed at her in a desperate attempt to keep his footing.

Then a hail of projectiles flew from behind the barricades, slamming into officers, knocking back helmets, jolting weapons out of hands.

The organized advance had become mass chaos.

The second wave or soldiers had seen what was happening to their companions. They slowed when they reached the ice, stepping carefully around the fallen advance soldiers, their shoulders hunched against the projectiles, weapons held close to their bodies.

Even on the uncertain footing, they advanced steadily.

Moments later, the first of them reached the barricade.

Ivan and Vera had iced the front of the barricade, too, but the soldiers were expecting it now. They fixed their grappling hooks and started grimly up hand over hand, boots slipping and scrambling under them, trying unsuccessfully for purchase on the slippery surface.

Nadia tensed, tightening her grip on the short iron bar in her hands.

The first soldier's head appeared above the barricades, and the kid swung. The soldier crumpled, blood streaming from the side of her face, and slid heavily to the ground, knocking two other soldiers loose as she fell.

Jez grinned. "Not bad," she said, and swung her broken-off table leg at the next head to appear over the wall.

All along the barricade, grim street kids and students were holding their own against the soldiers coming up the barricades.

But it wasn't going to last forever. These soldiers were bloody professionals, and already they'd found the place where the defence was the weakest and were focusing their attention there, while still keeping pressure on the rest of the barricade so the defenders couldn't afford to focus their efforts.

"You stay here," Jez hissed to Nadia, and she jumped to her feet and sprinted along the top of the barricade to where the soldiers' attack was strongest. She dropped beside Dmitri, who was swinging a broken stool to impressive effect, and brought her own makeshift weapon down on a soldier's hand. The woman grunted in pain, and before she could recover herself, Dmitri dropped her with a blow to the head.

Jez grinned at him. "You're not too bad at this, you know."

His face was pale, but he returned her grin. "How much longer, do you think?" he whispered

The officers were tangling up at the bottom of the barricades—a few of them still climbing the wall, most of them trapped behind the fallen bodies of their comrades, who were struggling to get back to their feet.

Someone shouted, and Jez looked around quickly.

A soldier had dodged a blow from one of the street kids and

grabbed his wrist, and as she watched, he yanked the boy over the barricades.

Jez swore and jumped to her feet. "I'm going down there," she snapped into her com. She stepped to where two soldiers were clawing their way up the icy side of the barricade. There was a split second where they realized what she was about to do, but it was far too late to get out of the way. She grinned, and slid down the barricade into them. One of them managed to raise his club, but she kicked his wrist hard, and all three of them landed in a heap on the icy cement.

She kicked someone in the stomach, planted her elbow in someone else's throat, and scrambled to her feet.

Felix was already on the ground, his face grim, and Nadia and two other kids were sliding down the barricade as well.

"Jez. You need a hand?" Caz's voice was sharp through her earpiece.

She ducked out of the way of a fist, and someone grabbed the back of her jacket. She snatched up one of the fallen knives and twisted, slashing at her attacker. The knife wasn't enough to get through armour, but it was enough to cause whoever the hell it was to let go. She followed up with a sharp kick to the side of her attacker's knee, and the soldier grunted with pain as he went down.

"Wouldn't say no to it," Jez panted. She stumbled forward, the spikes set into her boots keeping her from losing her balance on the ice, and swung her table leg into the head of a soldier who'd lifted his knife and was starting towards Felix.

The soldier staggered, and she hit the woman's wrist hard enough to feel a crack. The woman's knife fell, and Jez kicked it out of the way and spun as another officer grabbed her by the elbow.

More street kids, and even some of the university students, had scrambled down to join her, and the entire street was turning into a damn kabak brawl. The soldiers were better equipped, with their clubs and knives and body armour, and better trained, but they were slipping on the thin ice, wasting precious attention staying upright. And everyone from behind the barricades had spikes on their boots and a damn lot of experience with people with bloody heat armour on trying to kill them, and the street kids were small enough to be unexpected.

Across from her, Felix shoved his way through the soldiers to get to where they'd grabbed the street kid. Jez ducked a blow to her head, grabbed the soldier's arm while he was still off balance from the swing, and yanked him forward, kicking the back of his knees at the same time. He went down, and she relieved him of his heavy club, kicked his helmet off with her spiked boots, and brought the weapon down on the back of his head.

She tapped her com against her hip. "Lev. How's Ysbel doing?"

"Can you hold them for a bit longer?" His voice was tense. "If you get into trouble, though—"

"Yeah. We'll hold them as long as we can," she gasped.

A club slammed into her shoulder, and she cursed, staggering sideways. The soldier stalked after her, raising the weapon to finish her off—and then a skinny figure stepped up beside him, shoving a knife hilt deep under the soldier's upraised arm, through a gap in the body armour.

He collapsed, and Nadia gave Jez a sharp grin, grabbing a clean weapon off the fallen soldier. "Told you we were killers," she said. Then she gasped, her pale skin going even paler.

Jez followed her gaze.

A soldier had Felix by both arms. The boy was struggling ineffectually, cursing and squirming to escape her grip, but the woman had raised her club, its metal end easily enough to break Felix's head wide open.

Nadia gave a choked curse and started towards him, but there was no way in hell she'd get there quickly enough.

"Sorry, Lev, time's up," Jez muttered. She yanked out a pistol, lined up, and, just before the woman brought her club down, she fired.

The soldier collapsed as the stun-blast hit her, and Felix staggered free, cursing. Nadia reached him a moment later, checking him desperately for injuries.

"Alright kids, guess it's not a surprise anymore," she said into her com. "May as well show them what we have."

Modded weapons appeared in the hands of street kids and students alike, and soldiers dropped around them, their heat armour no protection against Ysbel's stun weapons.

"What the hell—" one of the soldiers choked.

Jez grinned. "Guess it pays to be friends with a tech genius. Who knows a hell of a lot about EMPs, and how to mess with them."

He barely had time to look surprised before she dropped him with a stun-blast to the face.

From the alley beside the barricades, Ysbel could hear, faintly, the muffled cursing as the soldiers reached the ice Ivan had set the night before.

She smiled to herself grimly.

Beside her, Vera was grinning as well. "Guess they weren't expecting that," she whispered.

Ysbel gave a brusque nod. "But we're going to get something we're not expecting too, if we don't hurry up."

Vera nodded, her face going solemn again.

Behind her were a handful of students she and Dmitri had vouched for.

Ysbel gestured with a quick jerk of her head, and they started forward silently.

She had a map on her com, but she'd studied it the previous night for long enough that it felt seared behind her eyelids.

If she judged correctly, this next side street should bring them up behind the guns.

She gestured with her head, and the students followed her.

At the end of the street, she paused, holding up a hand, and when she was sure the students understood, she crept silently forward and peered out.

Half a dozen soldiers had stayed back to guard the weapons.

She grimaced. It was more than she'd hoped, but not unmanageably so.

She took a deep breath and tightened her grip on her pistol, then stepped silently out of the alley.

With the chaos from the barricades, she was almost close enough to touch the first soldier before he heard her.

He spun, his shout of alarm cut off as she fired. He dropped, and she turned quickly, firing a series of stun-blasts in rapid succession until the soldiers were lying senseless on the ground.

She tapped her com. "Alright," she whispered. "Let's go. We don't have much time."

The students stepped out from the narrow street, expressions grim. Vera and three other students began to gather the dropped guns, lashing them together to make them easier to carry, and the rest took the explosives Ysbel had handed out earlier and spread out, tipping them into the mouths of the weapons that were too big to be hauled back behind the barricades.

Ysbel watched them with affection.

Considering how they'd behaved in her chemistry class a few months back, they'd come a long way in being comfortable around her explosives.

She caught sight of Vera's face for a moment as she turned, the exhaustion behind the girl's eyes, the tension in her posture.

Still—they'd had to grow up quickly these past few weeks.

She bit back her anger at the thought, and set to work.

She'd thought, once, they were so young. They weren't anymore. Facing live rounds and gas bombs daily, watching your friends shot down in front of you, fear for your life a dull undercurrent to every moment—that wasn't something that anyone could come through unchanged.

They worked as quickly as they could, but with the sheer number of weapons, it was taking longer than she'd hoped.

"Ysbel." Jez's voice through the com was sharp with pain. "Got some coming back your way. Sorry."

"How many?" Ysbel snapped.

"Fifteen, twenty? We held them as long as we could, but—"

Ysbel glanced around quickly. The students were almost finished, but there were still guns scattered on the ground. "Hurry," she said in a sharp whisper. "We're going to have company."

And then the first of the soldiers came into view through the mist. He was bleeding, and his helmet had been knocked askew, but he'd shoved it back on enough that a heat-blast wouldn't get through it.

He stumbled to a halt as more soldiers appeared on either side of him.

The soldiers took in the sight—the ragged students, Ysbel, the stacks of their guns. Then a woman who must have been their leader yanked out her melee weapons, and the others followed suit.

"Charge!" she snapped, and they started forward at a steady jog, spreading out to block off the students' retreat.

"Go," barked Ysbel. "Back the way you came, take all the guns you can with you."

Vera hung back, glancing around quickly. She grabbed one of the students who'd stooped to pick up another gun, shoving him down the street, away from the approaching soldiers.

And then a soldier, who must have come around the edge of the building, appeared from the mist behind Vera. Before Ysbel could shout, he'd grabbed the girl by the elbow and spun her around. She struggled, but in a moment he had her in a headlock, his knife pressed against her throat.

"Stop, all of you, or I cut her damn head off," he shouted.

The other students froze, glancing at Ysbel.

Vera, and the soldier holding her, were too far away for Ysbel's stun gun to be any use.

She gave a slow shake of her head. "Do as he asks," she said curtly.

Slowly, one by one, the students turned, raising their hands.

"You. Drop your weapon," the soldier snapped, turning to Ysbel.

She did as she was told.

He must have either seen the soldiers sprawled on the ground, or Jez had had to pull out her own weapons.

Ysbel held out her empty hands placatingly. "You can see I'm unarmed. Let the girl go."

"No." The soldier's voice was harsh. "I saw what you were doing. You'll disarm every one of these explosives. If any of them goes off, the girl dies. And when you're finished, you'll come back as our prisoners."

She hesitated for the briefest moment, and the soldier jerked

Vera's head up, pressing the knife harder. A thin line of blood appeared on the blade, trickling off the end and dripping onto the icy cement.

"Very well," said Ysbel. "I'll do it." She glanced over her shoulder at the students. "Don't move, any of you."

There was a cold fury hardening in her chest, but she kept her face completely impassive as she stepped forward, empty hands outstretched.

The leader gestured the soldiers to step back from the weapons, to be out of range if she were to try anything.

Ysbel took a deep breath and peered into the muzzle of the first gun.

The explosive had fallen far enough inside that it would be difficult to retrieve, but—

She glanced over her shoulder.

Vera would die at the first hint of anything but blind obedience on her part.

She sighed, and reached down into the mouth of the gun as far as she could, straining with her fingertips.

From behind her, she heard Vera's quick, laboured breathing, loud in the utter silence that had enveloped their small company.

Her fingers touched the explosive, and by dint of straining painfully with her fingertips, she braced it against the inside walls of the gun barrel and worked it high enough that she could grasp it.

She pulled it out carefully, holding it out in an open palm as she turned, so the soldiers could see she meant no threat.

And with their eyes fixed on the metal sphere in her half-open palm, they wouldn't have the attention to spare for her other hand, or the small packet she'd shaken loose into it from the sleeve of her jacket as she worked.

She bent, hand still half-open, and placed the sphere carefully on the ground in front of her, then stepped back from it.

"Now the next," commanded the soldier.

Ysbel half-turned, as if obeying.

The soldiers were out of range at the moment, yes. But—

She flipped the gel packet over in her hands, tearing it open as she did so, and sprayed it in a thin line that arced through the air and splashed down on the street in front of the soldiers. They stepped back in alarm, but the looks on their faces were annoyance, rather than fear.

The soldier holding Vera opened his mouth to shout something.

He didn't have time to form the words.

Ysbel tossed the empty packet away from her and hit the controller hidden in her sleeve.

The *boom* that followed shook the walls of the building around them, knocking chunks of prefab from decrepit windowsills and sagging doorways and sending soldiers flying backwards like blocks in a children's game.

The officer holding Vera half-turned, staring at the place where his comrades had stood, his helmet knocked back from the force of the explosion, his jaw slack with shock.

His hand on his knife had slackened too, for just a moment.

Ysbel stepped forward, yanking a heat pistol from her boot, and shot him squarely in the face. He fell, the knife clattering to the ground, and Vera stumbled forward, coughing and choking.

Ysbel caught her and steadied her on her feet. "Are you alright?" she demanded, tipping the girl's head back to examine the injury.

It was only a scratch, and she felt suddenly weak with relief.

On the other side of the crater she'd blown in the street, the soldiers were dazedly climbing to their feet.

"Professor?" asked one of the students carefully. "What—"

"You see," said Ysbel with grim satisfaction. "This is what I warned you about when I was teaching your chemistry class. If one of your experiments had gone wrong." She turned to the soldiers. "You can put your hands up now, and come in. We'll take you in alive. Or—" she shrugged. "I still have some of that gel left."

"You wouldn't actually—" one of the students asked, his voice mildly horrified.

Ysbel raised an eyebrow. "They were threatening my students. I don't like it when people threaten my students."

Vera stared for a moment at the crater in the ground, then put her face in her hands and began to giggle hysterically.

Ysbel sighed and gave her a small shake. "Alright, that's enough. Let's go. They'll be waiting for us behind the barricade."

When the students, with as many of the gathered weapons as they could carry, and the bound soldiers in front of them, had started off down the street, Ysbel replaced the explosive she'd removed from the mouth of the gun and followed, dragging the rest of the unconscious soldiers behind her with an antigrav. Outside the barricade, she paused for long enough to hit the controller for the explosives they'd planted in the cannons.

The explosion that followed, as she slipped into the barricade, was loud enough to make her ears ring.

Vera was waiting for her just inside. Dmitri had joined her, and had a steadying hand on her shoulder. Vera's face was haunted, and there was a smear of blood on her jacket.

"Thank you, Professor," she said quietly, as Ysbel came up to them.

"Like I said," said Ysbel. "I don't like people threatening my students." She paused. "Or my friends," she added quietly.

They ducked into the shelter. Most of the others were already there. Jez was sitting leaned up against a wall, and Lev, with gritted teeth, was fixing a bandage along a cut on her thigh. Her left arm hung limp, and Ysbel could tell at a glance it was broken, and at another glance that she and Lev had discussed this, and that Lev had wanted her in the medic tent to get it patched up, and that she'd insisted she wasn't damn well going anywhere until after their meeting, and that she'd won.

Ysbel smiled slightly as she took her seat on one of the rickety camps stools. Vera dropped to the ground beside her, putting her face in her hands, and Dmitri crouched next to her, his hand on her shoulder.

Vera's shoulders were shaking slightly.

Tae ducked into the shelter a moment later, Ivan close behind him. He looked utterly exhausted, the circles under his eyes dark as bruises, and Ivan caught him, his arm around Tae's waist, as Tae swayed on his feet.

They'd all been up all night. But Tae had been working non-stop to create and set the EMP device, and tune the implanted blocker to his and Ysbel's tech signature so the pulse wouldn't affect their weapons. It had been nightmarishly complicated, and she wasn't sure he'd paused for long enough to breathe.

He dropped wearily to the ground and leaned his head back against shelter wall with a long sigh. At last, though, he blinked his eyes open and straightened. "What—" he began. Then he must have noticed the blood on the collar of Vera's jacket, because he jerked upright. "Vera! What happened? Is she—"

"I'm fine," said Vera, with a weary attempt at a smile. "I—don't really want to talk about it right now." Her voice broke a little, and Tae's face tightened with worry.

"She's not hurt," said Ysbel quietly.

Tae sighed. "Thank the Lady for that, at least," he said, voice dull with exhaustion.

"How bad was it?" asked Lev at last.

Tae shook his head. "We lost five street kids, and two students. A couple dozen more injured, two or three who might not make it to tomorrow." His voice was flat and toneless.

"I'm sorry," said Jez. Her voice was quiet, and almost as grim as Tae's. "I—I tried to—"

"Jez. It's not your fault," said Tae. "We knew we wouldn't get through this without casualties, we all knew that. We did the best we could."

Jez nodded, looking away quickly. Lev put an arm around her waist, pulling her close, and she sagged against him.

"How many prisoners?" asked Ysbel.

"Seventy-two, as far as I know," said Tae quietly. "Which means they lost around twenty-eight. I don't think any got away."

"No," said Ysbel. "None got away."

She should probably feel satisfaction.

She wasn't sure why now, she simply felt sick.

Finally, when they'd all stood and moved off to their various tasks, Ysbel walked over and knelt beside her wife.

"My love. Are you alright?"

Tanya nodded wearily. "Yes. I'll be fine. But I think I'd like to lie down, if that's an option."

"Of course it is," said Ysbel. She stood and helped her wife to her feet, and Tanya leaned against her as they walked through the gates of the university, and into the lobby of the administration building, which they'd turned into a long, open dormitory.

"Mama! Mamochka!"

Ysbel looked up in time to see Olya and Misko hurtling towards them. She scooped them up before they could plow into Tanya.

"Hello, my loves," she said, smiling despite herself. "Did you have fun with Dimas?"

"Yes, Mama," said Olya primly. "But Misko got into trouble."

Ysbel glanced at Misko, trying to make her face stern.

He pouted. "I don't like Dimas. I want Aunty Masha to watch us."

Ysbel closed her eyes for a moment. "I'm—sorry, Misko," she said at last, in a voice that was somehow steady. "Aunty Masha isn't here right now."

Misko gave a loud, aggrieved sigh, and slithered down from her arms.

Tanya had seated herself on one of the cots, and looked capable of handling the six-year-old, so Ysbel let him go.

"Mama?" asked Olya softly, once Misko had clambered up on the cot beside Tanya and was loudly airing his grievances.

"Yes, my love?" asked Ysbel.

"What happened to Aunty Masha?" Olya's voice was small. "I thought—I thought she was our friend."

Ysbel looked down at her daughter for a long moment, trying to gauge from the girl's face how much she knew. At last, she shook her head. "Olyeshka. I'm—sorry. Your Aunty Masha has ... something she thinks is very important. But to do it would have involved hurting people we cared about, so we didn't go with her."

"Does she hate us now?" Olya's voice was even smaller. "Is that why she's trying to hurt us?"

"I—don't think so," said Ysbel at last, quietly. "I don't think she hates us. I don't know why she wants to hurt us."

"Do you hate her, Mama?"

Ysbel looked down at her daughter again, the hurt and confusion in her small face. She reached down and lifted Olya into her arms, pulling her into an embrace, and Olya relaxed into her arms.

"It will be alright, my Olyeshka," she whispered. "You'll be alright, and we'll figure this out somehow. I'm sorry it's so hard."

She hadn't answered Olya's question.

She wasn't sure she could.

17

Masha, day 8, evening

Masha leaned back in her office chair, pressing her fingers into her temples.

On the holoscreen in front of her, she could hear the muffled shouts from the special ops troops, replaying in the video she'd watched at least four times.

She'd known that going after the crew would be difficult. And she'd made contingency plans.

But the ease with which they'd halted her first foray was disconcerting.

A setback, certainly. Still, she'd dealt with worse.

There was a tap on her door. She sighed, opening her eyes. "Yes?"

"Acting Minister?"

Radka sounded nervous.

Masha shook her head. "Yes, Radka? What do you need?"

"It's Minister Branka. She—she requests that you call her over the com. She said she's tried to call you, but she couldn't get through." There was a moment's pause. "Acting Minister?" The girl asked at last. "Is everything alright? Are you going to be—will there be—"

Masha sighed again.

The girl needed to figure out what she was doing in government. A question like that could get her killed.

"I appreciate your concern, but everything is fine. Thank you for the message. You may go."

For a few moments, the girl hesitated. Then, at last, her footsteps retreated down the hallway.

Masha shook her head ruefully.

When had she become someone who was so obviously soft?

She took a deep breath, and tapped her com through to Branka's line.

"Alonya." Branka was clearly furious.

"Yes, Minister Branka?" asked Masha. "I assume you called me to speak about the insurrection."

"Believe me, Alonya," said Branka through gritted teeth. "You and I will speak about the insurrection, at length. However—" there was a momentary pause, and Masha raised an eyebrow.

Whatever it was the Branka was about to tell her, she clearly did not relish the task.

"However, the individuals behind the barricade have contacted me. They wish to speak to you specifically, Acting Minister." There was ice in her tone, and for half a moment, Masha had to bite back a smile.

Of course. Jez would still have the codes to get through to Branka's private line.

She could imagine how that conversation had gone.

"Of course," she murmured. "I assume you will be listening in on the line?"

"Unfortunately, no." Branka's tone was even icier than it had been. "They have requested that the line be private. And unfortunately, it seems they have encoded their line such that our standard decryptors can't pierce it."

Again, Masha had to bite back a small smile. "Very well," she said. "Transfer the call through to my com line, then, please."

Branka didn't bother to answer. There was a sharp click of her com disconnecting, and then Masha's com buzzed.

She tapped it, pulling up the holoscreen, and looked into Lev's face for the first time in weeks.

"Masha." His expression was grim, and he looked exhausted, dark circles under his eyes and face drawn and weary.

Something tightened in her chest at the sight of him, but she plastered on the calm smile she wore like a mask. "Lev," she said pleasantly. "As always, I'm impressed."

He gave her a grim smile. "As am I. You've done well for yourself over the past few weeks, Acting Minister."

She gave a noncommittal shrug. "You're very kind."

He sighed, and for a moment she saw the strain in his face. "Listen, Masha," he said wearily. "Neither of us has time for games. I have something you want, and I'd like to bargain with you."

She raised an eyebrow and sat back in her seat. "You have something I want," she said. "What might that be?"

"Seventy-two special ops soldiers," said Lev in a flat voice. "They're here, in one of the university buildings. They're alive, at the moment. And they can stay that way, and I can send them back to you. Or, I can set off one of Ysbel's explosions in the building where we're keeping them."

She watched him for a moment. "And what is it you'd like in exchange for seventy-two lives?" she asked at last.

"Oh, I have a list," said Lev grimly. "But we can start with medical supplies and a week of cease-fire."

She couldn't help the spike of panic at his words. He must have seen it, because he gave her a sardonic smile. "Worried about us now, Masha? After you tried to gun us down, you're worried that one of us got hurt?" He leaned forward slightly. "You'll have to keep worrying. You'll get nothing from me. No information, no pity, no quarter. If wondering which of us you killed and which you only injured keeps you up at night, I damn well hope you don't sleep for the rest of your life."

She just watched him, without speaking.

He was right—the thought of who might be dead, who might be injured, would haunt her.

And, in the end, it wouldn't matter.

"So," said Lev at last. "Are you willing to negotiate? Or do I kill your soldiers?"

Masha took a deep breath, and leaned back slightly in her seat. "Lev," she said at last. "As I see it, you have two problems—first, convincing me that you would actually do what you're threatening to do. Tae's behind the barricade, and Jez, and Tanya. Even you—I believe killing seventy-two unarmed people is not within your typical repertoire. And even if you were to convince me of that—" she gave him a small smile. "You'd still have to convince me how the lives of seventy-two people who have served their purpose, although not, I'll admit, as effectively as I'd hoped, would convince me to change my plans."

"To answer your first question," Lev said quietly, "When I came behind the barricade, it was with the person I love more than you can possibly imagine. And unlike you, that means something to me. Since that day, you've been trying to kill her. Ysbel came back here with her wife and her two children. Misko is six, Olya's eight. You've killed people Tae cares about, deeply.

"I won't try to convince you of what we will or won't do to protect the people we love. But I will warn you that if you gamble on that assumption, you may find you're not holding the tokens you thought you were."

There was a coldness in Lev's tone Masha hadn't heard there for a very long time.

"As to your second point," he continued, still smiling that small smile. "You must think I'm very stupid if you didn't assume I'd taken that into consideration. So——" he gave a small shrug. "Here's why you're going to care about the lives of seventy-two people who were captured trying to carry out your orders. I know you have no loyalty, and no conscience. But there are people in the government who do. The Minister for External Defence, for instance. I'm recording our conversation now, as we speak. And when I kill the soldiers, I'll broadcast it live on the general channel, along with your commentary.

"The Minister for External Defence will get a front-row seat. Every soldier's family members will see it streamed through their private line. I've gone over the information on their family members —some have their very powerful connections. It might be worth looking up yourself, if you have the time. The police will watch too, of course, and the rest of the military. You've played this game a long time—tell me, how long will you last after something like that?" He leaned forward, placing his forearms on the surface of the battered table he was sitting at. "I've played this game too, Masha. And in this instance, I believe I'm holding the better hand."

She watched him for a while. He met her gaze, and she found herself trying to read in his expression what was happening behind the barricades.

But then, that wasn't what she should be concerned about at the moment.

She took a deep breath, and then let it out slowly. "Very well," she said at last, her voice soft. "I'm willing to negotiate."

Lev nodded grimly. "In that case, I'll send through my list of demands."

She raised an eyebrow. "I'm sorry, Lev. If this negotiation is to take place, it will have to be in person. Any discussion over coms will hamstring what I am capable of agreeing to."

"And I am afraid I'm not capable of agreeing to you coming behind the barricades," said Lev through his teeth. "If you can't negotiate, I'll happily tell Ysbel to hit the controller on her explosives."

"Lev," she said patiently. "You could do that. And you're right, it would damage my standing. But you'd lose your bargaining chip, and I suspect that you need one at this point. Tae will confirm what I'm telling you. You can encrypt the message from your end, but there's no way for me to send a return message in a manner that will not be traceable, and if we are doing this negotiation while I'm physically in the government offices, I will be forced to run each of your demands up through a committee. Your actions yesterday have marked me as a persona non grata at the moment. I believe an in-person meeting is our only option."

"And as I said, that's not an option." Lev's voice was flinty.

Masha took a deep breath. "I'll send another minister—a neutral party, who you could negotiate with in good faith."

There was a moment's hesitation, and she could see the uncertainty in Lev's eyes.

He must be more tired than he was letting on—usually he was better at hiding his indecision.

At last, though, he sighed. "And if I agree? What's my guarantee that this person wouldn't shoot us down the moment they were behind the barricades?"

Masha gave a small smile. "I understand that you are very well-equipped to keep anyone from shooting at you. And my security will be that, if for any reason you attempt to harm the minister I send, or take them hostage, I will instruct my people to shoot down, one by one, the families of the students who are currently behind your barricades with you. I have not done so to this point, because it would be politically inconvenient. But if you try to take a minister hostage, the calculus would shift."

There was a long moment of silence. At last, Lev gave a brusque nod. "I'll consider it. I'll let Branka know within twenty-four hours whether or not your proposition is agreeable. If it's not, I'll assume we have no further need for negotiations, and I'll set off the controller for Ysbel's explosives."

"And I shall sincerely hope that it does not come to that," murmured Masha.

He tapped off his com without responding.

She stared at the blank holoscreen in front of her for a few moments, trying not to think too hard about the painful jolt the sight of Lev's face had brought, the way something inside her twisted at the coldness in his voice, the enmity.

She'd made her choice, and so had he. And both of them were convinced they were correct. And both, apparently, were willing to commit atrocities to bring about their preferred ends.

She still wasn't certain he would have done it, killed the soldiers in cold blood. But she wasn't certain that he wouldn't, either. If Jez had, in fact, been killed—she cut off the thought quickly.

It wasn't a possibility she was willing to contemplate, and she would prefer not to admit that, even to herself.

At last, she sighed and tapped her com to a private line.

"Acting Minister Alonya." Zhenya's voice was the same as always, that hint of amusement, as if everything in the world was a joke that they were the only person clever enough to understand. But under the amusement, she heard a hint of genuine admiration. "I see that talent rises to the top. You've made the most of your time here, certainly."

"Thank you," said Masha. "I was calling you, however, to discuss a proposition."

"Indeed," said Zhenya, but she could hear the tinge of interest in their voice. "I believe you already owe me a favour."

"I do," said Masha quietly. "But I suspect that my proposition maybe as beneficial to you as it is to me."

There was a moment of silence on the other end of the com. At last, Zhenya said, "I assume that this matter would be simpler to discuss in person?"

"I believe it would," she said, smiling slightly.

"I'll be there shortly, then."

They arrived a few standard minutes later. Masha was still staring at the holoscreen when they entered, replaying how the tiny, ridiculous band of students and street kids had taken down the system's most elite military force.

She glanced up as they sat in front of her desk. She was expecting, perhaps, a smug look as their eyes caught the screen she was watching. But their expression was grave and calculating.

"I'd express my condolences," Zhenya said as they took their seat. "But I suspect they're not necessary. You've planned for this contingency, haven't you?"

Masha kept her face completely blank.

"I've underestimated you before. And I wouldn't have survived as long as I have if I made a habit of making the same mistake twice.

So." They leaned back in their chair. "What do you need from me?"

Masha studied them for a moment. "Lev contacted me," she said at last. "He has the hostages they took when the soldiers made an attempt on the barricade. He wishes to use them to bargain for various concessions—a period of cease-fire and medical equipment being among them."

Zhenya's expression was speculative.

"I've managed, I think, to convince him that this is best done in person, but I will need to send someone to negotiate. Someone with the ability to grant concessions, if necessary, and to bargain for concessions of our own. Someone I trust to carry out the interests of the government."

She could see the understanding dawn in Zhenya's eyes. "So," they said after a moment. "You want me to go to the barricades."

"Yes," said Masha. "And, as you might expect, there is— something I wish for you to do for me while you're there."

Zhenya nodded slowly. "And in return?"

"And in return—" Masha paused. "I have information that I believe you'll find very interesting indeed."

Zhenya raised an eyebrow. "If the information is sufficiently valuable, I believe we can come to an arrangement."

Masha gave them a small smile. "I'll let you judge that." She leaned forward, swiping across the screen of her holoscreen to the still-shot of the footage from the burning of the apartment complex. She expanded the screen, pulling up the signature on the police captain's com. "Do you recognize this symbol?" she asked softly.

Zhenya's brow creased in a frown, but they shook their head.

"Then I'll refresh your memory." She tapped her com again, bringing up another screen.

She shouldn't have access to this particular information, not with the security designation she currently possessed. But she'd spent a long time in the government, and there were some security designations that did very little to keep her out.

"Viernest Protocol," read the words at the top of the screen. And underneath, there was a list of names, with their com signatures beside them.

Zhenya peered closer at the last name on the list, then sucked in a quick breath.

"Is that sufficiently valuable?" asked Masha quietly.

Zhenya looked up at her, genuine concern in their face. "Evka," they said shortly.

Masha nodded. "Yes. She's going by the codename Myrni. She happens to be a former professor and mentor of our mutual friend Lev. She's exactly as deadly as her reputation suggests, and exactly as intelligent as her position as mentor to Lev implies, and I assume she's causing chaos because the worse things get, the more desperate the government will be for her solution. They'll give her whatever she needs to finish it."

Zhenya's face was tight with worry. "If you're correct—" they shook their head, lips pinched. "We can't let her finish the Protocol. That's the doomsday option. If you were telling Grigory the truth, everyone in the city breathed in her metal substrate—politicians, police, soldiers, everyone. Once her program syncs with the metal in their brains—once she's controlling the commands that will kill whoever steps out of line—she'll control the system." They paused. "She was a former mentor of Lev's?"

Masha nodded.

"You need to tell him."

She frowned. "I don't believe I do."

Zhenya leaned forward on the table, their eyes piercing. "You're very clever, Masha. So am I. But Evka is not a person we can afford to take chances with, if what you're telling me is correct. Lev knows her. He may be able to come up with a solution neither of us can see. Whatever happens, she has to be stopped."

"You honestly think Lev will agree to help us?" Masha snapped.

"To help us? No. But to keep that pilot alive? I think he'd be willing to do almost anything. You told me, Masha, that all of you breathed in the metal, correct? Even the pilot."

She watched them for a moment, her heart beating strangely.

Zhenya was right—they needed all the help they could get to stop Evka, or at least delay her. But the thought of warning Lev, while at the same time going ahead with her plan, felt like more than she could bear at the moment.

"I know what you're planning," said Zhenya quietly. "You're going to keep your crew alive, aren't you, right up until the end. And then you'll betray them in exchange for whatever position you're angling for. The more dangerous they are, the more valuable your final betrayal will be—that's why you're not as upset as you should be by this setback. A crew who's proven they can defeat the military special ops—how much would the powers that be owe the person who could bring them in? But you can't use them as leverage if they're dead. I've heard enough about Evka. She'll go after whoever is a threat. And if anyone in the system is a threat to her right now, it's not you or me—it's Lev."

They sat back in their chair, still watching her. "So, Masha. What will it be? I'll go to the barricades as your ambassador, and I'll get you what you need from the crew. And I'll warn Lev that Evka's involved in this somehow. Or, I don't go, and Evka kills Lev, and with no one to stop her, finishes the Protocol. She gains the power to kill, instantly, anyone who disagrees with her. You're left with nothing, and so am I."

Masha studied Zhenya for a long time.

There was a sharp ache in her chest, and a sickness coating the back of her throat.

But Zhenya was right. She did need her crew alive, right up until the moment she betrayed them.

It was all for a good cause. Once she was in position, she'd have the power to halt the bloodshed on the streets. No more pleasure planets, no more political prisons, no more mafia tightening its hold on the poorest and most desperate and most vulnerable. No more government programs experimenting on street children, no more families freezing to death in their own apartment, when the under-under-undersecretary over City Resources accepted a bribe from a gang leader and diverted their sector's energy to some favoured politician.

And to do that, to save the system, she'd sacrifice her crew. Although there was a chance that if she worked fast enough, she could save at least some of them.

She saw again Lev's weary, drawn face in her holoscreen.

Who had she injured, in this last attack? Who had she killed?

"Very well," she said softly, at last. "When you go back there, warn Lev. But don't mention the information came from me."

"Don't worry," said Zhenya, a small smile playing on their lips. "I don't wish to sabotage my own interests. I have a feeling your crew no longer holds you in high regard."

She gave them her blandest smile, but she wasn't sure even that was enough to hide the sharp stab of pain at their words.

Save her crew, or save the system. It had come to that, at last.

But then, that was exactly how she'd planned it.

18

Lev, day 9

"Twenty or so. Coming in from Solovey street." Jez's voice was sharp, her words clipped, and Lev jumped to his feet, tapping his com.

"Jez? You alright? I'm on my way."

"Relax, genius," she drawled. "We got this. Just give me specs."

Lev tipped back his head, gritting his teeth.

Jez was fine. Jez was perfectly capable of taking care of herself, even with a broken arm, and no damn sleep since—

He sucked in a long breath, flipped up his holoscreen, and pulled the readouts from Tae's sensors.

"Twenty-two of them," he said quietly into the com, trying not to let the fear show through his voice. "No riot gear, it looks like. If they have heat shields at all, they'll be minimal. Ysbel's mods should cut through them."

He expanded the screen, squinting at it. "As far as weapons, just army standard-issue. If I were to guess, I'd say this is a squadron that's working unofficially."

"Well then," said Jez, and he could hear her grin. "Guess we'll just have to unofficially kick their damn butts."

He closed his eyes again for a moment as the sound of a heat-blast crackled through his earpiece, and Jez swore delightedly.

Damn it, damn it, damn it. He did much better at this on a full night's sleep. And—he sighed, pushing the heels of his hands against his eyes.

He had no idea when was the last time he'd had a full night of sleep.

Not that he could anyways. The thought of what would happen tomorrow morning—what Masha might have planned, how she might sabotage the negotiations, how she might trap them or trick them somehow—was enough to keep him staring blankly at the dark ceiling long after he should have been unconscious.

He glanced back down at the readout.

Jez, and whatever motley array of street kids she'd rounded up, were showing up on the sensors now, their heat signatures bright spots along the barricades.

It had been thirty-six hours since the attack, and this was the third unofficial retrieval mission they'd faced. And of course, no one had been able to talk Jez out of helping, broken arm or no.

On the screen, the white flash of heat-blasts burst from both directions—defenders on the barricades, and soldiers in the streets.

He squinted closer at the screen and cursed. Five soldiers had slipped down an alley, and would be coming up behind Jez's position.

"Jez!" he said, tapping his com. "They're coming through an alley, and they have long-range rifles. They're going to try to take you out from behind."

"On it," said Jez, her tone disturbingly cheerful.

He shook his head and crossed to the door of the shelter.

He could see the fight from where he was standing. His holoscreen was still open, and he was monitoring it with half his attention, but the other half was fixed on the lanky figure lying on her stomach at the edge of the barricade, firing with what looked like absolute delight.

He glanced at the screen.

The five who'd come around would be in range any second now.

He gritted his teeth.

Jez knew what she was doing. Jez damn well knew how to take care of herself.

She tensed, then jumped to her feet, running in a half-crouch along the top of the barricades until she was in position to have a view of the soldiers as they emerged from the alley.

The first shot hissed out from the alley, and Jez enthusiastically returned fire. Lev bit back a curse.

Then he noticed a soldier, who'd apparently crept through before Jez arrived.

They were halfway up the barricade, right below where Jez was laying.

He hesitated for half a second, swore, and took off running.

If he shouted to Jez, he'd distract her, and it was only her answering fire that was keeping the soldiers from getting into position to pick off the street kids from behind the sheltering wall of the alley.

He scrambled up the barricade and threw himself down on his belly beside Jez. She glanced up in surprise as he yanked out his heat pistol and fired a blast directly in the face of the soldier, who was maybe half a metre from the top of the barricade.

The man crumpled, tumbling from the barricade, and Jez raised an eyebrow at him.

"Thanks, genius."

"Let's just take care of this," said Lev through his teeth. "Can you keep them busy?"

She nodded, and he slid backwards to the ground and sprinted around to where the edge of the barricade jutted out.

From here, he was pretty sure—

Yes. There was a crack between two of the buildings that formed the small alley where the officers were hiding.

He lined up the shot carefully.

If he'd been Tanya or Jez, he'd have been able to drop one of the soldiers, but he'd never pretended to be a sharpshooter. Still, a heat-blast from the unexpected angle did its work—a moment later, the shots from the alley ceased.

He pulled up his com screen and paged quickly through the scanner readouts.

Sure enough, four heat signatures were fleeing back down the alley the way they'd come, and one, heat slowly fading in the cold of the winter air, lay crumpled at the base of the barricade where Lev had shot him earlier.

The rest of the soldiers appeared to have concluded this wasn't a fight they could win. They were retreating down the street, leaving their fallen comrades lying on the cobblestones.

He closed his eyes and drew in a long, shaky breath of relief.

They'd have to find a solution to this—there were too many places on the barricades where someone could get behind you, if they knew the streets well enough. For now, the sensors gave enough warning to keep anyone from being killed, but that required someone to be watching the sensor readouts at all times. And with the number of people injured and exhausted, and the number of people required to hold back an attack, it was becoming increasingly untenable.

By the time he'd come back around the barricades, Jez was waiting for him, and his shoulders slumped in relief.

There were dark circles under her eyes, and her face was drawn with pain—all the scrambling she'd been doing couldn't have been good for her broken arm—but she grinned at him. "Not bad, genius," she said, and he put his hands on her waist, inspecting her carefully for injuries, then pulled her into an embrace.

She sagged against him, and that, more than anything, told him how exhausted she was.

"Are you alright?" he whispered.

"Yeah," she whispered back. "I'm good." But there was a tone in her voice that told him that she was approaching her limit.

He drew back, finally, and she gave him another weary smile. "Better go check on the street kids."

He nodded and kissed her, then she turned back towards the barricades, a hint of swagger in her step even through her obvious fatigue. He watched her for a moment, affection and worry struggling in his chest, then shook his head and started towards the university administration building.

With how cold it had been the last couple days, they'd all but abandoned the small outdoor shelters. Even the roaring fires didn't provide quite enough heat to combat the cold air that seeped in from outside, and—well, they were running out of things to burn, to be perfectly honest.

Among other things they were running short on.

Tae waited for him in the building's outer lobby. Through the arched doorway behind him, Lev saw bodies sprawled on cots, people too exhausted to know or care what time it was. They'd been on full alert since the attack, which meant no one had slept more than a couple hours at a stretch.

Even then, the barricades were large enough it was difficult to keep a full watch.

"Is everyone alright?" asked Tae, voice tense.

Lev nodded wearily and dropped into a seat. "This time, yes."

Tae rubbed a hand across his face, shaking his head. "Thank the Lady." He sighed. "I don't think Ivan's left the medic tent since yesterday. And since they shut off the heat to the university buildings, we're running out of furniture to burn to keep warm. When is the minister Masha sent supposed to arrive?"

"First thing tomorrow morning."

"And if we can't strike a bargain? You told her we'd kill the soldiers."

"I—don't know that we have another option," said Lev quietly.

When the hell had it come to this? He'd just decided there were lines he wouldn't cross, things he wouldn't do. He'd just decided having a moral code, whatever that looked like, was worth the cost.

And then this.

What was the moral thing in this situation? Let the soldiers free, and let Masha murder everyone behind the barricades, if they didn't starve first? Keep the soldiers alive, and feed them with food pulled from the mouths of starving street kids? Kill them—enemy soldiers, yes, but bound and helpless—to save the lives of the kids and the students who were trusting him to find a solution?

They were silent for a few moments. At last, Tae sighed. "People are coming to the barricades every day now. They've heard about what's happening, and they want to join us."

"How are they getting past the police?" asked Lev, frowning.

"They're sneaking past, some of them," said Tae. "Or using their connections to get the officers to turn a blind eye. Some are bringing supplies, but they're also bringing more mouths to feed." He shook his head. "I don't know what to do with them. I can't turn them away. If the police find out someone's come to join us, they'll shoot them. They risked their lives to join us. But—" he trailed off.

Lev drew in a deep breath and pinched the bridge of his nose, trying to stave off an exhaustion headache. "I'll keep that in mind when I'm bargaining with whoever Masha sends." He stood. "I'm going to get a firm count on supplies, see what we have left."

Tae nodded. The kid looked tired enough to sleep standing up, but he managed to blink his eyes back open. "I'll go talk to Misko. Maybe I can convince him to stop crying for a bit, let Tanya get some rest."

Lev shot him a look. "Don't give Misko all your food. You need to eat too."

Tae scowled, and Lev smiled ruefully. "At least give him some of mine, too. I'm not already sharing half of my rations with street kids."

Tae just shook his head and stumbled into the makeshift dorm. Lev watched him go, then slipped out the door.

He was in the back of the medic tent, sorting through the pathetically small pile of supplies, when a small sound made him look up quickly.

Jez stood there, watching him. There was a soft look on her face, tenderness and affection together. And suddenly, all the exhaustion of the day broke over him at once, and all he wanted was to collapse, Jez in his arms, and sleep for a week.

She came over and crouched down beside him. "How's it coming?"

He shook his head, too tired to come up with the words.

She gave a small smile. "Hey. Genius. It'll be alright. I don't know how, necessarily, but hell—" she shrugged wearily. "We've survived everything so far. Figure we can do it again."

She dropped into a sitting position and pulled him down beside her, an arm around his waist. He didn't resist, just collapsed next to her and let his head drop onto her shoulder.

"Genius," she said finally, her voice quiet. "Look, I'm worried about you."

Something about the tone of her voice cut through all the damn shields he'd built up for the last—well, so long he couldn't remember.

"I can't do this, Jez," he said quietly. "I—I can't. Everyone behind these damn barricades is counting on me to somehow outwit Masha, keep us all alive. And—I don't know if I can do it."

She was silent for a few moments, and he could feel the slow, steady rise of her breathing. Finally, she said softly, "You remember back in prison? When Tae thought it was his job to get all of us out all by himself, and when the prison lock system was a damn mess and he couldn't get through, he thought he failed all of us?"

Lev turned his head and opened his eyes, glancing over at her. She wasn't looking at him, just staring ahead at the tent walls.

"It's not just us anymore though, Jez," he said at last. "It's—" he shook his head. "It's Tae's street kid friends, it's those damn students, it's the whole city. Everyone who risked their lives to stop this. And if I guess wrong, make the wrong decision—they'll die. All of them."

Jez give a soft laugh. "See, now you're sounding like tech-head." She paused again. "Thing is, genius, we are who we are. We do the best we can, and then when the tokens drop, we see how we've come out." She turned a little, so she was facing him. "And who you are— well, you're a good person. You're—" Her voice wavered slightly, and she cleared her throat. "You're maybe the best damn person I know." She gave him that soft smile and leaned in, and he kissed her, desperately, as if maybe she was the only thing keeping him from going completely mad.

"I love you, Jez," he said, when they finally pulled back. "I—I love you." His voice choked slightly, because the words were so painfully inadequate.

Jez brushed her sleeve across her eyes, blinking. "Always figured you were a little crazy," she said, trying for a jaunty grin. "Anyway, you should probably go see your family."

Her words were so unexpected that for a moment he just stared at her, not entirely certain he'd heard correctly. "I—I'm sorry, what?"

She rolled her eyes. "I said, you should probably go see your family. You know, your mom and dad?"

"I—perhaps I should," he said slowly, still staring at her. "I'm—not entirely certain they'd want to see me, considering I was the reason they were thrown in jail, but maybe when all this is over—"

She sighed, pushing herself to her feet, and held out a hand to pull him up as well. "I mean," she said patiently, "you should probably go see them right now. And I'm guessing they do want to see you, considering they've been asking for you since they got here."

He was still staring at her blankly.

Jez snorted with amusement. "They showed up at the barricades half a standard hour ago. Thought I told you that. That's why I came looking for you."

It took a moment for her words to register. Then he had to reach out and catch himself on the tent wall, his legs suddenly too shaky to hold him.

"Genius?"

Jez's voice seemed to come from a long distance.

He took a deep breath and straightened, trying to smile through the sick horror twisting in his stomach. "I'm—I'm sorry."

She grabbed his arm to steady him, concern in her expression. "Hey. You OK?"

"Yeah." He took another deep breath. "I'm sorry. Yes, I'm fine. I just—I wasn't expecting—"

This. He hadn't been expecting this.

Honestly, he'd tried, very hard, not to think about meeting his family again, ever since that day he'd watched on the holoscreen as they were escorted out of prison and to safety, to a location he didn't know and hadn't asked.

And some small, cowardly part of him had been hoping it could remain that way—his family safe, he unaware of where they were or what they were doing. Impossible for him to find. It wasn't that he wasn't doing his duty as a son, he simply had no way to contact them.

He could still remember the look on his mother's face as they'd escorted her into prison. He hadn't been able to speak to her, of course, but he'd been able to watch through the plexiglass shield.

She'd been looking around frantically, face grim, fear and confusion in her eyes. It had been months since he'd visited them, because seeing the tiny, shabby apartment they lived in made him almost sick with a mixture of guilt and resentment—at the fact they were there, and he was in a government apartment, dingy as it may be, with all the food he could eat, because even though he sent most of his wages home, the government food-stamps were non-transferable.

At the fact he wasn't teaching at the university, and it was because of them.

He'd watched, swallowing down the bile in his throat, the heavy ache of tears in his eyes.

And then, just before she was led away, she'd caught sight of him. He'd seen her eyes widen in recognition, her face go bloodless. And
—

And he'd turned away, unable to bear looking at her.

Her last sight of him, as she'd been led away to her cell on his account, was of him turning his back.

Even now, the memory made his stomach twist.

"Lev? I can tell them you're busy. Hell, I'll tell them you got shot, if you want me to—I sure as hell wouldn't want to see my parents if the bastards showed up." She paused. "Not that they would. Probably forgotten my name by now anyways."

The concern on Jez's face somehow made it worse.

He should be thrilled his family was here. If he wasn't a damn coward, he would be.

He tried to force his mouth into a smile. "No, it's fine. I—should go see them. They've come a long ways."

She was just watching him, head cocked to one side. Her dark eyes held no condemnation—just sympathy.

"Genius," she said finally. "I don't know your family. But I know you. And—hell, figure you should at least go talk to them. Because whatever it is is gonna damn well eat you up from the inside until you do."

He closed his eyes for a moment.

"Yes," he said quietly. "I suppose I should."

He took another breath to steady himself and stepped around her to the door of the supplies tent.

She kept pace with him, slipping her hand into his, and he clutched it, desperately grateful for her presence. Even if it meant she would see the dirtiest, ugliest, most shameful parts of him.

He saw his parents at once, waiting patiently by the edge of the barricade, and his heart skipped strangely.

They were so much older than he remembered. His mother's hair was streaked with grey, and his father's hair and short beard were grey all the way through. Their clothes were warm, at least, but ragged, and there was a drawn look to their faces, lines of worry cut deep into skin leathery from Prasvishoni's harsh winters and damp summers.

They hadn't noticed him yet, and for a small, shameful moment, he almost turned around. But Jez was holding his hand, and that gave him just enough strength to keep walking.

"Hey," called Jez cheerily. "Found him for you."

His mother and father turned quickly, and he watched the blood drain from his father's face, saw his mother reach out a hand as if to steady herself on some invisible support.

"Lev?" she asked at last, her voice cracking slightly with emotion. "Is that you?"

"Yes," he said, swallowing hard against the knot in his throat. "It's —it's me. I—"

Damn it to hell, why did it have to hurt this much?

Jez squeezed his hand tightly.

"You—look well," said his father, clearing his throat. "I'm glad to see that. Your mother and I were worried."

His voice was a deep baritone, a similar timbre to Vitali, but rougher, less cultured. And Lev felt again that small, unexpected pang of bitterness.

Brother of one of the wealthiest men in the system. And his children had grown up in poverty, barely scraping together enough food to survive. Shivering under their thin blankets in their tiny, dilapidated apartment, much too small for all of them.

He heard Vitali's scornful words: *"Pity your father was still too proud to ask me for help. He was willing to sacrifice you rather than his principles."*

His father had chosen the right thing. He'd had a line he wouldn't cross, and he'd held to it. Something Lev was still trying to learn.

But ...

"Thank you, Father," he said, keeping his voice polite. "I was worried about you, also. But you're well?"

"Yes, we are. The apartment where we're living now is much more comfortable than the one we left. I understand we have you to thank for that."

He nodded, somehow holding onto his smile. "Not me, particularly. The woman I was working for. But I'm glad to hear it."

"I heard you'd been in some sort of danger," said his mother, shifting her weight slightly. She'd managed to paste a smile onto her face as well, and it was odd how easily he recognized the pain behind it.

It had been a long, long time since he'd seen her. Longer still since he'd visited her and not felt like it was a damn burden. Evka had been more of a mother to him than she had.

She'd probably known that would happen when she let him go, as a seven-year-old. And she'd done it anyways. He pictured Olya, her bright, inquisitive eyes, the solemn enthusiasm in her voice. She wasn't even family, not by blood, at least. Could he have given her up? If he'd thought it would make her happy, could he have?

"Yes, a little," he said, trying to keep his voice light. "But we made it through. I was working with an excellent team."

"Good," said his mother, trying again for a bright smile. "I'm glad you found good people."

There were a few moments of awkward silence. Jez was glancing back and forth between Lev and his parents, a skeptical look on her face.

At last Lev's father said, "And who's this young lady? I don't believe we've been introduced."

"Oh. Yes. Of course. I'm sorry." He extracted his hand from Jez's and slipped his arm around her waist. "This is Jez. My ... partner."

He glanced at her quickly as he spoke.

They hadn't actually discussed this, but he was fairly certain that, based on the sheer amount of time they'd spent kissing, she wouldn't object to the term.

She gave a small, happy sigh and leaned into him, her arm tightening on his waist, and he decided he'd surmised correctly.

"Jez, these are my parents."

"Nice to meet you," Jez said, with a jaunty grin in their direction. "Halfway decent son you've got."

They both gave her looks of polite puzzlement.

Lev bit back a quiet curse. He hadn't actually thought through this meeting. At least, not in anything other than his nightmares.

"Well, you seem like a lovely person, Jez," said his father. "I'm glad you took pity on us when you saw us stumbling around lost."

"Yes," said his mother, the brightness in her tone only slightly forced. "And I'm so glad my son found you. He—you both look very happy."

"Yep," said Jez. "Just gonna say, he's a damn good person to have around in a fight. Hell, I'd probably have been a bloody spot on the pavement just this morning if it wasn't for him."

There was a moment of silence.

"Ah," said Lev's mother, finally. "I'm very glad to hear that."

"It's good to have someone who has your back," said Lev's father, with a quick glance at his wife. Lev was struck, suddenly, by the affection in his look.

He'd seen it as a child, but he'd never really understood it. Not until now. Not until Jez.

"Well, and that's not all he's good at," Jez continued cheerily. "Because I'll tell you what—genius here is damn good in bed. And I've had plenty of lovers, so I'm speaking from a hell of a lot of experience. I mean, he can—"

"Jez," he hissed, cheeks heating.

"What?" she turned to him, raising an eyebrow. "It's true. Pretty sure I've mentioned it to you a time or two."

"Jez." He was speaking through his teeth. "I … appreciate that. But—"

She shrugged, turning back to his parents. "Just saying. If I was a parent, figure I'd want to know about my kid's talents."

Lev's mother and father were staring at them, expressions frozen.

He groaned inwardly.

"So," Jez said. "You live in Prasvishoni?"

"Just—just outside the city now," Lev's mother murmured, tone slightly stunned. "We did live in Prasvishoni. When … When Lev was—" She broke off, her voice trembling.

Jez looked between her and Lev. Then she shook her head, rolling her eyes upwards, and pulled her arm from around Lev's back. "Oh, for the Lady's sake, go on," she whispered. And before he realized what she was doing, she'd placed her palm between his shoulder blades and shoved him, hard.

He stumbled forward, caught off-balance.

And then his mother caught him in an embrace, and the familiar, homey smell of her, the feel of her arms around him, hit him like a physical blow.

He froze, unable, somehow, to pull away, the guilt swirling through him paralyzing, cutting off his breath.

"My son," his mother whispered, voice thick with tears. "My son. My Lyovushka. I was so worried—" She pressed his head against her shoulder, rocking back and forth like he was a small child that needed comforting.

He closed his eyes, fighting back his own tears, shame rising in his throat like vomit.

She should hate him. She should push him away, spit on him, curse him. He'd damn well sent her to prison, and his father, and his younger sisters and brother—

"My son. My baby." She stroked his hair with trembling hands. "I've missed you, my Lyovushka. I've missed you so much."

His breath caught in a strange sort of hiccup.

And then he was sobbing, choking, gasping sobs that shook his whole body. He squeezed her, his face buried in her shoulder, his eyes closed at the pain and the shame and the hurt of it. "I'm sorry," he choked. "Mother, I'm so sorry—"

"My Lev ..." She was crying too, her voice catching. "My Lev. There is nothing to be sorry for."

"I bloody sent you to prison. You let me go away to school, and I didn't even come back to visit you. I—"

His father stepped closer, pulling them both into an embrace, and Lev was suddenly completely enfolded in their arms.

Like he'd been when he was a child. Before everything. Before he'd learned to despise them, and given them reason to hate him in return.

"Lev," his father said at last, his voice barely a whisper. "My solnyshka. My child—"

Lev drew back slightly, wiping his sleeve across his eyes in a futile gesture. He could hardly see through the blur of tears.

"How—" he began, but his voice choked off into another sob. He swallowed, and tried again. "How can you still—I thought—" He blinked hard, and wiped his eyes again. "Look what I did. Look what I did to you. I thought you'd hate me. You should—You should have —"

"Lev," said his father, voice thick. "You're our son. There's nothing to forgive."

His mother seemed still unable to speak, her face stained with tears, her lips pressed together against the sobs, but she looked at him, her eyes soft, and shook her head, and he had to swallow hard to keep from breaking down completely.

"Your father is right," she whispered at last. "There is nothing to forgive, Lyovushka. There never has been."

And this time he did break down, the sobs catching painfully in his chest, and she held him, and his father put his arms around them both.

They talked for a long time. It wasn't about anything important—they asked what he'd been doing, and he told them—at least, the condensed and slightly sanitized version. And they told him about his siblings—his sister just younger than him and his brother just older had both found husbands, and his oldest sister had a new baby—and how mild the summer had been outside the city. Twice, he saw Jez or Tae and started guiltily, but Jez rolled her eyes at him and tapped through to his com, *Talked to tech-head. We have this handled. I'd damn well better not see you working until tomorrow morning.*

And he knew he probably should protest, but he didn't.

It was well past dark, and the cold was biting through their clothing and stiffening their muscles when Lev finally stood, scrubbing at the salt-stains on his cheeks. "Mother, Father. I'll show you where we sleep. It's not much, but ..."

His mother embraced him again. She couldn't seem to stop touching him, as if she were trying to make up for the years and years he hadn't come home.

The thought should make him feel guilty. But something about the past few hours had changed things. Changed him. There was still regret, lingering in the back of his mind, and sorrow. But—not guilt, anymore. At least, not for now.

"Lev," said his father, voice cracking slightly with tears. "Please. Tell us what we can do to help."

Lev sighed shakily. "Nothing, for now. Unless you know how to treat burns and broken bones."

Lev's mother turned to him, her face set and slightly grim. "Believe me, son. I've treated more than my share. Your father, as well."

He looked at her in surprise, then managed a rueful smile.

Of course. They hadn't exactly had the funds for a doctor.

"Alright. Ivan will appreciate that," he said finally. "But sleep first. You won't get much of that around here."

They looked at each other and nodded, and he led them to the long row of cots. Then he left, and wandered outside in the frosty air for a long time, staring up at the smear of stars, barely visible through the city's force field.

Finally, when he was shivering enough that no amount of walking would keep him warm, he reluctantly returned to the administration building and slipped through the doors.

It was pitchy dark, and the room had the faint tang of wood-smoke, cut with the bitter, chemical smell of the varnish from the ancient university furniture. He made his way by memory over to the corner where Jez would be sleeping, and for a few moments, stood looking down at her sprawled out on the cot they shared, a dark shape against the darker background.

He smiled despite himself as he pulled off his boots and jacket—they all slept fully clothed now, to conserve heat—and slipped into bed beside her.

She stirred, and murmured, "Genius?"

"Yes, just me."

She rolled over just enough to kiss him, and he kissed her back, and her hand slid down the side of his face, pausing for a moment at the rough salt-stains on his cheeks.

She rolled up on her elbow. "You OK?" He could hear the concern in her voice.

He cleared his throat. "Yes," he said finally. "I'm—I'm alright."

She tapped on her com light and studied him in its dim glow. Finally, she leaned forward and kissed him again, gently.

He tried to smile, and somehow ended up having to swallow back a sob. She pulled him close, and he ran his hand through her tangled hair and she brushed his tears away and kissed the places where they'd been. And when he finally fell asleep, tangled together with her, his head ached from crying, but he felt, strangely, lighter than he had in a long, long time.

Somehow, by the next morning, he'd managed to compose himself.

His father and mother were already hard at work in the medic tent, and he'd seen the relief in Ivan's eyes when they'd come. But it wasn't enough. They needed supplies, or people would start dying.

"Lev." It was Matija, speaking through the com. Their voice was quiet and tense.

Lev tapped his com, heart rate spiking. "Yes?"

"There's someone here. They say you're expecting them."

Lev closed his eyes and took a deep breath. "Thanks, Matija. Tell them to wait. I'll come out."

They'd discussed this all morning—going out would mean the possibility of getting shot, and he wouldn't put it beyond Masha to decide the easiest way to deal with this situation would be to take him out of the equation completely. But Jez and Tanya would both be up on the barricades with Ysbel's sniper guns, and it was still probably a better option than letting whoever it was behind the barricades.

"Be careful, OK?" Jez grabbed his arm, pulled him around, and kissed him, the kind of kiss that turned his stomach into pleasant knots and left him gasping for breath. He stood blinking for a moment as she turned and scrambled up the barricade to her post.

He gave a small shake of his head and forced the slight, unconscious smile from his face as he turned back.

"I'll tell you to be careful too. I'm not kissing you, though," said Tae, and Lev gave him a reluctant smile. Then he turned and ducked out the small opening in the barricade.

A bundled figure waited for him outside, under the dim light of a streetlamp. Through the early morning fog it was hard to make out details, and it wasn't until he got closer that he realized, with a jolt, who it was.

"Lev," said Zhenya, pulling down their scarf to reveal their face.

He could hear Tae's sharp gasp through the com.

Zhenya looked the same as they had on Grigory's ship—slender, self-possessed, the hint of a beard on their face, the traces of grey in their hair the only hint of their age.

"Zhenya." He forced his voice to remain calm. "I didn't know you worked in government. You move quickly."

Zhenya smiled. "I didn't, until a few weeks ago. I have our mutual friend Masha to thank for that."

"I don't recall having a friend named Masha."

"Ah." Zhenya studied him. "A shame when friendships break."

"If Masha sent you to convince me that she's really on our side, and this was all a misunderstanding, you're wasting your time and mine. So. Why don't we discuss the reason you came?" Lev's voice was hard.

"Of course," said Zhenya smoothly. "Business before pleasure." They paused a moment, glancing around. "Are you going to invite me in?"

"I think you know I'm not."

They smiled. "I suppose I can't blame you."

"I don't care if you do."

Zhenya sighed, their expression growing serious. "Very well." They paused a moment. "I am supposed to bargain with you. I'm authorized to offer you two days' ceasefire, fifteen self-powered heatsinks with enough combined BTUs to heat one quadrant of the university buildings, and enough food and supplies for a month. It's more than Masha wants me to agree to, but I'm authorized to give it."

Lev frowned in sudden disorientation.

He'd spent the last day and a half trying to figure out how to force Masha to give them the bare minimum they needed. And then, for Zhenya to open the bargaining with this?

Objectively, the offer was much higher than it should have been. Which meant either Masha was so desperate for a deal that she'd miscalculated—which he found difficult to believe—or Zhenya was indeed offering something that was near the limit of their authorization.

"And why would you tell me this?" he asked finally.

Zhenya made an impatient gesture. "Because I'm hoping you'll accept it in exchange for the soldiers you've taken prisoner," they said. They were watching him, their gaze intent. "And I'm hoping you'll take it as it's meant—as a token of goodwill."

Lev narrowed his eyes, and Zhenya shook their head wearily. "This is nothing to do with Masha. I had to barter my cooperation to tell you what I'm going to tell you."

"Don't try to make me believe that you have any interest in our wellbeing."

"No. But I have a great deal of interest in my own." They paused a moment. "Evka's back. She knows all of you are here. She's the one behind the gangs' attack on the apartment complex, and behind much of the disturbances in the streets. I don't know her reasons, but if the relationship between you and Evka is what Masha tells me it is, she'll be hunting all of you—and you in particular."

Lev stared at Zhenya for a moment. He understood their words, but something in his brain was trying desperately to make them mean something other than what they did.

He'd known Evka was somewhere, presumably working on repairing the damage he and the others had done to her Viernest Protocol when they'd broken into the university months ago.

But this?

"Why tell me this?" he asked finally, voice hoarse.

"Because if Evka succeeds, I'll be as much at her mercy as you will. I do not intend for that to happen." They paused. "And you're the only person I know of with a chance of outwitting her." They shrugged slightly. "I must admit, I've grown somewhat fond of the seven of you. The eight of you, I suppose I should say—give my best wishes to Tae and Ivan. But your deaths are entirely irrelevant to my interest. In the matter of Evka, though, I believe our interests align."

They straightened slightly, raising their voice to be overheard. "You're a hard bargainer. That's my final offer—and believe me when I say, I don't have authorization to go higher. Two days' ceasefire, covering today and tomorrow, the heatsinks, and food and medical supplies for a month, in exchange for the prisoners."

"I accept," said Lev at last, not taking his eyes from Zhenya's.

"Good. I hope you'll forgive my presumption, but I'd hoped we'd come to an agreement. I have the supplies waiting two streets down. Shall we discuss the logistics of the exchange?”

When Lev stepped back behind the barricade at last, Tae grabbed his arm. “Are you alright?” he whispered.

“I’m fine.” Lev’s tone was dazed.

He could feel, again, the sick jolt of panic as a knife, aimed at him, buried itself in Jez’s arm, as she collapsed, pale and shaking, on the floor of their apartment.

“Genius. What’s wrong? If I need to shoot the damn bastard—”

He blinked and looked up into Jez’s worried face. “I—I’ll tell you in a minute. We need to get the prisoners together, get them ready to send out.”

The sun had slunk almost midway up the horizon by the time they’d gone through the monotonous process of the actual exchange, moved the supplies in behind the barricades, and scanned them for bugs or traps.

“Alright,” said Jez, when they were finally finished. Lev could practically feel the tension steaming off her. “What the hell did Zhenya say to you? Because you damn well look like someone killed your grandmother.”

“Evka,” he said quietly. “She was behind the attack on the apartment building. Behind at least some of the assassination attempts when you were in the government, Jez.”

They stared at him. Ysbel looked shocked, Tae looked horrified, and Jez looked furious.

“I—don’t know what she’s up to,” he continued softly. “But I can guess. If she lets the situation get bad enough, they’ll need her Protocol. They’ll give her whatever resources she asks for. This is her life’s work, and she’ll see it done or die trying.”

“What do we do?” asked Tae. He sounded almost shell-shocked.

"You mean, besides leave the bastard in pieces in the bottom of a damn bomb-crater?" asked Jez. Her tone was sharp with anger. "She damn well tried to kill you, Lev. And I'll be damned to every hell in existence if she gets away with that."

Lev sighed. He still felt, a little, like the ground had turned suddenly soft under his feet. "We have two options, I think," he said finally. "First, we abandon our friends to go after her. We can't do that. So that leaves the second." He paused. "We take down the government as quickly as possible. We throw it into so much chaos that her work is paralyzed. And—I think I have an idea of how to do that."

19

Masha, day 10, evening

Masha jerked her head up in momentary panic, then blinked hard, shoving the heels of her hands into her eyes.

It felt like days since she'd had more than an hour or two of sleep in a stretch, and she wasn't sure how much longer she could keep going.

Zhenya had struck a much-too-generous bargain. Masha knew them well enough, though, to know they wouldn't have done it if it hadn't advanced their self-interest somehow, and beyond ensuring it didn't affect her plans, she had no interest in Zhenya's ambitions.

And if Zhenya had been attempting to buy their way into her crew's good graces, she doubted they'd succeeded. She'd seen the look on Tae's face when he'd come back from his meeting with Zhenya on the pleasure planet.

Tae would happily watch Zhenya burn alive.

Masha sighed, and looked back at her holoscreen.

She should go home, get some rest. She'd have to present a plan to Branka and a cadre of high-ranking ministers tomorrow, and that would be easier if she'd slept more than two hours beforehand.

But—

But Evka was still out there. And Masha still needed to go through every scrap of footage Zhenya had procured in meeting with Lev, trying to find any hint as to what her crew's next move would be. Because she knew Lev, and he almost certainly had a plan.

The images on the holoscreen were blurring in front of her eyes. She blinked hard, trying to bring her focus back.

She was crouched beneath a table, the splintery wood rough against her hand. She could smell the laundry soap her father used when he washed clothes in the brush of the tablecloth against her face. He must have washed it recently, because the smell was fresh and strong.

Almost enough to obscure the thick, metallic tang of blood.

Almost, but not quite.

A figure stood over the two bodies on the floor, turned away from her. There was a knife in their hand. Other weapons lay on the floor where they'd fallen, stained with blood.

Mari's heartbeat pounded in her ears, her stomach knotted so tightly it hurt. There were other people in the room, but she could only see them as shadows—the only person she could focus on was the silhouetted figure standing over the bodies, rimed in light from the sun pouring through the narrow kitchen window.

One of the bodies on the ground moaned, and the figure turned, considering. They crouched, lifting their knife …

Masha started awake, heart pounding, acid coating her throat.

She stood quickly.

It didn't matter, anymore, what was on the holoscreen.

She needed to get outside, needed the long walk back to her frigid apartment, the snow blowing sharp and cold against her face.

She shut down her screen with a quick motion, gathered the information chips into her bag, and stepped into the hallway.

She would have checked first, probably, if she'd been thinking. If she'd been less exhausted, less unsettled.

The only warning she had was the faintest *click.*

Even in her exhausted state, it was enough to send her diving for the floor.

The impact of the heat-blast knocked her sideways. The heat flickered through the heat shield she wore, burning against her skin, and then she was scrambling to her feet.

One glance told her they were coming from only one side of the corridor. There was still a chance she'd get away.

She wasn't finished with her plan yet. She couldn't afford to be killed, not now.

She yanked out her own heat pistol and fired off three quick shots.

Even the best heat shield didn't completely stop a blast, just spread it out enough that it wouldn't kill.

It would still hurt.

She turned to run. She was halfway down the hallway when she stumbled as something slammed into the back of her leg.

She tried to put weight on it, but her muscles wouldn't obey. Damn it to hell, she didn't have time for this.

It wasn't until she glanced down and saw the gutting knife embedded in the back of her calf that she realized what had happened.

It wasn't until a few moments after that that the pain registered.

It was white-hot and sickening, and she sucked in a shallow gasp.

She couldn't afford this, she couldn't afford to be killed, not now. But when she tried to take a step, her leg wouldn't hold her weight.

Her attackers were coming down the hallway towards her, faces grim behind their heat-visors. Another heat-blast hit her in the back, sparking and glowing as her heat shield dispersed it, and then another. Her skin under the shield burned.

And then an arm was shoved around her waist, and someone

yanked her after them. She stumbled, and they shrugged her arm over their shoulder, taking her weight off her injured leg.

"Run!" they hissed, and Masha leaned her weight on her rescuer's shoulder, and they took off in a stumbling run down the corridor.

Whoever it was clearly knew the building well—they dragged her down a side-corridor, and then another, and then down a longer, wider corridor that led to the main building lobby. Even at this time of night it would be unusual for guards not to be posted there.

Their pursuers must have come to the same conclusion, because their footsteps faded behind them.

Masha stumbled, suddenly dizzy, and her rescuer caught her and helped her gently into a sitting position, leaning her up against the wall.

"I'll be right back," they whispered, and even with her head spinning sickeningly, Masha recognized the voice.

"Radka?" she croaked, but the girl was gone.

She returned a moment later with a first-aid kit from one of the emergency cupboards. "Acting Minister, are you alright?" she asked as she knelt beside Masha. Her voice was trembling.

Masha swore. Her whole body felt shaky, and something icy was coating her veins. "What the hell were you thinking?" she hissed.

Radka pulled out a self-sealing bandage and a disinfectant spray and looked up at her stubbornly. "You were going to be killed."

"You idiot. I've told you a hundred times. That's not your damn concern. If you want to stay alive here, you learn to mind your own plaguing business."

There was hurt in Radka's face now, along with the fear, but her jaw was set. "You were going to be killed."

Masha swore again and took the disinfectant spray from the girl's hands, but her own hands were shaking so hard she almost dropped it.

Radka watched her for a moment, then gently took it back from her. "Here. Let me."

Masha closed her eyes for a moment.

There was no reason to react like this. If the kid had died, it wouldn't have made any difference in the long run.

But the shakiness in her muscles and the ice in her chest told her she didn't believe that.

It was because she was tired. She was exhausted, and stressed, and that was the only reason she was reacting this way.

Radka sprayed the disinfectant on her wound and sealed on the bandage. "Do you need painkillers?" she asked.

Masha took another deep breath before she opened her eyes. "No," she said, keeping her voice flat. "I don't. I have work to do tonight, and I don't need—"

"Acting Minister," said Radka in a low voice. "You are damn well going home. I'll call the guards if you won't go yourself, I'll tell them you're drunk."

Masha stared at her for a few moments in complete astonishment. Finally, despite herself, she gave a faint, exhausted chuckle.

"Alright," she said. "I'll go."

Radka stood grimly and helped Masha to her feet. "I'll come with you."

One glance at the girl's face told Masha nothing she could say would deter her, and she realized suddenly that she was too weary to try. So instead, she gave a faint nod.

"I'll—I'll have to—" Radka hesitated a moment.

"It's fine," said Masha wearily. Her head pounded dully, and she felt almost like she was floating, the pain in her leg the only thing keeping her tethered to the ground.

Radka put an arm around her waist, and Masha leaned on her, and they made their slow, painful way back to within sight of Masha's apartment complex.

"Are you alright from here?" the girl asked.

"I'm fine," said Masha curtly. "Go home. I'll ask Branka to reassign you. You're not working for me again."

"I don't care," said Radka softly.

Masha glanced at her. She was staring at the ground, but there was a stubborn set to her face that told Masha nothing she could say would convince the girl of the stupidity of her actions.

So at last she turned and stumbled her way into the complex, up the stairs, and into her tiny, grungy apartment. She hit the lock, and then the security lock, her hands trembling so much she almost couldn't manage it, then stumbled to her bed fully clothed, too exhausted even to treat the angry blisters around the edges of her heat shield.

She didn't remember hitting her pillow.

But even in sleep she couldn't escape the nightmares, and she watched her parents die, over and over, her hand on the splintery table leg and the smell of fresh laundry soap in her nostrils.

20

Tae, day 11

"Be careful, Tae," said Lev quietly. "I'll be on the com if you need anything. If there's trouble, get out—we can always come back another time."

Tae nodded.

Lev was lying, and they both knew it.

Their discussions the evening before had ended with the inescapable conclusion—they were running on borrowed time. The ceasefire ended tomorrow, and once it was off, their ability to leave the barricades would shrink to virtually nothing.

Their plan was simple, but born of pure desperation—he wasn't sure he'd have agreed to it in other circumstances.

Lev had information on where the high-ranking government officials put their family members when there was an emergency situation in the city. And they were going to take the building, take the people inside hostage. Force the government to negotiate, force them to disavow Evka and disenfranchise Masha, and possibly save the lives of their ragged revolutionaries.

Normally, he would have balked at the idea of holding innocent people for ransom. But he'd spent too long these last few weeks watching police and soldiers shooting at defenceless kids, and at this point—well, Lev's plan was probably kinder than what he'd have wanted to do, given the chance.

"You have the explosives?" asked Ysbel.

He nodded.

"Good luck, then," she said.

He and Ivan slid through the barricades and set off quickly down the almost-deserted street. There were few police officers out, and fewer civilians. Those who were in the streets had scarfs pulled low over their faces, shoulders hunched defensively, as if that would protect them from a heat-blast or a beating.

Tae and Ivan pulled their own scarfs lower, and tried to blend in.

Tae slowed as they got closer to the edge of the Northeast Sector. He could tell when they were approaching the police cordons—the short, sharp blip of sirens, turned on and off quickly in warning, the way people who were supposed to look like civilians, but were far too obviously officers in plainclothes, lounged at street corners and impromptu checkpoints, the way the very, very few actual civilians, who were desperate enough or unlucky enough to step out into the streets even now, glanced around in nervous, jumpy apprehension at every sound.

And then, ahead of them, the street was barricaded off.

He ducked quickly into a side alley, hitting the scanner on his com, and Ivan slipped in beside him.

Tae peered down at the scanner readout. "Thirteen officers, it looks like. The way the force field is set up, it looks like they're more worried about people getting in than people getting out. But they're not going to let us walk through." He blew out a quick breath. He had Ysbel's explosives, but blowing the hell out of a police barricade would likely be taken as breaking the ceasefire.

Ivan was frowning, and there was an odd tension in his posture. Finally, he glanced over at Tae with a quick smile that didn't reach his eyes. "Listen. I used to live around here, back in university. I—might know a way through. Follow me."

Ivan led them down the alley, out into the street, and a few blocks north. Then they slipped into another alley behind an apartment complex, and Ivan paused at the back door. He bent over the lock pad, frowning, and typed in a quick code.

The door clicked and swung open, and he beckoned Tae inside. "Friend's old place," he whispered.

Tae give him a quizzical look, but stepped through the door.

They climbed a dingy staircase, pausing at the fourth-floor landing. Ivan seemed to know exactly where he was going—he didn't hesitate on the stairwell, just led them down the narrow, mildewed corridor to the very end, where a grimy window looked out over the street.

He paused a moment at the window, facing away from Tae. At last he turned, a small smile on his face, but Tae could see the tension in his shoulders, the way his hands clenched and unclenched.

"There's a metal decorative ledge outside the window that goes around the building. It just so happens that the ledge on the building across the street has come off the wall a bit and swung out over the gap. As long as you're not afraid of heights, we should be able to get across between them. It's more stable than it looks." He paused again, and gave another faint smile. "Or it was. Either that, or five years ago I had a much lower sense of self-preservation than I do now."

He turned away again, his whole body tight.

Tae took a deep breath.

This was going to kill him. Seeing Ivan like this was going to actually kill him.

He reached out and put a hand on Ivan's arm. For a moment, Ivan's body remained tense. Then his shoulders dropped, and the expression on his face was thick with pain.

"It was your boyfriend, wasn't it?" asked Tae quietly. "The one who was killed."

Ivan nodded wordlessly, and put a hand to his face in a gesture that Tae recognized all too well.

"I'm sorry," Tae said.

Ivan brushed his hand quickly across his eyes and turned to Tae with a forced smile. "It's—fine. I should have gotten over it years ago." He cleared his throat. "Anyways," he said, clearly trying to lighten the mood, "the point is, he and I were stupid college kids, and we thought it was very romantic to visit each other by climbing across between our buildings. And—" he turned to Tae, and this time his smile was a little more genuine. "And this time, if I can use it to keep the person I love alive? Well then."

Tae managed a smile back, and Ivan leaned over and gave him a quick kiss. Then he turned to the window, fiddled with the latch, and pushed it open.

The freezing wind outside carried the scent of snow mingled with the faint, ever-present chemical stink of Prasvishoni air. Ivan frowned, peering out. "We'll have to be careful. It'll be slick, and who knows how much wear and tear five years has put on it? But—" he gave a wry shrug. "I think it's our best option, if we want to live through this."

Tae took a deep breath.

He wasn't afraid of heights. Hell, between the police and the gangs and the street kids who'd become killers, he'd hardly had the time to be afraid of things like heights. But—he glanced out at the narrow path Ivan had indicated.

The ledge on their building was crusted with snow, forming a slippery, diagonal slant bordering on vertical, and the ledge across from them, jutting out from the old apartment block, was shiny with ice. And the gap between them was a solid metre and a half.

"I'll go first," said Ivan, his voice calm and businesslike. "You follow me, step where I step." He paused. "Unless I fall. In which case, I'd advise finding a different place to step."

Tae scowled, the worry a tight band around his chest. Ivan chuckled, leaned in and kissed him again, then stepped out onto the icy ledge, balancing there for a moment.

Tae had to force himself not to look away as Ivan started along the ledge, kicking the snow with the toe of his boot as he went to form footholds.

When he'd gone a few steps, Tae climbed up as well, balancing on the ledge for a moment.

At the very least, if he was close enough, maybe he could grab Ivan if he slipped.

Although more likely that would send both of them tumbling to the ground.

He took a deep breath, steadfastly avoiding looking towards the street, much too far below him, and started along the ledge.

The wind caught at him as he stepped out, trying to tear him from the narrow pathway. The ledge was maybe twenty centimetres wide, and there was nothing to hold on to, only the bare prefab-block wall. He inched along, trying instinctually to be quiet, although in the blowing wind it was unlikely that the police below would be able to hear them anyways.

Ahead of him, Ivan paused for a moment at the gap between the buildings. He waited until Tae had caught up, then whispered, "I'm going to jump first. I think it will hold me, but like I said, I don't know what five years has done to it. I'll give you a signal if it's safe."

Tae gave a tight nod, resolutely avoiding looking at the gap. Ivan hesitated a moment, his body tensing slightly. Then he gathered himself and jumped lightly across the gap.

He lost his footing as he landed, and Tae choked back a curse as Ivan's feet slid out from under him and he landed hard on his stomach on the slippery surface. His hands scrabbled at the ice, and Tae braced himself to jump, as if perhaps, somehow, he could grab Ivan before he fell—and then Ivan caught himself, and lay still for a moment, panting. The narrow ledge swayed in the wind, dipping slightly at his weight. Finally, Ivan pulled himself up on his elbows and got carefully to his feet, glancing back at Tae.

"Alright. Jump, and I'll grab you. I don't know how much longer the ledge will hold."

Tae closed his eyes, offering up a quick prayer to the Lady on the off chance she was bloody listening, and then leapt across the gap.

He landed, and his feet slid out from under him on the icy surface. For one heart-stopping moment he was sliding towards the edge, then Ivan's hand caught his jacket and hauled him back up.

The broken ledge swayed ominously under them. Ivan grabbed Tae's hand and dragged him at a half-run along the narrow, slippery surface, finally pulling both of them up into the meagre shelter of a windowsill.

The ledge groaned again, and broke ponderously free from the building.

They sat frozen for a moment, listening to the shouts and exclamations from the street below as the ledge crashed down and the police officers leapt out of the way.

Then Ivan bent quickly, feeling for the latch on the window. It popped open, and they fell inside, panting.

Tae scrambled to his feet and leaned against the wall for a moment, his entire body shaking from a combination of cold and nerves.

Beside him, Ivan was shaking as well, but after a few long breaths, he managed a small laugh. "Either that was a lot more exciting than I remembered, or I truly had no nerves to speak of five years ago," he said.

Tae chuckled shakily. "I didn't realize how dangerous it was to be a government brat."

"I think that only applies if you're a very stupid government brat." Ivan's voice was amused, but still slightly shaky. He took another long breath and straightened. "We'll have to find a different way back, I suppose. But we're on the right side of the police cordon now, at least."

Tae shuddered. "Honestly, even if that damn thing hadn't gone down, I think we would've been finding a different way back."

Ivan chuckled. "I wouldn't have argued." He paused a moment, then leaned forward and gave Tae a quick kiss. And something about the combination of the shaky adrenalin from the jump and the warmth of Ivan's lips on his left Tae breathless, his legs so shaky he had to grab for the wall again when Ivan drew back.

"Tae? Are you alright?" Ivan's eyes were dark and concerned, and for one ridiculous moment all Tae wanted to do was pull Ivan's mouth back down to his and kiss him until they were both dizzy.

He closed his eyes and swallowed hard.

They had a damn job to do. There would be time for that later. Maybe when they weren't all about to die.

"I'm … I'm fine," he said, but he wasn't sure how steady his voice was, and when he opened his eyes, Ivan was still watching him with concern.

They made their way down the grimy corridors, almost identical to the ones in the previous building, down the dilapidated staircase, and through the long hallway to the main lobby. When they reached the door to the outside, Ivan paused. "Remember," he said quietly. "You belong here. You're not a street kid, you're some under-minister, or an undersecretary to an under-minister."

Tae nodded, his whole body still shaky with adrenalin from earlier. Ivan pushed the door open, and Tae followed him into the streets.

A police officer glanced up quickly, glaring at them as they stepped outside. "Where are you going?"

Tae felt his muscles stiffening, but Ivan said smoothly, "My apologies. Today's our day for the ration lines, and we barely had enough for the week. We'll make the trip as short as we can."

"If you were smart, you wouldn't make it all," the officer growled. "Hard to eat when your insides are cooked solid from a heat-blast."

Ivan raised an eyebrow, his voice taking on slightly imperious tone. "I hadn't heard there was a citywide curfew. Perhaps I should call in to my superiors, let them know about the new development."

The police officer scowled at him, clearly unhappy with this turn of events. "There's no curfew," she grumbled. "If people are idiot enough to walk out in the streets like this, they deserve what they get." She stepped back grudgingly, and they walked past her out onto the main street.

Ivan's pace was unhurried but purposeful, the walk of someone who knew exactly where they were going and how long would take them to get there.

When they were out of sight of the officer, they slipped into a narrow alley, and Tae let out a long breath of relief.

"What now?" asked Ivan, face grim.

Tae closed his eyes for a moment, feeling under his shirt for the bag of explosives Ysbel had given him.

How the hell had putting explosives in a bag around his neck become something he did?

"We can't put the explosives too close to the apartment block, because we need them to provide a distraction," he said quietly. "But they need to be close enough so that the EMP casings I put on them will take out the weapons of the guards in the building. So he gave us a list of potential places to plant them that could look like something that would be our actual target. And hopefully, with Jez running distractions up by the government buildings in the next few days, they won't think about checking here." He pulled up his holoscreen, and they bent over it.

"I'm a little familiar with that end of town," said Ivan at last. "I think here—the city transport infrastructure building. That will be the easiest to get to, and the least likely to kill someone when we set it off."

Tae nodded wearily. "Alright. I guess we get walking, then."

By the time they reached their destination, Tae's boots had rubbed a blister on one heel.

The building was squat and unimpressive, the prefab bricks cracked and crumbling, the roof sagging as if under the strain of too many heavy snowfalls. Tae studied it carefully from the mouth of the alley where he and Ivan were sheltered.

He'd spent too much time around Ysbel not to know how to take down a building.

"Here," he said at last, pulling out the bag of explosives. "You take half, and I'll take the other. You know where to set them, right?"

Ivan gave him a small smile. "Ysbel made very certain I knew where to set them."

Tae pulled out three of the explosives, tucked inside the EMP shields he'd created. They should, if all went as planned, trigger the EMP pulse at the same time the explosives went off.

"Meet back here when we're done," said Ivan.

Tae nodded, and they slipped off in opposite directions.

Setting the explosives was the work of a matter of minutes, and Tae sucked in a quick breath of relief when he placed the last one carefully at the base of the wall and turned quickly back to the alley.

When he reached it, Ivan was waiting for him. "We need to go," he said, his voice tight. "I think they've noticed us."

"What happened?" asked Tae sharply.

Ivan shook his head. "Nothing, yet. But—"

Tae grabbed Ivan by the jacket and shoved him backwards against the wall, the conscious part of his brain realizing only as he did it what he'd heard. A moment later, the ground at their feet erupted in a blast of flame.

"What the hell—" Ivan choked, and then Tae had dragged him forward, shoving him ahead of him, and they were running down the alley as fast as they could.

"Weapons drone," he panted.

He pushed Ivan down a side street and turned, grabbing for his heat pistol, but a blast from the drone knocked him sideways, flinging the heat pistol from his hand. He swore and scrambled after it, but Ivan got there first, snatching the gun as another heat-blast charred the cement in front of them. He tossed it at Tae, and Tae grabbed it out of the air, rolling onto his back to point it at the drone. A laser blast hit the street where he'd been, and he fired blindly. There was a hiss and whine of overheated metal, and he scrambled to his feet as the drone collapsed in on itself, falling to the ground with a metallic clang.

He turned quickly. Ivan had staggered to his feet as well.

"They'll send another drone," Tae snapped. "Once they figure out this one was shot down."

Ivan swore softly. "We'd better get the hell out of here, then."

Tae nodded, and they took off down the street.

Behind them, the ubiquitous screech of police sirens was drawing closer, and now Tae could hear the high-pitched, almost inaudible whine of drones.

He led them down alleys and through back streets, keeping an eye over his shoulder to make sure that Ivan wasn't falling behind.

There was no way in hell they'd make it back before they were caught.

He turned over his shoulder, raising his heat gun, and shot twice as a drone appeared at the mouth of the street behind them.

The drone exploded.

"This way," panted Ivan. He grabbed Tae's jacket, pulling him down a side street, and Tae followed without asking questions.

The police officers were close enough that he could hear their shouts now, over the whine of their skybikes. And then he heard, ahead of them, the low-pitched, gurgling rush that was so much a part of the noise of the city he'd almost blocked it out.

He knew, suddenly, where Ivan was taking them. He wasn't sure if he was impressed, or horrified.

Moment later, they emerged onto the banks of the river.

The concrete embankment was coated with solid ice, creating a smooth surface that fell almost two metres to the surface of the river itself. The river wasn't completely frozen yet, but thick ice edged both banks, and had formed a smooth sheet over the detritus that had accumulated along the bottom of the river over the years.

"This should get us past them," said Ivan grimly. "There's cordons set up on either bank, but I doubt they're watching the river, and if we stay low, they shouldn't notice us."

Tae stared down at the sluggish water, tasting sharp, acrid fear. Every damn year he'd hear of another street kid, or more than one, who'd died in the river—trying to cross it, trying to get away from police, just fallen in and been unable to get out. He'd almost lost a kid there two years ago. Sergei had been sobbing and shaking and half-drowned by the time he and Peti had managed to pull him from the river. And that had been in the summer.

Behind them, the sirens were growing louder.

"Just trust me on this, OK?" said Ivan softly.

Tae took a deep breath, and nodded.

"Keep a hold of my jacket," said Ivan, turning to the bank. "Your body's going to seize up when you hit the water. Whatever you do, don't let go of me."

Tae nodded again, grabbing the back of Ivan's jacket. Then they slid down into the icy river below.

The impact of their feet sent a sharp crack through the ice, but it didn't break, and they staggered on the slick surface. For just a moment Tae had the brief, irrational hope that maybe they wouldn't have to swim after all, maybe they could stay on top of the ice—and then the ice cracked again, and they plunged into freezing water up to their chests.

The cold was so intense that for a moment Tae couldn't breathe, his muscles frozen, the water like a knife against his skin. Ivan's head went under, and panic unfroze Tae's muscles, and he yanked up on Ivan's jacket, bringing him to the surface coughing and spluttering.

Ivan's lips were purple, but he managed a quick, strained smile. "Thanks."

Tae nodded, although he was shivering so hard by now he could hardly manage it. He'd never bloody learned to swim, and the water clutched at him, grabbing his clothes, dragging him down.

"Just relax." Ivan's voice was shaking. "I won't let you go under."

Tae forced himself to go limp, leaning his head back into the icy water against Ivan's arm and letting his feet slide across the icy surface below him.

Through the narrow cement embankments, he could see the blue glow of the police force field, and the tips of the helmets of a couple officers, leaning up against the wall near the bank.

He was shaking so hard he could hardly breathe, and the pain of the icy water cut into him, stabbing through his muscles, aching in his joints.

And then he glanced up again, and they were on the other side of the police barricades.

He yanked on Ivan's jacket with clumsy fingers, pulling them towards the edge of the bank.

The river drew them along relentlessly, but as they fumbled towards the edge, Tae grabbed at a heavy iron ring set into the cement, rusty and thick with ice. His hand was almost too cold to grab it, and when he did, the river nearly jolted Ivan's jacket out of his grasp, but he hung on grimly.

Ivan struggled against the current, and finally came up beside him, grabbing the ring as well and clinging on with both hands, and for a few moments they stayed there, panting and shivering.

They had to get out, soon, or they'd die here.

But it was hard to think about that when a strange, creeping warmth was replacing the numbness in his muscles, clouding his mind and making him feel, suddenly, sleepy and almost content.

"Tae!"

He looked up sharply. Ivan was watching him, concern on his

face. And the sight of Ivan's face, his blue lips and glassy eyes, brought Tae back to himself.

"We have to get out," he mumbled through frozen lips.

Ivan nodded. "I'll help you up first, alright?"

Tae was too cold and exhausted to argue.

Ivan bent, somehow making a step from his leg, and between them they got Tae's foot onto the frozen iron ring.

"Ready?" Ivan asked, and when Tae nodded, he pushed Tae up, and Tae managed to straighten, grasping desperately at the icy banks and finally catching his fingers in a crack between two blocks of cement. He clung there for a moment, his arms almost too weak to lift him, but finally he managed to haul himself up onto his stomach on the bank.

He turned back, and a sudden horror jolted through him.

Ivan's head was tilted back in exhaustion, his eyes half-closed, and as Tae watched, his grip loosened a little on the iron ring.

"Ivan!" he shouted. He scrambled clumsily to his feet, panic granting him new energy.

Ivan blinked his eyes open, and his voice, when he spoke, was faint, and a little dreamy. "I'll be fine," he mumbled.

Tae cursed, stripping his jacket off with hands that trembled so badly he could scarcely manage the buttons, and dropped down on the edge of the bank.

Ivan was too far below to be able to grab his jacket sleeve, even if his grip was strong enough to hold on.

Tae fumbled with the laces on his tunic, pulling it off over his head. His hands were too clumsy to form a knot, but by bracing one end of the material against the cement with his knee and using his teeth to pull it tight, he managed to knot the jacket and the shirt together and craft an awkward slipknot in one end. Then he dropped onto his stomach again and leaned over the bank. "Ivan!" He hissed.

For a moment Ivan didn't respond, and Tae's heart caught in his throat. At last, though, he glanced up, and Tae slumped in relief.

"Ivan. I'm going to toss this down. Put your wrist through the slipknot and hold on, I'll pull you up." He wasn't sure how he'd manage that, honestly, but he didn't have time to worry about it.

Ivan nodded weakly, and Tae tossed the trailing end of the jacket towards him.

He was never quite sure afterwards how he managed to pull Ivan up—all he knew was, Ivan would die if he failed, and so he couldn't fail.

At last, though, Ivan fell onto the bank and lay gasping. His face was grey with cold, and he wasn't shivering anymore, and that frightened Tae more than anything.

"You go on," Ivan mumbled at last. "I'll catch up."

Tae rolled over and shook him roughly by the shoulder. "Get up," he said through his teeth. "You're going to die."

Ivan gave a small, soft laugh that chilled Tae even more than the frigid water. "I'll be fine," he murmured, eyes still closed. "It's not nearly as cold as it was." His fingers fumbled at the buttons of his jacket, and Tae realized with sick horror he was trying to pull it off.

"Damn you to hell, Ivan," he choked. He stumbled to his feet and grabbed the front of Ivan's jacket. Ivan was taller than he was, and heavier, and Tae's muscles were still weak and shaky from the cold, but panic gave him a strength he didn't realize he had. He hauled Ivan to his feet, and Ivan stumbled, almost falling again, eyes still shut.

"I swear to the damn Lady, Ivan—you come with me, or we both die here."

At his words, Ivan's eyes blinked open. "Tae?" he mumbled. "No, you go back. I'll—I'll come later."

"You come, or we both die. Because I'm damn well not leaving you." Tae's whole body was shaking from cold, his teeth chattering, and he wasn't actually sure he'd be able to walk anyway.

Maybe Ivan had the right idea.

Ivan swayed again, and Tae grabbed him to keep him from falling. "Then—then I guess we'd better get going," he murmured, with a sickly attempt at a smile.

Tae made a choking noise halfway between a laugh and a sob, and somehow he forced his legs to move, and they stumbled forward.

It should have been about a twenty-minute walk to the barricades from where they were, but it seemed to take hours. He'd long ago lost feeling in his hands and feet, and by the time the barricade finally came into sight through a narrow back alley in the place that was least likely to be watched, Ivan was leaning on him so heavily Tae was practically carrying him, Ivan's skin cold under Tae's numb fingers.

They stumbled to a halt outside the barricade, and for a moment Tae stared up at it.

He'd never be able to climb that, and he was far too exhausted to think of a way around it—

Finally, he remembered his com and slapped it clumsily against his thigh. "Lev," he mumbled. "We're here, outside the barricades. North side, in the alley." His words were slurred and thick with cold.

"Tae?" Lev's voice was sharp with worry. "Ysbel and Jez are coming. What happened?"

Ysbel appeared on top of the barricade a moment later, Jez right behind her.

Jez swore and jumped down beside them, taking Ivan from him in a gesture that was surprisingly gentle. "Plaguing hell, Tae, you bloody trying to get yourself killed?" she asked through her teeth.

Then Ysbel was supporting him by the arm, half dragging, half carrying him through the gap in the barricade. She was muttering into her com, outer-rim accent thickening, like it always did when she was worried, and he could barely understand her words. Tanya must have, though, because she appeared in the door to the medic tent, took one look at them, and disappeared back inside.

By the time Ysbel pulled him through the makeshift door, a fire blazed in the centre of the room, and the heat of it told him that a blast from one of Ysbel's modded guns had likely been the impetus.

Lev came into the room a few moments later with an armful of blankets and dry clothing.

"Here," he said. "Let's get you into something dry." And Tae was shivering so badly, his mind so numb from the cold, that he hardly protested as Jez sat him down, yanked off his sopping boots and trousers, and shoved a blanket at him.

He managed to mutter, "Jez—" through chattering teeth, but she just gave him a sharp grin.

"There's being an innocent, and then there's being an idiot. You were always the first, but I never figured you for the second." She paused a moment. "Not most of the time, anyways."

He glanced over to see that Ivan had received the same treatment, and was huddled in a blanket close enough to the fire that steam rose from his wet hair. He looked so close to dead that for a moment Tae's heart almost stopped. Then Ivan turned his head slightly and gave him a small smile, and Tae slumped in relief and let Jez position him closer to the flames.

Finally, when he and Ivan both had stopped shivering enough to talk, Lev said, "What happened?"

Tae managed a tight smile. "We got the explosives planted. But we ran into a drone, and—" he trailed off, too tired to continue.

Lev came to stand beside Jez and Ysbel, and they were speaking in low voices, but he was too exhausted to make sense of their words. His eyes were falling shut despite his best effort, his head nodding.

"Tae."

He jerked his head up.

Jez leaned over him, face concerned. "Come on, tech-head. Let's get you somewhere you can get some sleep." She bent and slipped his arm over her shoulder. "Come on."

She pulled him to his feet, and he stumbled after her into a small, comfortable-looking room that had been fitted with two cots. Ivan was already asleep in one of them, face drawn and exhausted.

"University president's office," said Jez, grinning. "Only the best for you two."

Tae managed a small smile.

Jez helped him over to the cot, and he collapsed onto it.

"Call if you need anything, OK?" said Jez, but her face wavered, and he was asleep before he remembered closing his eyes.

Tae's whole damn body ached.

He groaned, his consciousness slowly trickling back, the memories filtering back even more slowly.

He was on a cot, in the university.

They'd survived, somehow, he and Ivan both.

He rolled over painfully, and sudden panic flooded through him.

Ivan wasn't in the other cot.

And then he noticed the figure sitting in the richly upholstered chair in front of the small fireplace, and he recognized Ivan's slender form, and his whole body went slack with relief.

There was something about Ivan's posture, though—his shoulders slumped, jaw set, the way his hands clenched the arms of the chair. He'd closed his eyes, and his face was haggard, drawn with exhaustion.

"Ivan?" Tae croaked, rolling stiffly into a sitting position.

Ivan started, opening his eyes, and turned to Tae. "You're awake," he said. But there was a pain in his smile that almost broke Tae's heart.

Tae pushed himself to his feet and crossed over to Ivan, steadying himself for a moment on the back of the chair. "Ivan," he said quietly. "What's wrong?"

"You mean, besides hypothermia?" asked Ivan, but the humour in his voice was forced.

"Ivan," said Tae again. He glanced around, and pulled up a chair next to Ivan, sitting so their knees were almost touching. "Please."

Ivan looked at him for a long moment, the smile fading from his face. There was a hopelessness in his expression that took Tae's breath away.

"Tae," he said at last, his voice unsteady. "I—don't know if I can do this anymore."

"Do what?" Tae asked, his voice coming a little harsher than he'd meant it to. "Ivan, what's the matter?"

Ivan tried to smile, but the way he was clenching down on his teeth told Tae more than words how close he was to breaking. He closed his eyes again for a moment, and something tightened in Tae's chest.

"I love you, Tae," he said at last, quietly. "I love you. All I want is to be what you need me to be. But—but being back here—" he broke off, voice choking. "Every time I close my eyes, I see Andres lying on the ground, bleeding from the mouth," he continued at last, in a low voice. "I have nightmares that one day that will be you, and I won't be able to save you, just like I couldn't save him. I wake up from dreams of you dying. And it's killing me." The raw despair in his tone cut through Tae like a knife. "It hits me sometimes, and I can't breathe, and the thought that maybe I'll freeze up when you're depending on me—I can't sleep, it scares me so badly. I—" He took a deep breath, dropping his face into his hands. "Yesterday, in the river. I—for a few moments, I was hoping I'd die. I was hoping I could get you somewhere safe, but—but that it would kill me."

Tae couldn't speak. He couldn't breathe, because the panic had tightened around his chest like a noose being pulled.

Ivan looked up at him, finally, and tried to smile. "I know it's selfish of me. I know you, Tae, and watching me die would hurt you. So in the end, when I'm not halfway crazy from the nightmares, I don't actually want to die. But—I can't be what you need, because I —I can't get past what happened four bloody years ago. I should be able to, but I can't. And you deserve someone who—"

Tae stood abruptly. "Don't you damn well talk about deserving." The panic and fear and worry in his chest had condensed into a white-hot anger. "Don't you dare talk about deserving. I will bloody well kill every damn police officer in this damn city who tries to hurt you. I will damn well burn this damn city to the ground, and I'll damn well burn bloody Masha to the ground for putting you into this damn situation." He was so angry his voice was shaking. "So don't. Don't even think about telling me what I do or don't deserve. Do you understand me?"

Ivan was staring at him, face slack with astonishment.

"I bloody want you, Ivan. That's all. I don't give a damn about what you think I need. You're what I damn well need, OK? I—" His throat tightened so he wasn't sure he could speak. So instead, he leaned in and kissed Ivan.

The kiss was gentle at first. But there was something about the feel of Ivan's lips on his, solid and real, something about knowing he'd almost died, damn it to hell, Ivan had almost bloody died—Ivan's lips softened under his, his hands coming up to rest on Tae's hips, and Tae leaned down farther, pushing Ivan back against the chair, deepening the kiss, his heartbeat pounding through his whole body.

When he finally drew back, he was breathing heavily, and so was Ivan. He noticed the clean lines of Ivan's body under his loose tunic and soft trousers, and then he realized he'd been noticing them, in the back of his mind, since he'd woken up.

Ivan's shirt was partly unlaced, and Tae could see the tight muscles of his chest underneath, his brown skin paler under his shirt.

He'd been noticing it for days, weeks, but he'd shoved it aside, because there was always something more important to do.

Damn 'more important' to hell.

He swung his leg over the chair so he was sitting on Ivan's lap, straddling him, and kissed him again.

Ivan's arms came up around his back, his hands pulling Tae close, and Tae could feel the tension in Ivan's arms, through Ivan's whole body. He wound his hand into Ivan's hair and tipped his head back, running his teeth down the tight line of Ivan's neck, and Ivan gave a faint, helpless groan, and another when Tae bit down on the place where his neck met his shoulder.

Tae had never bloody done anything like this before, and he didn't bloody care.

He brushed his lips down Ivan's throat, yanking his tunic untucked, and ran his hands along the warm skin of Ivan's waist. Ivan's hands clenched in Tae's hair, his arms tightening reflexively, and he pulled Tae's mouth back to his, and there was a hunger in his kiss that left Tae breathless and dizzy.

Finally, Ivan drew back, gasping. "Tae," he said, his voice thick. "I'm—I'm sorry. I—I'm not sure how much longer I'll be able to be a gentleman if you—if we—"

Tae glared at him, breathless and shaky. "Ivan," he said, when he could speak. "What have I done in the last ten minutes that makes you think I want you to be a gentleman?"

Ivan stared at him for a moment. Then he groaned, arms tightening around Tae, and stood abruptly, pulling Tae to his feet as well. He was swearing softly, but his tone was a mix of tenderness and desire that made Tae's head spin. He crossed to the cot in a few quick steps, shoving Tae ahead of him, then paused there, the muscles in his arms trembling as if he was on the edge of his control. Tae was pressed close enough against him that he could feel the tension in the lines of his body, feel the way his heart pounded.

"Tae," he said, his voice rough with strain. "Are you sure you want to—I don't want you to think—"

Tae grabbed the back of Ivan's neck, pulling Ivan's mouth to his, and pulled them both down onto the cot. They landed tangled together, and Tae's body was tingling, everywhere it was pressed up against Ivan's, and his heart pounded, and Ivan's skin was warm under his hands, and he'd never wanted anything so badly in his entire damn life.

When at last they sprawled out on the cot, panting and exhausted, Tae was floating, every muscle turned to water, his whole body aching contentedly. The warmth of Ivan's body, where it touched his, was an anchor.

"Ivan?" he whispered at last.

Ivan turned his head, and there was a softness in his smile that tightened Tae's throat. He rolled up onto one elbow, studying Tae with that soft look, then pulled him close, holding him like he was something rare and precious and treasured.

After a few moments, he buried his face in Tae's hair, his whole body shaking softly, and it took Tae a moment to realize Ivan was crying.

"Ivan," Tae whispered, his own voice choking a little. "I'm—I'm sorry about—about everything. I'm sorry for bringing you here, and making you live through that again. I'm sorry—"

Ivan took a deep breath, wiping his eyes. He brushed back the hair from Tae's face and kissed him gently. "Tae. I came because I wanted to. I came because I love you."

Tae closed his eyes for a moment. "I—I thought maybe I could fix it for you. Make it better. I wish I could, Ivan, I wish—"

Ivan pulled back a little, and there was still a hint of that pain haunting behind his expression. "Tae, no. It's not you. It—I don't think I can be fixed. I—I just wanted to be not broken. To actually keep you from getting hurt. To be there for you, and maybe I— maybe I wouldn't fail, this time—" He broke off with a soft, choked sob, dropping his head.

Tae held him, tracing his fingers along the lines of Ivan's back, and Ivan pulled him close, almost desperately.

"Ivan," he whispered. "I hate that it hurts you. I hate it. But if I can't fix it for you, I just—at least let me be with you in the middle of it. I don't care if you're broken, I love you. And I'll never bloody stop loving you."

Ivan closed his eyes and pulled him close again, and Tae relaxed into him. Because even if the entire damn system burned down tomorrow—he'd never regret one moment of this.

21

Masha, day 12, early afternoon

The alert on Masha's com beeped, and she jumped to her feet, ignoring the cold jolt of pain through her injured leg, jerked up her holoscreen, and flipped rapidly through the pages.

There.

She cursed quietly. "Fedir," she snapped into his private line. "There's someone coming in on a bike, under Pravital street. Get soldiers out there."

"Are you—" the man's voice was heavy with doubt.

Masha swore. "You'll do as I ask, or you'll never work in government ever again, do you understand me?"

There was a moment's hesitation. "Understood, Acting Minister." His voice was cold.

One person, at least, who'd oppose Alonya's being raised to full minister after this was over.

Of course, if they could survive the next few days, that would be irrelevant.

She was so close. Despite her exhaustion, despite Lev, despite everything, she was close enough to her goal she could almost touch it.

One final move. One last move between her and what she'd been working for her entire life.

But she knew her crew. They'd declared war. And they were perfectly capable of making certain that surviving the next few days wouldn't be a given.

She turned back to the screen, expanding it so she could see more easily.

The streets that led up to the back of the government building complex were flooded with officers and soldiers, but a figure on a skybike wove easily between the heat-blasts.

Masha narrowed her eyes, her pulse speeding up.

There was only one person in the city—one person in the system, likely—who could fly like that.

A fresh wave of soldiers appeared on the edge of her screen's viewpoint, dropping to their knees and steadying their weapons, and the air was distorted by heat as they fired. Masha found her heart was in her mouth, but whether it was fear that Jez would get hit, or fear that she wouldn't, she couldn't say.

The heat-distortions faded, and once again she could see the pilot. She was holding one arm close against her body, and the expression on her face was grim, but she was still on her bike.

Masha let out a shallow breath of relief, closing her eyes for a moment.

Then she glanced back at the screen, and cursed, expanding it farther.

There was something in Jez's hand, something small and glittering. As Masha watched, she drew her arm back and tossed it. It made a long, glittering arc in the air.

"Leave her," Masha snapped into her com. "Get to the explosive, now."

Half a dozen of the soldiers jumped to their feet and ran for the place where the explosive had landed. One of them grabbed it up and tapped it to her com, and Masha tapped through to the general line.

"Ysbel," she said quietly. "This is Acting Minister Alonya. I know you're ready to hit the controller on your explosive. Before you do, please know I've wired the signature into every heatsink you possess. They'll explode at the same time your bomb does. I don't know how many it will kill. But possibly enough to be a deterrent."

There was a long silence, and Masha's stomach was so tight it hurt.

And then, at last, Ysbel's voice came through the com. "Thank you for warning me, Acting Minister," she said, her tone heavy with irony. "I appreciate your concern. I do hope you manage to disable the bomb before Tae disables your hack."

Masha tapped off the com and closed her eyes, trying to keep her breathing steady.

Less than a minute later, a voice came through her com. "We have it, Acting Minister. It's disarmed."

She let out the breath she'd been holding and dropped into her chair, boneless with relief.

Every damn day her crew came closer to succeeding. She'd stopped them, so far. But all it would take was one moment of inattention, one miscalculation, one of her security measures failing …

She closed her eyes and tipped her head back against the back of her chair for just a moment.

Not long enough to doze off. She'd been doing that too frequently, and she couldn't afford it.

And she wasn't sure how many more times she could watch her

parents being killed and not go mad.

Finally, she straightened wearily and tapped her com.

"Alonya." Branka's voice was sharp.

She took a deep breath, forcing her voice to steady. "The insurgents made another attempt to bomb the government compound. I have people analyzing the explosive, but I doubt we'll find anything of value."

There was a moment of silence from the other end of the com. "What do you suggest we do?" Branka snapped. "You were brought in to solve this problem. It appears to me it's only gotten worse."

Masha closed her eyes for just a moment.

She'd been waiting for just this question. But somehow she had to force herself to say the next words.

"Since my negotiations with the insurgents, I—believe I have acquired information that could end this disruption completely."

"What is it?" Branka's voice was almost desperate.

"That is a matter I'm willing to discuss, but—only with the Secretary General."

There was a moment's silence on the other end of the com.

"Secretary General, is it?" said Branka finally, her voice dripping with scorn.

"Imagine what the Secretary General might do for someone who'd discovered an Acting Minister might have information that would end this rebellion, and brought her to him," said Masha quietly.

There was another long pause.

"Not nearly as much as he'd do for someone who brought him that information in the first place."

"Perhaps not," said Masha. "However, that is not an option available to you at present."

Branka sighed, but Masha could hear the strain in her tone. "Very well. I'll attempt to get you a meeting with the Secretary General," she said at last. "But if the information is not what you've led me to believe, the blame will fall on you, and you alone."

"Of course," said Masha.

She tapped off her com and stared blankly at the wall in front of her for a few moments.

So close. She was so close. Just a few more days.

She started to pull up her holoscreen, then hesitated for a moment. At last, with a wry shake of her head, she tapped a button on her com to summon Radka.

A few moments later, the girl tapped at her door.

"Come in," said Masha, managing to make her voice pleasant as she hit the lock.

A moment later, the door swung open, and Radka's eager, anxious face appeared in the doorway.

"Acting Minister?" the girl asked.

There was worry in her voice, and concern in her expression, and it took Masha a moment to realize they were for her.

She managed a smile. "I'm fine, thank you. Please come in, and close the door."

Radka hesitated, then did as she was told.

Masha took a deep breath.

She was being stupid. She knew that. And yet—

And yet, somehow, she couldn't help herself. As if maybe this would make some atonement for what she was going to do next.

"Radka," she said quietly, looking the girl directly in the eyes. "Something is going to happen soon. Something dangerous."

"And you're going to be part of it," the girl said. It wasn't a question.

Masha nodded. "Yes. And if anyone hears even a hint of it, I'll be killed."

"Why are you telling me, then?" Radka asked.

She looked so young and eager that it was easy to forget her stubbornness, her quick mind. But she had to be intelligent, or she'd never have gotten a job in the government, and it would behoove Masha not to forget it.

"I'm telling you so you can get out," said Masha softly. "Take a leave of absence. Tell them you're sick, whatever you need to do. Just get out. Get out, and stay out until things calm down."

Radka was still watching her. "I thought you told me not to stick out my neck to keep someone safe," she said. "Two days ago, you were yelling at me for that."

"I was right then," Masha snapped. "I'm wrong now. But either way, now you know. Do as you wish. Now, get out."

Masha sat for a long time after the girl had left, her breaths coming fast and shallow.

It didn't matter. She'd been an idiot, and perhaps she'd pay for it with her life.

But somehow, she didn't think so.

And somehow, the thought that, regardless of the outcome, at least Radka would be safe, was a sick relief so strong she couldn't bear to admit it to herself.

At last, she turned back to her desk and, with brusque, matter-of-fact movements, pulled up the footage Zhenya had taken from their negotiations with Lev.

For a moment, she hesitated.

But there was no point in putting it off.

She tapped through to a hidden file under the video.

Zhenya hadn't been wearing their own com when they met with

Lev. They'd been wearing Masha's.

Which still contained the mods Tae had installed. Mods that could grab Lev's com signature, when he was close enough, and from there, pull the com signatures of the others.

She had them, under the recording. And now it was simply a matter of copying them onto a chip, and their lives—or deaths— would be in her hands.

Her fingers were cold as she pushed a clean chip into her com and tapped in the command. Her whole body was cold, despite the coat she had wrapped around her shoulders.

Perhaps she could still save one or two of them. It was possible, if things moved as quickly as she hoped they would, that the Secretary General would decide to take them in for interrogation, rather than have them killed outright. And from there, it was possible that one or two of them might still be alive by the time she'd seized control of the government, and survived the messy, chaotic disaster that would be the transfer of power, even with all of her preparations.

It was possible.

But she knew, deep down, it wasn't likely.

It was to save the system. She'd prepared for this her entire life. There was no reason the memory of Jez's face in her holoscreen should haunt in front of her exhausted eyes like a ghost.

There was the soft *ting* from her com, and she looked down.

It was done.

She typed in another command, wiping the data from the recording, and took a deep breath, closing her eyes for just a moment ...

She was crouched under the table, splintery wood under her hands.

She wasn't alone, though. There was someone else with her, someone small and frightened, their tiny body shaking against hers. She turned her head from the awful scene in front of her long enough to gesture whoever it was to silence.

She didn't want to turn back, but she couldn't help herself.

Her parents lay on the floor, bodies still and bloody. Her mamochka's long brown hair was clumped and matted, thick with clotted blood. Beside her, her mama's shaved head was bruised and bloody, blood hardening across long gashes in her pale skin.

Her mamochka stirred, slightly, and the figure standing over the bodies hesitated, then crouched, a knife glittering in their hand.

And for just a moment, as they crouched, the figure turned their head.

"Olya?" Misko whispered, clutching her hand.

But she didn't speak. Because she recognized that face.

"Olya, what is Aunty Masha doing?" Misko said again, his whisper so quiet she could hardly hear it.

And in front of her, the woman, her battered pilot's coat now covered with spattered blood, looked appraisingly at the two still forms on the floor.

She raised her knife, and Olya—Mari—Masha—closed her eyes as it plunged home …

A loud knock on the door jerked Masha awake, and she started upright, gasping.

She brushed a quick hand across her eyes and cleared her throat. "Yes?" she called out, but her voice shook.

Olya, watching her parents die by Masha's hand. Like Masha had watched her parents die by Grigory's.

It was a dream. Just a dream.

"Acting Minister?" Radka's voice was high and frightened. "Acting Minister, I'm sorry to disturb you. Only, Branka called me and told me to find you. She said the Secretary General wishes to see you immediately. I'm to bring you to his office."

For a moment, panic flooded through her.

But this was what she'd been preparing for since she was seven years old.

Masha rose from her chair, supporting herself on the edge of the desk. She felt older than she should, and tired.

"Thank you," she said quietly. "I'll grab my things, and we can go."

22

Jez, day 12, late

Jez tipped her head back against Lev's knee and ran her fingers along the smooth lines of her heat gun, her foot tapping a rhythm against the hard floor.

"Do you think Tae's alright?" asked Lev. "He was still asleep when Tanya checked on them this morning …"

She glanced up. Lev's face was tight with concern, and his hands on her shoulders were still, but she could feel the tension through his fingers.

She grinned. "Ysbel tapped on their door ten minutes ago, and they still have ten minutes before she told them to be down here."

He shook his head. "I know. But it isn't like Tae to—"

She half-turned, twisting from where she was sitting on the ground in front of his chair, and raised an eyebrow. "Genius. Tae and Ivan almost died yesterday."

"Yes. That's what—"

"And now they're recovering. In a room. With a bed. Just the two of them. Tae, and Ivan."

There was a moment's pause. "Ah," Lev said at last with a small smile, and she could feel the tension drain from his fingers. He started rubbing her shoulders again, and she sighed blissfully, leaning back against him.

"Our tech-head is growing up, I suppose," said Ysbel. She was smiling too, holding Tanya, her arm around her wife's waist.

"Hey genius," Jez said, closing her eyes. "You think we should almost die? I'm starting to think that's the only way a person can get some alone time with their damn lover these days."

Lev's hands on her shoulders squeezed a little more tightly, and she gave a small moan as his fingers found the place where her muscles were knotted.

He leaned forward slightly, his mouth close to her ear. "At this point, I'm ready to do just about anything, up to and including storming the government buildings and assassinating the Secretary General single-handedly, if that's what it would take," he murmured. "But I'm warning you, we may need more than a day or two with a private room."

"You do realize that we're still here," said Ysbel dryly.

Jez opened her eyes a crack and grinned. "Figure you'd know if we'd forgotten you were here. Mostly because I wouldn't be wearing any clothes right now, for one thing, and—"

"I don't need to hear any more, but thank you," said Ysbel, even more dryly.

Jez closed her eyes again and sighed heavily.

Damn it to hell, she hadn't actually thought it would be easier to overthrow the damn Svodrani System government than to get an acceptable amount of private time with Lev, but apparently …

"I found my wife again, after not having seen her for five years, and I've been either stuck on a ship with you lunatics or trying not to be killed by some criminal mastermind ever since then," said Ysbel. "So you'll excuse me if I don't feel particularly sorry for you two."

Jez opened her eyes again and shot Ysbel a mild glare. Ysbel grinned and pulled Tanya in for a kiss, and Jez was debating relocating to Lev's lap for a similar activity when the door to the small repurposed classroom creaked open.

Jez grinned widely as Ivan stepped inside, closing the door carefully behind him.

From the look in his eyes, she was pretty damn sure her guess had been entirely accurate.

"Ivan? Where's—" Lev began.

Ivan turned, and gave Jez a level stare. "Jez. Tae is waiting outside in the hallway. When he comes in here, you are not going to say one. Damn. Thing. Do you understand me?"

Jez's grin widened. "Don't have any idea what you're talking about."

His expression didn't change. "Not one damn word, Jez. Not one."

"Wouldn't dream of it," she said innocently.

He gave her a last warning look, then stepped back outside and returned a moment later, his arm protectively around Tae. He was watching Tae with a soft look in his eyes, and Tae glanced up at him with a small smile, pulling him close for a moment, and Jez wasn't completely sure that either of them realized that there were other people in the room, or possibly in the entire system.

She found she was smiling, and when she looked up at Lev, he was smiling too.

"Tae. How are you feeling? Are you and Ivan going to be able to make it tonight?" Lev asked after a moment.

Tae blinked and looked over at Lev, and there was a soft, dreamy look to his face, under the usual worry, that made Jez's smile broaden, and for some odd reason, made something choke a little in her throat.

Tech-head deserved to be a bit dreamy, for once in his damn life.

And something warm and comfortable was expanding in her chest at the sight of him like this, dreamy and happy and not quite focused on anything but Ivan.

"I'm—I mean, I guess—I—" He cleared his throat and gave a small shake of his head. "Sorry, Lev. I—Yes. I'm—We're—"

Ivan pulled him closer and kissed his hair. "We'll be fine," he finished quietly.

Tae glanced up at him again, and again, Jez figured they'd forgotten about every other person in the damn system.

"Good," said Ysbel. "If it were up to me, you two could have some more time to … recover. But unfortunately—"

Tae glanced reflexively at Jez at Ysbel's words.

She gave him a small shrug, still grinning.

"Go ahead, Jez," he said resignedly after a moment. "You might as well just say it."

"Say what?" she asked. "Don't know what you're talking about."

"Jez—"

She shrugged again. "Don't have a single thing to say."

He scowled at her suspiciously.

She was grinning so wide it hurt, but she just raised an eyebrow at him innocently. "Anyways, if we're going to head out, figure we should probably do that at some point before tomorrow, yeah?" she said. "I mean, figure the bed will still be there when you get back."

Ivan shot her a look.

"Since you'll probably be pretty tired. Seeing as you basically just about froze to death two days ago," she added, still grinning. "Probably need to spend a bunch of time in bed. Warming up and whatever."

"Jez—" began Ivan warningly.

"So probably better get going," she said. "Right genius?"

Lev sighed and stood reluctantly, holding out his hand. She took it, and he pulled her to her feet. His arms slid around her waist, and she closed her eyes, breathing in the smell of him, the feel of his body, the rough stubble of his cheek pressed against hers.

She'd never realized, before, what it would be like to have someone like this. Someone who was just … there. When you needed them, and even when you didn't know you needed them. Someone who steadied you when the world around you was going mad, who you'd smile unconsciously just hearing their voice or catching a glimpse of them from the corner of your eye.

She'd always assumed she'd feel trapped, and crazy, and desperate. Like she always had before, when she'd thought about being with someone for more than a few weeks, because that would be like a cage, and even the thought of a cage made her heart start beating too fast with panic.

But the thing about Lev was—he wasn't a cage. She knew, somehow, that he'd never try to hold her for one second longer than she wanted to be held.

And so for the first time in her life, she didn't need to run away. She didn't even want to.

She sighed and kissed him on the cheek before she straightened, and he squeezed her tightly for just a moment. Then he let go, turning back to the others.

"Ysbel, Tanya, I assume you have everything ready?"

Tanya nodded. "I've talked to Vera and Dmitri. They know what to do."

"Alright." He looked around at them, his face tight with worry, and gave a small, humourless smile. "I suppose there's nothing we're waiting for, then."

By the time they'd slipped out from behind the barricades, the streets were pitchy black. Whatever Masha had planned next, it didn't appear to be an outright attack—a small contingent of police had surrounded the barricade again that morning, when the cease-fire lifted, but there were few enough of them that, with Tae's knowledge of the alleys, they were able to slip past them without their notice.

The night was clear, and there was no wind to blow the snow up around their faces, but the ever-present Prasvishoni mist curled around their feet as they walked, the snow crunching under their boots.

Jez shivered slightly.

Damn city was always cold. But something about the dark, foggy night made it feel even colder than usual, and the dampness seeped through her jacket and under her scarf, through her skin and into her muscles, chilling every part of her.

The fog was thick enough that even the streetlamps didn't cast their typical desultory light on the frozen streets, instead forming odd orange globes that were a self-contained world of their own.

There was something tight in her stomach, and the tension bled through her muscles.

This was it. Either they'd planned everything perfectly, outwitted Masha and the rest of the whole damn government—or they'd die. There wasn't another option. Because if they didn't win, quickly and decisively, Evka would. And then they'd die, Masha or no Masha.

The streets were eerily silent, without even the distant whine of police bikes. Not really a surprise, considering how much hell they'd raised in the last few days—police were probably taking advantage of every moment of peace.

But it wouldn't last.

Ivan, who was walking in front, held up a hand, and the rest of them froze.

"We're a couple streets away from the police cordon," he said quietly. "Assuming they haven't changed it since Tae and I were here, there'll be a physical barricade blocking the street, and five or six officers watching it. They'll be able to hear us after this, so watch where you put your feet. Be a shame to all get shot to death because someone slipped on a patch of snow."

His words were light, but Jez could hear the tension in them. She glanced at Tae.

His jaw was set, his posture tense.

He and Ivan had almost died here.

And they were coming back again. Because they didn't have a choice.

Because none of them had a choice.

Lev nodded at Tanya, and she stepped away from Ysbel. For a moment her slender, graceful form was silhouetted against the faint starlight, then she disappeared into the darkness, not even a sound marking her departure.

Jez tightened her grip on her heat pistol.

Hell, she was crap at waiting, mostly because every damn second seemed to turn into a standard hour, and her whole body itched to move, and the waiting was an insect crawling under her skin, biting and stinging, that she couldn't slap and she couldn't ignore.

A hand on her shoulder made her start, and then she recognized the touch and leaned into it. Lev didn't say anything, but somehow, the pressure of his hand on her shoulder made the waiting just a little more bearable.

Even so, she was pretty sure she must've been standing in the damn street for about four and a half years by the time Tanya's voice hissed through her earpiece. "Come on, quickly."

Jez grinned, every nerve in her body tingling as they started cautiously forward. She could see the barricade ahead of them now, the flickering light from the flares the police had set around it letting off a sputtering, wavery glow. The officers' weapons were drawn, their postures tense as they stared out into the night, away from them, in the direction Tanya had disappeared.

Cautiously, their ragged groups stepped over the street-barriers.

The officers didn't even turn.

They reached the shelter of an alley, and Tanya joined them a few moments later, slipping in so silently that it took Jez a moment to realize she was there.

Ysbel kissed her wife. "What did you do to them?" Her voice was amused, but Jez could see how her hands shook.

"Nothing permanent. But I doubt they'll want to walk alone in the dark for a while," said Tanya.

"Let's go," said Lev quietly. "We don't have much time."

They crept through the silent streets, Jez's whole body singing with something that was probably anticipation, but could have been fear. Up ahead, the alley they were following ended. Tae peered out, then beckoned them forward. "There's another alley half a block that way," he whispered as they stepped out into the street beside him.

Then he stiffened, and she heard the faint, high-pitched whine.

"Go!" he snapped, shoving Ivan ahead of him, and then a police drone appeared at the end of the street, weapon ports open.

Jez jerked out her heat pistol as the sharp whine of laser blasts cut the air around them, planting herself between Lev and the drone. Lev grabbed out his own pistol and stepped up beside her, face grim.

Ysbel was firing too, and moments later, the drone was nothing but a twisted heap of metal. But—

Damn it to hell.

"Tracking drone," she muttered. "We have to get out of here."

They turned and sprinted across the uneven, cracked cobblestones for the mouth of the alley.

When they slipped inside, Tae was leaned against the alley wall, holoscreen open, typing frantically. At last he looked up. "The drone got a signal out before we hit it, but I've jammed the tracker. It won't hold for long, but it'll give us a few minutes before they can track our location."

"A few minutes is all we'll need," said Lev grimly.

They were only a few blocks away now. The buildings here had an air of luxury about them, the streets clean, the streetlamps shining brightly instead of guttering and flickering.

Those government bastards took care of themselves, even if the whole damn rest of the city burned.

For a moment, she pictured Caz and Peti, that little street kid girl the Tae was always so worried about—even that bastard Felix.

Protect the people the damn government cared about, and send the damn police after a bunch of starving kids. Maybe Masha had been right about that, at least—this whole damn system was rotten.

Ahead of her, Tae slowed. "It's just around that corner," he whispered. He'd reached out and taken Ivan's hand, and Jez could see the way he held it, as if he was terrified to lose him again.

She bit down hard on her teeth.

This had to work. This had to bloody work, because she couldn't lose these bastards. She couldn't lose a single damn one of them, or it would break her heart wide open.

They slipped silently into the cramped alley, waiting a moment for everyone to catch up and catch their breath. She leaned up against

Lev, and his arms came up around her waist, and she smiled, despite everything.

There were some benefits to tight spaces, turns out.

Finally, Lev turned to Ysbel. "Alright," he said.

The small metal controller was already in Ysbel's hand. She gave Lev a quick nod and tapped it sharply.

Nothing happened.

Ysbel frowned, tapping the controller again.

Nothing.

"What's going on?" asked Lev quietly.

Ysbel shook her head. "I don't know. They must have found the explosives and disarmed them."

Lev looked ahead of them at the heavily guarded building, face tense with indecision. At last he sighed, and Jez could hear the strain in his voice. "We knew this was a possibility," he said at last. "We'll have to go in. It will mean guards with weapons, but we've gotten past guards before."

"I don't think we have a choice," said Tae shortly. "I jammed the tracker from the signal the drone sent out, but someone's found my hack. They'll have our location pinpointed any minute now."

Ysbel smiled grimly. "Well, I think I can make enough noise to get us inside."

"Hey Ysbel," whispers Jez. "I ever tell you you're hot?"

Ysbel scowled at her. "Piss off."

Jez gave her a wink.

Ysbel reached for the padded bag of explosives she kept around her neck, kissed Tanya, and stepped out into the street.

For a long moment, they waited.

Then there was an explosion, and the officers in front of the building jerked up, staring around.

Another explosion rocked the streets. The commanding officer shouted orders, and half a dozen soldiers started towards the noise.

"Go!" Lev hissed, and they took off running.

They were halfway across the open space when someone shouted the alarm.

The remaining officers turned in their direction, and soon the air around them burned and glowed with heat. Ivan grunted and stumbled, and Tae gave a choked curse, and then they were in front of the doors. Jez dropped down behind a decorative planter, yanking out her heat pistol, and took aim at their attackers, grinning like a damn maniac. The blasts around them slowed for a moment as the officers dived for cover.

She risked a glance over her shoulder. Tae was bent over the lock, face set in concentration.

"Got it," said Tae, voice tight.

Jez jumped to her feet as the door swung open, following the others inside. Lev was whispering urgently into his com, and she ducked behind the door frame and kept up a steady stream of fire at the officers outside.

A figure sprinted across the square, and then Ysbel reached the door and stumbled through. Lev slammed the door, and Tae hit the lock scrambler, and a moment later, the lock clicked shut.

They were in.

23

Masha, day 12, earlier

"Acting Minister Alonya."

She recognized the Secretary General instantly, although she'd never met him in person.

He, too, had aged more than she'd expected. He had never been a large man, but his posture, when he stood, was hunched, and the veins on his hands stood out against his brown skin. His head was shaved, but his short beard and moustache were stark white. There were puffy bags under his eyes, and his face had the slightly bloated, unhealthy look of someone who'd spent weeks or months under too much stress and with too little sleep.

Not dissimilar to herself.

Thank the Lady Lev wasn't there to notice the toll these last few weeks had taken on her, and file it away in his impressive memory to use against her later.

She realized, belatedly, that she hadn't responded to the man's greeting. She ducked her head respectfully. "Secretary General. It's a tremendous honour."

"Sit," he said brusquely, gesturing to a chair. She did as she was told, sinking gratefully into the proffered seat.

Her legs were still shaky from the nightmare. Even if it weren't for that, she was, for the first time in a long time, at the very edge of her physical endurance.

As she sat, she noticed the other people, around the edges of the room.

Branka was there—that was, honestly, to be expected.

But there were others, too, who she didn't recognize. One person in particular caught her eye—a slight woman, older than Masha by a few years, with an intelligent face and sharp, piercing eyes that seemed to take in the room.

Masha didn't recognize her, but there was something uncannily familiar about her expression.

She was too exhausted to parse out the connection, so she simply turned back to the Secretary General, pasting the bland, pleasant expression on her face that had served her so well through the years.

Her heart was pounding in her chest, a sick mixture of anticipation and dread for what she was about to do.

"It was very kind of you to come so quickly … Masha," the man said quietly.

It took her tired brain half a moment to realize what he'd said.

Then something heavy and sick settled in her stomach.

She'd been too late.

She tasted acid in the back of her throat, but she managed, somehow, to keep her expression neutral.

"Don't bother denying it," the man said. His voice, too, sounded weary. "Evka has confirmed it for me, and has shown all of us all the evidence we need."

Evka.

Again, that tightness in her stomach.

She turned, her eyes finding the slight woman.

That expression. It was Lev's, when he was analyzing a problem or studying out an issue. Had he picked it up from her, or she from him?

Masha managed a slight smile. "It's a pleasure to finally meet you, Evka."

Evka's smile was sharp and calculating, measuring her. "The pleasure is mine. How have you enjoyed working with my star student?"

Masha kept her smile impassive.

Evka had won her game, then.

She turned back to the Secretary General. "Evka is correct," she said at last. "I apologize for the deception. I'm Masha Volkova."

He narrowed his eyes. "And you're trying to destroy us. This revolution—I assume you're behind that? And this is after you sabotaged our relationship with Vitali Dobrev, and with Grigory Korzhakov. What are you after, Masha?"

She studied him for a moment, then gave him a small smile.

Evka had won her game. But Masha had one final token left to play.

"I am not behind this revolution," she said quietly. "I've done everything in my power to end it—even Branka would have to admit that. The rest? I destroyed Grigory's relationship with Vitali Dobrev. I sabotaged his relationship with the government, his greatest source of power and influence. I bankrupted his organization, killed his boyeviki, took him down completely. Since I'm certain by now you know my history, you'll know why I did it. And now?" she shrugged. "I've had my revenge. I have no need of a revolution."

"You also sabotaged my project," said Evka, a bite to her tone.

Masha raised an eyebrow. "Your project would have let you kill us without lifting a finger. I wasn't quite ready to die."

The corner of Evka's mouth twitched in wry acknowledgement.

"So," said the Secretary General. "You claim your sole aim was to take down the mafia. Very well. Let's assume I believe you." He stood and leaned forward, placing his hands on the desk in fists. "That still leaves you a very dangerous woman. You took down Grigory Korzhakov and Olyessa Janovik, shattered their organizations, killed everyone on Prasvishoni who worked for them. You threw the government into madness. And if not you, at least your handpicked crew are driving the revolution in the streets. So tell me—why should I not have you tortured and killed?"

"Because," Masha said quietly, "you still need me. My crew, as you said, is leading this revolution. They ignored my advice and turned against the government, and if you know their histories, you'll know they have good reason to hate you. I know them better than anyone else. As Alonya, I've so far been able to keep them from destroying you. And as Alonya—" She paused. "As Alonya, I've obtained something rather valuable. My crew's com signatures. With this information to set into our new weapons, it will be an easy matter to capture them. And then, I imagine, this revolution will collapse under its own weight."

"Give them to me, then," the Secretary General said, holding out a thick hand.

Masha shook her head, smiling slightly. Her heart was pounding harder than ever, the rush of it loud in her ears.

This was it—her final play.

"No. This is currency, and I'd like to buy myself a position."

"A minister's position?" Branka snapped. "You think that would keep you safe?"

"No," said Masha. Her voice was calm. How was her voice calm? "Not that." She turned back to the Secretary General. "I'd like the position of undersecretary. Specifically, your personal undersecretary."

There was a long moment of silence.

"Why that position?" asked the Secretary General. "It's important. But you'd have no independent authority."

"But I'd have what I need. As your personal undersecretary, I'm protected. Against my crew. Against the survivors of Grigory's and Olyessa's gangs on other planets, who I'm certain will want my blood. Against Evka, who, I believe, would be happy to see me dead. After a career like mine, that is the only position where I could possibly be safe, and as I said—I'm not quite ready to die."

He watched her for a few moments, looking suddenly very, very old. At last, he shook his head wryly. "I would bargain with you. But my government is falling apart. Prasvishoni is in an uproar. My ministers are assassinating each other. We are on the verge of collapse. Evka tells me she thinks she's found a solution, but I can't afford to take chances, not now. So. You'll hand me the chip. I will ensure that it contains what you say it contains. And the moment your former crew is dead, I will sign the documents to grant you the position."

"You—won't take them for questioning?"

It shouldn't matter.

It didn't matter—they'd die either way, she'd always known that. She'd been able to pretend otherwise, but she'd always known it.

He shook his head brusquely. "You know better than that, Masha." He held out his hand for the chip.

They'd be dead.

And she'd have won.

The Secretary General was an old man, tired and unhealthy—no one would think it strange if he suffered a heart attack in the next few days. And even if they did—Masha would be the only person in the system with full access to his files. She'd be, de facto, the one to keep the government running while the ministers gathered to decide on a replacement.

A brief space of time, perhaps. But with everything she'd set up— it would be enough to do what she needed to do.

Enough for her to call in the favours she'd been so carefully collecting, ensuring that before the ministers could gather, those who needed to die were killed and those she could work with put into places where they'd be useful. Enough to negotiate with the remaining revolutionaries, give them the justice they were demanding. Save their lives.

Enough to destroy from within the corrupt government that had been sucking the lifeblood from the system for almost a century.

And then, with the leverage she held, she'd ensure she was appointed Secretary General. She'd have the power, finally, to make things better, not just for her, but for everyone in the system.

He was still holding out his hand.

Slowly, she slipped the chip from her com.

Her hands, she noticed absently, were shaking.

From the corner of her eye, she saw Radka, eyes wide.

Olya, crouched under a table with Misko, watching Masha raise her knife.

Had Grigory thought, once, that leading the mafia would be enough? That the methods of getting there were less important than the end result?

Slavenka had, certainly. Slavenka, who'd given the order that led to Masha's parents choking on their own blood, pleading for their lives in the kitchen of their small, cheerful apartment

"Well?" the Secretary General asked impatiently.

She could do so much good. Save so many lives.

There was something bitter in her throat as she held out her hand with the tiny, delicate chip.

He reached out to take it.

She hesitated for the briefest moment. Then she opened her fingers.

The chip dropped to the floor with a delicate *ting*.

Decades of planning. A lifetime of sacrifice. And in the end—the one thing she hadn't prepared for.

Her own damn weakness.

She stepped down hard, crushing the chip under her heel.

Everyone in the room started forwards at once, but it was too late. Even Tae would find it impossible to retrieve anything from the mangled innards of the chip now.

Branka was shouting, the Secretary General cursing loudly, every heat gun in the room trained on her.

"What the hell are you playing at, Masha?" the Secretary General hissed, his voice shaking with rage. "I agreed to everything you asked. Make me another copy of that information, now."

"I can't," said Masha. Her voice was, somehow, still calm, and she felt the strangest desire to laugh. "That was the only copy in existence."

"Take her and the aide away," he snapped to the guards. "Kill the aide, but keep Volkova for questioning."

Masha glanced at Radka from the corner of her eye, saw the girl, face bloodless, expression terrified, but laced with that stubbornness Masha had come to know so well.

She shook her head wryly.

She'd already failed. She'd already failed everything that mattered. It hardly mattered now. She pulled the tiny heat pistol from her pocket, her hands, for once, completely steady.

"Let her go," she said quietly. "She has nothing to do with this. Let her go, or I kill myself."

The guards froze.

"And if we let the aide go?" the Secretary General asked. He didn't look afraid—just curious.

"Then I drop the pistol, and go without a fight," said Masha. "You can question me. I know you want to. The girl's no one. Look up her history if you like. She's not mine."

"Then why do you care?" he asked.

Masha shrugged. "Because it's a shame for her to die for obeying Branka's orders."

"A wise government official doesn't let herself get attached," he said, smiling slightly. "You've grown stupid in your old age."

"Perhaps I have," murmured Masha.

"Go on," the man said, gesturing to the doors. "Let her go. Masha's right, she's unimportant."

Radka was staring at Masha, face horrified.

Then two guards shoved her out the door, and locked it behind her.

Masha waited a moment, listening for the telltale hiss of a heat gun.

"I'm not having her followed and shot, if that's what you're afraid of," said the Secretary General, a hint of amusement in his voice. "I have no reason to. The moment you put down the pistol, she goes free. As you said, she's nothing. You, however—"

Masha nodded. Carefully, she stooped, placing the heat pistol on the ground. She straightened and stepped back, hands held out to show she was weaponless.

"Go on, then," said the Secretary General, and the guards leapt forwards.

Despite everything, she tasted the iron tang of fear sour in her mouth.

She knew, very, very well, what questioning meant. She'd brought that pistol, after all, so she could kill herself before they could take her, if things went wrong.

But … at least now there was one less death she'd have on her conscience.

Maybe that was enough, in the end.

Her hands were bound roughly behind her, her pockets searched, legs clipped together with walking-cuffs. They were taking no chances, it appeared.

Not that they had to. Now that Radka was safe, Masha found her legs shaking so badly she wasn't sure she'd reach the torture rooms without assistance.

The guards jerked her towards the door, and she made no attempt to resist.

She deserved everything that was coming.

Everything she'd painstakingly set up, every death her actions had caused, had been for nothing. Her parents' deaths had been for nothing.

And yet—

And yet, as they dragged her out the door, a heat gun shoved painfully against her back—she couldn't, somehow, bring herself to regret what she'd done.

24

Lev glanced around, counting quickly to make sure everyone was in, then drew in a shallow breath, his whole body sagging with relief.

Everyone had made it.

"Ivan!" Tae's voice was frantic, and Lev straightened as the kid stumbled to his feet. "Ivan, are you——"

Ivan looked up with a weary smile. "I'm fine. Better than I expected, honestly, considering the amount of firepower we were running through." His voice was tight with pain, though, and Lev gritted his teeth in sympathy.

He had first-hand experience of how badly a heat-blast could hurt.

Jez was holstering her heat pistol, and he had to look away for a moment to tamp down the memory of the desperate panic seeing her in danger always brought.

He trusted her, and trusted her judgement, and trusted her abilities. This was a purely selfish reaction—he didn't think he'd actually survive if anything happened to her.

He crossed over to where Tae had knelt beside Ivan, his face tight with strain. Tanya had come over as well, and Lev turned on his com light while she examined a singe-mark on Ivan's leg.

"It's not nearly as bad as it could have been," she said gently, putting a hand on Tae's shoulder. "It probably doesn't feel very good, but he'll be alright." She stood, pulling a miniature first-aid kit from her pocket. "This isn't a heat kit, but it will help."

She tore the wrapping from a cooling sheet and sealed it carefully over the burn. Ivan's posture relaxed as the cooling pad began its work, and Tae's shoulders slumped in relief.

Lev bit back a small, humourless smile.

Tanya was right—this whole thing could have gone much worse than it had.

But he wasn't entirely sure how much more of watching his friends get hurt carrying out his plans he could take.

He sighed. "Let's go. Every moment we stay here gives them more time to prepare a response."

They walked through the echoing emptiness of the lobby and stepped into the corridors.

There was something odd about the quiet. After the explosions and the firefight outside, even the heaviest of sleepers should have woken up. If the people inside the apartments were too afraid to come out, he should at least be able to hear movement from inside.

But there was nothing.

Unease tickled in the back of his brain.

It had been too easy. For a place as heavily guarded as this— they'd gotten in far too easily. And the guards outside—they should have been pounding at the doors already.

"Tae," he whispered. "Can you do a scan?"

Tae nodded, his face tight with worry as he pulled up the scanner.

The look on his face as the readings scrolled across the screen told Lev everything he needed to know.

"What is it?" asked Ysbel.

Tae shook his head and hit the scanner again. "I'm going to check the whole building. I only had it set to this floor." His voice was tight.

Lev watched him, feeling a little like someone had punched him in the stomach.

He knew already what the scan would show.

How the hell had Masha tricked him again? He'd been so damn careful. They'd put so much work into setting distractions. He knew Masha, and she should have been so busy that there should have been no way she'd guessed what their real target was.

When the scanner beeped again, Tae's posture sagged slightly. Lev closed his eyes, his muscles so tight they hurt.

Damn it to hell. Damn that plaguing Masha to hell.

"Lev—" Ysbel's voice was sharp and impatient with worry.

"The building is empty," said Lev quietly, without opening his eyes.

"What do you mean, the building is empty?" snapped Ysbel.

Lev shrugged, and tried to smile. "Exactly what I said. The building is empty. Masha must have figured out what we were planning and moved everyone out."

There was a moment of silence.

"We've got to get out, now," said Ysbel, her voice sharp.

"We're going to walk right through the middle of those guards again?" Ivan's voice was tight with strain. "I hate to say this, but—"

"You have a better idea?" Ysbel snapped back. "I have enough explosives that I can make them think twice about coming after us. I'll kill every last one of them if I have to, but we've got to get out of here. Come on!"

They turned and sprinted for the exit.

When they reached it, Tae yanked a lock scrambler from his

pocket, clipping it to the lock. He waited a moment, frowned, and pulled it off again, tapping it sharply against the door frame.

Panic was rising in Lev's stomach.

Tae rummaged in his pocket, pulling out another lock scrambler. He studied it for a moment, and then his shoulders slumped, ever so slightly.

"What is it?" snapped Ysbel.

Damn Masha to hell.

"Lev, check your com," said Tae sharply.

Lev frowned, but lifted his com.

It was blank.

"What's—" he began.

"Jez? Yours?" There was a tone in Tae's voice that was on the point between hysteria and despair.

"Damn thing's not working," said Jez a moment later. "Tech-head. Tell me what's damn well—"

"EMP pulse," said Tae.

Lev stared at him for a moment. "I thought you put in blockers on our equipment."

"I did." Tae's voice was dull. "The only way someone could have done this was to have it set to my signature."

Lev closed his eyes, biting back the despair. "Listen," he said finally, his voice strained. "There has to be something we can—"

"I'm afraid there isn't."

Lev's head jerked up at the new voice, and he glanced around wildly for a moment before realizing it must have come through the building com.

And then he realized what was wrong with the voice.

It wasn't the one he'd been expecting, the pleasant, bland tones of the woman who'd once been part of their crew.

But it was familiar. Suddenly, sickeningly familiar.

He took a shallow breath, feeling like a sleepwalker in a nightmare.

"Evka," he said quietly.

"Lev." Her voice was matter-of-fact, sharp and crisp, just the way he remembered it.

"What have you done to our tech?"

"I'm certain you could figure it out, given a few moments. You were always very good at that." She paused, her tone slightly amused. "Is that girl still with you? Jez?"

For a moment, the rush of anger made him almost lightheaded. "I swear to you, Evka," he began.

She laughed, and he could hear the fondness in her laugh, and somehow, it made it worse. "I am sorry, Lev. I sincerely wish there'd been another way. But, as you proved last time we encountered one another, you are much too intelligent for me to work around. So I had to deal with you first. If you haven't guessed yet, I got a scan of the EMP tech your friend used when Masha sent the special op forces after you. It was—ingenious, honestly. I was impressed. No wonder you enjoy working with these people." She paused again, her voice tinged with amusement. "If I recall, the sixteen-year-old Lev I worked with did not suffer fools."

He gritted his teeth. "The sixteen-year-old me believed we were friends, Evka," he said quietly. "The sixteen-year-old me was a fool."

"You say that now, perhaps," she said, her voice still amused. "I don't think you really believe it, though. At any rate, while even the best of my people couldn't match the sophistication of your friend's device, they were able to mirror-copy it. It's set opposite to the one he created—it won't affect any of my soldiers' devices, but everything with his signature is dead. And the field will continue rapid-pulsing, so even if you managed to shield one of your devices, it will die the moment you attempt to use it." She paused. "I'm telling you this, because I want you to understand that your best option—your only option—is to wait quietly. I'd still prefer not to kill you if I can avoid it."

The others were staring at him, their faces bloodless. Jez slipped her hand into his, and he clutched at it as if it were the only thing holding him up.

"So. You've trapped us, then." He tried to keep his voice light. "You think that you will stop the insurrection? I'm flattered."

Evka laughed again, that familiar, dry laugh that made something twist in his stomach, years' worth of memories—fondness, affection, worry. Guilt, for years and years, thinking she was dead, wondering if he could have done anything to prevent it.

And underneath it, burning, white-hot fury.

"No, Lev. I do hold you in the highest esteem, certainly. But I don't assume trapping you here, on its own, will stop your revolution." She paused. "But I think I have what I need from you," she finished briskly. "Thank you, Lev."

He frowned, chest tightening.

What had she needed? Not their com signatures, she could have grabbed those without having to say a word. But—

For a moment, the world spun, and even with his hand against the wall, he thought he might fall.

Jez tugged her hand from his and slipped her arm around his waist. "Lev?" she asked quietly, voice concerned.

He leaned in to her for just a moment, trying to gather his strength.

"I'm a damn idiot, Jez," he whispered. "My voice. She was scanning it while I talked. Trapping us isn't going to stop the insurrection—I am. I imagine she'll send out a message to Vera and Dmitri in a few hours, in my voice, telling them we've won, and to come out without their weapons. A gesture of good faith or something. And then—"

"And then she'll have the damn soldiers gun them down," Jez finished, her voice sick.

There were a few moments of horrified silence.

"The building com?" asked Ivan at last. "Tae, can you hack into it, warn them?"

"I doubt it will change anything," said Lev quietly. "I'm sure she's slaved the building's com system. There's no way she left it connected to the general lines."

"So what do we do?" asked Tanya at last. The tone in her voice told him she already knew the answer.

"I suppose," he said quietly, "we wait."

Tae, day 18, late

"Tae?" Ivan looked up at him from where he was seated, leaning back against the wall, injured leg stretched out in front of him.

Tae gave a short shake of his head and sank down against the wall. "Lev was right. I managed to find something and hack through, but it's slaved to Evka's signature. If I had my equipment, I could try to rig something, but the moment I changed the signal, it would pick up my signature. The EMP pulse would take it out before we had time to get a message through."

He tipped his head back against the wall.

Caz and Peti. Mila. Olya, Misko. Dimitri. Vera. Everyone behind the barricades.

They'd be murdered. Maybe they already had been.

Ysbel looked sick, and Tanya's face was deathly pale.

Ivan put his arm around Tae, but Tae could feel the strain in his muscles.

This was Ivan's worst nightmare. And Tae couldn't fix it. He couldn't damn well fix anything.

He took Ivan's hand in his, knuckles cracked and bloody from the cold, palms calloused and scarred, and brought it to his lips, choking back the sudden sting of tears.

The com above them crackled, and he looked up sharply.

"Calling the crew of the *Ungovernable*."

The voice wasn't Evka's.

He sucked in a quick breath. "Zhenya?"

"Tae." Zhenya's voice had that same lazy, self-confident note it always had, along with that hint of genuine pleasure it always seemed to take on when they were talking to Tae. "I assume your friends are there as well?"

"Are you working for Evka now?" Lev's words were quiet, but there was ice in his tone.

Tae shivered involuntarily. Lev in this mood was not someone he'd want to be on the wrong side of.

"Of course not." Zhenya sounded amused. "As I told you, Evka in power is my worst nightmare. Which is why I'm speaking with you right now."

"Zhenya," said Tae through his teeth, lifting his head. His voice was shaking with fury. "Don't you dare. You've damn well done enough. Don't you dare come here and pretend to be a friend."

"Tae," said Zhenya after a moment. "I understand your—"

"Shut the hell up!" He was so angry he felt dizzy. "You mud-sucking rat. You filthy, plaguing, Lady-damned bastard. You worked with Grigory, and now you're working with Masha, or Evka, or both, I really don't care. So go choke on your own damn vomit."

There was silence for a moment.

Tae closed his eyes, his whole body shaking.

"Tae." Zhenya's voice was quieter now, his tone serious. "I understand you hate me. I don't blame you. But I need you to listen." They paused. "I only found out what Evka did a few minutes ago. There are enough people who owe me favours that I could get a few moments to talk with you, but I don't have much time. Your friends behind the barricade are still alive—she's waiting until daylight, so there's less chance for people to escape under cover of darkness when the shooting starts. She's going to start pulling the army into position in the next couple of hours, I believe. And—" They paused again. "Masha's been captured."

Jez gave a small, quick gasp.

Something twisted in Tae's chest, but he ignored it. "So you called to give us the good news," he said, his voice cold.

"In the end, she wouldn't give you up to be killed," said Zhenya quietly. "That's why they arrested her."

Tae laughed, the sound harsh even in his own ears. "I see. She's waiting for a more advantageous time to betray us."

"They've taken her away for torturing. I doubt there'll be a more advantageous time. She won't come out of that alive."

Tae glared at the com, heart pounding.

He should have felt triumphant.

Instead, he just felt sick.

"Why are you telling us this?" asked Lev at last. His voice was strained, but calm.

"I was hoping you'd save her," Zhenya said quietly.

Tae gave a snort of disbelieving laughter. "You thought we'd save her? Why the hell would we risk our lives to save the woman who's been trying to kill us? Even if we weren't trapped in here."

"She could have killed you, this afternoon." Zhenya's voice was still quiet, level. "It would have given her everything she wanted. But she didn't." There was a pause. "There was an aide with her, too. Masha had a hidden weapon. She could have killed herself, avoided the torture. I'm certain that's why she was carrying it. But she used it to ensure the aide was let free. And—" Tae could almost hear them shrug. "The aide came to me. She knew Masha and I had dealings in the past."

"What's your interest in this?" asked Lev.

Tae was grateful Lev was asking the questions. He wasn't sure he'd have been able to. He was lightheaded with anger.

How dare Zhenya suggest that he and the others owed Masha anything?

"My interest is what it is always been," said Zhenya. "I'd like to survive this. Once Evka gets her Protocol working, she'll be the de facto ruler of the system. And I doubt there's room for anyone else on her narrow pinnacle of power."

"I'm not sure you realize this," said Lev, his voice dry. "But it may be difficult for us to rescue anyone at this point."

"So I'd heard," said Zhenya, the amusement back in their tone. They paused a moment, and when they spoke again, their voice was deadly serious. "I understand your mistrust. And so, I'll give you the code to the door. You can walk out. I doubt there will even be guards outside—Evka seemed quite confident you wouldn't escape. Are you ready?"

"Ready," said Lev after a moment.

Zhenya read out a list of numbers and letters in their measured tone.

"Why are you doing this?" Lev asked again, his voice still soft.

"As proof of my good faith. And because I know as well as you do,

Lev, that if anyone is going to defeat Evka, it will be your crew." They paused a moment. "Your whole crew."

"Masha isn't part of our crew," Tae snapped. "She forfeited that when she tried to kill us all."

There was a moment's pause. At last, Zhenya said, "Tae. Do you remember back on the pleasure planet, when you thought I'd killed the street kids?"

Tae gritted his teeth. He'd never forget that moment, the sick, choking horror of it, not if he lived to be a hundred.

"I'd like to say that what I told you then was true," Zhenya continued quietly. "That I'd had a change of heart and decided not to kill them. But it was a lie."

Tae's heart was pounding. "What are you saying?"

"I'm saying," said Zhenya, "that Masha begged me not to kill them, and promised me something very valuable in exchange. My current position in government is the result."

Tae stared at the ceiling com. He felt dizzy, disoriented.

What Zhenya was saying didn't make sense.

No. It did make sense. There'd always been that nagging question. He didn't know Zhenya well, but he knew them enough to know they wouldn't suddenly become sentimental when faced with killing street kids. Street kids who joined the boyeviki had that sentiment stripped from them early on.

"Why?" he asked at last, his voice sounding strange in his ears.

"Because she didn't want to see you hurt, Tae," they said softly.

Tae's chest ached, and he couldn't draw in a breath.

"I can't force you to do this," said Zhenya. "But you're the only ones I know of who can. She's in the government complex, building four, room 1443. I understand Jez and Lev are familiar with the place. Either way, you have the code to the door now. I'll leave you to think it over."

The com clicked off.

There was a long moment of silence.

"She's getting tortured." It was Jez. Her words choked, just a bit. "They're bloody torturing her, Lev."

Tae glanced over at her. Her eyes were closed, but he could see something shining in the corners of them.

"Jez." Lev's arm was already around her. "I'm sorry. I truly am. But—she tried to kill us." His voice was tight, thick with uncertainty.

"I know," Jez said quietly. "Maybe she's a damn bastard." She opened her eyes, blinking hard. "Maybe she deserves every damn bit of it. But—but hell—" she swallowed hard. "Anyways, not like she could hurt us anymore, not if they've done that to her. And we can't just—" she broke off, voice wavering. "She's our damn crew. And they're going to let her die screaming, and we can't just leave her."

Tae glared at Jez, his heart pounding painfully.

Plaguing Jez. Plaguing naïve innocent Jez, of all the damn people in the system—

"She was going to blow up your damn ship," he spat. "What the hell the does Masha know about being part of a crew? I bloody trusted her. We all bloody trusted her. She damn well deserves—" he stopped, his throat too tight to allow him to continue.

Damn it. Damn it to hell. Damn that plaguing Masha to hell. He'd finally, finally learned to start hating her, instead of letting every damn thing she did stab him like a knife in the damn chest.

She'd saved Caz and Peti. She'd put her whole damn plan at risk to save them.

Why the hell had she done that? Why the hell had Zhenya told him? He'd just bloody learned to hate her.

He squeezed his eyes shut against the heavy, burning tears.

"Well," said Lev at last. "At least we can check if Zhenya's door code works."

Tae heard him stand and cross over to the door, but he kept his eyes closed. If he opened them, he'd start crying, and he couldn't afford that right now.

He had to hate her. If he stopped hating her—

If he stopped hating her, it would break him wide open.

"Tae."

He turned. Ivan was watching him with that expression he always had when he looked at him.

Tae swore, blinking back the tears, trying to shove back the heavy ache in his chest. "She lied to me. I damn well trusted her, and she lied to me. To all of us. She damn well used us. We were just tools to her. And I—" the words caught in his throat, and he couldn't continue.

"And you cared about her," Ivan finished softly.

The words were knives, cutting open the damn wounds he been carrying around ever since that moment on Gregory's ship.

He had cared about her. He'd worried about her, and worked himself exhausted to keep her safe, and damn well cared about her.

That's why it bloody hurt so bad.

He still bloody cared about her, even after everything, that was the worst damn part of this. She'd lied to them, and hurt them, and—

And like the bloody innocent fool he was, he couldn't stand the thought of leaving her to be tortured to death.

Even though she bloody deserved it.

A soft click made him look up.

Lev turned, face slack with relief. "It worked," he said softly. "We're out. And we still have—" he glanced at his com, then shook his head ruefully. "I have no real idea how long we have. But,

judging by how dark it is, I'd say—maybe four hours to sunrise. So."
He paused. "What are we going to do?"

25

Masha, day 13, early

The pain was a whining, high-pitched undercurrent, humming through Masha's veins. Even unconscious, she couldn't escape it. And as her mind slowly returned to awareness, it strengthened into a sick, breathtaking, overwhelming thing that swirled through her and pressed around her like atmosphere.

She blinked her eyes open.

Even that movement left her lightheaded, and she had just the strength to turn her head to one side before she vomited blood in a dark, sticky pool around her face.

She was lying on cold concrete, but even though the chill was enough to suck the strength from her muscles, the cold was a sort of afterthought.

Cold was something you could become numb to, eventually.

Torture—was not.

Her breaths were shallow, painful things.

The people questioning her knew their business. They hadn't hurt her badly enough to kill her. They knew exactly where that edge was, and pulled back just before.

Her ribs screamed with the agony of each breath, her body

bruised and aching.

They weren't trying to get information anymore. The Secretary General would have enough information on her file to know she'd have destroyed any information she didn't want them to see. And he'd know as well as she did the inherent unreliability of any confession extracted under such extreme, excruciating pain.

This was only punishment. Only revenge. A demonstration to anyone who might consider a similar course.

The room was lit by a bar-light overhead, painfully bright.

It would be on, night and day, for as long as she was in the tiny, windowless cell.

How long would they leave her alive? Possibly long enough to give a confession over the newscoms. They liked that. But they'd wait until they'd taken down the insurrection in the streets.

They'd told her, over and over, while they were torturing her, that the crew had been taken and killed. They'd described it in detail, every last murder, down to the children, screamed it into her face between blows.

Whether it was true or not, she had no idea. There was nothing she could do about it now, anyways.

She liked to think she'd refuse any confession they gave her to read. Tae would, possibly, or Jez.

She almost smiled.

Jez would spit blood in their faces and laugh.

But Tae and Jez had something they believed in enough to die for.

And she didn't. Not anymore.

She'd betrayed herself and everyone else because she couldn't bear that two children should lose their parents the way she'd lost hers.

She'd seen her mother and father, for a few moments, earlier that day. She'd been hanging in the cuffs between beatings, before they'd thrown her back here, her toes just touching the floor, enough that she couldn't help but try to shift to put weight on them and take the excruciating pressure off her shoulders, even though it was impossible, and shifting only made the pain tear through her muscles.

Her mother had been standing in one corner talking to her father. Their faces were kind and concerned, the way she'd seen them so often as a young child.

It was odd—she hadn't remembered them like that for a long time. All she'd seen was their mangled, bloodied corpses, splayed out on the kitchen floor. This was the first time in a long time she'd seen them like they'd been before Grigory.

She knew, somewhere in the part of her mind that clung tenaciously to reality, that they'd been hallucinations, brought on by pain and stress and exhaustion. But—

But it had been so long since she'd seen them as anything other than a horror of blood and gore.

What would her life have been like, if things had gone differently? Would a girl named Mari have grown up in a small, clean, cheerful apartment, praying three times a day to the Lady, trying not to harm anything living? Would she have been a merchant, like her mother?

Not that it mattered. What happened had happened. Mari had died that day, as irrevocably as her parents, and Masha had failed them all.

But there hadn't been condemnation in the faces she'd seen, although she'd looked for it.

She closed her eyes for a moment, the pain strumming through her body like a current. She longed for the black of unconsciousness, but the pain and the brilliant white light wouldn't let her drift off peacefully, and her mind clung stubbornly to consciousness.

When she opened her eyes in weary defeat, Jez bent in front of her. The pilot's face was concerned, and Masha smiled.

"I didn't betray you, you know," she croaked.

Somehow it was important that the image in front of her know that, even if the pilot herself never would.

"I know that, you dirty bastard," Jez said, her voice sharp with worry. "Not really the damn time to discuss it right now. Where are you hurt?"

It was—odd. Her parents hadn't spoken.

But then, her memories of her parents were old and long past. The last time she'd spoken to Jez was only weeks ago, although it felt like centuries.

She let her eyes drift shut again.

"Tanya, get over here. I have no idea—"

The words floated through her mind, and she blinked her eyes open again.

Lev was crouched beside Jez now, and someone's hands ran gently along her neck and then down her arm.

She blinked, then gasped as whoever it was touched her leg.

"It's not good," said a grim voice, in a familiar outer-rim accent. "She's hurt badly. They've broken her knee in enough places I'm not sure she'll ever walk on it again."

Lev looked up at whoever was speaking. "We don't have much of a choice. We're running out of time. Can we stabilize it enough to keep her from passing out while we're getting her out of here?"

"Not sure how conscious she is right now anyways," said Jez. "Masha? Can you hear me?"

"Move. I have some painkillers. It won't do much, but it'll help."

Ysbel's accent was even heavier than usual, and a moment later, she was crouched beside Jez and Lev. "Open her mouth," she commanded, and then Masha felt strong hands gripping her bottom jaw and gently pulling it open.

She whimpered at the pain, her vision going momentarily hazy, and she could see the sudden sick look on Jez's face.

Something small was placed on her tongue, and she swallowed reflexively as it dissolved.

"I gave her two—it might be enough that we can move her," said Ysbel, standing. "It will take ten or fifteen minutes before it starts working, though, so in the meantime, Tanya, my love, you and Lev work on stabilizing her leg. Tae and I will get the mag cuffs off her."

Someone touched her leg again, and the wave of pain took her breath away, and for a moment her vision went black.

"Masha, stay with me, OK?"

When her vision returned, Jez was still there, crouched beside her.

And that nagging, stubborn part of her mind that could still view the world rationally realized that this wasn't a hallucination or a fever dream.

She choked in a breath, and the pain of it almost blacked out her vision a second time.

"Jez?" she managed to mumble through her bloody mouth. "Jez, is that—are you—"

The pilot tried to smile. "Hey, you bastard, welcome back. Miss me?"

For a moment Masha stared, her bruised consciousness trying to make sense of what was happening.

"Why—" she started at last.

Jez rolled her eyes. "Why the hell do you think, you damn plaguer? Because you're part of our crew, OK?"

Tears gathered in Masha's eyes, and she didn't have the energy to fight them back.

Another jolt of pain from her leg, and she let out a choked scream.

Jez looked up, glaring past her. "Be careful, dammit."

"We're doing the best we can," came Tanya's sharp voice. "Perhaps you'd like to fix the splint?"

She hadn't dreamed Tanya either, it seemed.

"What … are you …" Masha's words were garbled through blood and broken teeth, but Jez seemed to understand anyways.

"We're rescuing you, you idiot. What did you think we were doing?"

And between the pain and the guilt and the sick, desperate gratitude, Masha found she was crying helplessly, short, painful, breathless sobs that jolted her chest like a shock-stick.

"Shhh. It's alright." Jez stroked Masha's sweat-soaked hair in a gesture that was oddly gentle, and Masha closed her eyes and wept.

By the time Tae and Ysbel had the cuffs off and Tanya had fixed an emergency splint on her broken leg, the painkillers had kicked in enough that she felt at least slightly more coherent.

"Alright, up you come," said Jez. There was something grim in her expression. "Figure you can't walk, but I also figure the way you look right now, carrying you will bust you up even more. Tanya said your arms aren't broken, so we're going to put you between two of us, and then we're going to get the hell out of here."

"Where … where are you going?" Masha muttered.

"Back to the barricades. Bloody Evka is going to kill everyone back there in about two hours, so—" She shrugged. "Basically, you're probably going to die anyways. But figure it's got to be better than this." She gestured with her chin to the bare cell.

Masha took a shallow breath, bracing herself against the pain. At last she mumbled carefully, "How is Evka planning to kill you?"

"Probably not the best time to chat right now," said Jez. "Ready?"

She slipped an arm under Masha's shoulders and lifted gently, and Masha sucked in a quick gasp of pain, and the room wavered around her, black crowding the edges of her vision.

When she could breathe again, she was standing, supported on either side.

"It's … important," she gasped when she could speak. "I—I may be able to—"

A wave of pain washed over her, and her head dropped forward as her body spasmed.

"You alright?"

The voice was tight and worried, and when she was finally in control of her muscles enough to lift her head, she glanced up to see who it was.

Tae was supporting her on the other side, his expression grim, hair tangled, exhaustion and strain sharp in his face.

She choked back a pathetic sound that might have been a sob.

There was resentment in his face, and anger, just like she'd expected.

But under that, there was a sharp concern, and his arm supporting her back was much more gentle than she would have guessed.

"Masha. Are you alright?"

She managed a weak nod.

Tae looked over her head to Jez. "Let's go," he said.

The rescue was a vague, nightmarish blur. Later, she could remember nothing but the pain, a faint, watery recollection that included shouts, and heat-blasts, being pulled along at a half-run with her feet dragging on the ground when she was too weak to move them, her broken knee screaming in agony. The black constricting her vision allowed her disjointed glimpses of people, guards, Ysbel calling something in a sardonic tone. There may have been an explosion at some point, but she wasn't sure that any of her memories were accurate.

And then they were out in the streets, and the icy bite of the wind on her face was enough to make her blink her eyes open again. She could make out the dim orange flicker of the streetlamps, the shades of grey and black that were Prasvishoni's streets at night.

Lev had pulled up a holoscreen and was studying it. "If Zhenya was telling the truth, the soldiers will be moving into position along these streets. So right here should be fairly open. I doubt anyone's expecting us to head back into the middle of that mess anyways."

"How—going to kill you," Masha mumbled. The icy air stung her broken teeth, but compared to the pain in her leg, it was hardly enough to take note of.

Lev turned to her, his expression one of faint irritation, but his voice was gentler than she'd expected. "She's set the military and the police around the barricades. She's going to send through a message that will be encrypted to look like it's coming from us, and lure them out. Then, once they're out from the barricades, the soldiers will gun them down." He glanced up at the dark streets. "To be honest," he said wryly, "even if we succeed, and the students don't come out when she expects, it'll only be a few minutes before she sends them in after us. And there's no time to set traps like we did when you sent the army." He gave a small shrug, but Masha could see the tension in his posture. "So I'm afraid that, like Jez said, we're only bringing you somewhere you can die a little faster. But I suppose it's the thought that counts, or something."

She closed her eyes again, fighting back the pain. "She's sending the army?" she muttered finally.

"Yes." Lev's voice was sharp with tension.

"I—I might have an idea," she managed.

And then, finally, she passed out.

26

Lev, day 13

The sky was barely beginning to grey as they set off through the empty streets of Prasvishoni. They'd wasted too much damn time on the rescue.

Lev still wasn't sure if he was glad they'd done it, or if he was already regretting it.

He glanced back. Masha was unconscious, her head lolling limply as Tae and Jez half carried, half dragged her down the streets.

Even looking at her made him feel slightly sick. He and Jez had come far, far too close to being tortured only a few weeks past, and the memory still glowed in his brain, a sharp, brilliant jolt of panic at the thought of what had happened to Masha happening to Jez.

He sighed.

He was lying to himself. The panic, the sickness in his stomach when he looked at Masha, wasn't from the memory of his and Jez's almost-torture.

It was the sight of this woman he wanted to hate, but couldn't, her body broken, blood running down her face and staining her clothes, her breathing laboured and unsteady.

"How close are we?" Ysbel's voice was sharp. She had her heat gun out, and was scouting the street in front of them while Tanya took up the rear.

He closed his eyes for a moment, picturing the map in his head. "Just over a kilometre."

"Where are all the police? I don't like this."

Lev sighed. "I'm guessing she's still getting them into position. She'll be concentrating on where the people will come out from behind the barricades first, get them into position. She'll set her forces up along these streets last, I assume."

Ysbel nodded noncommittally and moved forward again, her posture tense.

He glanced up at the sky.

They should still have time before Evka's call came through. Even at this pace, they should make it with time to spare.

He hoped.

He shook his head wryly. Somehow, he'd come to a point where the thought of being slaughtered behind the barricades with his friends was a more comforting one than the thought of being alive, outside the barricade, and watching it happen.

Who would have thought? He certainly wouldn't have believed it, however many months ago when he first joined on with this ridiculous crew.

As they neared the barricades, Ysbel held up a hand.

"Let me go ahead," she said quietly. "It looks like they have a guard set up." She paused. "When you hear an explosion, go as quickly as you can. I doubt it will distract them for long."

Lev nodded and fell back beside Jez and Tae.

Jez's face was strained, and sick with worry. Tae's, too, as much as he was obviously trying to hide it behind a scowl.

"How's Masha?" Lev whispered.

Jez shot him a tight look. "I think she's still alive. That's about all I can say."

He nodded, trying to ignore the sickness coating the back of his throat. "We'll have to move fast when Ysbel's ready for us."

Ivan glanced over, worry sharp in his face. "I don't know how much she'll be able to handle. She's—not in good shape."

Lev sighed. "I wish we had another option."

Behind them, Tanya watched the streets where they'd come, her posture tense.

An explosion shook the street, and Tae and Jez started forward at a stumbling half-run, Masha's limp body sagging between them. Lev and Ivan kept pace with them, pistols out, but whatever Ysbel had done, it seemed to have distracted the guards' attention. When they came around the corner to the barricades, there were half a dozen soldiers in view, weapons drawn, but all of them were facing in the wrong direction.

They reached the barricade and slipped inside, followed shortly by Ysbel, and for a moment they stood there, panting.

"What the actual hell—"

Vera was staring at them. Dmitri joined her a moment later.

When he saw Masha, his face grew grim. "Medic tent," he said shortly. "Questions later."

When they reached it, Jez and Tae lay the unconscious Masha on one of the few empty cots. Lev had to look away for a moment—under the generator-lights in the med tent, Masha's wounds looked even more gruesome, her skin an even sicker shade.

"Lev?"

He looked up as his father stepped out from the back of the tent, worry creasing his face. "Are you alright? What—" he caught sight of Masha, and sucked in a quick breath. He disappeared back from where he'd come, and emerged a few moments later with a first-aid kit and an armful of medical supplies.

"What happened to her?" he asked softly, coming over to stand by the cot.

"Torture. The government did this," said Lev shortly.

His father nodded, his expression grim. "This is a job for a real doctor," he muttered, pulling out the medi scanner. "But it seems those are in short supply around here." He looked up at Lev. "I'll do what I can," he said in a businesslike tone.

Lev nodded, not trusting himself to speak. His father's voice, brisk and efficient and familiar, brought back a sudden, overwhelming memory of his childhood. Of being young enough that there was always someone older who knew better, and decisions that could cost a life or save it were made by other people.

But that had ended a long, long time ago.

"Thank you," he said quietly. "If she wakes up, and she's coherent, send someone to get me. She may have information we need."

His father nodded absently, mind clearly already focused on the task at hand.

Lev sighed, and gestured the others out the door. "Let's go somewhere warm," he said quietly when they were outside. "We have a lot to discuss."

They reconvened to the small, makeshift conference room.

"What happened?" asked Vera once they'd all pulled up their mismatched chairs around the battered table. "I assume the plan didn't work?"

"You could say that," said Lev wryly. He explained the events of the last six hours as quickly as possible. As he spoke, Vera's face drew into a frown, and the crease between Dimitri's eyebrows deepened.

"So we have—" Vera glanced down at her com. "Forty minutes or so before Evka springs her trap, and then maybe ten, twenty minutes after that before she comes in and kills us all anyways. Have I got it right?"

"Tries to kill us all anyways," said Jez, but there was strain behind the jaunty tone in her voice, and her face was drawn with exhaustion.

"I still have some explosives," said Ysbel at last. "I don't know if it's enough to save us, but we'll have company on our way to see the Lady."

"You think any of us have a chance of seeing the damn Lady? You're a hell of an optimist." Some of Jez's native cheerfulness was creeping back into her tone.

"I don't suppose you have any ideas," Lev said quietly, turning to Tae.

Tae shook his head. He looked so exhausted that Lev wasn't entirely sure how he was still conscious. "Not off the top of my head."

For a moment, no one spoke.

It was just possible that between them, they could come up with some slapdash way to save everyone's life. He wouldn't put it beyond them—they'd certainly done it enough times before.

The problem was, Evka wouldn't stop. Even if they survived this, she'd kill them sooner or later. Probably sooner, honestly. And unless they could cripple the government to the point that she couldn't get the resources she needed, they couldn't stop it from happening.

Tanya glanced over at him. "Our only way out of this is to stop Evka. Am I correct?" she asked quietly.

Lev nodded.

Tanya gave a small shrug. "I suppose, then, we'll have to

assassinate the Secretary General. That ought to cause enough confusion to stop her for a while."

Vera and Dimitri had both turned, and were staring at Tanya open mouthed.

"You—mean the actual Secretary General," said Vera. "The head of government. Of the entire Svodrani System. That Secretary General."

Tanya nodded.

There was a moment of silence.

"I—think I understand why you and our professor got married," said Dmitri finally.

Lev grinned to himself, then sobered quickly. "Tanya. I don't disagree. But—" he gestured around. "We're trapped. Even if one of us could get out, we couldn't do something like that alone. He'll be guarded, probably by your old schoolmates."

"Perhaps if all of us went," began Ysbel slowly. She paused. "We still wouldn't have much of a chance, I know. But then, we don't have much of a chance as it is. And I could find a way to keep the soldiers busy back here. If we can set something up and lure them inside—my students are learning to be very good at explosives. It wouldn't hold them forever, but for an hour or two, maybe."

There was a slightly flattered look on Vera's face, and a slightly horrified one on Dmitri's.

"It's—not a bad idea," said Lev slowly. "But it doesn't solve our main problem, which is, by now, Evka will have every street between here and the government buildings completely blocked off."

"You have a better idea?" Ysbel's voice was sharp.

He sighed in exasperation. "If I had, I would have already told you. All I'm saying is—"

"Lev?"

He looked up.

The door was open a crack, and his father peered through, concern written across his face. "The woman you brought in," he said. "She's awake, and she wants to talk with you. She says it's quite urgent."

Lev clenched his teeth.

Damn, bloody Masha.

Still—they could plan as well in the medic tent as here, he supposed.

He pushed himself to his feet. The others were doing the same.

"Vera, Dimitri," said Ysbel. "You know where I keep my explosives? Bring them to the conference room. We may as well get started."

The two students nodded, the looks on their faces something between apprehension and raw terror.

Outside, Lev paused for a moment at the door of the medic tent.

His father must have seen the look on his face, because he'd slipped away to attend to his other patients, leaving the four of them to visit with Masha alone.

Lev wasn't sure if he was grateful, or resentful.

But—there was no point in putting it off.

He stepped through the door.

Masha's eyes were open, and she was propped with pillows into a semi-seated position, but he could see how her body trembled.

He glanced at Jez involuntarily. She looked like she was going to be sick.

"Masha," he said, turning back to the woman on the cot. Somehow, his voice was steady. "I'm glad you're awake."

"I'm not certain I share your sentiment," said Masha wryly. "But I thought it important to speak with you as soon as possible, considering your time constraints."

He closed his eyes for a moment. "I … suppose I should say I appreciate your offer of help," he said quietly. "But I don't. I don't trust you, and I don't think that following any suggestion you might have would be wise, considering our history."

Masha was watching him, and even through the pain in her face, her eyes were cool and perceptive. "I thought you might feel that way," she said at last.

"And do you blame me?" he snapped, suddenly furious. "If you have some justification for what you've done, something that lets you sleep at night, that's fine. But the rest of us have work to do."

"I—" her voice faltered suddenly, her eyes going glassy.

Jez stepped forward, face creased in concern. "Easy there, you bastard," she murmured, straightening the pillows propping Masha upright.

Masha took a deep breath and gave Jez a weak smile. The sight of it set an irrational anger burning in Lev's chest.

Jez trusted Masha. Jez had always trusted Masha, and Masha had used that to hurt her.

He wasn't sure he could ever forgive Masha for that.

"I've been—contemplating how I could demonstrate my good faith," said Masha last. Her voice was strained. "Would you be more comfortable with my suggestion, Lev, if I agreed to accompany you?"

"You can't," he said shortly. "You can hardly talk without bloody passing out."

Masha gave a small sigh. "I am fully capable of coming, if necessary. And I currently don't see how I could prove my good faith without being willing to come. Therefore—" she spread her hands. "Your father has given me a strong painkiller. Once it takes effect, I should be able to sit up without fainting. I believe that will be everything that's required."

"How do you know what's required?" he was speaking through his teeth. "How the hell do you know anything about us, or about this, or about our situation?"

There was something approaching fondness in her expression as she looked at him, and for some reason, it made him even angrier.

"If you recall, Lev, I've worked with you for some time now. With all of you." Her voice was painfully weak, and she paused a moment, as if gathering her strength. "What you care about, more than anything, is to keep the people you love safe. With my threat neutralized, your most pressing enemy is Evka. Your most pressing concern is that she'll kill everyone behind the barricades—but your next most pressing concern is that she somehow uses this battle to gain the resources to finish her protocol. You'd have two options—assassinate Evka, which, unless I am mistaken, is not currently a possibility, as you have no idea of her whereabouts—or, kill the Secretary General." She paused. "Am I correct?"

He turned abruptly. "Come on," he said, his voice sharp. "Let's go. She doesn't need to hear anything else."

"Lev."

Reluctantly, he turned back.

Masha's face was drawn with pain, and her eyes still bore the shocked, glassy look of someone whose body had been hurt beyond their mind's ability to comprehend it.

His stomach twisted, looking at her.

He'd been stupid enough to trust her, once. And he'd sworn he'd never make that mistake again. But—

He hesitated a moment, then crossed to her bed and crouched to her eye level. "Masha," he said quietly. "Zhenya told us that in the end, when you were almost in reach of everything you'd been working for, you chose not to sell us out. I—don't know if they were lying. I certainly wouldn't put it beyond them. But I can't deny the fact that you were tortured. So." He paused a moment. "Why?"

There was a long moment of silence. The others were still, waiting for Masha's response.

"I—would prefer not to talk about it," she said at last, quietly.

He gave a sharp shake of his head. "No. You don't get to decide anymore what you tell us and what you don't. Because so help me, I'm this close to sending you out into the streets to give the soldiers something to shoot at."

He was almost shocked at the bitterness in his voice.

For a moment, he thought Masha might tell him to go ahead, rather than answer his question. But at last, she dropped her eyes. "I—suppose you're right," she said quietly. "I suppose if there was a time for secrets, it's long past." She paused again, and when she spoke, her voice was reluctant. "I—was caught, by Evka. She realized who I was, and notified Branka."

"And?" he said quietly.

Masha drew in a shallow breath. "And, I had your com signatures on a chip I'd prepared. I'd instructed Zhenya to copy them when they were negotiating for the return of the hostages."

Lev sucked in a quick breath. Of course that had been the reason she'd sent Zhenya.

"And then what?" he asked. "Don't expect me to believe that after everything, you had second thoughts. Because there were so many times you could have had second thoughts—" His voice choked, and he broke off angrily.

There were a few moments of silence. Finally, Masha raised her head again. There was a look in her face that he couldn't entirely read, but looked something like despair. "I couldn't," she said quietly. "I thought I could. Up to the end, I thought I could, but—" She turned away. "I couldn't."

For a long time, he stared at her.

He'd expected her to exaggerate her heroics in saving them, use it to guilt them into doing as she asked.

Instead, she seemed ashamed. As if the words were being dragged from her against her will.

He looked over at Jez, but her she was watching him, and he could tell by her face that she'd let him decide.

He swore and stood abruptly, turning to face the tent wall. His breath was coming too quickly, and he was lightheaded with anger.

Damn Masha to hell. Damn her to hell, damn her, damn her, damn her.

At last, he turned, wiping his eyes quickly on the back of the sleeve. "Alright, Masha," he said through his teeth. "What's your idea?"

27

Jez, day 13

"Vera, Dimitri, I need you." Lev's voice through the com was calm, but there was an urgency under it. "We're safe, and everything went as planned. They've tentatively agreed to our demands, but they want a show of goodwill. I've told them I'd contact you, ask you to come out from behind the barricades without your weapons. They've sworn you'll be safe, and—" Lev paused, voice wry. "We have our hostages. They know what they'll be sacrificing if they don't keep their word. The streets should be clear now. Wake everyone up, come out. The sooner we can prove we're negotiating in good faith, the sooner this will be over."

Jez raised an eyebrow at Lev. "You're pretty persuasive there, genius."

Lev scowled at her.

It was actually almost disturbing how much Evka had managed to make the voice in the message sound like the scholar-boy standing beside her.

Might have worked, too, if he wasn't, in fact, standing beside her, glowering at the world in general. And if they hadn't spent the last however many damn minutes coming up with yet another ridiculous plan.

It wasn't much—she'd lure the soldiers in after them, whatever the hell Ysbel had set up with the students would show them it wouldn't be as easy as they'd planned, and while they were hunkering down trying to figure out a way in behind the barricades without getting the hell blown out of them, Jez would fly them out, in one of the university's ancient transports, through a place where one of Masha's friends was commanding soldiers, and would turn a blind eye to an ancient piece of crap transport flying through. Once they got to the government offices—it was basically Tanya's plan after that, with the rest of them as backup. Well, a hell of a lot of backup, considering they were trying to kill the damn Secretary General.

She glanced around. Dmitri and Vera were gone, setting up explosives with Ysbel, and Tae and Ivan were doing something with tech. Well, Tae was doing something with tech. Ivan might just be for emotional support, but hell, tech-head looked like he needed all the emotional support he could get at this point.

They'd all meet at the ancient ship Dmitri and Vera had dug up from somewhere, as soon as she got back. Tanya hadn't straight-out said it, but there was no way she was getting through to the Secretary General without every last damn one of them, and their skill-sets, along to help. But right now, it was just her, Masha, and genius-boy.

"Anyways, guess I should get going," she said. She leaned over and kissed him, and—well, OK, maybe she got a little carried away, but the point was that she stopped kissing him eventually. And if she couldn't quite tell whether she was walking or floating afterwards— well, that wasn't the worst result in the system.

She gave Lev a slightly foolish grin and turned towards the skybikes.

"Jez," he managed, his voice slightly hoarse. "Be—be careful, alright?"

She turned back and winked at him. "Hell, genius, you think I'm going to let myself get shot to pieces after a kiss like that? I'm not that stupid."

He sighed, worry written across his face. "I love you, Jez," he said quietly.

"Yeah," she said. "Guess I love you too."

There were a handful of students waiting for her at the skybikes, faces wan and frightened.

She winked at them as she swung on. "You ready? Mostly you'll just have to stay back, don't get into trouble, and let me do the flying. Soon as the shooting starts, get the hell back inside the barricades."

They nodded mutely.

Vera and Dmitri had chosen them as probably the best skybike pilots of the group, but she had to be honest, she wasn't particularly impressed.

Flying skybikes was one thing. Flying skybikes while getting the hell shot out of you was something completely different, not to mention a hell of a lot more fun, and these idiots looked like it would scare the damn pants off them.

She shrugged internally.

No accounting for taste.

She glanced behind her one last time to make sure they were following, then started forward at a sedate pace over the wall.

Let those bastards outside think she was just another damn weak-kneed student, and coming out on Lev's orders.

She reached the end of the street without incident, and turned onto the next.

Nothing—no police, no soldiers, no sign of anyone watching

them. She swore quietly, and tapped her borrowed com. "Listen," she whispered to the students behind her. "Looks like they want to wait until they're more of us. So I'm going looking for them. Follow me close, but not too close—plaguers need to think maybe they can kill the whole lot of us off before we can get word back. And like I said before—once the shooting starts, get the hell out of here. I'll keep the bastards busy."

There were murmurs of stricken, frightened acknowledgement through the com.

She heaved a sigh.

A shame, really, to waste an experience like this on people who clearly wouldn't appreciate it.

"Genius," she said, tapping through his private line. "Need specs. Gonna go in after the bastards, but it'll be easier if I know where I'm going."

"Sending it through." Lev's voice was grim. A moment later, a scanner readout popped up on her screen.

She scanned it quickly, grinned, and leaned parallel to the street, shooting forward in a burst of speed that tied her stomach in knots. The grin on her face was stretched so wide she could hardly stand it.

She whipped around a corner, and then another, and behind her, faintly, she was aware of the sound of other skybikes following—or at least, trying to keep up, which honestly was about as much as she'd expected.

And then she shot around another corner, and yanked back on the bike's handles, jerking to a stop directly in front of rows upon rows of grim-faced soldiers.

There was a moment of shocked silence. Then the soldiers scrambled for their weapons.

She shoved her bike's handles forward, buzzed her bike low over their heads, then yanked it around and gave them a cheeky grin. "Guess there'll be some people behind the barricades interested in finding out what the hell you're doing here," she called over her shoulder.

The first shot sang over her head, and she yelped and flattened herself on the bike as she shot out of the alley.

Heat-blasts followed her out, and then she heard the unmistakable sound of skybikes powering up.

She grinned. "They're on their way," she whispered into the com. "Let them see you, then get the hell out of here."

A dozen skybikes appeared in the street behind her, followed by a group of soldiers on foot, running with their weapons drawn. They paused, dropping to one knee, and fired off a blistering volley, heat-blasts singeing the walls of the buildings around her and turning the temperature of the alley air warmer than a Prasvishoni summer.

The students, who'd almost caught up to her by now, yanked back on their handles in a frantic attempt to turn their bikes.

"Think they saw you," said Jez with a grin. "Go on."

The students' bikes shot back towards the barricades.

A dozen other skybikes appeared in the opposite end of the alley, and Jez yanked up on her handles, sending her bike skyward again as heat-blasts burned the air around her.

The scum-suckers had anticipated her move—a handful of bikes idling in the shipping lanes dove towards her, clearly trying to block her ascent.

She leaned farther forward, her bike shaking on the very edge of its control, and shot between two of them, so close the handles of her bike grazed them on either side.

There was shocked swearing behind her, and then they were after her, but she kept her bike's nose pointed firmly towards the city force field.

They stayed on her tail for longer than she'd expected, honestly, but at the last minute they peeled away, and she yanked her handlebars down and leaned to the side, skimming the force field so close that she could smell the cuffs of her trousers burning from the friction.

Ahead of her, six of the bikes pulled into formation, four more coming up behind, with another handful hovering below her. Now that she was up against the force field, they were clearly trying to pin her in.

She slowed a little, letting them come in close. Then she leaned back abruptly, shoving down on her handlebars and cutting the bike's power.

Her pursuers shot past her, going far too quickly to stop, and a moment later she was tumbling in free fall.

The air caught her bike, sending it spinning wildly as it fell from the sky. The ground below her was a dizzying, twisting mass, but hell, she'd been drunk enough times to be actually pretty damn decent at figuring out where things were when she couldn't see straight. She timed her revolutions, and at the last second, twisted upwards in her seat, yanking the bike upright, and pulled back on her handlebars at the same time as she hit the power. The bike coughed, then hummed to life and jerked forward. The toes of her boots scraped along the top of the building, and then she was back in the sky.

She risked a quick glance behind her, and grinned at the soldiers' stunned faces. "Think I made 'em mad," she whispered into her com. "On my way back. Hope you're ready."

She leaned forward and shot towards the barricades.

The soldiers on the ground had clearly realized they didn't stand a chance, and they'd stopped where they were, contenting themselves with firing rounds after her. But the soldiers on bikes were still firing, and they were still close enough to pose a threat.

She weaved in and out of the heat-blasts, rising as high as she dared so the bike would provide some protection and flattening herself against her seat.

A shot slammed into the back of her bike, sending it haywire, and for a moment she fought for control. The choking sputter of the machine told her it wasn't going to take much more fancy flying, but she was in sight of the barricades now, far below her.

"Ten seconds out," she whispered through her com.

Another shot hit the bike.

 It sputtered, and died.

She swore as she plummeted towards the cement, yanking frantically on the handlebars.

She was not going to damn well die because some crap police bike couldn't hold up to a damn heat-blast—

She glanced down at the rapidly approaching ground.

On the other hand—

She took a deep breath, closed her eyes, and pulled out her heat pistol.

This had damn better work.

She aimed as carefully as she could with the wind tearing at her, and fired a blast into the ignition, hit the power with her other hand at the same time, and kicked up with her knees, jerking the handlebars back.

For a moment, nothing happened.

She closed her eyes—

And then the bike sputtered, coughed, and choked to life at the shock of heat to the power core, just in time to keep her from turning into a damn smear on the concrete only metres below.

The engine was choking again, on the verge of dying, but she just needed to get over the top of the barricade, through the gap the students had made in the wires …

And then she was in, and she yanked back on the handlebars as the bike choked and died for the final time. She hit the restraints and rolled off as it crashed into the pavement, skidding across the square with a painful squeal of tortured metal and sending students and street kids diving out of the way before it finally came to a crumpled halt.

She lay on her back for a few moments, breathing heavily, and trying to decide if she'd actually survived that.

She was pretty damn sure her arm wouldn't hurt this much if she was dead, so maybe she'd made it after all.

And then there were running footsteps, and someone dropped to the ground beside her.

"Jez?" Lev choked out, and she opened her eyes and grinned up at him.

His entire body went slack with relief, and he pulled her into an embrace, kissing her hard enough that for a moment she completely forgot about her broken arm.

"Jez. Are you alright?" he asked when he finally pulled back. His voice was shaking.

"I'm fine, genius," she said breathlessly. Honestly, she wasn't sure how much of her breathlessness was from the near-death experience, and how much was from the kiss. "Probably be sore tomorrow, though."

"Thank the damn Lady you're alive," he said, pulling her back into an embrace.

Finally, he stood and helped her to her feet, his face tight with concern. "I saw what happened. Are you sure you'll be able to—"

She gave him a look. "Am I dead? If the answer's no, then I can damn well fly a ship. Come on."

From behind her, she could already hear the fizz and whine of heat guns as the bikers who'd been pursuing her met the defenders on top of the barricade.

She took in the ship as they sprinted towards it.

Old beater, Pelican model. Probably fifty years old, and not very well kept up. Hadn't been run in a while, from the look of it.

But it was a ship. And hell, flying for Lena, she'd learned how to fly all sorts of crap.

Tae shoved open the door from the inside as they approached, and she dived through, Lev close on her heels.

"Strap in," she called over her shoulders, hitting the controls.

"Believe me, pilot girl, we are," came Ysbel's dry voice.

The ship coughed to life, and she closed her eyes just for a moment, resting her fingers on the controls, letting her whole body soak in the beautiful, beautiful feeling of a ship ready to take her whatever the hell she wanted to go.

Then she hauled back on the ancient controls, grinning in ecstasy, and the ship rose reluctantly into the air, grumbling and groaning.

The moment they rose above the level of the university buildings, the air around them lit up with heat-gun fire.

She hit the throttle, and the geriatric ship swung to one side and lumbered off down the shipping lanes.

She nudged the controls, sending the ship swerving back and forth for a moment.

Always had to learn a new ship, figure out how to talk to her.

Except for the *Ungovernable*. Jez figured she must have basically been created just to fly that lovely, exquisite, perfect angel-ship.

Still, she could basically fly just about anything. And once a ship started talking to you—well, that was the whole damn point of flying.

Something slammed into them from behind, and the ship lurched and rolled like a drunk. Jez swore softly through her teeth. "Easy there, sweetheart, stay with me—"

"Jez," Lev's voice was a studied calm. "I don't mean to rush you, but we're going to have company."

"Don't worry, genius," she murmured. "This little sweetheart still has a trick or two up her sleeve."

She shoved the throttle again, and the ship lurched forward. "Sorry, beautiful, don't mean to be rough," she whispered. "Just trying to get you out of the way of those bastards with heat guns."

"When you're finished explaining the situation to the ship, it would be nice if you got us somewhere we weren't being shot at," said Tae through his teeth.

She winked at him over her shoulder.

The ship swung drunkenly from side to side, Jez's fingers flickering over the controls the only thing keeping them pointed in relatively the correct direction as they staggered along. She pulled up the ship's com with her free hand, studying it quickly.

A handful of bikes—fast, but not a lot of firepower—and … She expanded the screen quickly.

Yup, three in-atmosphere ships. Two police and one military, looked like.

She grinned.

To think she'd been worried this might turn out to be a boring job.

"Give me specs, genius," she said.

Lev's face had taken on a distinctly greenish shade, but he nodded grimly and pulled up his own holoscreen.

The ships were approaching rapidly. And apparently they'd either guessed who was flying this thing, or had learned a lesson or two from her stunt on the bike, because the skybikes were following below her, clearly intending to cut her off from the streets below the shipping lanes.

"Two are MPX 20 models, and the third is a Yastreb," said Lev, sounding a little like he was going to be sick. "They'll have ion—"

Jez caught the flash on her screen from the corner of her eye and yanked the control stick backwards, pointing their nose at the sky. The ship groaned, and she patted the panel reassuringly. "You've got this, beautiful," she whispered.

The ship rocked with the aftershock as the shot passed beneath them. They'd clearly been expecting her to dive, but even so, the shot skimmed her ship so close she could smell the burning wiring.

"Alright," she said into the internal com. "Guess that's enough of me and this little sweetheart getting acquainted. You ready for some flying?"

She didn't wait for Tae's swearing, Ysbel's grumbled curses, or Lev's resigned sigh, just pulled the ship into a tight backflip a scant few dozen metres from the force field, sending the blood rushing to her head. Then she pointed their nose at the ground, and dived.

The police bikes realized what she was doing moments later, and there was a mad scramble as the officers and soldiers tried to yank their bikes out of the way of the descending behemoth.

She whooped gleefully as the walls of buildings flashed past. Beside her, Lev made a sound like he was trying not to vomit, and from the back seat, Tae was cursing in a strained monotone.

She yanked back on the control stick about three seconds before they'd pancake into the street below.

The ship continued her dive.

"Jez?" asked Lev through gritted teeth.

Two…

One…

The ship straightened out abruptly, skidding along the pavement so close that if she put her feet out, they would have dragged along the ground.

"What in the actual hell—" began Tae in a strangled voice.

"Just got to learn the lag time, is all," she said cheerfully.

She glanced at the screen. The bikes had scattered at her descent, but were regrouping now to come after her. The bigger ships, though, were holding back in the shipping lanes, clearly leery of following an absolute lunatic through the narrow alleys of this part of Prasvishoni.

Which—fair enough, really.

She yanked on the controls, leaning the ship onto its side and skimming around a corner so close she left a streak of paint across the white prefab. "Tanya? You have your gun?" she murmured.

"I have my gun, you complete lunatic." Tanya's voice was strained. "I don't know if I'll live long enough to use it, though."

Jez grinned. "Ah, leave that to me. You worry about shooting."

Tanya muttered something that was probably uncomplimentary, but Jez didn't have time to listen. Already, heat-blasts sparked off the walls around her.

She yanked the ship into a staggering weave, hopefully enough to at least make them a more challenging target for the bastards, and eased the throttle gently forward. Her little sweetheart strained and pulled to do as she asked, ancient body shaking with the effort.

"Just a little farther," Jez whispered. She hauled up on the controls, manhandling them around another corner. "Ready,

Tanya?"

"Yes, you idiot," Tanya snapped through her teeth.

Jez glanced over her shoulder. "Hey, no need to—"

"For the Lady and the Consort and all the bloody saints' damn sake, Jez, focus on flying!" Tae ground out, voice strained.

She rolled her eyes and turned forward. "Don't know if you noticed, tech-head, but I'm actually doing a damn good job of flying."

The alley ahead of them ended in a dead end, and she pulled back on the throttle. The ship grumbled in protest, but did as she asked, jerking up into the shipping lane for a brief moment before diving down again into another alley.

The street bikes followed.

Jez had been increasing their speed so gradually the bastards probably hadn't even noticed how quickly the buildings were whipping past them.

Jez patted the side of the control panel appreciatively with her free hand.

Little sweetheart could get up a pretty good head of steam, given time and some sweet-talking.

A dozen or so more bikes had joined the chase, and the ships were following her low over the top of the alley, determined not to let her jump into the shipping lane again. They'd probably start using their harpoons and nets in a minute or two, and no matter how much heart this little darling had, she didn't have the power to pull into a roll and force them to cut the cables.

Now or never.

"Might want to hang on to something," she called over her shoulder.

The pack of skybikes was maybe half a block behind her, coming up fast.

And ahead of her—

She yanked the throttle towards the blank wall of the warehouse next to them, and Lev gave an involuntary yelp. But hell, she was a damn pro at flying ships with a steering lag.

The ship veered sharply, just as an alley wall cut the side of the warehouse, and she'd already yanked back on the throttle and hit both stabilizers into reverse.

The ship came to a smoking, steaming halt in the mouth of the alley. Tanya flung open the door and leaned out, her sniper rifle tucked against her shoulder.

The skybikes shot past a split second later. Tanya's finger on the trigger hardly seemed to move, but blistering lines of laser-shot streaked after the skybikes like a swarm of stinging insects.

It was only moments before the last of the bikes collided with a building in a bone-jarring crunch of metal, and tumbled to land with the others on the street below.

Jez grinned. "I ever tell you how hot you are, Tanya? Because you're pretty damn hot."

"Piss off, Jez," said Tanya through her teeth, resuming her seat beside her wife.

"There are still ships after us," said Ysbel grimly from the back. "Please don't forget that."

"I haven't," said Jez, still grinning hugely. "You ready, genius?"

"I'm—not entirely certain I am." Lev's face was several shades paler than usual. "However, I'm not certain that I have an option at this point."

He cracked the door open, lean halfway out, then glanced back over her shoulder Jez. "You're—sure that—"

She rolled her eyes. "Genius. Trust me."

He sighed heavily, dropped the heavy percussion explosive out the door, so it landed directly under their ship, and slammed the door again, bracing himself.

"And…" said Jez, closing her eyes, feeling the faint vibration of the ship humming through her bones. "Now."

Lev hit the controller for the explosive.

For a moment, nothing seemed to happen.

And then there was a noise that was loud enough that she could feel it in the marrow of her bones, and a shockwave flung the ship skyward at a pace that the little beauty had probably never dreamed of even brand-new.

Jez whooped and screamed, laughing in pure delight as the ball of flame from the explosive surrounded them in a cradle of fire, the ship's outer walls beginning to glow a dull orange. They blasted past the three ships who'd been pursuing them. The pilots, clearly panicked, were yanking back on their throttles, trying to get out of the path of the ever-expanding explosion, but they were far too late. Their ships rocked and bucked as the shockwave hit them, and they hadn't been damn well planning for it like she had.

The last glimpse she caught of them, over her shoulder, was the pilots fighting for control, their ships' electronics fried by the heat of the blast, their controls haywire.

When their little ship was close enough to the city force field she could just about spit on it, she yanked on the stick and engaged the stabilizers, shoving them sideways and out of the path of the explosion. Behind them, orange flames flattened against the force field, expanding like a swamp lily in full bloom.

The ship pulled and jerked under her for a few moments, but by the time she had back into the streets, it was purring under her as gentle as a kitten.

"And that," said Jez, grinning at Lev, "is the advantage of having a ship so damn old half the controls are manual." She paused. "The important ones, anyway. Don't figure our com will come back online anytime soon."

Lev let out a long, shaky breath, rubbing his hands across his face. "Jez," he said at last. "That was simultaneously the most incredible feat of flying I've ever seen in my life, and the most terrifying thing I have done, or dreamed of doing, or hopefully will ever do again."

"Come on, genius, I was just warming up." She gave a snort of laughter at the look of sudden terror that flashed across his face. "Nah, I was joking. I think we lost the bastards."

"I certainly hope so," grumbled Ysbel from the back seat, her voice shakier than usual. "Because I think I'd rather be shot down than do that again."

Jez pulled the ship into a sedate speed—she figured the poor little darling could use a break at this point—and turned to Masha. "So," she said. It was hard to tell whether the sick look on the woman's face was from pain, or from Jez's flying, but hell, they'd asked her to do the job—"You talk to your army friend, then, you bastard?"

She still wasn't entirely sure how she felt about Masha. And she sure as hell didn't have time to stop and figure it out right now, so she figured the best compromise was not to think about it, and to call Masha 'bastard' at every opportunity.

"Yes," said Masha. Her voice was calm, but there was a weakness in it that made Jez's stomach lurch, just a little. "I spoke with Rafail. He assured me that his soldiers will clear our path through to the government buildings. He will also do everything in his power to slow down the other units, to hopefully give our friends at the barricade an easier time of it."

"Speaking of our friends at the barricade—" Jez began.

From behind them, a massive *boom* rattled the windows on the surrounding apartment buildings, and made her little ship jerk and tremble under her hands like a frightened moon-deer.

"Easy there, sweetheart," Jez murmured, running a comforting hand along the dash. "Just some friends of ours having fun."

"Hopefully that will make the soldiers think twice about coming over the barricade again, at least until we get finished," said Lev.

"Let's hope," grunted Ysbel.

"Well," said Jez cheerfully. "Guess now we pay Masha's friend a visit."

28

Ysbel, day 13

Ysbel leaned shakily back in her seat.

Not a lot frightened her. But after that flight, she wasn't sure she'd ever voluntarily get into an in-atmosphere ship with Jez as pilot again.

Tanya, beside her, looked sick to her stomach. "Remind me again why we all agreed to let Jez fly the ship?" she whispered.

Ysbel chuckled, pulling her wife in for a kiss.

"What the hell—"

She looked up abruptly at the tone in Jez's voice, something tightening in her stomach.

Ahead of them, the entire street was blockaded off. Military ships patrolled above street level, and grim-faced officers on skybikes blocked the space between the buildings.

Jez's posture had gone tense, her hand tightening on the controls. For a terrifying moment, Ysbel thought she might try to make a break for it.

But she didn't, just brought the ancient ship to a gentle halt.

Ysbel let out a breath of relief.

Even Jez wouldn't have been out able to fly them out of

something like this, not in this ship.

"Masha." Lev's voice was hard and cold. "What is this?"

Ysbel cast a quick glance at Masha, slow anger welling in her own chest.

But Masha, pale faced and exhausted, looked as surprised as any of them.

"I'm—not entirely certain," she said at last. "Although I expect we'll find out shortly."

Ysbel glanced out the window.

A grim-faced officer was walking towards them, and behind him came a handful of soldiers, weapons drawn. He paused a few metres in front of the ship, pulling up a voice amp that was loud enough they could hear it inside the ship. "Drop your weapons and come out, please."

Jez tapped the ship's com, then shook her head in disgust, likely because she'd just remembered they'd blown the majority of the ship's electronic components. Honestly, Ysbel wasn't completely sure how they'd survived the explosion in the first place.

Still, it was probably just as well. Judging from the look on Jez's face, whatever she'd been about to say would probably have gotten them all shot.

"Bastards," Jez muttered.

"If I may, Lev," said Masha quietly. Her voice was weak, and somehow, Ysbel didn't feel nearly the satisfaction in hearing the weakness there she'd once thought she would.

Lev was watching her. "If this is a trap—" he began.

Jez turned to him wearily. "Genius. If it's a trap, she's already caught us. May as well let her say what she's going to say."

Lev nodded tightly. "Alright, Masha. Talk to your friend."

Masha tapped her personal com. "Rafail," she said. "I was under the impression that we had an agreement."

"I'm sorry, Masha." The soldier's voice was tense, and slightly unhappy. "But—I was—approached by someone who has more pull than you do. She made it very clear to me where my duty lay." His words were stiff.

"Evka," said Masha, her voice still, somehow, calm.

The man nodded. "Yes. And I was instructed that you were all to be killed on sight."

For a long moment, no one spoke.

Jez's eyes darted to Lev, and there was a look on her face that told Ysbel that losing Lev, now, would do to Jez what losing Tanya would do to her.

Lev's expression was cold and furious.

"Masha," he said, his voice hard. "You planned this, didn't you? This whole thing. How long have you been working with Evka?"

"I don't know that it will do any good to answer, as I doubt there's anything I could say to make you believe me." Masha's voice was weary.

"Perhaps if you hadn't spent the last few months lying to us—" Lev began

"Lev," said Ysbel.

He turned to glare at her, and she sighed. "Lev. I don't think this is Masha's doing."

She wasn't sure, even now, why she'd said it. Why she felt the need to defend Masha, of all the people in the system—the woman who'd been trying to kill them, over and over and over, for the past thirteen days.

But there was something about the exhaustion in the woman's posture, the blank despair in her face and the pain in her eyes, and for some reason, Ysbel was certain that this wasn't something she'd planned.

"I'm sorry, Masha," said the officer. "I need you and everyone with you out of the ship, now. Weapons down. Otherwise, I'll be forced to instruct my soldiers to shoot you where you stand."

Masha took a deep breath. "Rafail," she said quietly. "I am as aware as you are that Evka has a tremendous amount of power at the moment. But—" Ysbel noticed how Masha's body tensed slightly, almost unconsciously. "But I'm sure she would be very grateful to you if you were to take me back for further questioning. And I believe that may be enough that she would disregard your failure to capture the remainder of my crew."

Ysbel watched her, frowning.

This, she hadn't expected.

She'd seen Masha's injuries, what they'd done to her in the torture rooms, and the memory still made her stomach twist uneasily.

To volunteer to go back to that?

"I'm sorry," said the captain brusquely. "I'm unable to do what you ask. Again, I must ask you to come out, unarmed."

Masha's posture slumped, slightly, as if whatever willpower she was using to keep herself upright was fading. "Captain," she began. "I'm sure I could make it worth your while. I have connections—"

"I have my orders," the man snapped.

Masha slumped in her seat, a sick hopelessness in the drawn lines of her face.

And for just a moment, Ysbel remembered Olya's words to her, back behind the barricades. *Do you hate her, mama?*

She hadn't been able to answer at the time.

But looking at Masha, broken and exhausted, the despair in her face and the tired droop of her posture, she could answer now.

She was angry with Masha, furious that the woman they'd trusted had put them through so much, hurt at her betrayal, disgusted at her lack of loyalty. But—she didn't hate her.

She couldn't, somehow. Jez was right—Masha was part of their crew, whether they liked it or not. And she couldn't find it in herself to hate her, even after everything.

"Hey, you bastard," said Jez, glancing at Masha. "You tried yours. Guess it's my turn now. You want to send that scum-sucker's line through to my com?"

Masha paused a moment, seemingly too weary to protest. At last she tapped something into her com, her fingers slow and hesitant.

"Hey there, you dirty plaguers," Jez began jauntily, tapping her own com on. "Here's the thing—I don't plan on being shot down the moment I step out of this ship, and I figure that's exactly what you're going to do. So, you want to shoot us? You'll have to get through twenty-five damn centimetres of ship-steel first, you plaguing mud-eaters."

The captain gave a curt gesture, and Ysbel ducked instinctively as the soldiers raised their weapons, heat-blasts and laser fire rocking the tiny, ancient ship.

It went on for what seemed like hours, but was probably less than five standard minutes. At the end of it, only Jez was grinning. Which wasn't exactly a reassuring sign.

"See," she said cheerfully over her shoulder, "that's the other thing about these old in-atmosphere junkers—they made their damn hulls thick enough to hold off a herd of stampeding swamp oxen."

The captain gestured again, and a soldier ran forwards, tossing something under the ship and then jumping back out of the way. The ship jolted, and Jez cursed.

"What is it?" asked Lev tensely.

"Mag-lock," said Jez through her teeth. "Bastard wants to make sure we don't get away, I guess."

Lev glanced around quickly, one eyebrow raised. "Where exactly does he expect us to go?"

"Stay in your ship, then," the captain's voice growled through the voice amp. "You think your mods or your shields or whatever else you installed will keep you safe, I assume. And I have no doubt they would, if I were to use my equipment."

"Guess he'd be pretty disappointed if he knew we hadn't given you a single damn mod, sweetheart," said Jez said a stage whisper to the control panel. "That was all you."

"But I doubt you have mods to protect against Ysbel's tech, which is what I'm going to use next. So, I'll ask you one more time—will you come out?"

"You wish, you bastard," said Jez through the com, her grin dangerous. "I know I'm hot and all, but if you think an ugly mud-sucker like you could get some—"

The captain glared at her.

Jez snickered.

He held up his hand, and Ysbel frowned, squinting to make it out. It was a familiar-looking silver sphere, but it took her a moment to recognize it, without the EMP casing she and Tae had placed on it.

"These were planted around the city transport infrastructure building," the captain continued. "One of our teams found them a few days ago, disarmed them and brought them back. I've re-armed this one. I expect it will be enough to take out even your ship, whatever you've done with it." He handed the explosive to one of the soldiers, who ran forward again, placing the explosive gently down beside the mag-lock, then jogged back to rejoin her companions.

The captain shouted a command to his soldiers, and they pulled back until the captain apparently deemed they were out of range. Then they dropped to one knee, weapons trained on the ship.

Ysbel glanced around the small cabin. "The explosive is on a timer," she said quietly. "Tanya? I suppose there's no way we could make it out of the ship?"

"If one of us stayed behind to provide cover, we could get to maybe the end of the street," said Tanya. "But they've blocked off the exits. Whoever got out would die the moment they tried to make it through."

Ysbel closed her eyes and pulled her wife close, kissing her gently on the lips. "I suppose you're right, my love," she said quietly. "You usually are."

29

Tae, day 13

Tae didn't have to glance at Ivan to know the look on his face—resignation, and worry, and fear, and probably, the faintest hint of self-deprecating humour. And under that, the sick, hollow despair he'd seen there far too often, when the demons in Ivan's head were too loud for him to drown out.

"Ivan," he said quietly. "It's not your fault. None of this is your fault. If we die, it's because we were trying to do something worthwhile. And maybe we die, but it doesn't mean—" he took a deep breath. "It doesn't mean that meeting you—that being with you—isn't the best thing that's ever happened to me."

Ivan turned to him and tried to smile. "Tae, I—"

"It's not your fault," said Tae, voice harsher than he'd meant it to be. "You're a good person, Ivan. You were doing something you believed in, and your boyfriend who died was doing the same thing. He knew the risks, and he did it anyways, and that wasn't your fault. And this isn't either, OK? If—" He swallowed hard. "Just—remember that, alright?"

Ivan didn't speak, just leaned over and kissed Tae, and Tae kissed him back.

His stomach ached dully from tension and from far, far too little sleep, but somehow, dying didn't really frighten him anymore. Not after everything they'd been through in the last few weeks.

The soldiers outside were standing tense and alert, weapons trained on the doors and windows of the ship, in case any of them should think to try to escape.

"Tae?"

He looked up at Lev.

"Can you tell how many minutes we have left?"

He nodded and pulled up his scanner. "It looks like we have just over seven minutes," he said at last.

"And I suppose there's nothing—"

Tae shook his head. He was so tired at this point that all he could feel was a sort of weary emptiness. "If I'd had time to prepare, maybe. But there's nothing I can do in seven minutes."

"I'm—sorry."

Tae glanced over in surprise. Masha was leaning back against the seat, clearly at the end of her physical endurance, but her eyes were open, and she was watching them.

"I know it's not enough. It will never be enough. And I don't expect you to forgive me, or to understand why it did it. But I am sorry. And I suppose I should say thank you, as well." Her voice was quiet. "I—understand you had no reason to come help me. I certainly did not expect you to, and in the end, I wasn't able to help you in return, as I had hoped. But—" her voice choked.

And then she'd dropped her face in her hands, and her shoulders shook gently.

Tae took a deep breath, then pulled himself gently free from Ivan's grasp and stood, crossing over to Masha. He hesitated a moment, then gingerly, he laid a hand on Masha's shoulder and crouched beside her.

She looked up in surprise, and when she saw him there, there was a look on her face that, for just a moment, was more full of pain than it had been when they'd found her in the torture chambers.

Then she closed her eyes and dropped her head back against the seat.

He left his hand on her shoulder. It was an odd feeling, comforting her—Masha, the person who'd always been, from the moment he'd met her, enigmatic, calm, competent. Completely in control.

"How many more minutes, you think, tech-head?" asked Jez quietly.

He glanced down at his com. "Six minutes now." His voice was tight.

"Ysbel," ask Lev quietly. "How will it affect the explosives, to have the EMP casings removed?"

Ysbel shrugged slightly. "The blast won't be nearly as contained." She glanced out the window. "A fact which our brave captain seems not to have grasped. Every building on this block will be turned to rubble when this goes off."

Lev nodded, with a small, wry smile. "I suppose I could have guessed as much."

Tae looked up, frowning. "Why would they have taken the EMP casings off in the first place, do you think?" he asked.

She shrugged. "I don't know. Likely, they didn't realize what they were. I've never seen someone build EMP shields like that."

He frowned. "Lev. If—listen, originally, we'd planned to use the EMP casings to detonate along with the explosives, to knock out the guards' weapons and communication, right?"

Lev was nodding slowly.

"We were going to take the families hostage, and then use them as leverage to force the ministers to negotiate," Tae continued, his mind racing. "We failed, because Evka was one step ahead of us. But the point of it all was to disable the government—throw it into enough chaos to keep the ministers from giving orders to take out the barricades, and keep them from giving Evka the assistance she needs. That was the point of what we were trying to do now, as well, assassinating the Secretary General."

Lev was still nodding, his expression puzzled.

He turned to Masha. "If they found the explosives, where would they have taken them?"

She opened her eyes and tried to raise her head. "To a unit in the government buildings to be dismantled and examined, I assume."

"And they would have taken the EMP casings as well, right? Even if they didn't know what they were, they would have brought them along to study." He could feel the excitement tingling through his body now.

"Yes, I assume so," said Masha.

He turned back to Lev. "We were going to use them in conjunction with the explosives to take out communications around the one building. But what if instead—"

Lev was staring at him, and Tae saw the realization dawn on his face.

"If we set off the EMP devices in the government complex—" Lev continued slowly. "If the communication were shut off, they'd have no way of contacting the soldiers or the police to give orders besides going out into the streets themselves. Unless we could physically stop them from getting out of the government compound as well."

"And it should shut off the com systems that the police and the military use internally. All their private channels. They'd have no way to communicate at all, except over the general lines. So no private communication to coordinate their assault."

Lev shook his head, smile fading. "It's a good idea. A brilliant one, really. But we're not close enough to the government buildings for you to grab the signals and rig a controller, are we? And besides, we have—" he glanced at his com. "About five minutes left before we're all blown to fragments."

Tae blew out a breath, his excitement fading. Lev was right.

"Hey. But what if someone got into the government buildings for you and sent the signal back?" asked Jez suddenly, turning to look at him.

Tae scowled at her. "That would be great, Jez, except if you remember, Tanya just told us anyone who tried that would be shot down before we could get to the end of the street."

"Yeah? Well, I might just have had an idea," she drawled. "You think you could write a hot-wire into my com for one of the military skybikes, hypothetically speaking?"

"I—"

"Look, we're running a bit short on time. Yes, or no?"

He scowled harder. "I could. But—"

"Because here's the thing. If you can, and if you can do it in a damn hurry—pretty sure I can fix all our problems at the same time."

Lev's face was suddenly tense. "Jez," he began. "Whatever you're thinking—" He closed his eyes for a brief moment, and Tae could see the strain in his expression. "Just—just be careful, alright?"

Jez turned and winked at him. "Here's the thing, genius," she said. "It's been about a million damn years since I've been able to get you into a room alone. And I'm damn well not about to let either of us get blown up before that happens." She turned back to Tae. "Alright.

Send a hot-wire through to my com. Because I figure we have about —" she glanced at her com. "About four and a half minutes before my plan won't be much good anymore."

30

Jez, day 13

"Are you ready, Jez? I'll cover you as well as I can. That should get you to the end of the street."

Jez grinned at Tanya. "You know me, Tanya—I was damn well born ready. Anyways, only need to get to the skybikes."

Tanya gave her a look of sorely tested patience.

"I'm going to open the door," said Lev in a low voice. "As soon as you're out—"

"Know what I'm doing, genius," she whispered.

He didn't look reassured.

She kissed him, which didn't actually lead to him looking any more reassured, but made her feel a hell of a lot better.

He sighed, putting his hand on the door handle.

"You have exactly three minutes and twenty-one seconds," said Tae, his voice tense.

"Got it," said Jez. She turned to Lev. "Alright, genius."

He took a deep breath and pulled the door open.

Jez jumped down as heat- and laser-blasts scorched the air around her, snatched the explosive from under the ship, and sprinted at full speed towards the nearest line of soldiers, the explosive in full view in her hand.

There was a moment's shocked pause, and then the captain was shouting, "Get back! Don't shoot, you'll set the damn thing off!" and the soldiers scattered.

Tanya's precision fire from inside the ship was already wreaking havoc, and the soldiers, even the ones with military-grade heat shields, were forced to dive out of the way, still scrambling to get out of range of Jez's explosive.

Jez stooped as she ran and grabbed a gun the soldiers had dropped, tucking it under one arm. A courageous—or exceptionally stupid—soldier stepped into her path, and she swung the explosive like she was using a damn knuckleduster. It connected with the side of his helmet, sending him staggering to one side. She assisted him with a sharp kick to the side of the knee, and he fell heavily, grabbing for her as he went down. She dodged out of his clumsy grasp, grabbed the handles of the nearest bike, and swung on, grinning like a damn maniac. The bike jumped to life as she tapped her com to its controls, and she spun it in a tight circle and shot off.

There were two dozen bikes on her tail in moments, but oddly enough, they were keeping a polite distance. Possibly owing to the fact she was holding an explosive with enough power to take out about three city blocks.

"Two and a half minutes." Tae's voice was tight.

"I know, tech-head," she said, with a long-suffering sigh.

She weaved in and out of buildings, diving through alleys so narrow her bike's handles scraped the walls on either side, popping above the rooftops for a brief jump into the shipping lanes, then diving down again into a different alley—but they were on her tight. They clearly didn't want to fire at her and risk hitting the explosive, but they also clearly saw taking out her bike as their best option, and it took every damn bit of her concentration to avoid the heat-blast fire.

A blast charred the edge of her boot, and she swore and yanked the bike to one side, narrowly avoiding another shot.

Damn it to hell, it was going to get pretty hot around here pretty quick.

"One minute."

She yanked up the bike's holoscreen, and pointed the nose towards the blinking red light indicating the coordinates Lev had sent.

At this speed—maybe thirty seconds out?

She dropped flat against her bike as a heat-blast slammed into the side of it, almost knocking her into the alley wall. The bike wasn't responding like it had been anymore.

Bloody idiots needed to learn how to make a damn skybike that could take some heat. The manufacturers had clearly never had to fly the things while a bunch of plaguers behind them were trying to turn them into plaguing barbecue.

It was still fast enough to keep ahead of the bastards, though, and that was all that mattered at the moment.

Besides, the soldiers behind her were dropping farther back.

They were probably performing the same countdown in their heads as she was.

"Jez? How close are you?" Lev's voice was almost sick with worry. "You have ten seconds."

She whipped around a corner and saw her destination at the end of the street—the building they'd been trapped in only hours before.

Better hope that damn Evka hadn't had time to worry about it with everything else she had going on.

She shot towards the building, dropped into the now-deserted courtyard, and yanked the bike to a halt.

"I'm in," she whispered through her com.

There was no response.

She glanced down, and realized it was completely dead.

The wave of relief that washed through her was enough to make her dizzy.

The EMP pulse Evka had set up was still active. The one she'd fine-tuned to affect only devices created or worked on by one of the crew.

Like, for example, the explosive she was currently holding.

The soldiers stopped when they saw she was off her bike, spreading out away from her at a sharp order from their commanding officer. They jumped off their bikes, taking cover behind them, rifles raised in case in case she did something unexpected.

She tossed the explosive casually into the air and caught it. Another barked command, and the soldiers backed still farther away. Although—she grinned to herself. If Ysbel was right, those bastards would be stains on the cement if this thing went off at this range.

Three seconds.

She dropped the explosive. It landed on the concrete with a *ting* that sounded abnormally loud in the silence.

Two.

She swung onto her bike, still grinning.

One.

The soldiers dropped to the ground, bringing their riot shields up to protect their heads, and she hit the accelerator, shooting forward and up, over the heads of the officers, and out into the alley.

She weaved in and out between buildings, sighing blissfully.

This was the kind of thing that damn well made life worth living.

After a few moments, she tapped the bike's com. "Hey Ysbel, how long do you think they're going to shelter in place before they figure out the damn thing isn't going off?"

"Jez! You're alright?" Lev's voice was sharp with mingled worry and relief.

"Figure you'd all have heard about it by now if I wasn't." She paused a moment. "Tell Masha I need the damn coordinates for that storage room crap. And tell Ysbel if she doesn't tell me where she wants her explosives planted, I'm just going to damn well start sticking them wherever I feel like." She paused. "Like maybe up the damn Secretary General's—"

"Jez—" yelped Tae.

She grinned.

The bike's com flashed a moment later. She pulled up the screen, studying the coordinates with half her attention while she flew.

"The officers are after you again," said Tae, voice worried. "I didn't have time to put a mod into the hot-wire to disable the tracking, so—"

"Relax, tech-head. I know what I'm doing. Be there in a couple minutes." She paused. "Listen, Lev said he wanted the government compound to be basically inaccessible. I'm going to do my best to get Ysbel's damn explosives from where they stored them and put them where they need to be before I start getting shot at. But I won't have a lot of time. Figure I'll have to park my bike close enough that it'll be in range of the EMP blast when it goes off. Evka's already killed my com, and Tae's EMP pulse will kill the bike, so I'll probably be walking back, and I probably won't have any communication. So when you hit the EMP, just go. I'll be fine, meet you back at the barricades."

There was a moment's pause. "Alright," said Lev finally, thought the com. "Just—"

"Hey, I'm always careful." She paused a moment. "You too, genius. I—look, don't want to have to—" her voice choked a little.

"I love you too, Jez," he said quietly.

She could hear the whine of bikes behind her as she rounded another corner. It didn't matter, though, because—

Yep. She was here.

She yanked her bike to a stop in the wide square across from the government compound.

Funny how familiar the place looked now, after weeks of going into the offices.

She jerked the com free from the bike and shoved it into her pocket. It would tell those bastards behind her exactly where she was, but she didn't really have much of an option at this point if she planned on getting the signatures from the EMP devices back to Tae.

She took a deep breath, and started off at a casual stroll towards the entrance of the nearest building.

Two guards stood outside, and they stiffened as she approached. "What are you doing?" one of them snapped. "Who are you?"

She raised an eyebrow skeptically. "That how you always talk to a damn minister?"

"Who are you?"

"Layla. That bastard Branka called me up, wanted me in the damn office, stat, and what I always say is, five minutes early is still late."

There was a snort from Lev through the com, hastily disguised as a cough.

The guards looked at each other in mild confusion. "Layla?" one of them asked. "I—don't recall—"

She rolled her eyes. "Look it up, then."

Hopefully they hadn't gotten around to changing her profile to 'scrawny, mouthy, disrespectful smuggler pilot who happens to be trying to blow up the damn government' yet.

"Anyways, not me who's gonna have to explain to Branka why they wouldn't let me in."

The officers conferred for a moment, com screens pulled up. At last they straightened.

"Your profile's here, but there's some mark on it."

"Yea, because Branka damn well asked for me to come in, and I'm not in there," she said.

Her heart was beating a little too fast, and she could feel the tingle of adrenalin through her veins, and whether or not this worked, it would damn well be worth it just for this.

"Alright, give me the code, then," said one of the officers.

"Svetlana," Masha whispered through her earpiece.

She repeated the code, and grudgingly, the guard stepped aside.

She gave them a cheerful grin and stepped past them into the building, just as the first of the military bikes burst out into the courtyard.

This particular building had an identical layout to the one she'd worked in, but was clearly set up for the higher-ranking officials. The corridors were mostly deserted, but lights shone from under the doors of pretty much every office she passed.

Couldn't blame the bastards. With what was happening in the streets, pretty much the only reason someone wouldn't be in the office shovelling through all the crap was that they were bloody dead.

She started briskly towards the end of the building Masha had indicated. Possibly those damn guards at the entrance would hold the soldiers up a few minutes—they looked like the type who might —but once they were in, it'd be a little harder to be inconspicuous with heat-blasts singing off the walls around her.

There were a few frightened-looking aides and grim-looking guards wandering the halls, but she made it without incident and slipped down the stairs.

The explosives were exactly where Masha had said they'd be, and beside them—

She grinned.

Half a dozen of something that looked like fabric lunch-sacks lay in a pile beside the explosives.

"Tech-head. Got something for you," she whispered into the com, touching it to one of the metal wires woven into the fabric.

"Got it," said Tae after a moment. "Get me the explosives, too, so I can set them into Ysbel's controller. Then let me know when you have them planted. Ysbel will blow the explosives first, and then I'll hit the EMP."

She did as Tae asked, then tucked the shiny metal spheres carefully into her jacket pockets, grinning.

Something about having enough damn firepower to take out an entire compound did a lot for your confidence, honestly. And your mood.

She could hear soldiers in the corridors by the time she got back up to the main level.

She grimaced and broke into a light jog, heading towards the back door of the building.

She checked the com again quickly and rolled her eyes. "Ysbel. Did you really need to tell me how many centimetres away from the base of the doors—"

"Jez," said Ysbel, "Put the explosives exactly where I told you. Exactly."

Jez grinned. "Figure if I just sort of scattered them around—"

Ysbel's voice was flat. "If you just 'sort of scatter them around,' then the moment I hit this controller, you will be just sort of scattered around the entire government compound, do you understand me? Which wouldn't do much to shut off the entrances and exits."

Jez heaved a deep sigh. "Fine, be that way. But honestly, don't know what kind of explosives these are, if they only work if you—"

"Believe me, pilot girl," said Ysbel. "It's not a question of whether or not they work."

She was just setting the last of them when someone grabbed her by the back of the jacket and yanked her around.

She spun to see a heat gun pointed at her face, held by a grim-faced soldier.

"Alright, you," the soldier growled. "You'll tell me exactly what you were doing here."

Jez grinned, letting her body relax. The soldier was watching her, narrow-eyed, but as Jez relaxed, the woman let the barrel of her gun waver, just for a moment—

Jez stepped back, yanking out a heat gun of her own, and now she and the soldier stood facing each other, both of them with fingers on the trigger of their guns.

The soldier didn't even look alarmed. "You went into that EMP pulse that was keyed to the weapon signatures you insurgents carry," she said, her voice heavy with scorn. "Shut down the bomb, yes. Very clever. But I know damn well it shut down your gun, too. So. I could shoot you, but I have a feeling someone is going to want to ask some questions about what you were doing in the government compound. Come easy, and you might not get a heat-blast in the face."

Jez's grin widened. "Yeah?" she drawled. "But here's the thing.

This gun is one of yours."

There was a split second where the soldier's eyes widened as she tried to take in the implications of Jez's words.

That was all the time Jez needed.

"And," said Jez to the solider, who was writhing on the ground, com melted off her wrist and a heat-blast through her leg, "I'm a hell of a lot faster than you." She paused. "Lucky you ran into me instead of Ysbel. But if I were you, I'd get the hell away from here as fast as I could. Tell your buddies too, and the damn guards. Because it's going to get pretty exciting right around the entrance and exits in a minute here."

She hit her com as the soldier rolled to her feet and hobbled frantically away. "Got it," she whispered.

"Alright," said Ysbel. "Stand back." She paused a moment. "Farther back then you think you should be standing." She paused again. "Farther back than that."

Jez rolled her eyes, but did as she was told.

"Are you ready, Jez?" Tae's voice was still strained.

"Born ready," she said, in her jauntiest tone. She paused a moment. "Genius?"

"What is it, Jez?"

His voice was worried, that familiar concern that always made her choke up, just a little bit.

"I love you, OK?"

"Jez—" His voice choked.

She took a deep breath. Across the courtyard, soldiers were approaching at a run, weapons at the ready.

"Alright, tech-head."

"On my count, then," said Tae. "Three. Two. One."

A massive wall of flame exploded from a dozen spots that marked entrances into the government compound, rubble and broken pieces of prefab falling like fiery rain from the sky.

31

Lev, day 13

Even from inside the dirty apartment building where they were sheltering, Lev could hear the chaos in the streets.

Probably everyone in the city of Prasvishoni had heard the explosion that preceded it.

Getting out of the ship and away from the soldiers had proved remarkably simple, with Jez's distraction.

He exchanged glances with Tae. The kid was smiling softly, leaning against Ivan with an affection that made Lev suddenly very aware of Jez's absence.

He sighed and shook his head.

She'd be walking back, which took a while at the best of times, and she wouldn't be able to call in, because the EMP wave would have taken out the bike and her com both. And they'd both known that, and there was no reason for him to worry, and there'd be time to think about how empty his arms felt without Jez in them later.

In the meantime—

He tapped his com through to the general broadcast line. "Hello. This is Lev. One of the insurgents. I have a message for the Head of Police and the Head of Military," he said. "As you'll have noticed, you have no communication between your forces. You'll also notice that you have no communication with your superiors in the government. They've been cut off completely, and will be so for the foreseeable future. We, however, have fully functioning communication, which gives us the ability to mobilize quickly. We have private lines, which you no longer do. And so, while you could certainly attempt to coordinate an attack as we listened in, I'd advise against it."

He paused a moment. "I could order my people to attack you. I'm under no illusions that you wouldn't do the same, given a reversal of our positions. But unlike your superiors, we don't want bloodshed if we can avoid it. So I'm giving you thirty standard minutes to lay down your weapons and surrender." He paused again. "We don't want bloodshed. But we are certainly capable of it. I'll leave the decision to you."

He tapped his com off.

Ysbel smiled. "You can be surprisingly intimidating, for a scholar boy," she said.

He grinned wearily back at her, then tapped his com through to their closed loop. "Vera?" he said.

"Lev." Her voice was sharp with relief.

"I think we did it," he said softly. "I suspect they'll surrender, but if we don't hear from them in half a standard hour—"

"We'll damn well be ready for them," finished Vera. She paused a moment. "Are you on your way back?"

Lev glanced over at Masha.

She was leaning against the wall as if she no longer had the strength to stand, and the tension in her posture told him clearer than words how much pain she must be in.

"We'll be there as soon as we can," he said quietly.

The streets outside were chaos, and Masha, at this point, was no more than half conscious, but somehow they managed to make their way through the back streets until they reached the barricade.

He'd expected it to be more difficult than it was. But with frightened soldiers and police officers arguing with their superiors, captains angrily shouting through the coms that no longer worked, and panic at the thought of being taken out by armed insurgents spreading through the ranks, no one seemed to have the time or attention to spare for their small, ragged band stumbling through the streets.

When they reached the barricades, Masha was fully unconscious, and something inside Lev hurt to see her like this. His mother came out and took charge of her, her face lined with concern, and between them, they got her settled into a cot. Her head lolled back on the pillows, her face wan and drawn with pain, but she was alive, at least.

It was almost more than he'd expected, honestly.

He lingered in the medic tent for a moment, and then reluctantly stepped outside.

He'd barely had time to get through the door of an abandoned dorm room, where he could at least hear himself think, before the first message came through on his com.

"147th company surrenders," it read.

It was followed by another, and another.

He sank back against the wall, closing his eyes for a moment in relief. Then he tapped his com through to the internal line.

"They've surrendered," he said quietly. "We won."

Coordinating a surrender, it turned out, was more complicated than it might appear—they had to come to an agreement on what a surrender entailed, and then an agreement on where the surrender should take place, and then an agreement on how the surrendering soldiers would be kept safe. Which was not an idle concern—news of the government's paralyzation had spread through Prasvishoni like a spring breeze, and citizens who'd been trapped inside their apartment for weeks were now flooding the streets, some of them joyful, some of them angry, all of them completely unwilling to obey orders from their former oppressors.

The next few hours was dealing with details—who would go where, what would happen when.

He still had no idea what things would look like once this was over —presumably, the people trapped in the government compound would extricate themselves sooner or later and regain communication, but it would likely be at least a day or two. By that time, if the insurgents had disarmed the army and the police, it was very likely that even the most intransigent government official would agree to negotiate. And hopefully, whatever settlement they negotiated would include dealing with Evka. But for now, the important thing was to get through the rest of the day.

He'd been so busy that an hour later he was still leaning against the wall of the small empty student dorm, without even time to find a chair to drag in.

But in the back of his mind, he was watching unconsciously for any sign of Jez. He told himself that she was fine, that from the government buildings, it was a good hour's walk to this part of the city even in the best of conditions, that since the EMP had almost certainly blown up her com, she'd have no way to contact them until she got back to the barricades.

But her absence sat like a weight on his chest, not quite letting him pull in a full breath.

Hours later, when the sun through the narrow dorm window was low on the horizon, there was a tap on the door. He looked up, but the door was shoved open before he had time to answer, and Jez stepped through.

She sported an impressive number of bruises, and her face was coated with grime and prefab dust from the explosion, but she was grinning. And when he saw her, his heart jumped, and a frantic relief washed over him, and he tapped off his com halfway through a sentence, crossed the room in three strides, and grabbed her into an embrace.

The relief of her body against his, the feel of her, and the smell of her, and the simple presence of her, felt like coming home after a long, long day.

"Jez," he said, face muffled against her hair, "are you alright? Are you hurt?"

She shifted slightly in his arms, pulling back so she could look at him. "I'm good, genius," she said at last, but her voice was much less snarky than usual. "At least—at least, I am now." She leaned into him, and he held her, and finally he could breathe again.

At last, reluctantly, he pulled back a little, still keeping his arm tightly around her waist, and tapped his com back on.

The military captain he'd been speaking with was sputtering with indignation, but after a few minutes Lev managed to talk him down, and work out one more absurd, ridiculous detail.

Jez leaned into him, letting her head drop onto the shoulder. When he finally finished with the call and tapped his com, she said, "The others? Everyone else alright?"

"Yes," he said. "I sent Tae and Ivan off to go sleep an hour ago, because they looked about dead on their feet, and Masha's in the medic tent. I don't know where Ysbel and Tanya are, but I suspect they're with the kids."

She raised a skeptical eyebrow at him. "So hang on a minute, so you're doing all this crap by yourself, basically."

He gave her a slightly rueful smile. "Vera's helping. And Caz, since he knows the streets. I think I'm mostly there for moral support. But considering I can't make weapons or hack tech or fly the way you can, there has to be something I can do to pull my weight." He paused a moment. "Besides," he said, a little more softly. "I—wasn't exactly going to be falling asleep when I didn't know where you were."

She looked up at him, her eyes soft, and leaned in towards him.

His com buzzed again, and he sighed and shook his head ruefully.

It was another logistics issue—there were weapons that had to be surrendered, but the captain of the division wanted to know how they were proposing to work out timing so that her people could drop their weapons without fear of being shot by the insurgents who were to be coordinating the drop.

It was difficult to keep his mind on the task with Jez beside him, though, when all he wanted to do was to sink down on the small student cot in the corner, pull her into another embrace, and never let her go.

She leaned over and kissed him gently on the temple, and he gave her a quick smile before trying to pull his attention back to the com.

"—will be acceptable, I suppose," said the police captain, her voice sullen.

"Vera," he said, "Would you and Caz please coordinate a location with the captain?"

Jez stepped in closer and kissed the corner of his jaw, then bit down lightly on the lobe of his ear, and for a moment, he lost track of the conversation completely.

"—as long as they don't mind—" Vera was saying.

Jez grinned wickedly. She kissed the side of his neck, her lips lingering on his skin, and he swallowed hard, every nerve in his body at full attention.

Caz said something, but Lev hardly heard him.

Jez's lips had moved around to the back of his neck, and she bit him, harder than he expected, and he sucked in a quick breath and tried to swallow through his suddenly dry throat. Her hand slipped under his shirt, sliding across his stomach, and she trailed her other hand lightly up his spine. Her lips had moved to his shoulder now, and he was suddenly having a very difficult time breathing.

On the com, somebody was saying something about Reka street. But Vera and Caz were perfectly capable of dealing with it, and besides, at the moment, he didn't have a single brain cell with any interest whatsoever in the locations of a weapons drop.

Jez was kissing the hollow of his throat, and down his chest, and his entire damn body was sparking like he just been hit with an electric jolt and the charge had nowhere to go.

The com clicked as the police captain signed off.

"Lev? Are you still there?" asked Vera, her voice sounding concerned.

He managed to mumble something in response, which hopefully made some sort of sense. He honestly had no idea.

Jez had kissed farther down his chest now and—and damn it to hell, she was undoing the top button of his damn shirt with her teeth, he hadn't even known you could do that. She ran her fingers down his back, sending goose pimples across his entire body, then grabbed his free hand and planted it firmly on the curve of her butt.

He tightened his fingers instinctively, and she gave a blissful sigh.

There might have been words coming through his com, but at this point, there wasn't enough left of his brain to decipher any of them. Every speck of his concentration was completely absorbed in processing, at length and in detail, every damn place Jez was touching him, and every other damn place he wished she was touching him.

Jez pulled her hand reluctantly from his stomach, and he bit back a groan just in time. She took his com hand in hers and pulled it towards her. "Hold on, Lev'll be right back," she said. "Something came up."

She tapped the com off, gave him a grin that shut off every remaining brain cell he had, and pulled his lips to hers.

The kiss was slow and lingering, and her fingers traced lines along his skin, and he pulled her to him hard enough that there shouldn't have been room for air between them, and it still wasn't nearly close enough. When the kiss ended and Jez pulled back slightly, he was gasping for breath, his legs so weak he wasn't sure they'd continue to hold him up.

The raw desire in Jez's expression was enough to take his breath away again.

She slid her hand down his arm, bringing his com up in front of them, and he twined his fingers with hers as she tapped the com. He slid his other hand up into her hair and tipped her head back and to the side, revealing the long, smooth line of her throat, and he ran his teeth along it gently.

Her eyes went hazy, and her body went soft under his fingers.

"Lev?" came Vera's voice through the com.

"Hey, Vera, it's me," Jez said, her voice breathless.

Lev tipped her head back farther, kissing along the hollow under her jaw. She moaned.

"Jez? Are you alright?" Vera sounded slightly worried.

"Yeah," Jez managed, then moaned again, a little louder, as Lev nibbled down the side of her neck. "Listen," she managed, "you and Dimitri know the area around here pretty well, yeah?"

"Yes …" said Vera cautiously.

"Good," gasped Jez. "Can you put Lev's mom and dad on?"

A moment later, Lev's mother answered cautiously, "Yes? What do you need?"

Lev slid his hand down Jez's neck and along her shoulders, pulling back her tunic to give him more area to kiss. Her eyes were closed blissfully, her head still tipped back, and for a moment the part of his mind that was still functioning wondered vaguely if she would answer at all.

The rest of him didn't actually give a damn, as long as he could keep kissing her.

He pushed her backwards, pressing her up against the wall, and stepped in closer.

"Jez?"

"Hey," Jez's voice was completely breathless, with a tone to it that would have driven him completely off his head if he hadn't passed that stage a long while back. "So, genius has been working his damn tail off for the last I don't even know how many hours, and I figure if you were—" she broke off with a sharp gasp as he tightened his hand on her butt. "… were smart enough to raise him, you can probably take over whatever the hell he's supposed to be doing right now, between you and Vera and Dimitri," she managed at last, her voice distinctly unsteady.

"I—suppose we could," said Lev's mother, after a moment. "I've been listening to the negotiations, and I think I understand enough that we can work out details." She paused a moment. "I'm sorry. I should have realized Lev needed some rest—"

Jez's grin grew wicked. "Don't figure he's going to be doing a lot of resting, per se. Mostly what I expect to have happen starts out with him and me locking the damn door, and ends up with neither of us being able to remember our damn names."

There was a long moment of silence on the other end of the com, then his mother's voice, in which, even in his completely hazy state, he could hear the small tinge of humour.

"I—suppose that's understandable," she said. "Tell Lev his father and I will take care of things for the next few hours."

"Knew there was a reason Lev liked you two," Jez said, tapping off the com.

She turned to Lev with a dangerous expression and gave him a wink that almost sent him into full cardiac arrest. Then she leaned up until her mouth was against his ear, and whispered, "Alright, genius. You made a hell of a lot of promises over the last few weeks. I expect you to pay up."

He ran his lips along the outside of her ear, and his hands down her sides, maneuvering her towards the cot, and she gave a small shiver of pleasure. "Believe me," he whispered back. "I fully intend to."

32

Masha, day 13, late

It was night. The sun had gone down hours ago, and the dim glow of the streetlamps through the walls of the medic tent was the only illumination from outside.

Masha looked around at her crew, gathered on the floor around her.

They all looked tired, to one degree or another, but a soft blanket of happiness seemed to have settled over them. Ysbel held Tanya close. The children yawned in their laps, but the two women were sneaking kisses when the children were distracted.

Tae and Ivan stood together, and she wasn't entirely sure which one of them was being held, which one of them was doing the holding, but there was a look of sleepy contentment on Tae's face, and soft adoration on Ivan's. She wasn't sure if they'd actually slept or not, but if they had, she was certain it had been in each other's arms.

Jez was seated in Lev's lap, seeming completely unembarrassed by the fact that it was abundantly obvious that neither she nor Lev had gotten anything that could be remotely considered rest. Or about the fact that both of them had a number of suspiciously shaped bruises along their necks that made it very clear, for anyone still left with questions, the tenor of their activities over the last few hours.

She sighed, smiling to herself despite everything.

And, despite everything, something welled up in her chest at the sight of them here.

She'd failed. She betrayed herself, and everything she'd always thought she believed in. But—seeing her crew here, safe, happy—she was heart-stoppingly, sickeningly glad. Unutterably relieved that she hadn't gone through with it after all. That Olya and Misko still had their mothers, that they'd grow up with parents who loved them.

That they wouldn't have to be another Mari.

And that somehow, despite her failure—her long list of failures—it had worked out.

There were complications, of course, but both the military and the police force had surrendered, although Lev's parents were still in negotiations. They were surprisingly effective, and she supposed that shouldn't be a shock—this was, after all, the family that had produced both Lev and Vitali Dobrev. On reflection, it would have been more shocking had they not been absurdly good at whatever they put their minds to.

"Alright," said Ysbel at last. "I've been waiting for Lev to say something about how we have to discuss what our next steps should be, but I'm not completely sure he remembers how to talk."

Masha suppressed a smile. Lev did look slightly less focused than was his wont—or rather, entirely focused, but purely on the lanky pilot in his lap.

He looked up, blinking slightly. "I'm sorry, Ysbel, what was that?"

Masha was secretly impressed that he'd gotten out an entire sentence.

Ysbel sighed deeply. "I said, I suppose it's time for us to figure out what we do next to keep everything from falling apart."

Lev took a deep breath and shook his head as if to clear it. Then he glanced reluctantly at Masha.

There was still that tension in his posture whenever he looked at her. She couldn't blame him.

"Masha," he said, his voice wary. "I don't know what's been happening inside the government. I—assume you do?"

"I believe I have some insights," she said quietly. The pain washed through her body like waves, advancing and receding, and the effort of speaking was enough to set the tent swaying around her. She reached out unconsciously to catch herself on the bed, and the movement sent another jolt of pain through her strong enough that for a moment, the entire world went black.

When she regained consciousness, Ivan and Jez were both bending over her, their faces creased in concern.

"Masha?" Jez's voice was tight and worried.

Ivan was holding a medi-scanner, and he scanned her quickly. He crossed over to Tanya and held out the readout, and for a moment, the two of them studied it. Tanya gave a short shake of her head.

"We have better supplies back on the *Ungovernable*," Ivan said quietly. "It's not much, but—"

"I think you're right," said Tanya at last. "If we want to keep her alive, that's our best bet. At least until we can find a medic who is not hiding in their apartment, trying to avoid being shot."

Lev glanced around the small tent. "I suppose there's no reason why we couldn't continue this conversation on the ship," he said, and Masha noticed the way he glanced at Jez, and the way he smiled at the look on her face at the mention of the *Ungovernable*.

It wasn't a far walk, but to Masha's unutterable relief, they took one of the ancient university transports. And to her even more unutterable relief, Jez kept to a staid pace the entire way.

By the time they'd half-supported, half-carried her into the ship and laid her on the cot in the med bay, she was gasping at the pain, dark spots constricting her vision.

"Here. Take this," said Tanya. Masha didn't have the energy to resist, so she swallowed whatever Tanya had given her.

For a while, the pain broke over her in overwhelming waves, turning the room into a wash of blurred lights and unintelligible sound. But slowly, as the painkiller took effect, the room steadied until she was able to follow her crew's conversation.

"Lev," she said, when she was certain she'd be able to form the words. "You asked me what's happening in government. Tell me your specific questions, I'll do my best to answer them."

Lev glanced over at her. His arms were around Jez protectively, but he'd regained his typical calm, intelligent look, although there was a dreamy cast to it.

He studied her for some time. "I assume, Masha," he said at last, "that you have a plan for what you want to happen next."

She watched him for a moment.

It had been a long time since she hadn't had a plan. It had been a long, long time since she hadn't known exactly how she wanted the future to look, and each individual step that would lead there.

With the government essentially paralyzed, Lev was right—there were a hundred plans that she could put forward, a hundred things that would bring her closer to what she'd been working for since she was seven years old, hiding under table, watching as her parents were murdered.

He was still looking at her, as if trying to figure her out.

"Lev," she said quietly. "Forgive me, but I have a question of my own." She paused. "Why did you rescue me?"

There was a long moment of silence. No one seemed inclined to speak.

Lev still hadn't taken his eyes off her. Finally, though, he gave a small, wry shrug. "I suppose Jez was right, after all," he said simply. "We're crew. We couldn't leave you to be tortured, any more than we'd leave any of the others." His gaze, still fixed on her, was piercing. "That doesn't mean I've forgiven you for what you did. It certainly doesn't mean I trust you. Trust is something that's earned, and you'll have your work cut out for you if you want to earn our trust back again. But—" he paused, and shrugged again. "But whatever you did, whatever you were going to do—we're crew. And we don't leave people. I learned that from a pilot I know." He pulled Jez closer, and she snuggled against him, a soft expression on her face.

The room had blurred again, and it took Masha a moment to realize it was tears, not pain, causing it. She blinked hard for a moment, and when her vision cleared, they were all watching her.

She could see in their eyes the truth of Lev's words.

How in the hell had she become part of a crew? She, Masha, who was supposed to have been above it all, who was supposed to have been able to use them without a second thought.

But she couldn't, in the end. Instead, she'd become one of them. In a way that, apparently, even everything she done wasn't enough to break.

She'd cried far, far too many times in the past few hours. But she found her breath catching in her throat, and the tears she'd tried to blink back dripped down her cheeks.

Lev gave her time to recover herself, for which she was grateful. At last, though, he said quietly, "Masha?"

She took a deep breath. "You're correct in assuming that I have plans—or at least, I had plans—that would cover this situation. But —" she paused. "But I think," she continued at last, quietly, "that we've spent enough time carrying out my plans. So. Whatever you choose to do, I'll do what I can to help. I'll use my connections, and my information—but not my plans, any longer. I—" she swallowed, and blinked again. "I suppose, if what you say is correct, and I am part of this crew, I—suppose it's time I start acting like it."

There was another long moment of silence. Masha closed her eyes against the dizziness, leaning back against the pillows someone had propped up against her back.

"In that case, then," said Lev quietly. "I—would appreciate hearing your thoughts."

She blinked open her eyes as he pulled up his holoscreen, paging quickly through to a chart she recognized, mapping out the government organization—or at least, what the government organization had been a few weeks prior, when Jez had somehow convinced everyone that she was a minister.

The memory still made her smile. Perhaps, after all the things they'd done, pulling that off was the one that still took Masha the most by surprise.

"I assume that there have been several personnel changes since this was current," said Lev.

"You mean, assassinations," said Ivan dryly.

Lev cracked a small smile. "I suppose you could use either term. At any rate, Masha, if you know who has stepped in to fill vacancies, or which positions are currently vacant, that would be tremendously helpful."

"And what is your ultimate goal?" asked Masha.

"I—" he ran a hand over his face, and Masha could see the weariness there. "At this point, anything that will keep the insurgents alive and give us a chance to stop Evka would be more than acceptable. However, I believe that will best be accomplished if we can enter into negotiations with the current leaders of government, and bargain for a new power structure. One that doesn't leave the street kids and the people in the projects at the mercy of the police. I'm not certain how that would look, yet, but between all of us—" he glanced around the small med bay, a small smile on his face. "I think we should be able to come up with something."

"I'm very certain you will," said Masha softly.

For a while, they sat in comfortable silence. No one seemed to want to move, and they were obviously far, far too exhausted to start a planning meeting then and there.

Just as well. With what they'd done, blocking off the government offices, negotiating the surrender of the army and police force, it would take at least a few days before anyone in government would regain control enough to negotiate.

Misko yawned hugely and leaned back in Ysbel's lap, snuggling into her, and she removed one of her arms from Tanya and pulled him close.

Then Jez looked up, glancing around the cabin. "Hey," she said. "Getting kind of foggy in here, don't you think? Didn't think it was going to be that warm tonight."

Masha glanced around as well.

The dank, slightly malodorous fog from the streets of Prasvishoni had wound its way into the smuggler bay and through the *Ungovernable*, filling the small cabin.

"Wait," said Tanya, her voice suddenly tense.

Lev was frowning as well, and Tae had a distracted look, as if he was trying to place something.

The pain still clung to Masha's thoughts, making her mind more sluggish than usual. But—Tanya was right. There was something about the scent of the mist, something familiar. And threatening.

She realized it just as Lev spoke the words.

"Evka," he said quietly, his voice tense. "This is her Protocol."

"How did she—" Tae began, his voice tight with horror.

Lev's com buzzed. He glanced down at it, and give a small, humourless smile. "I suspect we're about to find out." He tapped the com. "Hello, Evka," he said quietly.

He'd answered on the general line, so they could all hear Evka's response.

"Lev," she said. Her voice was businesslike, but tinged with affection. "I'm impressed by what you've done."

"I have no interest in small talk with you, Evka," said Lev, voice still quiet. "Say what you're going to say."

"You always were one to go straight to the point," said Evka, and again, there was that note of fondness in her voice. She paused a moment. "I won't waste either of our time, then. I repaired the damage you did to my Protocol, as was always inevitable. The gas with my metal substrate, as you've surmised, has been re-broadcast throughout Prasvishoni. Personally, I think it unnecessary, as I believe the dose last time was sufficient, but I'd hate to be brought down by a miscalculation that easy to guard against. So, you've failed, ultimately. Within a few hours, the machine will have finished calibrating and will be fully functional. There's nowhere left for you to go, you or your friends. You put up an impressive fight, but in the end, it was unsuccessful. However, you are still undoubtedly the most brilliant student I've worked with. You could contribute a great deal to the development of this protocol. It's a new system, and it will take tweaking to perfect, and there is no one in the system I would prefer to work with."

"And you expect me to agree?" asked Lev, his voice still soft. "You expect me to forget that you tried to have me murdered—tried to have Jez murdered—and are currently threatening to kill me and everyone I care for?"

Evka laughed softly. "No, Lev. Give me more credit than that, please." She paused a moment. "I've been watching you, since you reappeared a few months back. You seem to have made friends since I knew you. Fallen in love, even."

"Evka." Lev's voice was controlled, but there was a warning in it.

Evka laughed again. "Lev. I've missed you, you know." She paused. "You and I are both intelligent enough that I don't need to threaten. But I will tell you this—you've known, for quite some time now, that the moment the Protocol was active, you and all your friends would die. It's active now, and you only have remaining to you the few hours it will take the machine to finish calibrating. I simply wish to present an alternative. If you come work for me, your teammates will be safe, whether or not they agree to come along. As long as you're working with me, I'll ensure they're protected.

"That girl who was sleeping over at your apartment in the university—I saw how terrified you were when you thought I'd kill her. I saw how motivated you were to keep that from happening. You've always had a strong streak of self-interest, and that's not a bad thing—in fact, it's one of the things I've always enjoyed most about you. Self-interest is what makes the system run, after all. But —" Masha could hear the smile in the woman's voice. "You seem to have lost that pure self-interest, at least when it comes to that girl of yours. So. What will it be?"

No one in the room spoke.

Masha could see the struggle on Lev's face.

Once, he'd been willing to do anything at all, no matter how many people he'd hurt, to keep Jez safe. To keep the others safe.

But now—

She wasn't sure anymore. It had been too long since he'd trusted her enough that she knew him.

Tae didn't speak, but Masha could tell from his face what he'd say if he did. And he clearly knew Lev already knew his position. Ivan— someone like Ivan, it wouldn't even be a question. There was a reason he and Tae had been drawn to each other. Odd, really, how two people who were that genuinely good had ended up part of a motley crew like this one.

But the crew had changed, since she brought them together, so many months ago.

She glanced over at the small family unit, huddled together on floor.

Even Ysbel. Ysbel and Tanya. She doubted even they would have agreed to this.

For a long moment, no one spoke.

Lev took a deep breath, closing his eyes for a moment. When he opened them, he was looking at Jez.

Jez turned her head and gave him a small, weary smile, something intimate and unspoken passing between them.

"Evka," Lev said finally, into the com. "I'm not who I was when I was your student. There are lines I won't cross. Working with you— helping you enslave the entire system—is one of them."

"Not even to save Jez?" asked Evka softly.

Masha could see the pain on Lev's face. But his voice was steady. "Not even for that." He paused. "A friend of mine once said, if saving the system requires you to betray your friends, betray everything you believe in—perhaps it's not a system worth saving. You're right. I love Jez. I love her more than you will ever understand. I love her far too much to betray everything she stands for, just to save her life."

There was a long pause from the other end of the com. Finally, Evka said, her voice once more brisk and businesslike, "Very well. I won't insult you by trying to talk you into something you've decided against. I'm very sorry to have to kill you—believe me, I'll take no pleasure in it. But I think you've worked with me long enough to know that I'll do it, regardless."

The com tapped off, and the room fell silent.

It wasn't despair Masha felt. She'd felt that too often, perhaps. It was something else, something beyond despair—a hollow emptiness that seemed to open inside her and swallow whole every emotion, every thought, every feeling.

Jez sat up, leaning back against Lev. He slipped his arms around her waist, holding her close. She put her hands over his, her head leaned back against his shoulder. Lev's eyes were closed, and Masha could see the strain in every muscle of his body, but he leaned his head against Jez's, his lips pressed into her hair. Ivan had pulled Tae against him, and Tae leaned into him, as if they were drawing strength from each other. And Ysbel and Tanya had gathered the children close, holding them. Masha could tell from Olya's face that she understood what was happening, at least part of it, but Misko looked sleepy and confused and bad-tempered.

"I'm sorry I couldn't stop this," said Masha softly. It didn't matter. The words didn't matter, and they wouldn't change anything, but somehow, she wanted to say them anyways. "I'm sorry I didn't prevent this. I'm sorry I couldn't save you, after everything I've done."

Jez opened her eyes and gave Masha the approximation of a snarky grin. "Hey, Evka took all of us by surprise. Happens to the best of us."

Lev managed a small smile as well. "I'm glad you're here, Masha," he said softly. "I'm sorry we're going to die, but I suppose I'm glad, after all, that if we're going to die, we'll at least die together, as crew."

They were quiet again for a moment.

And then Jez sat up, and Masha could see the tension in her muscles, the grin spreading across her face that always seem to appear when things were going sideways.

"Hold on just a damn minute," she drawled.

They all turned to look at her.

"Jez?" asked Lev after a moment.

Jez turned to him, still grinning. "Screw that crap," she said. "I mean, you said it, didn't you, genius? We're here as a damn crew. That Evka bastard thinks she can kill us all? Well, figure she's tried that a few times before. Never quite succeeded yet."

"Jez," said Lev gently. "The program is already working. We've breathed in the gas, twice now. And this time, we have no way of hacking into the system. We don't even know where the servers are, or where Evka is—she's clearly not in the government buildings. Four or five hours for the machine to calibrate, and Evka can kill us with a flick of her finger."

Jez gave an easy shrug. "We've dealt with worse crap before."

Tae looked up, glaring at her. "When?"

She paused a moment, considering. "OK," she said finally, "maybe we haven't. But hell, nor has that bastard Evka. We have what, four hours before that plaguing scum-eater can do anything? Which is basically like four years, honestly."

"It's not anything even approaching four years," Tae grumbled, but Masha could see the hopelessness beginning to lift from his expression.

"Sure as hell feels like four years, hanging around with you bastards," said Jez, with another shrug. "Anyways, figure we have at least an even chance. Hell, you believe in the Lady, right tech-head? I don't, but if I'm wrong, you don't figure she'd let a bastard like Evka kill someone as hot as me, do you?"

The corner of Lev's mouth was twitching, even under his grim expression, and Tae was fighting back a reluctant smile.

"I agree with Aunty Jez," said Olya importantly, sitting up. "My mama and my mamochka are very, very smart. Probably smarter than Evka." She paused a minute, glancing at Lev. "You're smart too, I guess, Uncle Lev," she added. "And anyways, Aunty Jez does whatever she wants, and she's very good at gambling, so if she thinks we can beat that damn Evka—"

"Olya …" Tanya began warningly.

"—then we probably can," Olya continued, ignoring her mother. "And I know Aunty thinks we can, because if she didn't, I know what she and Uncle Lev would be doing for the last few hours before we all got killed."

Lev looked distinctly uncomfortable.

"What would they be doing?" asked Misko plaintively.

Olya rolled her eyes to the ceiling, and whispered loudly, "Kissing."

Masha bit back a smile.

"I don't know what I could possibly do, not without having access to Evka's servers," Tae grumbled. "But I guess Jez isn't going to leave us in peace for the last four damn hours of our lives unless I at least pretend to try something." He gave a long-suffering sigh, but there was the hint of a smile on his face.

Jez was still grinning hugely. She rolled to her feet and held out a hand to help Lev up. "Hell, can't even keep track of how many damn bastards tried to kill us so far. And no one's managed it yet." Lev stood, and Jez winked at Olya, then grabbed him and kissed him thoroughly.

Olya gave them a disgusted look.

"When you are quite finished, Jez," said Ysbel dryly. "I thought we were on a time limit here."

Reluctantly, Jez broke off the kiss. She sighed deeply, then grinned. "Figure that bastard Evka isn't going to know what hit her," she said.

It was hopeless. It was completely hopeless, and they were all going to die, and no amount of bravado could change that.

But somehow, looking around the small cabin at the crew she'd assembled so long ago—against all facts and reason and logic, Masha couldn't quench the small, absurd flicker of hope sparking in her chest.

TO BE CONTINUED …

ENJOYED THE BOOK?

I HOPE YOU'VE ENJOYED Threat Agent, the eighth book in The Ungovernable series. Thank you for reading!

I have a small favour to ask you: Would you please leave a review on Amazon? It may seem like a silly thing, but reviews are very important to authors like me, as they help other people find my book, which in turn helps me to keep writing. Even a line or two would be unbelievably helpful.

If you haven't read it yet, Zero Day Threat is the first book in the series. The ninth and final book, Attack Path, is available on Amazon.

In the mean time, if you subscribe to my mailing list, I'd love to send you an exclusive short story prequel featuring Jez Solokov, *Devil's Odds*. I'll also let you know about future launch dates, giveaways, and pre-release specials. And I always love to hear from my readers, so feel free to drop me a note!

If you'd like claim your free short story and subscribe to my newsletter, head over to my website: www.rmolson.com

Also, feel free to connect with me on Facebook: https://www.facebook.com/rmolsonauthor

or Instagram: https://www.instagram.com/rolson_author/